WINTER

WILLIAM
HORWOOD

MACMILLAN

First published 2013 by Macmillan,
an imprint of Pan Macmillan, a division of Macmillan Publishers Limited
Pan Macmillan, 20 New Wharf Road, London N1 9RR
Basingstoke and Oxford
Associated companies throughout the world
www.panmacmillan.com

ISBN 978-0-230-71263-8

1 3 5 7 9 8 6 4 2

A CIP catalogue record for this book is available from the British Library.

Typeset by SetSystems Ltd, Cambridge, CB22 3GN
Printed and bound by CPI Group (UK) Ltd, Croydon, CR0 4YY

Visit **www.panmacmillan.com** to read more about all our books
and to buy them. You will also find features, author interviews and
news of any author events, and you can sign up for e-newsletters
so that you're always first to hear about our new releases.

WINTER

PART I
END OF DAYS

I

VIGIL

One cold November dawn a solitary hydden stood before the thundering surf of Pendower Beach in south-west Englalond. He was lost in thought, as he had been since the night before. But now the stars had given way to black clouds and the wind had turned to a cutting northerly that heralded a bleak and bitter winter.

Bedwyn Stort was tall for a hydden, over three feet high, and had he been solidly built and stood straight and true he might have seemed a match for the roughening sea he faced.

As it was he was thin and gawky and stood skew, swaying first one way then another, then another yet again, as if helplessly caught amongst flows of thought and feeling every bit as powerful as the currents and tidal races in the sea before him.

He had nothing under his pale cotton jerkin, which was damp and rough from the brine in the air. His trews served him no better for they reached only just below his knees and were worn and torn. He had no hose to cover his bare, freckled legs and his boots were little more than tatters of material held together with wire and string. The tops were canvas and the soles fashioned from scraps of worn black rubber tyre scavenged from human roads.

Nor did he wear headgear of any kind, the winds playing havoc with his red hair, while his ears were blue with cold.

He had followed the sea's rise and fall since the night before, first up the beach through the dark hours and then down it again to the dawn. The waves had continually sent greedy, roaring races of water at him, trying to catch him, tumble him and drag him to their fatal embrace.

The more he had tired and grown cold, the more they caught him and knocked him down. But each time, though now more slowly and with increasing difficulty, he picked himself up and continued his self-appointed vigil.

Stort came from Brum in far-off central Englalond, land of freedom, city of hope. He might, had he been less modest and innocent, have laid claim to be one of the most famous people in the Hyddenworld. He was certainly the most beloved.

He was a scrivener, inventor, traveller, savant and searcher after truth and solutions to problems scientific, secular, spiritual and paradoxical. In fact anything that caught his imagination and fired his insatiable curiosity about how things worked and in what – and exactly where – the answers to Mother Earth's mysteries lay.

It mattered not to Stort whether the problems he dwelt upon were great or small. Though only in his early twenties, he was wise beyond his years, as if in some other life a wide and benign experience had accrued to him. For he understood that since all things of Earth and Universe are vivified by a common energy or harmony, which wise folk call *musica universalis*, everything, however incidental it might seem, has a bearing on the whole.

So when some notion or other caught his attention, even if others might see it as a waste of time, he pursued it wherever it took him. As a result of this unending wonder about the world, and his occasionally strange scholarship, impractical experiments and seemingly hapless travels for the greater good, Stort inspired affection and respect. Though his attributes were not those normally associated with great and heroic leadership, a leader he indubitably was.

Like most hydden, he believed in the Mirror-of-All, in whose vast universal reflection we live our lives, as smaller parts of the whole, which is to say as reflections which come and go. But in that belief he went further than most, thinking that perhaps there were many parallel universes, many Mirrors-of-All. For which his only evidence was that he sometimes felt he had been the same way before in a similar but different world, not necessarily as a hydden.

But it was not for such problematic philosophical musings as these, which passed over the heads of most hydden, that Stort was most renowned. No, he owed his unwanted celebrity to the fact that many hydden had come to believe, rightly or wrongly, that the world was now in real danger of coming to an end and that it would be upon his bony, slender and seemingly frail shoulders that the future of them all, of both Earth and perhaps even the Universe, now finally rested.

For these were troubled times.

In nine short, terrible months, all had changed.

Spring had ended with the extraordinary and fearful birth of the prophesied Shield Maiden, the avenging agent for an Earth angry at its centuries of mistreatment at the hands of mortalkind. Summer heightened people's fears with unnatural threats of all kinds, climatic and seismic, in the sky above and the Earth below. Autumn saw threat turn to frightening reality as Englalond's beauteous land was riven by earthquake and ruined by fire.

Now Stort stood on Pendower's shore as winter and the End of Days began. But though the wind grew steadily stronger and the driving waves ever closer and more eager to destroy him, he seemed intent on staying right where he was until he had worked out a way to save the Hyddenworld, our Mother Earth and, perhaps, the Universe as well.

2
GOOD FRIENDS

Lonely though Stort looked down on the shore, he was not alone.

Among the dunes above the high-tide mark, barely visible amidst the fluted banks of sand and tussocks of marram grass, were five of Stort's friends and helpers. They had been keeping a watchful eye on their companion since he ventured onto the beach the evening before, insisting that he be left by himself until his vigil was done.

They knew well that he was in a crisis of uncertainty and personal doubt. The pressures on him were great and might easily cast down his spirit and even his body to illness and despair.

In the past tempestuous months, Stort's fame had moved from the local to the global when it became known that he had achieved what generations of hydden had only dreamed of being able to do. This had to do with a prophecy made fifteen hundred years before by Beorn-amund of Mercia, considered by most to be the greatest CraftLord, or maker of powerful objects, who ever lived.

He had blamed the gods of those days for the death of Imbolc, his betrothed. Her name meant 'Spring' and he was angered that she died before the first flush of her life, and his own, could be fulfilled.

In his rage he fashioned a sphere of crystal and metal so perfect that the gods feared to see such skill in mortal hands. They thought its existence threatened the Mirror itself and tried to destroy it. But four fragments survived, each a gem of great beauty, each carrying the colours of its respective season and something of the Fires of the Universe.

The CraftLord found three of the gems, but never that of Spring, despite a lifetime of searching. In time he repented his pride and arrogance in defying the gods and they forgave him. They sent Imbolc to him on a White Horse, saying she must journey the Earth as its Peace-Weaver to earn her place at his side, until the day came when the lost gem of Spring was found by a mortal. In that moment her task would be completed.

Beornamund accepted their decision but prophesied that by the time Spring was finally found the End of Days would be approaching. He fashioned a golden chain and hung from it a pendant in which he made four settings, each for one of the gems. He placed in it the three gems he already had, those of Summer, Autumn and Winter. He put the pendant round Imbolc's neck and by his skill and artifice ensured that each gem would fall to the ground and be lost as she passed beyond that season of her journey.

So it happened: when her Summer was over, that gem fell from the pendant; with Autumn, that season's gem fell; so too with Winter and its dark, shimmering gem of icy fire, which fell to Earth in a place none knew, not even Imbolc.

For the next fifteen hundred years hydden after hydden set forth to find the gem of Spring – and failed. Which was, perhaps, as well. For Beornamund had warned that the gems held power beyond a normal mortal's strength to bear. Whoever found them must be sufficiently pure of heart and spirit that they would not be corrupted by the gems and try to keep or covet them. Instead they must return them to Imbolc's sister, the fearful Shield Maiden.

It had been Bedwyn Stort's wyrd or destiny to find the gem of Spring and seek out the the strange and angry Shield Maiden. When he found her he fearlessly placed the gem in the pendant she wore, which had been made by Beornamund and which Imbolc had passed on to her.

Stort had done the same with the gems of Summer and Autumn, but the toll on him had been great, for their power was such that they sapped his strength. Now he had to find the last and most challenging of the gems, that of Winter. He knew, as did his friends, that if he failed then universal disaster would ensue.

But Bedwyn Stort was, after all, a mere mortal and so prone to those weaknesses which beset the mortal life. In his case nothing was more troublesome and painful than the fact that he suffered that most common of ailments – an unfulfilled love. Wise in many things he might be, but in matters of the heart he was innocent and ingenuous. So it was that, though many a female would surely have been glad to spouse such a good-hearted hydden, he eschewed them all in favour of the one – the only one – he could *never* have, though he might live a thousand years.

Mirror help him but he fell in love with the Shield Maiden herself and, to make matters worse, she fell in love with him! It was, they knew, an impossible love, for how can a mortal and immortal ever be united? It is against the very nature of the Universe that it be so and no amount of soul searching, or vigils by the dangerous sea, can ever resolve a problem such as that.

Yet, doomed or not, he loved her still, the wild confusing love of inexperience which seeks a way to resolve the endless, irresolvable torrents and passions of the heart, the mind and the body.

The truth was that it was this dilemma, as well as the need to find the gem of Winter before the End of Days destroyed them all, that had been the two driving impulses for his solitary vigil.

Innocent he might be, but Stort believed to the very depths of his being that if only he could find a way to resolve the impossible, to achieve what all common sense and natural law said was beyond even his considerable talents, and so satisfy that deep and abiding love he and she felt for each other, then the problem of Winter, and therefore of the End of Days, would be somehow solved.

Certainly it needed to be – and very soon. For the times were tempestuous, literally and metaphorically. The worsening weather, the ever-growing incidence of earthquakes and tremors, recent devastations of human and hydden life by natural disasters of fire and flood, seemed to most hydden simple confirmation of what the legends and prophecies all said, that Beornamund's gems would be found only at the point when the extinction of all things was nigh.

The hydden now huddled up amongst the dunes and watching over Stort were a very extraordinary group. Each was in his or her own way quite exceptional in terms of the personal sacrifices they had made for the good of the Hyddenworld.

They had stayed meditative and silent through the night apart from occasional forays down the beach to see if Stort had reached a point where he was ready to return to the companionship of their circle.

But now, as dawn broke, they became as concerned for their own safety as for his. Human society had begun to collapse in recent months and they were aware of many dangers in the hills and vales immediately behind them, as across Englalond itself. It was all very well to stand in darkness on the shore but doing so in broad daylight was not the hydden way.

'It seems to me,' said one of them, breaking the silence, 'that Mister Stort's vigil has gone on long enough and in these harsh conditions might already have lost all point or purpose. He is also now easily seen from the cliffs above and though humans have some difficulty seeing us hydden, surely even *they* cannot fail to notice him out there on the shore if they look that way!'

The one who spoke was Slaeke Sinistral, the former Emperor of the Hyddenworld. He was now very old, older it seemed than time. His head was so devoid of flesh that it was little more than a skull covered by skin so papery-thin it showed an intricacy of blue veins beneath.

Sinistral was tall, taller than Stort, and his hands were skeletal. He was strangely beautiful, like an exotic plant that the long decades and seasons had withered to barely more than a husk of what once was, but one in which life still flowed, whose form is an exquisite echo of what went before. He held himself erect and his eyes shone with a compassion, intelligence and command so powerful that but a few moments in his company rendered his age and frailty immaterial.

It was not hard to see why this compelling yet intimidating hydden had forged an Imperial might, nor guess from the spirit that still shone from him that his journey was not quite finished and might yet bring to the world wonders as great as those he had brought it before.

His first words had been to no one in particular but now he turned to the two hydden nearest him.

'The sea is growing rougher by the moment and we would not want it to take Stort from us before he delivers the fruits of his mental labours through this long night! Eh, Jack? Do you not agree, Blut?'

Jack was the sturdy and well-built Stavemeister of Brum, an office whose emblem he held in his right hand – a carved stave of wood so hard and ancient and shiny that it caught in its convolutions the sun and the stars as well as the glint and sleek light of dawn. His dark hair was ruffled by the wind and at eighteen he seemed too young to hold such high and important office. But though so different in every way from Sinistral he, too, was intimidating. A bullish strength and sense of inner purpose emanated from him and commanded instant respect.

In addition to his stave, a sheathed dirk and crossbow hung from his belt. He gazed down the beach towards Stort, who was one of his best friends, and his eyes narrowed, considering. But he stayed silent, as yet uncertain what to say or do.

It was Niklas Blut who finally replied.

He was Sinistral's reluctant successor as Emperor and at first glance looked like what he had until so recently been, no more than a bespectacled bureaucrat, a shadowy Imperial administrator, a knower of facts, an anonymous shaper of policy and maker of decisions, a manager of budgets, a manipulator of people and committees. He was a hydden another might pass by without ever guessing the power he held.

But the moment Blut spoke, and his steely, grey eyes showed through the round spectacles he wore, it was plain that he too was more than ordinary. He had a clipped voice but a pleasant one, he spoke thoughtfully and rounded his sentences as he did his thoughts, with care and logic and weighty intellect, as if his words were the fruit of hours of contemplation, not seconds.

'My Lord Sinistral,' he replied coolly, 'we have all tried our best, but it seems to me that Mister Stort is not one easily dissuaded from what he chooses to do. I doubt that even the sea itself could master him.'

'If it did,' added Jack matter-of-factly, 'he'd somehow escape to live another day. No hydden I've ever met has a stronger instinct for survival than Stort. But I'll admit it now begins to look as if we should get him and ourselves to safety – and very soon.'

Blut blinked, took off his spectacles and wiped their flat glass orbs. It was something he usually did at moments of tension or thought but just then, in such a place, in such a wind, it was practical. The glass was fogged by salty condensation from the chill sea air.

'Unless . . .' he continued, glancing at another of their number who sat quietly some way from them, 'we might prevail on . . .'

'Ah! Yes! Barklice!' cried Sinistral, whose conversation and debate with his former aide was often a marvel of half-thoughts understood and notions fast-developed, as each shared the other's intellect, like great raptors that gyre together on an upwind above the common land. Though on this occasion their shared idea was plain enough.

'Indeed, Lord,' murmured Blut, '. . . Mister Barklice.'

They looked as one at Jack, who nodded and got up, muttering, 'I suppose it's worth a try.'

He said this as much to his consort Katherine, who was nearby, as to himself. She was as fair as he was dark and at eighteen the same age as Jack, but her face bore such signs of trial and suffering that she looked ten years older. She gazed thoughtfully down the beach at Stort.

'*I'll* talk to him,' she said, getting up and going to the far lee of the dune, where Barklice had squatted down and half-turned away to studiously avoid their earnest gazes and pretend he had not heard a word they had said.

3
BARKLICE

Mister Barklice was Chief Verderer of Brum, which meant that he journeyed about southern Englalond, and sometimes further afield, on official business. This had to do with rights of way, scutage, accounts and forest matters that required a firm but diplomatic hand.

He was wiry and thin, with wispy grey hair and the mild look of one skilled in the art of quiet negotiation and compromise. He walked with an easy, regular step, uphill and down dale, his grey eyes ever watchful of the path ahead, escape routes to right and left, and of such shifting vegetation, fallen branches, holes and conduits and the slant of shadows and whispering wind as might give a wanderer cover and protection.

The stave he carried was a light one, more as a walking aid than defence, and his canvas portersac, though old and patched, was always tidily packed, neatly buckled and so well balanced that if put on the ground it stayed upright and did not fall forward or back. He was intensely practical and as practised a camper as any hydden alive, able to set up, strike down, brew up or extinguish a fire in a trice, without sign or trace. He arrived at a place unnoticed and his departure was as unremarkable. Often it was nearly impossible to tell he had been there at all.

He was generally regarded as the greatest route-finder in the Hyddenworld, his knowledge of the green roads and hydden ways of Englalond being unrivalled. As was his knowledge of hyddening, which is the art of not being seen by others, especially humans.

These two skills made him the perfect companion and guardian of

Stort, who possessed neither. But what Stort did have, better even than Barklice, was an encyclopaedic knowledge of the railway lines of Englalond, both those still in use and those now abandoned but useful as green roads, short cuts across difficult terrain and reference points where few others existed. Taken together, these two hydden were a formidable pair when it came to working out the best way to go and which mode of transport to use.

When Stort had nothing better to do, or wanted respite from the dusty tomes of the Main Library in Brum, or his laboratory at home, he often accompanied the verderer on his rounds. In consequence, the two had become close friends and in matters of the heart neither had a better confidant. Their times on the green roads of Englalond were ones of friendly debate, interesting discourse on their different specialities, bickering and complaint about trivial matters of habit and routine, gossip by the cheerful fire and murmured memory under the mysterious stars.

Barklice respectfully deferred to Stort on matters of scholarship while Stort paid his friend the same compliment regarding routes and the wide range of skills and stratagems travellers and hyddeners must call on if they are to avoid the attentions of enemies and remain invisible to humans.

The evening before, when Stort began his vigil, Barklice had settled himself a little way from the others in a sheltered spot which had no view of the beach. Instead of watching Stort, he busied himself with the making of a fire, of the surreptitious well-turfed kind that humans cannot see. This kept him warm and enabled him to make various brews and nourishing fare to which the others gratefully helped themselves.

He did not join in the initial chatter and concern about Stort and had continued to ignore him as the night deepened and the wind veered. Even when the temperature plummeted just before dawn, he showed no interest or concern for the continuing exposure of his friend on the strand. He knew that when in pensive mood, with a problem or problems to solve, it was best to let Stort be. He had no doubt that he had been pained by his most recent encounter with the Shield Maiden, on the last night of October, when he had delivered to her the gem of Autumn.

He had observed the tender looks they gave each other and saw how they held back from touching, even each other's hand, as if even so simple and natural an intimacy would open floodgates of frustrated emotion and regrets that could not be requited.

Barklice understood too, as did Jack and Katherine, that though Stort carried the gems so lightly, and gave them up willingly, each one took an ever-greater toll. They aged him inside and put into him feelings of profound loss.

All this Barklice felt empathically, knowing time was the only healer, even if it was time spent on the bleak, windswept, dangerous beach. Unable to directly help his friend through so personal a trial he chose to doze, or poke the fire, or ruminate on parental love and duty, twin themes he took very seriously indeed.

After years of silence and denial he had, very recently, confessed to Stort that he had a son. The lad was called Bratfire and was the result of a brief and wondrous liaison with a Bilgesnipe girl, one of those folk who lived by and on water in wandering, gypsy style. Whatever the rights or wrongs of the matter, Barklice had finally accepted responsibility for his boy, now twelve or thereabouts.

The recent quest for the gem of Autumn, and an invasion of Englalond by mutinous Fyrd, the army once led by Slaeke Sinistral, had forced Barklice to leave Bratfire in Brum.

He missed him greatly and when sitting by himself he had taken to removing from his belt the sheathed dirk he kept there, not to take the blade out but rather to gaze with joy upon the rudely made sheath itself, which was crudely decorated with tufts of red string interwoven with red and green paper. His son had made it for him as a parting present before Barklice headed south-west with Stort on the journey that had brought them to Pendower. The verderer valued it very highly as a gesture of filial love which, if truth be told, he felt he barely deserved. But there it was, and here it was, and through the long cold hours of that night, while Stort stood upon the shore, the glints of fire in the sheath's decorations gave Barklice pause for pleasant paternal thoughts and a yearning for reunion.

This was the remarkable hydden to whom Jack's partner Katherine now went, urging him to try doing what the others had failed to do and persuade Stort to come back to them to take refreshment and rest.

'He's tiring visibly before our eyes,' she said, adding a sudden 'oh!' and involuntarily reaching toward Stort as a particularly high and formidable wave came down on the shore near him. From their fore-shortened view it seemed almost to crash on Stort himself. But then another race of green and foamy water raced up the beach and caught his legs so that he tumbled sideways, saving himself only by reaching an arm and hand into the sodden sand and holding himself steady as the water swept back under him to the waves.

'Sinistral and the others are worried that if humans made their way near Pendower they might easily see him on the sands . . .' added Katherine.

Barklice studied Stort awhile before saying stubbornly, 'He hates to be disturbed when he is pondering things.'

'Pondering!' cried Katherine. 'He looks half dead with fatigue and in danger of being swept away!'

'For Mirror's sake, Barklice,' added Jack, joining them, 'if you don't bring him back to safety I will go down there myself and haul him out of reach of the waves whether he likes it or not! What's he playing at? We need him to complete the quest for the gem of Winter. Without that the End of Days will engulf us all. Sometimes Stort risks too much and goes too far!'

Sinistral and Blut exchanged glances. They knew the others were close friends and understood each other well. The bond between them was deep and in it lay the secret of how Stort had already been able to recover the gems of Spring, Summer and Autumn.

'We must not interfere, my Lord,' murmured Blut, 'Barklice knows Stort better than most. We must let things be.'

Sinistral nodded grimly and said no more.

But their confidence was tried again moments later when another wave shot in and Stort was tumbled once more into the water, his ragged clothes left dripping and sodden as he righted himself before finally retreating at last, if only a yard or two.

Barklice, observing this and considering the plea made to him, seemed to reconsider.

'Hmm,' he mused, 'I think perhaps . . . it might be as well . . . *yes!* Katherine, kindly stoke that fire once again and boil a fresh cannikin of water.'

He scrabbled about in his portersac, muttering, 'I'm sure it's still here somewhere,' and finally withdrew a small tin on which was scrawled in white paint the abbreviation 'MedB7'. Underneath was a single word in red: 'Caution'.

'Needs must,' he pronounced warily.

'What's in the tin?' asked Katherine, curious and not a little alarmed. She recognized that the scrivening was in Stort's hand and knew very well that in his complacent parlance 'Caution' usually meant 'Extreme Danger'.

Barklice looked shifty.

'I can tell you it's a brew,' he replied, 'but more than that I know not. It is one of Stort's own invention and I believe that the letters stand for Medicinal Brew No. 7. He gave it to me years ago against the day when someone was in danger of death from extreme exposure and cold. That day has now come, for I think when we get him back here Stort will have need of something more than an ordinary brew if he is to recover himself!'

He was about to say more when their conversation was interrupted by two urgent whistles from further inland. Jack reacted first, as in circumstances of danger he usually did.

He came over to them and ordered Barklice to go and get Stort at once.

'Hurry! I want you both here and out of sight inside two minutes . . .'

Without more prevarication Barklice set off down the beach as Jack gathered the others around him, awaiting a further signal.

It came almost immediately.

The warning, which had been made by a lookout a little way inland, was followed by three more whistles then three more of different durations. A code.

'Humans are approaching,' murmured Jack, 'and we may need to leave fast.'

Moments later the lookout appeared.

He made a very extraordinary figure. He was a young hydden of Bilgesnipe stock, his legs bare, brown and muscular, with a turban-like wrapping of blue and white cotton about his head, a loose-fitting pale jerkin covered by a sleeveless blue padded jacket such as mariners wear, and a loin cloth. The Bilgesnipe were famed for their expertise with craft and trading on inland waterways and the high seas. They had been accepted and well settled on Englalond's water courses for generations.

'Hail and well met, my jubbly friends!' he cried. 'Who they'm be I know not. What they'm be about is unclear but dark, dark as death hissel'n. Where they'm headed is this-a-way, more or less. So I whistled you to come inland a pace or two.'

Arnold Mallarkhi was a Brum boatyboy, heir to the greatest family of Bilgesnipe mariners Brum had ever known and, without doubt, one of the most skilled handlers of watercraft ever born and raised in Englalond.

He was quick-thinking and had as steady a head in a crisis as adventurers and questers like Jack and the others could ever hope to find.

'What exactly have you seen?' asked Jack.

The expression on Arnold's face was one of almost perpetual good cheer but for once he looked grim, his eyes glittering and touched with anger.

'Humans,' he said. 'Coming down the lofty valley with a group of sorry folk runnin' afore 'em so scared I'll dare swear their teeth'll drop out. Killin's the game.'

'Killing what?' asked Jack urgently.

'Humans killin' humans,' said Arnold matter-of-factly.

An angry roar carried to them on the cold wind, then screams, male and female.

'They'm not likely to come this way a-bitta-yet but come they will. I'll be off to see what's what about!'

As Arnold retreated to investigate further, Jack and the others looked seaward, where Barklice now appeared to be trying to persuade Stort to return to the dunes. Whatever the outcome of that discussion might have been it was pre-empted by the arrival of a wave bigger than all those that had gone before. It swept the two right off their feet.

Jack and Katherine raced down the beach, waded into the swirling water and hauled them upright. They thumped them on their backs to rid their mouths and throats of water and then, half carrying, half dragging them from the rapacious waves, got them back at last to the safety of the dunes.

4

STORT'S PROPHECY

It took some minutes to get Stort and Barklice into dry clothes and administer the medicinal brew to them both.

While they waited for it to take effect Arnold reappeared. The humans were still further inland but heading their way and towards the shore.

'They'm a-taking their time, a-hurting as they go.'

'"A-hurting?"' repeated Jack.

'Torturing,' said Arnold quietly. Such a thing was beyond his, or any Bilgesnipe's ken.

Jack moved them further in among the dunes to a place from where they could still keep the shore in sight.

'I want a clear view of who they are and to be sure that when we retreat back to the top of the cliffs we are not likely to run into others of their kind.'

They all nodded grimly, understanding immediately what was on his mind. The evening before, they had accompanied Stort from the cliffs above to the shore for his vigil, and had left several more of their party behind in the protective shadow of Veryan Beacon, an important local landmark. It was near there that Stort had found the gem of Autumn and passed it into the safe-keeping of Judith the Shield Maiden.

It made no sense for them all to come down to the shore but now Jack, whose role as Stavemeister made him responsible for the security of them all, saw that by allowing them to be split into two groups he had weakened them and exposed them to the very danger from humans that now presented itself.

Obviously they must get back together and decide as a whole what to do next, even if it finally proved best to split up once more and make their different ways back to Brum.

'The sooner we get away from this cursed part of Englalond,' he growled, 'the better . . . Arnold, continue keeping a close eye on things while we attend to Stort and Barklice.'

Whatever the nature of the scrivener's special brew, it worked with such effect that very soon Stort seemed almost his normal self. He stretched, he rubbed his eyes and he began to hum, always a sign that his mind was settling down again. He was already so far recovered, indeed, that instead of having endured a difficult and challenging vigil through the long, exposed hours of the night, he might have simply been having a recuperative sleep.

When he finally came back to full consciousness he stared at them all with blank astonishment.

'Whatever are you doing here?' he cried out cheerfully, oblivious of the care and devotion they had shown him.

'Worrying about you,' said Katherine.

It had not occurred to him that they had been holding a vigil in parallel to his own, one concerned as much with his health and safety as with those same matters of the gem of Winter and his love for Judith which he himself had been wrestling with.

He found it very hard to understand concern for him or to think that hydden other than Barklice would think twice about his safety. His actions always seemed logical and reasonable to him and in no way eccentric or matters for others to waste their time over.

'Well, well, I am sorry if I caused you anxiety!'

'You are already quite recovered, then?' asked Blut with amazement.

Stort nodded casually before staring hard at Barklice, for whom the brew had been less immediately efficacious. He now sat hunched and pale and holding his stomach.

'Ah!' said Stort with some unease. 'I fear that if you plied my hapless friend Barklice with that brew of mine he might feel ill for a little while. You see he has a weak stomach and it may act as a violent purgative! I am made of sterner stuff and in rude health! Indeed, I may . . . I may say . . .'

He turned suddenly pale and a look of pain and discomfort came to his face as he too grabbed his stomach, turned from them, and staggered off behind the nearest dune, from where they heard the retching and groans of one who is being violently sick.

Strangely, these sounds of illness had a restorative effect on Barklice, who perked up on hearing them and immediately began to recover. A short while later he leapt to his feet with his ear cocked in the direction of the dune behind which Stort had gone to ground and observed, 'If that is the sound of what I think it is then, gentlemen and lady, I cannot say I feel sorry for him! He should have warned me! Let him be as sick as I have been. Let him experience at first hand the effects of his untried inventions. Pity him not, for he will bounce back from his self-inflicted trial, claim it was a necessary part of the experiment and, when he discovers that all his warts, pimples and moles—'

'I did not know he had any,' said Katherine.

'Well then, when all his various excrescences and suchlike disappear, you may be sure he will re-label this vile brew as a curative for Cow Flux!'

That this was unjust and unfair Jack knew, but it was also uncharacteristic of Barklice to say such things. Clearly the brew had not yet worked itself right the way through his system.

'And do *you* feel yourself again, Mister Barklice?' asked Sinistral, eyes twinkling.

'Never better, Sinistral, Lord of All, never better! Incidentally, out there on the shore Stort was threatening to make a prophecy. Has he made it yet?'

They looked puzzled. But as they shook their heads a frail-looking Bedwyn Stort reappeared, a shadow of what he had been moments before, yet, as Barklice had predicted, a shadow recovering.

'Interesting!' he murmured. 'I do believe my freckles have faded somewhat. Hmmm! Of that, more later. Meanwhile . . .'

His demeanour became sombre and serious now and he seemed about to speak. Silence fell but for the hiss of the wind in the marram grass and sand about them and the grumbling roar of the surf down on the beach. This made sufficient noise for them to draw closer in together so that they might more easily hear him.

'No doubt,' whispered Blut to Lord Sinistral, 'we will now receive the fruits of Stort's mental labours on the beach.'

Stort stood frowning, his hair lank with brine but his colour brightening.

'Not so many days ago some of us here, indeed all of us with the exception of you, Lord Sinistral, were present at the natural destruction of a small human town named Half Steeple,' he began. 'At the time one of us said, or perhaps only thought, that we were mute witnesses to the beginning of the End of Days . . .'

It had happened barely two weeks before, two hundred miles to the north. Jack and his friends had then been heading south in pursuit of the gem of Autumn and found themselves on the bank of the River Severn, near a human town called Half Steeple. A great fissure had appeared in the ground into which the town, the river and all the humans thereabout were swallowed as if into the maw of Mother Earth Herself.

This sequence of events was so rapid and horrible that they had no time to make sense of it before the fissure closed, leaving barely a trace of the lost town. The Severn began its normal flow again and it almost seemed to Jack and the other hydden witnesses as if it had never happened at all.

Yet so strange and shocking had it been, and so demanding their subsequent journey on south to where the gem of Autumn was found and returned by Stort to the Shield Maiden, that the truth was that they had never come to terms with the incident. All the more so because in the days following they had to deal with the fact that one of their number, the much-loved Arthur Foale, the adoptive father of Katherine, had died. He had done so on the night when October gave way to November, which marked the start of the season hydden call Samhain, which humans call winter.

Then, while Katherine had to deal with Arthur's death, Jack was suddenly faced with the arrival by sea on this same Pendower beach of a family and in particular a brother he did not know he had. Blut too, who had thought it likely he might never see Lord Slaeke Sinistral again, was astonished to have him appear at the same time and by the same route. Which meant, to his relief, that, having been elevated to the Imperial throne but three months previously, he now had support in that role from the person who understood it better than anyone else. This he welcomed, though Mirror knew he had performed the highest office in the Hyddenworld with remarkable skill and leadership.

Now Stort's sudden and unexpected recall of what had happened at Half Steeple had subsequently stilled them all, himself included.

'You too have suffered change and loss,' said Katherine suddenly, going to him and bidding him sit down, for he looked tired and weak once more. He did as he was told, his attachment to Katherine being deep and special.

He was never easy with the touch of others, growing awkward and wishing to withdraw, as if so simple a thing as a hand on his arm might rob him of something of himself. But Katherine, who was herself inclined to be prickly and uneasy with intimacy, had that art to perfection where their friend was concerned.

He accepted her hand gratefully. The night had been a hard one, and the day as well. Recalling the night of Samhain, when the gem of Autumn was returned, Katherine said, 'Judith had no sooner come than she was gone, Stort, and you must have found that very difficult.'

With a sad nod of his head he conceded that he did.

Judith was the strange and terrifying daughter of Katherine and Jack, born six months previously but grown to an adult in that short time and, too, into a near-immortal. She was the prophesied Shield Maiden, though whether guardian of the Earth or protector of mortals against the Earth, no one was sure. It was she alone who could receive and wear the gems, in the pendant Beornamund had made fifteen hundred years before.

Only Stort seemed able to give them to her without harm, for anyone who even touched them risked a heavy sickness of body and mind. As Jack, for one, had discovered the previous summer, nearly dying after coming into contact with one of the gems.

The expression on Stort's face showed clearly that it had indeed been upsetting to meet Judith again. She aged at a much faster rate than ordinary mortals. The girl he first knew had become a beautiful young woman that summer, if a difficult one, but by autumn she was already ageing and by Samhain she was old and worn and plainly unhappy. Age had gripped her and they could all see how terrible was a wyrd that aged someone a whole lifetime in a single human year.

But he had felt her distress more than any of them. For he of all living beings seemed to understand rather than fear her. Only with him did she feel that, for all her fearsome, maddened passion as the ambiguous agent of the Earth, and her rapid withering, she was not entirely alone.

On the night when he gave her the Autumn gem, up by the Beacon on the hill above the beach, where others of their friends now awaited them, that night . . .

'She challenged me,' he said, 'or perhaps I did her. She said our love is impossible, for never could a mortal and an immortal . . . well . . . you know . . .'

He smiled uneasily, shy as he was about matters of love, about which he knew so little, especially physical love.

'Never did such a love come to be. It is impossible. But fool that I am, driven by desires that are not entirely . . . well . . . you know . . .'

They could guess but had no need to put into words what he found so hard, deep and natural though his yearnings were.

'Fool that I was, as I placed that alluring gem in the pendant she wears, I said I'd find a way for us to be together one day, somehow, somewhere, and . . . then . . . well . . .'

'We know,' said Katherine gently, reaching a hand to his shoulder.

'But one of the conclusions I came to last night out there on the sands, is that I will not, I *cannot*, find the last lost gem, which is that of Winter. I do not know how to do it, and if I did I would not know where to look, and even if I did know that I would not be *able* to give it to her.'

He paused, shaking his head miserably as he wrestled with duty and doubt.

Then, in barely more than a whisper, he continued, '. . . and even if I did succeed, which I will not, at the moment that I place the gem of Winter in that immortal pendant, the End of Days may come upon us quite another way. For by then the Mirror will have cracked and all will be as if it never was, lost in the darkness of a trillion reflections of endless night in the shards and fragments of what once was.'

They looked at each other in bewilderment, uncertain if what Stort was saying was prophecy or warning. What he said next left no room for doubt.

'Oh yes,' he explained, 'once the four gems are conjoined again, the

Fires of the Universe will re-ignite and that can only mean the end of those whose mission it is to find the gems and return them, namely ourselves.

'So,' he concluded heavily, 'one way or another I have lost Judith forever. Not that I ever truly had a chance of winning her except, notionally as it were, up there in the constellations of the stars, as if my love for her, as hers for me, is in some imagined pattern of those irritating points of light, which are, I suspect, not what they seem at all. I yearn for her and that yearning will drive me on to the doom that I have seen awaits us all. Even if . . .'

Barklice, fully recovered now, sat next to him.

'Even if what, Stort?'

'Even if she comes trotting along on that White Horse as if she were no more than another pilgrim on the green road, like the rest of us.'

'Is she?' asked Blut.

'She is.'

'And will she?' said Sinistral, adding a question of his own.

'She will.'

'And all that . . .' said Jack after a pause and feeling bewildered, 'is your prophecy?'

Stort stood up once more and said, 'I think I've just made several prophecies.'

He looked out to sea as a brief shaft of sunlight broke through the clouds and turned a patch of water dark blue.

'But, of course, whatever may happen to each one of us in the days and weeks ahead, we'll all have to contend with those unpredictable shifts in time we have experienced through these months past. They are the inevitable consequence of the Mirror cracking and the greatest evidence that it is doing so.'

In recent weeks especially and latterly on their journey to Veryan Beacon, such shifts in time, though mainly slight and barely noticeable, had occurred more frequently. A lost few seconds here, a shift in the hours there, differentially from one place to another and probably, according to Stort and Sinistral, right across the Earth. When time itself ceased to be predictable the end as mortals knew it was certainly in sight.

'Then,' continued Stort, who after so many hours of silence seemed all too ready to talk, 'there is the question of humans. They are mortal too. They will be as affected by all this as we hydden, which throws into doubt the centuries-old lore that there are no circumstances in which we should interact with humans, except of course those who, like Katherine and Arthur Foale before her, found a peaceable way into the Hyddenworld. Indeed . . .'

They heard Arnold's warning whistle once more and as Barklice immediately turned towards the sound, scaling a dune to see what he could spot, Stort finally fell silent.

Barklice lay down, parted the grass at the top and studied the valley inland from which, in times past, the stream that issued forth just there had created the outlet and small estuary that was the bay.

After a while he said in a low voice, 'There are seven or eight of them being chased by four others, all heading down the path from the Iron Age fort on the hill above to this very beach. If they continue on that course they'll arrive two hundred yards to our east in a few minutes much as Arnold predicted. There's no one westward unless humans have got into the buildings we scouted out yesterday . . .'

Arnold reappeared and confirmed what Barklice had said.

Jack signalled for them all to lie low and it was as well he did. Soon they heard the unhappy sounds of the humans more distinctly. Soon after, a straggle of ill-dressed humans, some bleeding, some helping others, spilled out onto the beach. There were indeed eight in all, being adult males and females and three children. After hesitating for a short while and sending terrified glances back up the stream down whose valley they had fled, they staggered down the hostile shore to where Stort had been standing a short time before.

There, unable to flee further because of the surf, nor having enough strength or will to help each other along the shore one way or another, they huddled passively together, awaiting their fate.

5

INHUMANITY

Jack and the others watched cautiously from the dunes as four more
humans appeared at the top of the beach. It was obvious from
their confidence and dark, well-made clothing that these were the
aggressors.

'I do not think we need worry overmuch about them seeing us,'
murmured Barklice. 'We are well hidden and they seem intent on com-
pleting their own unpleasant business.'

In fact the risks of being seen by humans were nearly non-existent,
for in the fifteen hundred years since hydden had ended all direct
contact with them, humans had forgotten not only that hydden shared
the world around them, but also even how to see that they were there.

When a hydden made a mistake or was caught out humans went into
denial at what they saw, insisting they must have been 'seeing things'
or, for want of a rational explanation, 'seeing fairies' or a whole host of
mythical creatures, such as elves, sprites, goblins, ents, orcs and many
more besides. There were few human societies that had not made such
superstitious myths of the simple truth that hydden had always existed
alongside them and still did.

The historic truth was more astonishing still. The 'giants' and 'ents'
and suchlike monstrous creatures so many human cultures created in
their stories were nothing less than they themselves.

But while hydden were able to see humans when they first came
into contact with them, they did not immediately see them as clearly
as humans saw each other. The hydden had no great interest in
humans and avoided contact with them as much as they could. They

saw human movement and general shape rather than their detail. Indeed, only humans like Katherine who had travelled into the Hydden-world, and Jack who had lived so long in the human one, were able to make out and describe the differences between humans in terms of age or sex.

Yet even they, in the relatively short time they had been in the Hyddenworld, had got out of practice. So, like someone who must adjust to sudden dark or light, Katherine needed time to be able to adjust to the humans clearly.

It helped that she was not over-sensitized to the hideous sweet-sour smell of them, as ordinary hydden were. Such odours were the result of the dairy products they consumed, which hydden rarely did, as well as their much higher consumption of dead meat and other decaying things and products with preservative chemicals and colourings whose scents sweated out foully from their skin. And then there was the odour of fear, which Arnold Mallarkhi had first scented before he spotted the fleeing humans earlier. Jack and the others now smelt this fear in all its unpleasantness: rank and sharp.

The others could only watch the scene that now unfolded as through a slightly misted glass, it being initially easier for them to follow the horror of it through the medium of scent and general movement, as extreme fear blurs a human image to a hydden even more than normal.

The four pursuers were nearer and easier to make out. Three of them were larger than even the largest of their quarry. They wore leather clothes and heavy boots as a form of armour and carried weapons of some kind. The fourth, a female and apparently their leader, began shouting commands.

'She's carrying a shotgun,' whispered Katherine.

'She's ordering her followers to herd the others further towards the waves,' said Jack grimly, signalling to the others to stay low.

Odours of a different kind now came to them. They were those of the pursuers and they were less rank, being that of the triumph of victors, heady and strong.

'They've been drinking,' murmured Katherine uneasily.

Two were armed with clubs and knives. When they had the bigger group trapped by the waves they stood still, neither side moving, the thundering waves the backdrop to them all. To the hydden the aggressors' voices seemed deep and jagged, their laughter like breaking glass, their movements jerky and unpleasant.

One of them turned back towards the dunes, stared at a point a hundred yards or so to the right of where Jack and Katherine lay, where a path came onto the beach, and whistled.

Almost at once another female appeared and she chilled the hearts of Katherine and Jack when they saw what accompanied her.

She had two strong dogs on leashes. They were squat, stumpy, muscular creatures and they did not bark but rather emitted low, deep-throated growls. At the sound of a second whistle from the beach they began straining at their leashes so powerfully that their handler had difficulty restraining them. Wet sand flew from beneath their scrabbling paws and drool hung from their snarling maws. One was brown, the other black flecked with grey. They were creatures of nightmare.

Jack whispered urgently, 'Katherine, we've no part in this. We must leave now. If those dogs came our way . . .'

Arnold Mallarkhi, who had briefly crawled to the top of a dune and looked inland, came back down to them.

'There be more humans upperway,' he said, his voice fading as he saw the dogs, 'but they'm avoidable. My good hearties, seeing them currish hounds, I'm thinking we best retreat right now and beat a path the long way round to our friends a-waitin' by the Beacon.'

'Do we know *they're* safe?' asked Blut.

'They be so I'd say,' said Arnold, 'being like to have scented these humans long afore they appeared and gone well to ground. Easy enough to get you all up there right-a-way. This'm mess down here bain't now for hydden eyes . . .'

Perhaps he was right and they should have followed his advice and left at once. But it was difficult not to watch in mounting horror what happened next.

At a third whistle the handler unleashed the straining dogs, which began their charge down the beach immediately, heads low, teeth bared, their yellow pig-eyes fixed on their prey.

The pursuers, female and male alike, followed after the dogs, swinging their clubs back and forth aggressively and occasionally smashing them with gusto into those of their colleagues.

A horrible pattern of attack developed, which suggested that the dogs were trained for just such work. They went for the largest and strongest of their quarry first, which meant the men. These had done their best to stand their ground while the women retreated with the children. Some went one way along the shore, some another and some fell among the waves where they stood awash and helpless.

When the dogs launched themselves at one of the men they did so so powerfully that their target fell back helpless onto the sand. As the others tried to haul off the dogs their enemies arrived, clubbing them down summarily, one after another, before beating the men into semi-consciousness.

A shout, some more laughter and a bloody cry from the woman leader, and the dogs began to feed on the exposed flesh of the fallen men. Their screams were high pitched yet muted as blood spurted onto the sand, and surf came up and retreated, made pink by what washed back with it.

The dogs were soon called off, their victims suffering pain and shock. One reached hands into the air as if seeking support from the brightening sky above.

At a single, whistled new command the dogs, which had obediently squatted down awaiting their orders, raised their heads, looked about and bounded off along the beach, this time targeting the only child left standing.

Then one of the dogs appeared to pick up the scent left by Stort and Barklice, for it paused, turned duneward and peered in the hyddens' direction. Jack's grasp of his stave tightened and they all stilled until the dog, distracted by the child, turned seaward again.

The surviving victims stood terrified, the lives of some of their kin already torn to pieces right in front of them, their terror etched on their faces and expressed through their screams.

6

COLD COMFORT

A cold rage overtook Jack.

He had no wish to attack humans but such outright cruelty and murder he could not stomach or ignore. He laid his stave on the ground, unbuckled the crossbow from his belt and calmly loaded it. He signalled to Katherine to do the same.

They had acquired the crossbows after defeating some renegade forces of the Imperial army, better known as the Fyrd. Though Jack preferred using a stave and Katherine had little fighting experience, they had both taken to the weapons. They were light, easy to load and aim and very effective at close range. The short hardwood bolts tipped with metal which they shot could easily fell a hydden and cause serious injury or death to a human.

The men with clubs now advanced severally on the women. When one of them turned to flee they simply threw a club at her and brought her down. The dogs were whistled to heel.

More human aggressors appeared at the top of the beach.

'They be the ones I saw blocking our way earlier,' said Arnold, 'which means we may have a clearer path now. Master Jack, it be time to leave. Let 'em cursed humans to ruin their own lives.'

Which even then Jack might have done, leaving the humans to their own wyrd or fate, had not one of the children surprised them all. He had been among the first to fall and had appeared lifeless since. The dogs had passed him by, the humans too. Now he rose up and began a desperate attempt, wounded though he was, to reach the dunes. The dogs heard and saw and turned as one towards this new victim. But the route up the beach just there was steep and the sand wet and thick, so the boy was able to negotiate it better than the dogs, whose short legs sank deep. He headed straight towards where Jack and the others were watching.

'Get Lords Sinistral and Blut back to the others and the safety of the Beacon above,' Jack now finally ordered Barklice and Arnold, stuffing his stave of office through his belt so that it was handy should the crossbow fail him. 'Now. Do it. Katherine, come with me and stay on my left . . .'

The others retreated at once while Jack and Katherine stepped forward into the open to meet the boy. Some instinct in the child told him that they were benign and he ran between them to the safety of the nearest dune.

Jack now turned to face the dogs.

'Bastards,' he said, eyeing not just the dogs but the surprised humans beyond.

'Agreed,' said Katherine quietly, readying her crossbow as well.

'You take the left one and I'll take the right . . .'

'Oh *yes*,' she said softly, sighting on the dog nearest her.

They were both exposed but the humans were slow to react, no doubt puzzled by what they saw.

The two strangers who had appeared to protect the boy were hard to scale in a natural landscape like the dunes without a human artefact to set them against. Hard even to sex, since both were dressed in similar clothes and these were unfamiliar. The gorse and marram grass behind them kept shifting in the wind, making things more difficult still.

Were they big or small, adults or children?

What were those things they held, which now they both raised slowly and with a calm and fearless assurance which the aggressors had never seen in any of their victims, especially when attacked by their beasts? These were trained attack-dogs and once off the leash all their victims could do was try to flee. But often they simply froze where they stood, so struck with fear that they did not even scream as the teeth of the bull terriers sank into them and they were savaged to the ground.

But the two strange people who had emerged from the dunes to rescue the boy were something else entirely. They stood their ground, calmly readying their weapons.

The leader of the aggressors, the female with the shotgun, was the first to react. She swung the barrel of her gun round and brought it to bear on the new arrivals. As she did so she moved towards them, shouting to those with her to follow suit.

But something wasn't right. Still the two by the dunes didn't waver and the closer they got the more the humans couldn't make out what they were. Their familiar world was suddenly unfamiliar. Their safe world of murder, rape and pillage had now been turned upside down and felt unsafe.

Choosing his moment, Jack took a step forward and fired at the dog that was coming straight for him.

His bolt hit the creature's breast and went through flesh and muscle and bone into the creature's heart. It dropped straight down, its legs spasming briefly before it lay still.

Jack turned as Katherine's shot drove into the right eye of the dog about to attack her. Shaking its head terribly it veered to one side and Jack fired his next bolt into it, shouting, 'Save your second for the men!'

'And women,' said Katherine grimly, turning her attention to the humans. It was as well she did for the female leader was already taking aim with her gun. The bolt Katherine fired next caught her in the chest and she fell, her shots going wildly but harmlessly into the air.

The attackers now stood still in surprise and growing fear, black against the sky and sea, their carnage about them, but for a man who was trying to rape one of the women near the waves. Hearing the firing he pulled himself into a kneeling position and turned to see what was happening.

He saw the two small figures advancing down the beach, dead dogs on the high-tide mark behind them, his leader prone in the sand and two more of the men wheeling away, one clutching at his groin, the other at his throat, from shots that Katherine and Jack, having re-loaded, had continued to fire.

As he struggled to rise, his loosened trousers tangling him so he stood hobbled, he saw two more of his friends, both trying to flee, fall to the ground, bolts in their backs.

The last one remaining but for himself threw his raised club aside and raised his hands.

'Shoot him,' said Jack mercilessly.

Katherine did so, in his fat belly, then a second shot the same. He screamed and wept as his victims had before him.

'Bastard,' she said, the blood-lust in her too. 'He was the one who clubbed that child.'

Which left the rapist alone, struggling to find his trouser top to pull it up and flee.

They might easily have killed him too but the woman he had been trying to rape did the job for them. She rose up behind him, grabbed the knife from his belt and brutally stabbed him in the back. He fell struggling into a surging wave and she, screaming her hate, plunged the knife into his back again and again.

When the next wave swirled about them both, the water turned to a mess of foaming pink, before he was dragged away and she lay weeping in the sand.

One of the other women called out to the boy Jack had saved and who now reappeared up by the dunes. They ran towards each other and embraced as the remaining survivors stood staring at Jack and Katherine in wonder.

'Our work is done,' said Jack bleakly, 'let's get away from here . . .'

They did so at once, first into the dunes and out of sight of the humans and thence up the valley down which the humans had come. They did not talk to each other. Nothing to say, nothing to think, the vengeful anger of minutes before fading into a dull sense of horror at what they had just done.

They felt tainted, unclean, soiled by the very inhumanity they had been trying to prevent.

'What have we done?' asked Jack.

'We have discovered what the End of Days must mean,' replied Katherine, her expression blank.

They stopped and tried to look at each other but their eyes could not meet.

'Come,' said Katherine, trying to reach to him but not quite doing so, 'it's time to go back to Brum.'

7
PARTING

The half-hour climb from Pendower Beach to Veryan Beacon, which sits on high ground a little way back from the cliff edge looming over the shore, was steep.

The human path was plainly visible all the way up the valley from the beach to an Iron Age fort. Then through its ramparts and on along the side of a field with a high bank to the right and a view across the wider expanse of the upper valley to the left.

The Beacon, which was an ancient human structure of earth and stone, on top of which a concrete emplacement had been added in recent years, was twenty feet high. It gave a commanding view over the land all about and far into the distance along the southward shore.

The hydden route from beach to beacon ran parallel with the human one, first through woodland to scrub on higher ground and finally by way of a plush green road. Their path rejoined the human route at the fort.

It was here that Jack and Katherine were met by Barklice. He had gone ahead with Sinistral, Stort, Blut and Arnold Mallarkhi, re-established contact with the group above and had returned to find his friends.

He was bleary eyed and breathless, which for him was almost unknown.

'That brew of Stort's did the trick for him,' he conceded gruffly, 'but was a mistake for me. I've really come to hurry you along because your . . . I mean to say your . . . um . . .'

Jack frowned and Barklice wavered, quite unsure how to continue.

The hydden he was trying to find a tactful way to refer to was Borkum Riff with whom Jack had only just become acquainted; feelings ran high and awkwardly between them.

'Riff is *what*?' asked Jack rather heavily.

'He is anxious to ready his sailing craft for the rising tide and set off for the east coast of Englalond. I think he hopes that you will sail with him.'

'Does he!' exclaimed Jack sharing a glance with Katherine. 'Does he indeed!'

'Er, yes . . . he does.'

A few days before, on the eve of the finding of the gem of Autumn and its returning to Judith the Shield Maiden, Riff had skippered one of three craft that unexpectedly arrived on the shore below. In his cutter had been Sinistral and his Shadowmaster and protector Witold Slew, along with two fierce Norseners, all stave fighters of great skill.

Jack had been shocked and astonished to discover that Borkum Riff, a powerful, dark and taciturn sailor who was widely regarded as the greatest of the North Sea mariners, was his father.

But that was not all.

The second craft was helmed by Riff's son Herde Deap, who many would have said was second only to Riff himself in his skill as a mariner of the treacherous and unpredictable waters between the Continent and the isles of which Englalond was the largest. It also carried the Lady Leetha, Riff's onetime lover and mother of Deap. She had also been for decades the close friend and confidante of Sinistral himself.

It was obvious to all but Jack, when he and Deap stood side by side, that they were twins. But neither had met the other before as adults, for Jack had been separated first from Riff when Leetha left him and then from her as well when it was realized he was the giant-born of prophecy who might help save the world from the End of Days. He was initially raised by Leetha in the Thuringia Wald in central Germany but sent to Englalond to be raised in the human world when he was six. Like Katherine, on his return to the Hyddenworld he was changed to hydden size, but in his case he retained the exceptional strength and qualities of a giant-born.

The early dislocations of his family and country had robbed him of all memory of his past. He had been appalled to discover that Witold

Slew, his mortal enemy in the struggle for the gem of Summer and killer of one of the most revered citizens of Brum, was Leetha's son by a different father and so his half-brother.

No wonder that Barklice was uneasy calling Riff Jack's 'father', even though he was. Jack felt uncomfortable too and it was therefore in dark and sombre mood that he plodded the last few yards to Veryan Beacon to join the others – and Borkum Riff – once more.

It was now nearly midday and the sky had cleared. The north wind was so cold that the group of hydden, fifteen in all, had moved their base to the sheltered south side of the Beacon.

'There be no humans any more, not near anyroad,' declared Mallar-khi. 'Brother Slew, his mateyboys Harald and Bjarne have looked hither-abouts and down and upperways. We'm safe 'n sound we be, for now.'

Safe they might be, but the mood of the gathering grew dark after news of the massacre of humans by humans on the beach was reported by Jack and Katherine, though they played down their own subsequent involvement.

After that Jack stayed silent, sitting down next to Deap and accepting a wooden bowl of good hot pottage from Terce, another of the party.

He was a large, broad hydden, gentler in nature and appearance than the two Norseners, whose self-appointed task was to sit high up the Beacon on either side to keep a watchful eye for strangers.

Terce's name was a clue to his origin. He had been a monk and was the last of two survivors of an ancient choir whom Stort had tracked down to a monastery in central Englalond during the autumn. His meister had died since and now he was the last survivor of a tradition that stretched back centuries, a chorister of such training and skill that Stort believed he had it in him to sing in perfect harmony with the Earth Herself. In short, to make audible, through his voice and its resonance with all things, that same harmony which was said to hold the Universe together and help keep the Mirror whole. But since, in Stort's view, the Mirror had cracked, the importance of Terce to them all could not be over-estimated, for he would surely be needed if universal harmony was to be restored and the Mirror repaired.

He was modest by nature, no more than twenty or so, with hair

shorn in a monkish way and physically courageous. A quality of innocence and goodness shone from him and in that he had a similarity to
Stort himself. He carried a large and sturdy stave, as monks often do,
and he was prepared to use it in the protection of others as well as
himself.

As for singing, he practised frequently, though rarely the sacred songs
and melodies he knew so well. He practised scales of all kinds, in keys
most musicians were unfamiliar with. His harmonies with wind and rain
and all things natural were beyond imagining until they were actually
heard.

But it was another large hydden, bulkier and older than Terce, who
took charge of the warm welcome that Jack and Katherine now received
and saw to it they were well settled and provided for. He was silver
haired and so magisterial in bearing and gaze that even in a company
as august as that one he seemed the natural host and leader of
proceedings.

This was Lord Festoon, High Ealdor of Brum, who, within the
bounds of his own city, took precedence over even the Emperor
himself. But here too, it seemed, they were happy to let him take
charge.

Satisfied that they were all safely present once more, he signalled
the new Emperor, Niklas Blut, over to him and the two conferred
in whispers for a while. Then, coming to a decision of some sort, they
nodded their heads and Festoon called them all to order, as if this were
a committee meeting in a city hall.

'Lady and gentlemen,' he said, his voice rich and warm, 'I think we
can agree that our work here in the South-West is done, and done
successfully. Mister Stort, whose researches far and wide led us here,
found the gem of Autumn and returned it to the Shield Maiden. That
was good. We lost a friend, and Katherine here a father in all but name,
when Arthur Foale passed on to the Mirror. For him we have grieved
these days past and we shall not forget him or ever fail to be grateful
for what, as a human, he uniquely gave to the Hyddenworld.

'But Arthur, who was my dear friend too, would have been the first
to want us to now move on. He knew, as well as any of us, the extreme
danger these times present us with. He feared greatly, and said as much

quite recently to Emperor Blut here and myself, that in such a turmoil as the Earth now is, humans might become a serious threat to the hydden. He said this as a human himself . . .'

Festoon turned to Blut and continued: 'My dear Blut, correct me if I am wrong, but did Arthur not say that it is the human habit to attack others when they are afraid, unlike the hydden?'

'He did,' said Blut, 'and also . . . if I may . . . ?'

Blut's memory was phenomenal and Festoon now deferred to him.

'Arthur's exact words were these: "Fear and hysteria will sweep the human world if natural disasters reach a point where it looks as if the Earth Herself is angry. Hydden understand that Mother Earth has feelings and is sentient but humans find that notion difficult. If they were able to see things differently then surely they would not hurt Her as they do. As it is, they blame whatever or whoever they can rather than themselves. If they were to discover that we hydden exist and live among them they would find a way to attack and destroy us."'

Blut paused before continuing with his own words.

'I can say with certainty that Arthur was very worried by the fact that he had left a great deal of data and other information about the hydden and Brum and even ourselves in and about his human home in Woolstone . . .'

Jack and Katherine both looked surprised. They had always assumed that Arthur would leave nothing that would give away the secret of how he used a henge to enter the Hyddenworld.

'I'm afraid,' said Blut, 'he *did* leave clues. He admitted as much to me during the time we were held in captivity by General Quatremayne, leader of the renegade Fyrd. I owe my life to Arthur and was in awe of him. He was, of course, the first human being for fifteen hundred years to solve the riddle of how to travel between the human and hydden worlds and back again.'

'He was so,' added Stort, 'and I could not have done the same without his instructions. But he was very much concerned about what would happen if humans discovered his secrets.'

'Yes he was,' confirmed Katherine, 'but he told me he had been careful to destroy his notes on that subject.'

'Perhaps he did,' said Blut, 'but I have a feeling that unfortunately he may not have had time to finish doing so. His last journey into the

Hyddenworld – something he had promised his wyf never to do again – was forced upon him by humans who were intent on holding him until he revealed his secrets.'

Sinistral looked surprised.

'Yes, indeed, my Lord Sinistral, it was so.'

'Tell us, Niklas.'

Blut nodded, recalling something which at the time he first heard it had seemed of no great significance.

'One of his former students was called Bohr, Erich Bohr I think. He was an important figure in what humans call the Union of America.'

'You mean the United States!'

'Just so. Well, when the number of natural disasters rose so suddenly earlier this year, Bohr contacted Arthur. Arthur guessed why: Bohr wanted access to the Hyddenworld, which Arthur had foolishly revealed was possible, though without revealing exactly how he did it. When Arthur realized that it was likely he was going to be taken to a place from which he might not be able to get away, he took steps to hide his remaining papers and anything else that might be a clue, however indirect. But he told me he had not completed the job.

'"Blut, my dear chap," he confessed, "we all allow our judgement to be clouded by sentiment and pride. The secret to using the henges as portals between our worlds is really simple. In fact, it can be written down on a single page. Well . . . not exactly written, drawn more like."

'He looked worried and I expressed horror that he might perhaps have left such a piece of paper at his home in Woolstone. When he fell silent I challenged him and he replied cagily saying, "Look, Blut, even if someone found it they wouldn't know what it meant. They couldn't do it."

'"So you did leave it somewhere?" I asked.

'"I . . . maybe . . . did . . . I . . . dammit, Blut, all right! I admit it! Sentiment got the better of me. I left it . . ." At this point I had to stop him talking. I did not want to know where or what it was.'

'You mean you never found out?' cried Katherine. 'And this bit of paper, this clue, is out there still for humans to find!'

'Hardly "out there", Katherine.'

'You mean it's in Woolstone, the first place anyone looking for it would go?'

'Yes,' said Blut unhappily.

'Well, then, the first thing we're now going to have to do after we leave here is to get to Woolstone and retrieve it, isn't it? Even before we go back to Brum!'

'I suppose one or other of us might have to,' conceded Blut.

'Otherwise the humans who let Arthur escape will go to Woolstone to try to find out what they can, won't they?'

'Probably,' admitted Blut, 'they might.'

'And the Hyddenworld will be invaded just like they invade everything else: wilderness, space, the sea . . .'

Jack and Katherine looked at each other.

'One of us, or perhaps both of us, needs to get to Woolstone as soon as we can and make sure that no secrets have been left there. Agreed?'

Jack nodded and looked at Festoon and Blut.

'Agreed,' they said together.

'Which means, Stort,' said Katherine, 'that while you're looking for the gem of Winter some of us will have our work cut out in the shadow of the White Horse!'

Woolstone House, where Arthur had raised her, sat in the vale just beneath White Horse Hill.

'Just so,' said Festoon grimly. 'But also, we left Brum in dire straits, in the hands of the Fyrd. With winter now upon us things will get no easier. But we should not be surprised at such challenges. Recent history shows us that no sooner has one quest been completed than the complexities of the next are upon us and most particularly upon our good friend and beloved Master Scrivener, Bedwyn Stort.'

Stort never did like being singled out in such a way. When he was he tended to fidget uncomfortably, to gaze at anything nearby like blades of grass, passing clouds or his own ill-shod feet, as if they were objects of great interest.

Festoon was aware of this and, having given this brief acknowledgement to their mutual friend, simply added, 'But of the search for the gem of Winter, which will concern us all and to which our combined efforts must now be bent, since Stort has led us to the first three gems so triumphantly, he needs nothing more now by way of help except what he asks for and warm encouragement from us all!'

'Humph!' muttered Stort.

'Now to matters more immediate. We are generally agreed then that it is imperative we return to Brum, some of us by way of Woolstone?'

'Definitely by way of Woolstone,' said Jack.

'Quite so. But our primary duty and, I believe, our future, lies in Brum. We can also agree that it makes sense and will be safer if we travel in two separate parties, one by land and one by sea. The question is: who goes in which party? Emperor Blut and I have conferred and, apart from three of us, it seems clear enough who goes with whom. First the sea travellers. Borkum Riff told us earlier that he wishes to sail with the afternoon tide along with Herde Deap, who will skipper the other craft. So far it is agreed that Lady Leetha, Brother Slew and the two Norseners will go with them.

'Travelling by land will be myself, Emperor Blut, my Lord Sinistral, who wishes to see a part of Englalond he never has, Terce and Barklice, whom we will need to help us with the routes. Stort, my sense is you would wish to come with us . . . ?'

'I would,' said Stort.

'Which leaves Jack, Katherine and Arnold Mallarkhi. The latter, of course, came in his own craft with Terce . . .'

'And a fine and chumpy hand 'ee wer to have aboard,' cried Arnold, 'but to save your breath my bones tell me the sea going will be hard if we'm headin' north and along the western shore in this season, so mayhap I'm a better stayin' with inland waters for now. I'll go wi' ye, my Lord Festoon.'

'A shame!' murmured Riff. 'A more natural-born sailor I never saw.'

'Maybe, maybe,' replied Arnold, 'but count me in with the shore party if you please! And anyway, there be another reason takes me along wi' you lubbers.'

'Yes?' said Festoon.

'I be a-watchin' for a spousible one to take home wi' me . . .'

Sinistral and Blut looked puzzled.

'He means he wants to find a wyf,' whispered Jack, grinning.

'. . . and ma allers said they'm a good few possibilities westward way. Meanin' the land we'm headin' back through. My spousal one will know me when she sees me.'

'Isn't it a case of you knowing her when you see her?' Blut could not help asking.

Arnold laughed.

'That b'aint the Bilgesnipe way. Tis the wyfkin do the choosing and the asking and the fellers who say yay or nay. Me? I bain't easy meat and willern't take the first I see, not by a long way. Not Arnold!'

'Good,' said Festoon mildly, 'then that's settled, Arnold, as far as you're concerned. You'll come with us. Leaving Jack and Katherine. Now I have no wish to suggest they be parted but . . .'

'Nor will we be,' said Jack, frowning. 'I'm travelling back overland. Agreed, Katherine?'

Jack had earlier observed Katherine having a brief conversation with Leetha and immediately after with Riff. Reading her mind, he was making a pre-emptive strike against something he had no wish to do. But she was not going to be deterred.

She shook her head and said, '*Not* agreed. It would do you good, Jack, to travel back with your family.'

Jack stood up peremptorily and said, 'I'm not talking about this here!'

She stood up too and they walked off across the field and engaged in what appeared, from the many gesticulations, raised voices, turnings-away and embraces and reconciliations, to be a violent disagreement. But finally, as suddenly as the argument began it ended with a very long hug, out in the cold wind. Then the two joined them once more and sat down.

'Jack has decided that he will travel with Borkum Riff and Lady Leetha,' said Katherine simply, adding, without much enthusiasm, 'which means that I'll go with your party, Lord Festoon.'

The decision finally made, and certain other matters agreed, Riff stood up and said, 'We leave in ten minutes. Jack, your brother will check your portersac to see you have what you'll need for a sea voyage. The sea makes different demands than land.'

Arnold ambled over and offered advice as well.

'Don't fight the deck, Jack, or it'll fight you. My grandpa allers said the boat be a woman and you be a man, and the best is when you work together. O' that I bain't been old enough till now to find out! Me? I say a boat is your partner in crime and your fellow crew your partners too. Listen to the water and the wind and listen hard.'

A short while later Riff summoned his party to him.

'Slew will lead us to the shore, in case there's still humans about down there. Jack, you're to take the rear. Let's be a-gone and away!'

There was barely time for Jack and Katherine to embrace and so be rid of any lingering irritations arising from their argument, in which Katherine had imposed her will.

'They're family, Jack, and it's time with them you need.'

'But Slew . . .'

Slew had killed Master Brief, Brum's Librarian and a friend to them all.

'Even Slew,' she said.

Then they were gone, with no more than a wave.

Katherine would have liked to linger and watch the craft set sail but Festoon wanted to get away as well. Their time in the West Country was done. It really was time to go home.

They struck camp, cleared the site of all evidence that they had been there, as hydden do, and were off north and eastward along the green road once more.

'Farewell,' they said to the place that had harboured them so well.

'Farewell, Arthur,' whispered Katherine, looking back at the hallowed place where he had died and his pyre had burnt, 'farewell.'

Farewell, my friends, farewell, the wind whispered in the high hedgerows and gnarled, bent trees, *farewell*.

Then they were gone, as the black-headed gulls hovered over the Beacon for a while before plunging to the ground to huddle against the wind, their breeding plumage long since faded with the coming of the winter.

Soon the day drew in and all that was left was the sound of the wind and the roar of the distant surf.

8

By Land and Sea

As night fell Jack found himself leaning heavily against the taffrail of his father's cutter, staring miserably at the rise and fall of the darkening sea and the pale wake that trailed behind.

He had never felt so sick in his life.

His head ached, his stomach churned and his throat retched in acidic spasms that had made it sore and horrible. Even the water he sipped was hard to hold down.

Katherine had persuaded him that it would be for his own good to travel with Riff and his family. Adding, 'And theirs too, Jack: they need to get to know you as well. It'll be a healing. It'll do you all good.'

So far it had done no good at all.

Borkum Riff was too busy skippering the craft through the strong winds and heavy seas to talk. All he said at the start was: 'Get below, lad, and clear up your vomit as you go.'

Later, Jack was so sickened by the fetid atmosphere of the cramped quarters below, and the hearty way the crew consumed food and drink, whose odours only added to his nausea, that he went back on deck.

Seeing him, Riff called out, 'If you must take the air, keep clear o' us and what we're doing.'

Now, beyond barking the occasional order at his crew, Riff said little and did not bother at all with Jack. The others ignored him too.

Riff he could understand. The safety of the craft and its crew and passengers must come first, especially in such difficult seas. But Witold Slew was another matter. He was chilly and indifferent, turning his back on Jack's early advances, after which the seasickness took him over and he gave up trying to be friendly.

Leetha and Deap were over on the other craft with deckhands to help, but where that was Jack had no idea. They sailed without lights, and how one knew the other's location Jack could not work out, though they seemed to.

'He'm riding hard a-port, sir,' Harald had cried out suddenly. Then, 'Here she'm wears, aye porterways!'

Sure enough, moments later, Deap's craft came racing alongside out of the dark, and father and son exchanged a few shouted words through the wind and spray. Jack felt jealous of their easy intimacy and respect for each other.

A shaft of light from a storm lantern had lit up the other boat and Jack saw Leetha on the prow, wet hair streaming in the wind. The look of ecstasy on her face, and her wave of delight at the weather, the sea and wild circumstance, and her cries and whoops of pleasure, had been enough to turn Jack away to be sick again.

So now he leaned on the rail for support, ill as a stricken dog, ready to give anything, even his life, to be on solid ground again. His wretchedness was made a thousand times worse by his instinctual feeling that he should not have left Katherine and the others to make the landward journey back to Brum without his protection. It was what he did, protect people. It was what he was trained to do and made to do by the fact of who he was, Stavemeister of Brum, and, he had no doubt, the errant genes that had cursed him to be the giant-born of prophecy.

'Playing happy families is not my style!' he swore to himself as the swirls of sickness came and went. 'Mirror be damned! I should be with Katherine and Barklice and Stort! They won't know how to protect themselves if it comes to a fight. I should never . . .'

He leaned over the side and was sick again, so far as he was any more able to be. He realized in that moment he could no longer see the sea itself. It had grown too dark and the clouds, which had lifted for a while during the late afternoon, were lowering now with neither moon nor stars anywhere in sight.

But what he could see, when he found the strength to look, was the black rise of the land to starboard, backlit by a paler run of sky and the diffused human lights of settlements and maybe roads. But not very many, which seemed strange. He thought the south coast of Englalond would show more human life than that.

Yet that was not quite all.

Here and there he saw the red-yellow glare of bonfires and thick smoke which swirled with light. Then, too, the sudden, brief rise of rockets against the night sky, bursting red and green and white.

A rough hand settled on his shoulder and turned him round.

Someone thrust a cannikin towards him and helped him wrap his chilled fingers around its handle.

'Drink this, Jack, it'll do you good.'

Jack sniffed the brew. Hard to say if its warm, rich aroma made him feel better or worse.

'What is it?' he gasped.

'Sailorman's tea,' came the reply, 'with a dash of something more.'

Jack sipped it and it was good.

'What's the something more?'

'Rum, by order.'

'Who's order?'

'Your father,' said Slew, whose blond, sleeked hair and black, glittering eyes caught the storm light and made visible his face and thin smile. 'Drink! You may bring some of it back up but it'll settle you until the sickness goes. *Drink* . . .'

He patted Jack's shoulder, rough again, and disappeared back towards the mast.

Jack turned to the rail, drank, watched the fires on the distant shore, and suddenly felt better about something deep inside himself than he had in a long time. They must have known how he would feel and that they could do nothing about it. In their way they were watching over him. Maybe that's what family did: support each other in things great and small.

He drank again, was sick, found himself grinning at nothing very much and for the first time since he climbed aboard hours before was glad to be right where he was.

It was in that same hour, when darkness became night, that the inland party, after a hard trek west, finally reached their first objective.

This was the major road east of Truro, the A39.

They were following Barklice's suggestion that the fastest way back to Brum was to get themselves to one of the human routeways heading north-east, towards central Englalond.

'The green roads are all very well,' he had declared before they set off, 'but that very welcome destination, the public bar of the Muggy Duck in Brum, is two hundred and fifty miles away. If the rain comes in and the going gets hard, which it will, I would estimate that if we rely on the green roads and hydden ways the trek back home will take us a month or more . . . We need to get there sooner than that!'

Some of the others, less experienced than he, were not so sure. Human roads and rail, though familiar enough to practised travellers like Barklice and Stort, were frightening to those whose lives had been more circumscribed. Terce for one; Blut for another.

But Katherine understood the verderer's argument.

'We'll have to follow the hydden ways initially anyway,' she had said, 'for there's no choice in this out-of-the-way place. Let us debate the matter again when we reach the main road . . .'

Now, after tramping over hill and down dale, through mud and mire, and scrambling through scratchy, leafless hedges and drawing blood, they had finally done so. Katherine suspected Barklice had led them by routes that were rougher than they needed to be to exhaust them so much they would agree to travel more on human roads. If so, his ruse was working.

'I am inclined to think,' said Festoon, looking back the way they had come, 'that another month of that would kill me, or so wear me down that I would be a shadow of my former self.'

Blut nodded, breathless and wan.

Sinistral waved a frail hand to indicate that he was willing to agree to anything provided he did not have to walk another step for a few days.

Barklice, on the other hand, was as sprightly now as if he had been carried all the way by porters in a palanquin, as royalty and rich hydden used to be. As for Katherine, she was used to walking and saw the hours past as little more than a brief stroll.

'However,' said Barklice, peering about and sniffing the air in the way a fox might who is seeking danger as well as advantage, safety as well as ease, 'I do not quite like the smell of things.'

They knew what he meant.

The night breeze, which blew from the north-east, the direction they were going, carried an acrid, sickly sweet scent that turned the stomach. The good, heady scent of burning wood or leaves was one thing, but this was paint, chemicals and the filthy, cloying stench of burning oil and, though none of them said so openly, charred flesh.

They had seen a fire or two earlier to west and east, but only now they were on the high embankment of the A39 main road with a view over the hedges and woodland all about, could they see that its source lay to the north. That portion of the sky was livid with the light of a great fire whose origin they could not actually ascertain.

'Looks like a whole town is burning,' said Katherine uneasily.

Barklice and Stort conferred, debating which town it was likely to be. Even though neither had ever visited that part of the coast of the south-west peninsula they knew its geography and the location and names of the major settlements.

'We think it's Newquay, a coastal town,' announced Barklice finally. 'We'll follow the A39 towards it for a few miles, but only as far as the A30, which will take us out of the South-West and on towards Brum.

Terce moved onto the hard shoulder of the road itself and observed, 'When we crossed this road two weeks ago there was human traffic to be seen. Now there is none.'

Barklice pulled out his chronometer.

'You're right. Were it three in the morning that might not be remarkable but it's only nine at night. Listen! Silence! There is not even the distant roar of traffic.'

'Are we surprised?' said Festoon, who was recovering fast. 'Given the rapid succession of storms, and 'quakes and puzzling time shifts in recent weeks and months, all of increasing severity, it would be astonishing if the lives of human beings had not been disrupted. We know of the violence on Pendower Beach. But we knew already from reports we were receiving in Brum before we left that the human transport systems of rail and road have been badly affected. Now they seem to have ground to a halt.'

Niklas Blut concurred.

'Our intelligence suggests that these events have caused humans to desert their settlements and make a general flight northward to the hills of the Peaks and the Pennines,' he said. 'That might explain why the South-West is deserted. But *so* much so?'

They had fallen silent, considering this mystery, when they heard coming from their left and west, the direction of Truro, the rumbling growl of vehicles.

They retreated to the cover of the embankment and waited. The sound grew louder, the growl more ugly, but they saw no tell-tale lights such as human vehicles normally have. So what appeared did so quite suddenly, out of the darkness. It was both shocking and frightening.

A great vehicle, with big wheels and a high chassis, the flat, steep glass of its great windshield reflecting the lurid sky ahead, loomed out of the dark on their left side. With a rush of air and clattering of sound it drove on by along the road showing only a single red fog light at its rear.

They had no sooner risen from their hiding places to go out onto the road and watch after it than they had to dive for cover again when a second vehicle, identical to the first, passed them by as well.

A torch shone briefly in the rear interior of the second vehicle and they caught sight of two humans in khaki, one with a weapon in his arms.

'They're military vehicles,' said Katherine, 'heading the way we want to go.'

'They seem in a hurry,' said Barklice ominously. 'But, decision made, we follow on. If more vehicles come up behind us, or we see anything ahead, we'll find cover along the verge. If worse happens and real danger looms, the fields beyond will be our refuge. But at least the going will be easier here and every step we take will bring us nearer home.

'We'll find out what's afoot with these fires ahead and maybe where those vehicles were going and what they were doing, for certainly they seemed intent on something serious.'

After a few more minutes of rest they moved off once more, now content to walk on the hard shoulder of the road.

More vehicles came by and, later, returned, and they soon got used to taking cover.

Further observation confirmed that the returning vehicles had been emptied of their loads for they bounced and rattled back along the road very noisily. It amused Blut to observe the different vehicles come and go in more detail and he worked out that there were nine in all.

The darkness across the land on either side of them was punctured here and there by much smaller fires than the vast one far ahead. The silence was broken only by the familiar cries of night creatures, except once, when Katherine herself stopped and cried out.

'I'm a fool!' she declared, as they spied another of the red-orange fires far off to their right and saw the glimmer of a rocket in the low clouds above. 'I've been in the Hyddenworld too long and had forgotten what date it is.'

They all stopped and turned to her.

'November 5th,' she said, 'Guy Fawkes Night, one of the few secular festivals humans have celebrated continuously for hundreds of years. Usually for good reasons but sometimes for purposes of riot . . .'

They looked at each other blankly but for Blut, who had made a point of studying human culture, especially that of Englalond, from where Slaeke Sinistral had originally come.

'It is a celebration of sorts,' he explained to the other hydden, 'commemorating the arraignment of a terrorist named Fawkes, caught red-handed trying to blow something up.'

'Blow what up?' asked Sinistral.

Blut smiled bleakly in the dark.

'I think, my Lord, as former Emperor, and therefore upholder of the Imperial might and all its institutions, you might prefer not to know . . .'

'Try me,' said Sinistral.

'An institution that harboured free speech,' said Blut.

They moved on, bantering as they went, easier in themselves now they felt they were heading home, distant though it might be.

When midnight came they agreed it was time to stop and rest. Which they might well have done, moving off the road to find a safe campsite in the fields and woods nearby, had they not once more been interrupted by the familiar roar of a military vehicle. It came from their left, and this time its front lights were on, for the good reason that it was on a winding, broken slip road which led up to the highway itself. It was moving fast, arrived at a gate, jolted over a cattle grid and accelerated up to the road they were on, joining it two hundred yards ahead of them.

It carried straight on in the direction they were going, again with just a red fog light to its rear, and it was soon out of sight.

'Interesting,' observed Festoon.

'If no more humans show up, that slip road might be a good place to rest awhile,' said Barklice. 'Easier than clambering down the embankment.'

They waited a little longer and saw no more lights, nor heard any sound. The air was acrid with smoke and the flickering glow of a second burning city showed up on the horizon far ahead.

They went off the road, quickly settled among vegetation adjacent to a concrete drainage conduit and brewed up.

Katherine was restless, the night lightening a little as the clouds thinned and revealed a few stars. She decided to explore the road from which the truck had come. Terce got up to go with her.

'Not a good idea,' said Barklice.

'I must,' said Katherine, making it clear enough what it was she needed to do.

'Me too,' said Terce, who had the same idea.

'We won't go far,' said Katherine, 'and we won't stray from this slip road. If you whistle we'll signal with my torch that we've heard and start straight back.'

Once through the gate and beyond the wire fence, curiosity got the better of them both and they went further than they needed to.

'It looks like an old airfield,' said Katherine, eyeing the expanse of concrete that stretched away to their right.

'There's a building ahead,' said Terce, whose night vision was exceptional. The dark, looming shape of a structure showed against the night sky a hundred yards ahead.

'And the smell of burning . . . I thought it was from the distant fire but it's getting stronger here. Come on . . .'

'I'm not sure . . .'

'Come on, Terce. Let's find out what the military were up to.'

They headed straight towards the structure silhouetted against the sky, past some tyres, a pile of unused fencing and empty wooden boxes with rope handles at either end, which set off a warning bell in Katherine's mind. It was unfortunately one too faint to act upon.

Two posts rose up to their right with a noticeboard on top whose writing they could not quite read. The structure ahead became clear and they saw it was not a building at all, but huge containers, their rear ends open, roughly dumped into a circle.

Beyond these there really were buildings, their windows barred. Not derelict but left secure, perhaps for storage use.

The smell of fire came from something smouldering between the buildings and the containers. Katherine flashed her torch momentarily.

The containers were filled with wooden boxes like those they had seen earlier. Their nailed tops had been levered off, the contents strewn. They peered more closely. There were boxes of bullets, hand-grenades, sticks of dynamite . . . and Katherine understood her earlier doubts. They were looking at unexploded munitions.

Terce, not understanding what they saw, advanced towards the smouldering fire. It flared, caught by the breeze, sparked and sputtered strangely and its light caught the frozen panic in Katherine's face.

She grasped Terce's arm.

'Come back,' she whispered, as if just the sound of her voice could set everything off. They had walked straight into a crude attempt by the military, or a militia group, to destroy dangerous ordnance.

'We get out of here now,' she said so urgently that he did not argue.

The fire began to roar as they retreated, lighting up the boards on the posts they had just walked past. She peered upward and flashed her torch for confirmation.

'Oh God,' she said, echoing an expression Arthur Foale used to use at moments of danger, 'oh dear God.'

The board was yellow. It had a skull and crossbones on it beneath which were the words: *DANGER. Ministry of Defence Restricted Area. UNEXPLODED ORDNANCE, Authorized Access Only.*

'Run!' screamed Katherine. *'Run for your life!'*

Jack was still weak but no longer nauseous.

The brew Slew gave him had settled his stomach. The endless motion of the deck and rails of the cutter, the ghastly see-saw of the night horizon no longer upset him. The once-revolting odour of cooked food in the galley seemed no longer so; he vomited no more and he had even managed a mouthful or two of stew.

He was able at last to breathe the good sea air with pleasure and gaze in wonder at the few lights across the sea, some winking, some yellow, a few near, most far. The shore might be almost dark but the lights of buoys and automatic lightships were still working.

Jack had never been at sea at night, either as human or hydden. Never seen the shore of Englalond as a nocturnal invader might see it, or an embattled, storm-tossed sailor seeking a safe haven in the centuries gone by might have done.

The landmass itself was a two dimensional black-grey wall, the night sky lighter now the stars and a clouded moon were up. As the black coast slipped by, its anonymous shapes and features shifted into new ones almost imperceptibly. Jack found comfort and reassurance in Riff's barked orders from the wheel as the crew luffed and reefed and kept the ropes tight and the canvas full.

Sometimes on the passing shore, occasionally on top of higher ground, they saw bright fires and the shoot of rockets heavenward.

These troubled the sailors until Jack explained that he thought it was November 5th, which humans commemorate.

'Why?' Slew had asked.

'Because on that night, in 1605, Guy Fawkes failed in his attempt to kill some important people,' he replied. 'Maybe this year it's being used as an excuse for something more violent.'

Slew slipped away, puzzled still. The hydden were not in the habit of drawing attention to themselves with fireworks.

Jack looked far to the west, the direction from which they had come, trying to work out where Katherine and the others might now be.

'Maybe about *there*!' he said aloud, pointing at what looked like yet another bonfire. Even as he did so there was a frightening flash, infinitely larger than any ordinary fire or rocket . . . and moments later the crashing, thumping, start of a series of explosions on an enormous scale.

As these continued a new and different sickness overtook him, one far more dreadful than before. With it came a horror that ran to his heart's core and churned it into feelings of absolute dread and fear.

'Oh dear God,' he heard himself say, 'I should never have left her side.'

He stepped back blindly from the rail without thinking, straight into the void above the galley and berths below. He felt himself falling, and heard the thump, thump, thump of his own head as it bumped downward on the wooden steps.

In the final moments, as darkness descended, Jack was overtaken by the conviction that what he had seen was nothing less than an explosion that had killed all his friends on the landward route, Katherine included.

9

RACK AND RUIN

Katherine's cry of 'Run!', when she saw the fire by the explosives, was intended for Terce, but it was fortunately so loud that it was heard by the others in their camp near the road.

The flames were bright enough for her to see that Barklice and Stort were trying to work out what was going on.

'Get back down!' she yelled as she and Terce desperately tried to escape and dive down into the protection of the deep conduit by their camp.

Barklice knew Katherine well enough to know that she meant what she said. Seeing the fire and guessing the nature of the danger they were in, he grabbed the seat of Stort's trews, pulled him backwards and shouted at the others to stay down and take cover.

They followed his lead, abandoning their food, their fire and their 'sacs and tumbled pell-mell into the open conduit in a tangle of arms and legs.

For a moment more there was silence, broken only by the drumming steps of the other two on the concrete road, their shadows a confusion of shapes on the embankment beyond where the others lay.

Then the light of the fire turned to a blinding white and the dark night was rent asunder by a succession of percussive, incandescent, murderous explosions, which shook the ground and deafened them.

Moments after that the dry, husky vegetation around them snapped off and two figures, like rag dolls caught in a hot, hurricane wind, shot over their heads and thumped sickeningly onto the steep side of the embankment beyond.

The air shimmered with heat, the vegetation caught fire, the explosions continued.

Festoon was the first to move, understanding at once that the flying figures were their friends. He might have tried to go to them but that the force of another explosion, as loud and bright as any before, slammed him back down again.

There was a crackle of sound, as of gunfire, and ordnance great and small shot about above their heads for several minutes before silence fell again and the white light turned a shade more orange.

Again Festoon rose, seeming to be less affected than the others and to understand the danger that Katherine and Terce were in, even supposing they could have survived the full brunt of the blast which carried them bodily onto the embankment.

Seeing the danger, Festoon ordered them to stay where they were while he and Barklice climbed up through smouldering vegetation towards where Katherine and Terce lay deathly still.

The crackling began again and bullets whizzed through the air and rockets shot across the airfield as showers of burning debris and shrapnel fell all around. Another series of explosions began and the two would-be rescuers buried themselves face-down in the vegetation.

'Let's get them to safety, Mister Barklice,' said Festoon coolly when the next lull came. He bravely rose to his knees, crawled up the slope far enough to reach the outstretched leg of Terce and grasped it. There was no time for niceties. He heaved at the leg, got Terce down the slope and helped Barklice roll him into the conduit.

They went up again and brought Katherine back to safety the same way. Neither she nor Terce was conscious but there was no sign of obvious injury to him, and nothing but a deep cut on Katherine's hand.

It was as well they got the two into cover when they did for now the explosions became as violent as the initial ones, and soon after flaming debris came sailing through the air which set the embankment alight where the two had fallen. For a short while the heat was intense and those with their backs nearest to the flames, who were sheltering the others, found their clothes smouldering.

Then, as suddenly as the explosions began, they were over, but for the fires and the drift of smoke, which had them coughing and spluttering for a while, leaving only the glimmering light and occasional flaring-up of a multitude of small fires, near and far.

Miraculously, as it seemed, Katherine came round, groaning in shock and discomfort, her right hand going at once to her left shoulder. This was evidently more painful than the injured hand. She stared at them uncomprehendingly when they spoke to her, eventually shaking her head. The explosions had temporarily deafened her.

Terce remained unconscious and seemed more seriously hurt. Stort examined them both and, having declared that Katherine had no broken bones or serious lacerations apart from the one on her hand, he shook his head grimly over Terce.

'He breathes, just about, but even in his state of unconsciousness he seems in pain. I think some ribs are broken. His back is pitted with a dozen small puncture wounds, but they do not appear to be deep or very serious. I think he must have sought to protect Katherine with his bulk, and small pieces of grit and suchlike have been driven through his skin by the force of the explosions coming from behind him.

'When he regains consciousness I would expect him to be in a state of confusion. He too may be deaf for a time.'

He stopped abruptly, having seen something more.

'What else have you found?' Blut asked.

'It may be of no import, I hope it is not. But I fear there is a trickle of blood coming from his right ear . . . I trust it is an indication of nothing more serious than a perforated ear-drum, from which a full recovery is to be expected. But . . . well . . . his balance may be affected too and . . .'

Stort could not bring himself to say what he really feared but Festoon guessed what was on his mind.

'His whole life has been and remains bound up with singing and music,' he said very sombrely, 'and in that department he is, as I understand it, unique in the Hyddenworld . . .'

Stort nodded, evidently upset.

'He may be our only way of reaching or finding that sound and harmony which is the *musica universalis*. We must hope he makes a full recovery and that his singing will be unaffected.'

None of them slept that first night, nor very much in the day and night following, while they waited for Terce to regain consciousness.

They decided to stay put, though smoke drifted continually in their direction, feeling it was unwise to disturb Terce until he was able to indicate to them the nature and extent of his injuries.

'Of course,' declared Stort on the third day, when the chorister was finally showing signs of coming round with groans and slight movement of hands and feet, followed by pained grimaces when he tried to sit up, 'it is self-evident that Terce and indeed Katherine here were effectively unconscious as they flew through the air. Otherwise they would have suffered something more serious. We sometimes fall most safely if we do not try to protect ourselves.'

Terce finally woke fully twenty-four hours later and, as they feared, he had suffered total loss of hearing. It was only by gesture and touch that they were able to explain what had happened. He was greatly relieved to see that Katherine was already recovered.

He could talk, though his voice was wild in its modulation, being now loud and now soft, but as yet he seemed unconcerned by his loss of hearing, perhaps too shocked to be so. Stort's diagnosis of his ribs proved correct: two at least were badly bruised or broken.

'Time will cure them,' said Stort.

Terce suffered a headache as well but by dawn of the fifth day that had gone altogether. With help, and grunts of pain, he was able to get up and they finally talked of moving.

They had long since realized that things could have been much worse.

'Had Katherine not gone exploring,' said Blut, 'we would all have been out in the open and those blasts would have affected us badly. I dread to think of the injuries we might have sustained.

'I suggest that we now continue our journey, but slowly and with caution to see how Katherine and Terce fare. Let us make a further assessment when we have travelled a few more miles.'

It was agreed and, the road being clear, the fields empty and there being no sign of other life or danger, they settled once again into a steady trek, though with more frequent and longer stops than before to allow Terce to rest a little and Katherine too.

Terce tried to sing and practise scales as they went along, as had always been his habit. But the voice that had been beautiful was an ugly, grating thing, and worse even than that, he did not know it.

10

STORM

Jack woke to noise and movement so violent and chaotic, with water sloshing about beneath where he lay, that it took him a long time to work out that he was below-decks and tight-strapped into a bunk. Even then he could not work out in which direction the craft was travelling and whether his head was facing bow or stern, the alternating visions of dark and light that spiralled around his eyes robbing him of all sense of the passage of night and day.

That first time he woke he drifted off again at once. Each time after that he came back to consciousness with a shock, but each time more and more aware of one comforting fact: a hand was holding his and it was not rough like a sailor's hand, but soft, gentle, like a female's.

Yet he knew it was not Katherine's . . .

Sometime in the course of this slow and sporadic re-awakening to life his mind became clear enough for him to believe that he knew where he was and who he was. He was Jack, he was eleven years old and he was in hospital because long before he had saved Katherine from a burning car and been burnt on his back and neck and ever since some things triggered feelings of old pain and panic.

The nurses had always held his hand like this before they put him to sleep again against his will because he didn't want . . .

'I don't want another one . . .' Jack heard himself cry out.

I don't want another operation.

They were going to cut his body and steal his skin and he would wake up to pain.

'No!' he cried out, sweat coursing down his neck as he felt the imagined pain of the coming skin graft.

I don't want another . . .

There was a crash above him, wind tore into where he was and freezing water crashed and splashed down and about and over his bare legs and the top of his head. The rest of him was protected by her and her warmth but he began pushing her off because the threatened pain of having what he imagined might be another skin graft was greater than the warm safety of her embrace.

Oh, but she was not a nurse.

'Katherine . . . ?'

'Leetha,' said his mother, 'it's your mother, Jack.'

Crash!

Thump!

Deep voices, shouts of command and a sudden heaving and yawing as the cutter went about.

'We're in a storm, Jack. You fell down.'

'But you're over there . . .'

'They brought me over from your brother's craft before the storm hit. To look after you.'

'Where am I?'

'You're here and now, not back then and there, my love. I never knew you had been burnt, I never saw your injuries before. For Mirror's sake, I never *knew*. What happened?'

'Katherine got trapped in a burning car so I pulled her out. That's what happened. When we were six. It took five years of operations . . .'

'I never knew,' repeated Leetha faintly.

He spiralled away into darkness, the sweat a hot sea, the pain the harsh land surrounding it, which meant he had no place to go and set his feet down that was not pain incarnate.

Her grip tightened and then, embracing him again, she opened a door that he had kept tight shut for years and years, ever since the accident.

He screamed and roared, not caring if his thrashing and kicking and punching at her broke his old scars open. Screaming now like he never did then.

'I didn't let them do it again.'

'No, you didn't, Jack, and now . . . now . . .'

The hot sweat was an ocean trickling beneath him which had another name: blood.

His scars felt as if they had all ripped open and Leetha was there holding his hand and talking, whispering in his ears, cooling his chest and brow, holding him tight through the crashes and bumps as, above them, Borkum Riff stood solid at the wheel, his crew as tired as he was, fighting to keep their craft afloat through the worst North Sea storm they had ever known.

The sea roared, Jack roared.

The wind screamed, Jack screamed.

The cutter bucked and yawed and Jack did just the same.

Then, blessed silence as he drifted off, his mother against him, and her tears, her warmth, her fear his own.

'Where's my brother?'

'Which one?'

'I can hear Slew's roar above us,' he said without much pleasure. 'Where's Herde Deap?'

'Fighting the storm in his own craft, like your father is doing in this one.'

Her voice trembled; her body too. He could feel the warp and the weft of her, the kin of her, the deep sense of blood and bone that came from her and into him, the flow and the smell of her, stretching away in time, back and back and back and then forward again to now.

He could feel his birthing in her, the scream out of her, and how she made his life with the power and love of Borkum Riff and how she didn't care that he was a giant-born. But Riff did.

'Why are you here with me and not with him?'

'Because you . . .'

Because you need me.

His hand gripped hers savagely to stop the lie being spoken. He shifted his bloody back. He didn't need her, it was the other way about.

'Because *you* need *me*,' he said, the emphases muffled by his turns and groans.

'I do,' she said simply, which meant everything.

'Are my scars bad?'

'Not so bad.'

'Have they opened wide?'

'No.'

'I can feel the blood, our blood.'

'It's mainly sweat, Jack. Two opened near your neck where you thumped your head falling below-decks like a novice.'

'Did Slew laugh?'

'We all laughed. The whole family but you has sea legs, especially your twin . . .'

Anger swept him. They were they and he was he alone.

'Laughed?'

'We did,' she said and her smile was so open and warm and welcoming that he felt the brightness of it in him.

'I . . . well . . .' And he smiled.

The sound of the storm and the creaking of the craft grew too loud for it to be worthwhile talking.

They held each other's hands in the dark, staring towards each other's face, seeing nothing until a slanting beam of light crossed between them.

It was Riff with a lantern, staring at them, his eyes glittering and deep.

'How is he?'

'Alive, Borkum, as alive as you or me.'

'Fell down the bloody steps you did,' said Riff, coming nearer, squeezing his powerful body between bulkhead and Leetha, the lantern swinging, the light dancing in all their eyes.

Jack eyed them, together and close to him for the first time in his life that he remembered. She so beautiful, Riff an uncut diamond, but together they looked as worried as only parents can.

'Them scars, lad, they be a sad sight. How'd you get them?'

'I got them,' he said simply, saying no more.

Which is just what Riff would have said.

It was his wyrd to get them. It was his wyrd to protect. He was made that way. He had no more need to speak of it.

'I want to get out of this bunk,' he said.

'You try and I'll knock you back into it,' said Riff, 'or Slew will. You get up when your mother says you get up. Has his bleeding stopped?'

'It's healed,' said Leetha softly, easing Jack further over before taking the light from Riff to hold it where he could see.

'That's blood,' he said gruffly.

'It's sweat, Borkum, coursing over old wounds. Here was where the damage was . . .'

Jack felt a coolness on his shoulder, a sliding caress like cold satin on his skin.

'What happened to the storm?' wondered Jack, now blissfully tired.

'We're in its centre, it's all around us but will soon o'ertake us once again.'

There was a shout from the wheel above, torn away by the rising wind.

'I must go.'

'Is it night or day?'

'An hour after dawn. We're 'twixt and 'tween and this blow has worse to come.'

Riff left them, his lantern swinging wildly as he went up into the wind and spray above.

'What did you want when you were ill?'

'Before Katherine?'

'What did you want and need?' she asked insistently.

He fell back, the night slanting with dark light, things swinging above his head, her long blonde-grey hair, her eyes and smile near laughter all the time, though etched with a concern that touched him.

'Deap told me you dance. Why?'

'I do, at home and along the shores of life, I dance the wonder that I see, the wonder of the Earth. And you, I feel there's dance in you, Jack, in your great, strong hands.'

He didn't answer that question but thought about the one before, about what he had wanted.

'Tell me about when you sent me away to Englalond.'

'I didn't . . . well, I did . . . I put you on the White Horse and your great-grandfather's 'sac upon your back and giant-like as you were, you were already near my size. Up there on the Horse's back you looked like the child you were, but brave . . . when they pulled me away, for I didn't want to lose the touch and feel of you, it felt like I was cutting off my own arm. I never wanted to lose you, Jack.'

Her tears were his own.

'I remember the White Horse but not you,' he replied, 'not the sight of you but something . . . after I was burnt I remembered something fading, a touch slipping away, a voice growing distant, a lovely scent blown from me by the breeze, all the parts but not the whole, the blood and the bone but not . . . *you*. I fought the pain by trying to remember, I fought the tears by reaching back for that memory of you I lost, I never wept because I feared that the pain of loss would be greater than the physical pain I felt . . .'

The hull crashed, Riff swore, Slew laughed into the wind above and a small sail cracked loudly as it filled the wrong way with wind.

'What do I call you? Mother? My Lady Leetha? Plain Leetha?'

His voice rose as the wind did, a roar of wild despair.

'What do I call a mother who never was?'

The boat yawed forward, back, and rocked and juddered and he tried to reach up, to get up, to stop being prone as he was when he was so ill, so many years before.

'You call me Leetha,' she said, her slender body still stronger than his weak one, the passion of her love more fierce, holding him down for safety as the boat reared up.

As if it were the White Horse trying to take him from her again, except that this time she would not let it do so, not now, not ever again.

'What did I want?' he cried out into the storm's fearful heart and he felt the greatest terror of them all, which is the pain the simple truth can bring. For Jack that was the raw, raw aching loss of her he had felt down all the years since the White Horse took him away forever.

What did I want?

The wind shrieked and the cutter creaked and the shouts and commands of Riff and Slew and all of them joining their voices to cry the cry he had cried from the beginning of his first consciousness.

What did I want?

'I wanted you,' he said.

11

THE WHITE HORSE

The progress of Barklice and the others after the explosion was necessarily slow. Katherine and Terce were in a poor way for days, the first more mentally than physically, the second the other way round.

Katherine's hearing soon returned but she was suffering the stress that follows such a violent trauma and her mind was dull and unresponsive, her body movements and expression like someone who has barely woken up.

Terce appeared more robust, as his brave attempts to sing again showed. But he remained stone deaf and his bruised and broken ribs made almost any movement involving twisting or getting up and sitting down very painful. As for sleep, it eluded him except in fits and starts, when his extreme fatigue briefly overcame the difficulty of finding a position in which he could comfortably close his eyes and rest.

Nor were the others their normal selves either.

As they journeyed on it became increasingly evident that something terrible had taken place in the human world. The killings they had witnessed on Pendower Beach and the panicky behaviour of the military over the ordnance which so nearly killed them were but symptoms of this

The glow of the Newquay fire in the night sky was soon behind them, but it was not long before they came across more fires and much wanton destruction in the towns and villages on either side of the A30. Carland Cross, Mitchell and Chapel Town were all seriously damaged, while many smaller settlements and farmsteads had been burnt to the ground, the ruins of houses and public buildings still smouldering.

It was when they reached Fraddon that they discovered more evidence of violent human strife and even civil war. Here they found bodies lying openly in field and ditch, garden and road. To the smell of the smoke that drifted across the A30 was added the charnel-house odours of burnt and rotting human flesh, creating a stench so nauseating that in some places they had to cover their mouths and nostrils with wet cloth scented with herbs.

The livestock in farms and fields on either side of their route had been abandoned wholesale, as if the farmers who had tended them had suddenly vanished off the face of the earth.

The doors of one hangar-like building hung open and the smell without and strange sounds from within caused Stort to take a look. The vast building was one of three that housed battery hens, tens of thousands of them. The air was thick with tiny flies and the fowl, many layers deep, were in various stages of life, dying and death. Some were long-dead and rotten, crawling with maggots. Others were near-dead, feeding on the maggots and putrid flesh of their dead comrades in captivity. A few, near doors and such ventilation as there was, were alive but maddened by the heat, feeding on the weaker ones, which uttered such cries of high-pitched despair that Stort hurried from the building, ashen-faced.

It was a struggle that night to find a location to stop and camp that was free from the sight and odours of death, and safe from half-crazed beasts of the fields. When they did, and darkness fell, their small fire and the aromatic scents of the stew they made attracted unwelcome visitors.

Feral green eyes were seen at the shadowed edge of their campsite, until a growling pack of dogs chased the creatures away and began advancing upon them. Thin, starved curs all of them, snapping at each other as if to find the courage to attack.

There had been a time when Stort was more frightened of dogs than any mortal on the Earth, but that had changed, completely. He leapt to his feet, grabbed his stave, and ran towards them with shouts and gestures so terrifying that they fled, yelping with fear.

The next day brought more evidence that some mass panic and flight, combined with a breakdown of order into chaos and anarchy, in which the military were in some way involved, had overtaken the humans and their world.

They found cows and pigs which had battered at their pens in the desperation of their thirst and starvation, horses dying in the fields and along the lanes, poisoned by drinking polluted water, and sheep, tangled helplessly in barbed wire.

There was no normal life, no humans but dead and occasionally dying ones, no healthy animals but feral dogs and cats, growling and hissing from the shadows of burnt buildings and woodland; or those horses and cattle that had succeeded in escaping their captivity unharmed and wandered the roads and paths, feeding where they could and instinctively avoiding the ponds and rivers in which the dead lay.

These wretched sights, combined with the different stresses and strains to which each member of the party had been subjected in recent weeks and days, rendered several of them silent and uncommunicative.

Barklice, as their route-finder, stayed alert and positive, as was his nature. He missed talking with Katherine about the ways and means of their journey as they went along, debating this or that option or considering when best to take a break. But she was much shaken by the explosion and she still walked like one in a daze.

Festoon and Blut, on whose respective shoulders lay the burdens of Brum and the Hyddenworld, sat and talked in low voices at the stopping points. But when moving Blut stayed close by Sinistral, ever watchful and protective.

Terce walked slowly and in evident discomfort. He never complained, but it was his pace and his need for frequent rest as well that slowed them down.

Even Arnold Mallarkhi, the youngest and normally most ebullient of them all, was now in sombre mood, the sights and sounds of so much death having been a severe shock to him. As was the sight of the filth and pollution in the waterways caused by dead animals and uncontrolled effluent. For a Bilgesnipe, water is a beautiful thing, whether still or flowing. It is a source of life and a medium of movement and celebration. Arnold's distress at what he saw was very real, and for the time being he was a shadow of what they all knew he could be.

Sinistral at least was more positive than the others, though death seemed sometimes to stalk across his frail face and watery eyes. He moved cautiously now, though with a kind of infinite, unforced elegance, like a great tree whose leaves still shine but whose branches have grown brittle and stiff.

His bleak gaze took in everything and he still found time and energy to comment on the natural beauty of the Earth and be glad that old though he was, the blood still flowed in his veins.

'Things will get better,' he said, 'and as a poet of my youth once wrote, "the snow falls, and the winds calls and the year turns round again." The winter may be upon us, it will no doubt get worse, but spring will come again even if I do not myself live that long! Eh, Blut?'

'Yes, my Lord. I mean, no, my Lord!'

'Just so, Blut, just so!'

'It would help,' said Barklice on the sixth day after the explosion, 'if we could get some intelligence. Normally I meet fellow hydden on my travels who are only too willing to talk, but almost everyone has gone to ground.'

In fact they had come across three or four hydden along the way, not including the dead ones, of whom there had been many more. With only one exception these had been no more than brief sightings of hydden making themselves scarce and resisting all attempts to come and talk.

The one they talked to was unfortunately a hydden in deep mental distress, maddened by some terrible experience affecting those he knew. He stood trembling before them and in an obvious state of fear. He wanted to talk but when he did his words were incoherent, his shouts and moans, tics and shaking very frightening. He sought to attack Barklice with his fists, broke free of Terce's grasp, ran off into woodland, and they saw him no more.

It seemed that whatever trauma the human beings had suffered had affected hydden too.

'Ourselves as well, perhaps,' murmured Sinistral in a rare moment, 'at least in some ways. Are we not now behaving with extreme caution and daily growing more anxious? Eh, Blut?'

'I fear that may be true, my Lord,' was Blut's reply.

It was as if a mass hysteria had gripped Englalond, a fearful mood made up of insubstantial fears and shadows fuelled by outbreaks of anarchy and violence here and there, perhaps by hydden as well as human.

Of all the sights they saw, the strangest – and in its way the most beautiful – was a horse that galloped past them one evening, along a metalled road. They heard the pounding of its hoofs approaching from behind and stopped and waited. Their reward was the sight of a stallion, big and strong, rushing by as if it, too, was in flight.

At first it was black against the setting sky, a silhouette. Then, its hoofbeats fading into the distance, the road curved such that the last sunlight fell upon its flanks and they saw that it was not black at all.

It was as white as snow, but for its flowing mane and flailing tail, which were pale gold in the evening sun. It turned for a moment and stared at them. Then it raced on once more, leaving them with a fearful, irrational feeling that if they did not hurry they might be left behind in the wasteland of lost and ruined life that the world about them had become.

That evening, Sinistral briefly took the lead.

'There is no enemy but we ourselves,' he said. 'There never is, there never was. Eh, Blut?'

'That is indeed so, my Lord.'

'Then we shall do the only thing we can, we shall carry on.'

Which they did, into the night, not sure if it was the horse or Sinistral that put strength into their legs and new hope into their hearts.

12

ACROSS THE GOODWINS

It was sixteen days since Riff and Deap had launched their craft into the waves at Pendower and the storm, which had never abated, was still getting worse. It was the most severe, according to Borkum Riff, there ever was or ever could be in all of time.

'As if he can possibly know that!' observed Jack, almost cheerfully. His seasickness was gone and he had recovered from his fall. His duties now were in the galley and occasionally helping on deck.

'Oh he *knows*,' shouted Leetha, anything less being inaudible against the howling wind and creaking of the craft. 'The Earth is made up of sea as well as land and from Riff's birth he's felt the sea like his own blood and through it the beat of the heart of Mother Earth. He believes this storm is the Earth's cry of rage and pain.'

Riff and Deap each worried for the other, each now so dog tired they were beginning to make mistakes. They fell asleep at the wheel at times, their salt-swollen eyes closing. The mouths and lips of both were bruised and bloodied by the freezing sleet and hail. Sometimes they spoke incoherently, their minds circling around towards the bliss of unknowing when they needed to be even more clear and focused. The crews as well.

Not a one among them but had not been hurt: a falling spar, a parted, thrashing rope, the swing of jib and the cosh of tackle, like thunderous fists coming at them without warning, putting clusters of bursting stars around their heads and the dull, deep pain of mounting injury.

Slew was thrown down and his leg and ankle so damaged that he could not use them without worse injury and he was sent below.

'Riff's going to need you, Jack,' his mother said, binding Slew's ankle up.

He knew that well enough but did not reply. He knew nothing of the mariner's art and had none of their experience and skills. But he knew exhaustion when he saw it and where his duty lay.

The storm was relentless and they seemed caught up now in its vast roundel of driving wind, forced to tack and gybe to face the shifting direction of the waves, harried far from the course they thought they were on.

One night a pillar of chalky cliff loomed out of the waters, needle like. There were more behind it, the waves breaking high over the top of them.

'Where the Mirror did *that* come from?' muttered Riff, staring at his compass in puzzlement. 'If it be what I think we'm way off course or the compass be wild. That was . . .'

The chalk scraped by before he named it and the water opened up once more and an hour later or maybe three, or maybe a whole day, they ran into a big red buoy, number plain in white.

'What's that doing here, it's . . . !?'

Wrong place again, the bearings all awry, Deap as confused in his craft as Riff in his.

Confused and bewildered, tired beyond the grave, they fought on and on. But now they were beginning to lose, even Riff, even Deap, greatest sailors of their day. Jack could feel their growing despair.

'Mortality has limits,' Leetha whispered in a lull, repeating, 'they need you now, Jack, they need all the help they can get. Take them this.'

He took them the food in a closed cannikin to stop it blowing away.

'You eat now,' he ordered his father, the first time he had done so.

Riff cursed and swore but took the mess of pottage she had made and gulped it down. He wanted more and Jack, still uncertain on the slippery decks, went and got it.

'Leetha make this?'

He nodded.

'She never were much good in a galley,' he growled.

'*I'll* do it next time,' said Jack. 'She's tired through. What herbs have you got?'

'Seaweed!' someone called out with a laugh.

'That's a start,' said Jack, who had learnt a lot from Mister Barklice about making do and doing that well along the way.

The next day Leetha rested and he did the galley work, serving them, brews and all, twixt stove and table, bulkhead and floor, making, serving, eating, drinking, one and together, crew as well, family every one of them.

It was there, doing that, being a part, keeping the craft surviving, that Jack found his sea legs. They came suddenly, from fighting the deck to being one with it, from being an alien and bumped about to joining himself to the cutter, as if he were one of its planks, or the mast maybe, one and all together.

'Where are we?' he asked, beginning to move and flex his body with the craft as Riff did.

Riff smelt the air like a fox at night.

Jack, whose sight was good, couldn't see a thing.

Riff listened, head cocking to one side.

Jack could only hear the roar and whine of the wind in the ropes and the spray thudding on the deck.

Riff caressed the wheel and felt the shiver of the boat.

Jack touched wheel and deck, rail and stanchion, and all he felt was cold.

'We'm round about and headin' where we've no business to be,' said Riff, slow now, his eyes vague.

'Where's Deap?'

'Half a mile to leeward and he's tired, more tired even than me.'

Riff's bulk swung with the wheel and the lean of the boat into Jack's hulking body. He stood his ground, supporting Riff awhile until he swung away upright again. His tiredness engendered Jack's growing strength.

'Aye,' said Riff, eyes closing again, 'he be more tired than me and . . . and . . .'

Jack saw new worry in the dark, creased, bearded features of his father's face, and alarm in his eyes.

'And *what*? What is it?'

'Ain't nowt.'

But Jack knew something wasn't right. He looked round the boat, eyes half shut against the stinging spray. He felt the boat, or it felt him.

Solid, strong, like his own blood and bone. It wasn't the boat that was worrying Riff.

Jack went to the side and stared through the breaking waves and spray in the direction Riff had cocked his head, to listen rather than look. The din was a chaotic mix of wind on water, water breaking, the slap of the bows against the sea, the fall of sea upon the decks, and the clatter and crash of things loose, things breaking.

'Canst hear it, Jack?' he said.

Jack listened and was about to shake his head when his eyes caught something through the spray, whiter than the spray, blacker than the night shadows.

It was . . . it was . . .

He strained to see, leaning out over the racing, raging water, and it turned and was gone, a massive horse's shin and hoof, streaming with water.

Then the flank of a horse vast above them, whose other parts – its head, its tail, its racing legs, he could not see.

But the shining, streaming, palely iridescent flank, and down it, plain as the spray that raced by it, a mortal leg, robe streaming behind. Then briefly, as the flank dipped and turned and the horse's legs raced through the great seas, her bare arm, her hand loose on the rein, her angry, bitter laugh.

'Canst thou?' whispered his father, pulling him back to safety, speaking lips to ear, 'canst hear it?'

'I saw it, I heard it, the White Horse and its Rider.'

Riff shook his head.

'Nay, 'tis an illusion. Listen, lad, and hear the soft, grating growl of the Goodwin Sands, which we call the Ship Swallower. That's what we saw!'

Jack looked and listened and had to shake his head. There was nothing for him there.

Riff slipped, let go the wheel and it spun momentarily out of control.

'Damn its eyes and spokes,' said Riff as Jack himself took the wheel and held it, stilled it, and helped Riff set it and their craft true with the waves again.

'Listen up, Jack, and you'll hear 'im soon enough. But now . . . now . . .'

Riff's eyes were closing, his body sagging.

'You take 'er, Jack,' he said, as the bow dipped deep into green water and the sails above their heads jolted dangerously about, filling and emptying, 'and keep her . . . so . . .'

Together they leaned into the great wheel, feeling the heft of the craft against them, a-playing to her play, their strength with hers.

'You take her,' repeated Riff, stepping back like he had when Deap was a scrap of a boy, teaching him his trade.

Riff's smiles were usually rare and grudging things but out there, as Jack took over, and unseen by anyone, even Jack himself, his smile was a joyful open thing.

You're getting your sea legs now, my lad, and by the Mirror true, afore this day be done we'll have need o' you!

A lull, and Jack at the wheel, watching to port where a wave steepened towards them, saw the Horse's head heave up out of the water, its mane a breaking waterfall, its exquisite cheeks two calms, its proud dark eyes the shadows beyond the waves.

'Why didn't we take shelter in a harbour along the coast?' asked Jack as the Rider, who was perhaps no more than the broiling sky, rode by.

'This storm came on too fast,' explained Slew, back on deck but struggling; his head was bleeding from a knock. 'It is safer staying out in open sea than trying to make land. Get it wrong and a single wave in weather like this will crash a craft onto sand or shore or the stage of a jetty so hard it will break in two.'

'What's *that*?' asked Jack, hearing a sudden grating sound.

'The Ship Swallower,' said Riff, eyes wild, 'right *under* us.'

'And that . . . ?' cried Jack, hearing a warning shout carried on the wind.

'That's Deap.'

Whatever it was, the keel had touched the bottom and at the wheel's turn the wind had brought them clear again. The white wall of savage surf, where the Horse and Rider went, loomed off to starboard before it was gone from sight.

The great seas rose and fell about them like the rise and fall of mountains, majestic and slow. Their craft now felt no more substantial than a splinter of sodden wood. It went heavily up with the waves, on and on, up and up until all that remained was the angry, grey sky ahead and the top of the wave beginning to break around them, driven by the wind into a million flying fragments of water. Then, cresting the giant wave, they slid back down and down to the furious, dark deep below, the craft losing way and steerage, slewing sideways, perilously near broaching, risking capsize absolute if they could not control it and bring it round, the bow back up the rise, bow to the new crest far above, up and up once more, each time more tiring than the last.

Sometime then came the shout again, and Jack, who was needed now at the wheel all the time because Riff had grown too weak, pointed forrard through the spray.

There, for the first time in hours, Jack saw Deap's craft and Deap at the wheel, hand raised, not in salute but to show he needed aid.

'He'm lost un' o'erboard . . .' cried Riff, head snapping round as not one, but two bodies, Deap's deckhands, shot by them overboard and gone in a moment, floppy drowned and dead.

'Not a chance o' getting 'em and no damn point,' said Riff, dismissing them because he needed to be alert to what lay ahead. 'He'll need you now, over there.'

'Me?' cried Jack, spitting out salt, cheek blown sideways. '*You* need me!'

Riff nodded his head and leaned to the wheel, letting the cutter slide up and down the great seas, swearing and cursing as, with a skill born of years of experience, he brought their craft ever nearer Deap's.

'Listen!' he said. 'Can you hear 'im now?'

'What is it?' asked Jack, who could hear the surf's fatal roar, a thumping, battering of sound.

'Watch to starboard now, as we crest this wave . . . There, lad! That's the Ship Swallower!'

It would have been unimaginable had he not seen it with his own eyes. A wilderness of surf straight ahead, just moments away, all darkened by sand and stretching to the horizon.

'It be the Goodwin Sands, and they'm never something you'd want t'see either side of your bow. Gybing or tacking's now too late and will only broach us down.'

Jack looked around but saw no way back.

'There be none,' said Riff, holding the wheel through the breaking waves, 'we'm to cross 'em or die in the trying.'

Another crest, another fragmentary view, before their bow dropped forward and down, down to the trough, deeper down than any valley Jack had ever entered.

Yet there, in its lowest part, incredibly, Deap awaited them, holding his craft besieged on all sides by the sea.

'Ready yoursel'n,' cried Riff, 'there'll be half a second to jump, if that. *Now!*'

Their craft rushed down, Jack got to the side, Deap's craft rose, its stern square and set and for a moment on a level, as neat as two peas in a pod.

'Jump!' cried Riff and Jack leapt, terrible broken water beneath, got a grip, felt the lower half of his body fall into the waves, saw the stern of Riff's craft rush on by, up the steepening, tumbling wall, felt his arm grabbed by a hand as strong as his own. Deap heaved him in, hauled him along, pulled him upright and got him back to the safety of the wheel in time to face the next gigantic wave.

A flash beyond, a sail briefly horizontal, its mast-top Riff's as he dared to gybe and, sliding back down and turning again, began following Deap up the opposite wave.

'Hold 'ern, Jack, hold 'ern now . . .'

He felt Deap's hand on his shoulder, his hand to his hand on the wheel. 'Hold 'ern to the wave and water, hold her now . . . where we'm going, which be hell itself, he'll need our good sail to see him through . . . *hold* 'ern . . . we bain't letting Borkum Riff our father drown in this forsaken reach o'barrenness along with Leetha. She'd be better dancin' on land than out alone on these wild sands.'

Then Deap was gone along the deck, past the flexing, creaking mast, which was cracked, its bulkheads split and broken, fragments of wood skittering along the streaming deck.

'Oh dear God,' murmured Jack, leaning to the wheel as he took command of the craft, a mortal fear coming on him as they crashed into the first huge surf of the swallowing sands, 'Mirror save us now . . .'

Loose ropes whipped and flew. A sail shot by and tore off in the wind and Deap was a hunched, oil-skinned, mortal thing fighting on the foredeck to raise a sail. Fighting against a fatigue that showed in every slow, clumsy movement he tried to make.

Hold 'ern, Jack, he had said, giving up the helm to Jack while he scrabbled along the deck, braced against the nearly impossible seas, swept aside one way, then another, then getting back, bringing metal eye to rope, frozen fingers turning to unwieldy thumbs, the rope flying up and away, his feet knocked sideways, his body bashed onto the rock-like deck and stabbed by a broken metal rail, blood flying free on the wind and reddening the foam for an instant of time.

Jack watched, horrified, as Deap struggled to set the sail they needed to get them through.

Then with a shudder and jump they touched the bottom again. The craft keeled over and the deck slewed one way and the other.

'Hold 'em, lad,' he heard Deap cry, as the wind took the sail and the craft was hauled bodily upright and forward once more as the seas tried to rush in and take her down.

Anger then, anger in Jack.

The anger he had always known he felt and feared.

Anger at the fire and the pain and the long loneliness of those early years.

An anger learned for this moment now, here, now and now and now again.

He turned for a moment and saw through the spray to port, across that ridged bank of sand they had touched further back, Riff at his wheel and Jack raising a hand to signal *Follow me*.

Riff stared, eyes wide with surprise, as Jack turned starboard a few points with another brief wave which Riff understood at once. For the first time in days he was able to relax and follow on, to rest his beaten body before the final fight and to watch as Deap crawled back along the deck, one-handed now but the sail released, the craft under Jack's stern, cool leadership.

'Get t'back o' Jack,' Riff urged, words that could never be heard above the surf's roar, even by himself, 'he'm our skipper now!'

But Deap needed no bidding, he knew the truth and felt it in his craft's new confidence.

As Jack grabbed him, heaved him upright and shoved him close behind, he set himself steady. Then he threaded a rope round himself, looped it and hooked it through Jack's belt so they could work as one.

Then, tired beyond fatigue, letting go command, he put his head so near to Jack's right ear that they touched, and roared, 'Arm's broke. Turn round in a lull, Jack, and make the knot fast.'

But Jack knew it already, as if their thoughts had overlapped, and moments later turned briefly to bind them close. The knot he tied was right, a shackling round, though he had never tied one before and did not know its name. But he knew it could be untied single-handedly in an emergency such that if one of them fell the other need not fall as well.

He turned back to the wheel, taking it again in his strong hands, and felt the Earth's rage reaching up from far beneath, up through the churning sea and sand, up to his arms and wrists, trying to force him one way when he insisted they must go another. Trying to founder them, when it was life they wanted to find once more. Trying to sink them, when they needed to float.

The wheel lurched clockwise, broaching the craft into a dangerous wave . . .

'Oh God,' Jack muttered as he bent his weight the other way, bringing the prow round and round, 'oh God, it's going too slow . . .'

God? He bain't hereabout, you fool, the Rider mocked Jack, aping Deap's accent, bearing down on him from behind in a deluge of water and spray, *and you won't get help from me!*

She rode on by, the Horse bigger than the coming wave, the hair of Judith, his daughter, grey and thick with sand and salt, her smile bleak and savage.

He helmed after her, sweating, angry, not believing her.

The sea tore under them, bucking the craft beneath their feet even as he saw a heavier sea was on portside and . . . if he . . . failed . . . to . . . bring . . . her . . .

He felt the deck rise up beneath him, pushed by Mirror knew what, watched helpless as the mast above his head tilted over, then back, creaking, something cracking as everything was lost to sight beneath the wall of solid water that ran diagonally through them.

He held on, unable to breathe; the stinging, bitter water in his mouth, up his nose, battering his eyes and head.

He held on, not knowing what would face him when it cleared, or even which way up, or round, or sloping the craft might be.

The way before them opened into a simple, smoking trough and the White Horse rearing, Judith raising an arm in acknowledgement as Jack had.

Follow me.

She was helping them get through the worst of the surf.

He steered her way and she was one with the Horse, turning across a flat race of water that looked like a pane of frosted glass.

'I can't . . .'

For out of the breakers thrust the jagged prow of a sunken ship. Rust-black, corroded steel as sharp as icicles and a skewed, unholy cross of metal that could scupper any boat. It was bending, thrusting, plunging towards them as if it were animate and purposeful, and Judith's laughter mocked them.

'Oh God . . .'

Deap's hand was firm on his back and his whisper quiet as thought itself . . .

It's all right, Jack, it's all right . . . become the sea, take her strength and play her into your arms, love her as the Earth does. Feel her now, feel her . . .

Deap's life was in him, thinking him, coursing through him.

It's all right . . .

'Yes, yes . . . can you see the White Horse? See its dread Rider?'

'Hold 'ern, Jack, just keep her true.'

He heaved the wheel and his weight to the left, just enough to scrape on by the gantry but not so much that the craft turned broadside to the next wave before she powered down the slope towards the naked, terrifying sand. Then bringing her round just in time, using the coming wave to bring her keel up to safety, straight . . . *oh God . . . oh Leetha . . .* straight into a rugged, ribbed, black viscous wall whose sides stretched away too far, whose base was a bulbous fist of death.

'Bastard!' cried Jack. 'Bastards!' As he drove them through the wall of water and out the other side, where briefly, before they dropped into the next savage trough, he had a momentary vision of the hell that lay ahead: a seascape of endless, killer surf and black sand banks like beached whales, the evidence of whose centuries of ship-murder was littered all around. The hulls of metal ships, the ribs of wooden ones, the tilted masts, gravestones all, through which raced and surged the surf and waves, continuously causing the maze into which they had sailed to change.

'Bastards!' he shouted again.

Feel what you must do, don't think it, thought Deap.

Feel it with your whole body, Jack, every sinew, every part.

Feel the cold as a reminder you are alive.

Feel the fatigue as a reminder that you are awake.

Feel your weakness so you know the sea's great strength and love for you.

Honour her and she will honour you.

Deap's grasp tightened and Jack looked round, a tremble in the touch to leeward. It was the other craft and Borkum Riff, lashed to right and left, the wheel in front supporting him, his body vanquished now but his spirit not.

Not yet.

He heard a shout, he raised his eyes to wakefulness and he saw Jack just ahead, Deap secure behind, and Jack was . . .

Jack was . . .

Grinning! Just like Leetha would have done. Just like Leetha was just then, from below.

'Bastards,' murmured Riff, revived, turning the wheel, following in Jack's broken wake on across the Goodwin Sands.

'Grinning at what, I'd like to know!' he rasped before shouting down the hatch to Leetha and Slew, 'Our lad's doing good and the Swallower don't like it!'

Later, the passage more steady, the surf less high, the waves more predictable, Riff said, 'And now he's singin' and laughing. He's as bad as you!'

Leetha laughed as well.

While out across the Goodwin Sands, where the stars began and the moon might rise, Judith pulled the reins and stopped the White Horse, watching after her family too, ragged with age, proud of them and ashamed of herself.

'There may be worse than this to come in the weeks ahead,' she said softly, 'may the Mirror help us all.'

She turned into the waves, rode them high and was gone unseen, a rider alone, longing for a touch she could never have, screaming unheard with the winter wind. Empty, sterile and bereft as the sand which scattered behind the Horse as it galloped across the banks, this way and that, looking for a way off before the tide came back in and covered them over again.

Of that fabled crossing of the Ship Swallower poets might pen a thousand rhymes and a teller tell a hundred thousand times, but none could ever describe the wyrd world into which Jack sailed those hours through. A place where his body and mind and spirit were the Earth's, where all that mattered was the present moment in which Jack found both doubt and new confidence.

He was there now, through the long hours of day towards another night; there, where raw skin was life, swollen eyes were life, hunger and thirst were life, no-time was life, nothingness was life, and he was the sea and the boat was him and Deap was the voice inside his head and heart and . . .

Cr . . . crash!

The craft was tossed up and taken by the wind, crashing sideways on the sea, the small sail filled with water, his left hand holding on to the unconscious Deap and Jack laughing, shrieking, roaring at it all, or with it, because he was part of it.

They had hit the bottom of an upturned craft, all rust and barnacles and streaming water. They were scraping along it, skewed over by the wind so Jack leapt off, feet on quaking metal, and heaved the prow up and round, before he leapt back on.

'Bastard,' he cried again, but affectionately now, almost lovingly, for he was that water, that sea, the wind, the pain, that wreck; and the Swallower meant him no harm, not really. It just wanted to drown them all because that's what it did, like hunters ate prey.

Bastard . . .

Jack smiled to feel Deap wake, muttering, his hand firm on Jack's shoulder as darkness fell and the first light showed ahead, out of the murk, beyond the breaking seas, a light at last.

Hold 'ern, his brother had commanded.

Jack had done just that.

'Judith,' he whispered, grinning in the night. Forseeing the angry, raging hustle of her on the White Horse as he had here and not somewhere else signalled to him that Katherine was still alive.

13
RECOVERY

The hurricane that so nearly caused the deaths of Jack and his family in the North Sea struck the whole of east and southern Englalond.

But its impact on Mister Barklice and those travelling with him from the South-West was delayed a few days, its great mass travelling down the North Sea coast before swinging westward.

So as the winds eased and Jack and Riff helmed their craft into the less violent waters of the Knock and Black Deeps beyond North Foreland, severe storms and flooding began battering the counties along the A30 into which Barklice and his party were just entering.

Conditions got worse and worse as they followed the road up into the bleak heights of Bodmin Moor. The wind came in from the east, but still had a cutting, northern edge. It carried with it swathes of sleet and hail, which soaked their legs and schuhe, stung their ears, ripped off their caps and ran down their necks and into the unprotected sleeves of their stave arms.

The only respite was where the road was sunk into the moor with high banking on either side but this decreased the higher they got.

Barklice called frequent halts, less because they were unwilling to go on than to make sure that Slaeke Sinistral, thin as he was, was not suffering from exposure; and that Katherine and Terce, whose recovery had been good, were not being pushed too hard.

'I'm fine,' said Katherine, 'and getting better by the day. But I think Terce is suffering.'

He was, indicating that the cold wind was getting into his perforated ears and causing severe pain. While Sinistral was wrapped up more warmly, Terce submitted to muffling bandages around his head.

'It is a very great shame, my friends,' observed Stort, at one of these stops and pointing westward, 'that the weather is not more conducive to travellers. Not far over there across the moor is a group of very famous stone henges. I believe one of them, the Stripple, might well be in sight of where we are sheltering, but for the driving rain.'

'No doubt these are interesting thoughts and this an interesting place, Mister Stort,' interrupted Niklas Blut wryly, 'but I think getting back to Brum is of more importance than visiting ancient monuments!'

'There is no need to dismiss this area as merely "interesting", my dear Lord Emperor!' cried Stort hotly. 'These henges offer us a way of transporting ourselves quickly back to Brum. They are portals after all, not only between our world and that of the humans, but from place to place. Jack and I and some others availed ourselves of that facility when we paid a visit to the Imperial headquarters in Bochum . . .'

Blut blinked at Stort's tactlessness but then smiled slightly, understanding that their scrivener friend meant no harm by it. The visit he was referring to had taken place barely three months before. He, along with Jack and some military personnel from Brum, had mounted a sudden and very effective raid into the heart of the Empire and recovered – or perhaps stolen – two of Beornamund's gems, those of Spring and Summer. The result was the invasion of Englalond and, through circumstances complex and strange, the journey of Stort and friends on one hand, and Sinistral and friends on another, to Veryan Beacon and Pendower Beach.

'I had not realized,' said Sinistral soothingly, 'that you used henges as a means of reaching Bochum. Neat and clever, eh, Blut?'

'Some might think so,' murmured Blut.

'And now you propose we use the henges near here to get us out of this bad weather and back to Brum?'

Stort shook his head.

'I merely moot it. If we could control where we arrive, and we could be sure of all arriving at the same time, in the same place, together, then the idea might have merit. But we cannot, and we might be scattered about and separated.'

'You really think that time shifts when folk use the portals?'

'I am as certain of it,' replied Stort, 'as I am the fact that the Earth's present turmoil is causing time shifts quite *apart* from the portals. But given these grim climatic conditions and the unpredictability of henge travel, it would be better if we could think of a less risky form of transport. Unfortunately the canals and rivers hereabout are thin on the ground, and so far we have seen no sign of human railways operating at all. In the past Barklice and I have often travelled under a train and got ourselves from A to B very speedily and without harm. But that option is not available.'

Barklice allowed them to rest a few minutes more before inviting them to rise and press on. They did so willingly enough but rather quietly, each trying to work out a better way of getting home than plodding along a road with no sign of life of any kind but for burnt-out human homes across the moors and the other detritus of violence and civil unrest.

It was no surprise that it was Katherine who saw a way out of their predicament. She was, after all, of human stock, had direct experience of that world and could see possibilities in ways the others could not.

They had just passed through the moorland village of Bodventor, with a miserable church on one side and a ruined inn on the other, and were heading downhill when she stopped short and cried out, 'I am an idiot! The answer has been staring us in the face ever since those military vehicles first passed us outside Truro!'

They looked at her blankly.

It had not occurred to any of them that they might solve their travel problem by commandeering one of the many vehicles that had been abandoned along the way. Assuming they had fuel and could start a vehicle, and the pedals could be adjusted to their hydden stature, they might in theory be able to get to Brum in a matter of hours.

Katherine wasted no time in telling them what she thought they should do. The more she talked the more blindingly obvious it was to her.

'We just need a vehicle large enough for all of us and a set of keys and . . .'

They stared at her blankly, not getting it at all. The human world and all its ways and means still felt alien to them. It was as if, though it was palpable enough, it was impossible for them to be part of its realm.

'Can't you see we'd get back to Brum a lot *faster*?' she said, exasperated.

'And a lot deader,' said Barklice darkly.

But after another rough, sleepless night of driving wet and cold and a miserable dawn-time start, Katherine had finally had enough.

To everyone's astonishment, when they stopped for breakfast, she simply said, 'I'm going to eat, I'm going to drink Stort's brew, and then I'm going to do it.'

'Do what?' asked Barklice.

'Take a vehicle and get away from this place.'

She looked around, glaring at each in turn, challenging them to tell her not to. None of them did.

Instead, the decision made it seemed, Blut said, 'Tell me, Katherine, exactly how a car is driven?'

'And how, pray, *exactly*, is the direction in which a vehicle goes *determined*?' wondered Stort.

'By a steering wheel.'

She explained how steering worked.

'Ingenious,' observed Stort, 'but rather subject to error, I would have thought.'

'You get used to it,' said Katherine.

'Then you will do what you call the driving . . . ?'

'Oh yes,' she replied very firmly, 'I'll do the driving.'

'No one is driving anywhere,' said Barklice firmly 'until we need to, and we don't need to yet.'

Which re-started the argument, a bickering, rumbling, bad-tempered thing, which dragged on half a day. Until Sinistral, who had stayed silent and was very tired, asserted himself.

'Miss Katherine,' he said very formally, 'you will select a vehicle from the many we find along the way and convey myself and Blut to Brum. The others may choose to come with us or not as they wish.'

'Yes, my Lord!' said Katherine.

The road took them steadily on into the open heath and moor. It was sterile and desolate and the only buildings were occasional farms, bothies and concrete erections that looked military. The strong wind grew ever colder, the chill factor making their progress increasingly unpleasant. Sinistral, who had proved remarkably robust for an old hydden, was growing pale and breathless.

'Time for another halt,' said Barklice.

Ten minutes previously they had passed a heavily gated private road with a sign which read: 'Bodmin Equestrian Centre'. They could see buildings half a mile away across the fields.

'Interesting,' murmured Stort examining it with his glass. 'Let us explore it, Katherine. It has possibilities.'

Despite the protests of Barklice, they set off to do so, assuring everyone they would not be long or do anything stupid. Time passed, the afternoon light faded, twilight came and with it no Stort or Katherine.

The only sign of life had been a light showing briefly by the cluster of buildings they had gone to explore and after that a white light nearby followed by a red one. Barklice grew restive and uneasy.

'My only consolation is that Katherine is with Stort and will prevent him doing something extreme. She is the personification of common sense. I would not have allowed him to go without her. I can only hope they have found some useful but heavy supplies which are slowing their return down.'

Darkness came and they began to get seriously worried. The last time Katherine went off the world exploded.

The silence was broken by the sudden starting of an engine, and two strong beams of white light shot out of the darkness across the fields from the direction of the equestrian centre. The engine sounds increased and decreased, stopped, started and stopped again. The engine started once more, the lights cutting through the darkness as the vehicle they had found, for that was surely what it was, began jolting and bouncing along the private road, gathering speed towards them.

'I hope that Stort is not at the wheel,' said Sinistral uneasily.

'He will have to stop at the gate,' said Blut, 'so do not concern yourself, my Lord.'

'Humph!' said Sinistral, eyeing the rapidly advancing lights and then the gate.

'He must stop,' said Barklice, his voice rising. 'Surely!'

But Stort, if it was he, did not stop.

Indeed, as they neared the entrance, the vehicle loomed ever faster out of the darkness, a great monster of a thing, as big as any truck, but high-sided, solid and long. Its side and roof shone darkly in the night and, as it approached, they saw no sign of Stort at the driver's seat in the cab. They could only see Katherine's face, lit by green-white light, peering through the window.

The vehicle lurched over the last few bumpy yards of the track on the far side of the gate and powered straight through it. The two parts splayed open, padlock and chains skittering across the road towards the watching hydden as the rear wheels of the vehicle, of which there were several pairs, rode over the fallen gates and skidded sideways. To avoid crashing into the central reservation, the vehicle made a sharp left with a clattering of metal and a burning of rubber, sliding to a stop with a squeal of brakes.

The vehicle skewed over on one side, the nearside wheels leaving the road and hanging briefly in the air before it thumped back down. Acrid smoke lingered as the engine stuttered to a stop, the passenger door swung open and Stort, small compared to the great passenger seat, tumbled down onto the tarmac of the road, swiftly followed by Katherine.

The others gathered around, lanterns in their hands, at once alarmed, awed and amazed.

'Not bad,' cried out Stort cheerfully, proffering Katherine a hand, 'considering.'

'Who was driving?' asked Blut very reasonably. He might equally well have asked: 'How were you managing to drive, given the distance between seat and pedals?'

Stort and Katherine looked at each other.

'We both were,' she said. 'Once the engine was on I turned the wheel to steer while Stort's height enabled him to have a foot on the clutch and accelerator and change gears.'

'And we may well have just made history,' added Stort, 'this being the first time, to my knowledge, that a hydden has driven a human vehicle.'

'It's against all the traditions,' said Barklice with a frown and somewhat feebly, 'and as Chief Verderer of Brum and leader of this particular journey I feel . . .'

But his voice was drowned out by the others, who hoisted each other up onto the seats to examine the steering wheel, dashboard and lights.

'It's a horsebox,' Katherine explained, 'which we found locked away in an outhouse. Very new, complete with a sleeping bunk behind the passenger seat, a television which doesn't work, a full tank and berths for horse handlers in the rear, accessed through a side door.'

Stort had put padding on the seat so Katherine could see out of the window. He had also stockpiled more fuel at the rear, in containers they had found. Now he built up the pedals with wooden blocks so she could reach them as well.

'The perfect transport on these empty roads,' he declared with satisfaction.

'Provided we don't run into humans,' said Barklice darkly.

Neither Sinistral nor Blut felt they should let the moment pass without comment.

'We have avoided human contact, and the use of their machinery, for centuries,' said Blut, 'and historical though this moment may be I am not sure it is entirely positive.'

'My dear Blut,' responded Sinistral, 'you delude yourself. We hydden have been living off human mismanagement of our Mother Earth for centuries. Borrowing one of these vehicles may seem a significant moment in history but in my view it is nothing more than an extension of what we already do.'

'My Lord, you always surprise me,' said Blut.

'Needs must,' replied Sinistral with a smile, 'and we certainly need to get on faster than we have been!'

They stowed their 'sacs in the rear and agreed it might be safer if they all travelled together in the cab.

'We might do best to wait until dawn to leave,' said Blut, ever the sensible planner.

'Indeed we might . . .' began Sinistral, as excited as the others by the prospect of speeding up what had become a troublesome and wearisome journey, '. . . but that . . . I fear . . .'

'What is it, my Lord?' asked Blut, following the former Emperor's gaze down the road behind them.'

'I fear we are no longer alone upon the road!' he announced.

Small lights were bobbing in the dark towards them, their distance hard to determine.

'Shutter the lanterns,' called out Barklice as Stort focused his monocular on the lights.

'Humans,' he pronounced, 'armed and running . . .'

'All aboard, me hearties!' cried out Arnold Mallarkhi, who was clear-headed at such moments. 'Katherine first, since she's going to be the main one driving this great craft. Stort next to her, since he be needed too, it seems. Up'n you all go,' he said, cupping his hands to give each of them in turn a bunk-up.

'Quick!' said Barklice.

'Start the engine!' commanded Stort.

'Give me a hand, my Lordship Emperor!' called out Arnold, the last left on the ground.

As Blut obliged and helped Arnold in, the engine started with a roar. The great vehicle lurched forward; they heard gunfire and the thumping of someone trying to board behind. Then they were gone, the offside tyre sending up a spray of gravel as they swung across the road.

Katherine righted the wheel, grazed the central reservation, swung the vehicle back, straightened up and accelerated into total darkness.

'It would help,' said Stort, 'if someone put the lights back on!'

'That's your job, Stort,' Katherine said, 'remember?'

The road ahead flooded with light and they saw a grey metal barrier on the passenger side swing towards them. Katherine turned the wheel again, and they were away.

14
THE HORSEBOX

An awed silence descended in the cab as Katherine drove the vehicle along the A30 dual carriageway. Gaining confidence, and seeing they were not pursued by another vehicle, she eased their speed to fifty miles an hour. They had to stop twice to pad out her seating and make it comfortable, and to re-attach the blocks on the pedals to the right angle for her to work them easily.

'Even were I back to human size,' she said ruefully, 'I'd have trouble driving this great thing!'

The others, whether on the passenger seat or perched on the spacious bunk behind, crowded forward with excitement, with one exception: Terce.

The strongest among them, he had already proved his courage in the face of danger. But naturally, since the explosion and consequent loss of his hearing and being badly shaken about, he had not been himself. Now, as the road rushed towards him, he sat terrified, covering his eyes with his fingers. Beads of sweat broke out on his brow, his heart raced and he muttered his thoughts aloud, unable to hear his own voice, 'I can't . . . it's too . . . we'll all . . .'

Because it was night and the lights were on low beam, items like emergency orange telephones, the occasional tree on an embankment and a cardboard box that had blown onto the carriageway, appeared to jump into view as they rushed on by.

Used as he was to a quiet, monastic way of life, he had no experience of human roads. These sudden apparitions or the disconcerting vibrations caused by the various bumps and turns, swings and slowings down along the way disturbed him.

Several times he cried out 'Oh!' and 'Nooo!' and then, when it suddenly got too much and he lost all confidence, he cried out, half-hitting those around him in his panic as if thinking they could not hear his cries, 'Please, stop! I cannot bear this any more.'

But Katherine did not stop.

Instead Festoon, at Sinistral's suggestion, moved his bulky frame alongside that of Terce and put a great and reassuring hand upon his arm.

The chorister finally calmed down, relaxed his body into the vehicle's motion and, before many more miles had passed, began staring with growing confidence at the continuously changing nocturnal scene.

Of the others not one said a word, so entranced were they by the flying spectacle of dark and light, white markings, barriers and abandoned vehicles before them. But for Stort. The scene beyond the windows soon bored him and he refocused his interest on the instrument panel and its appealing array of knobs and buttons of things unknown.

'Don't touch!' commanded Katherine and for a short time he did not. But like a child to whom temptation is presented, he surreptitiously reached a finger out here, and prodded something there, to see what would happen if he . . . if he . . . pushed that thing, there, just a wee bit . . . just enough to make it . . .

The temperature in the cab suddenly began to drop and in moments the air was icy and a draught blowing in their faces.

'Stort, you've turned on the air conditioning and the fan as well!'

'Ah! Interesting, I wondered what that was for.'

'It cools the air.'

'Amazing.'

'Turn it off!'

He pressed a button and turned a knob.

The temperature rose and rose some more and then more still.

'*Stort* . . .' said Katherine warningly.

'This is so interesting,' he said unabashed. 'This panel here appears to show the temperature.'

'Turn it down . . .'

'Please Stort,' said Blut suddenly, 'my Lord and myself are beginning to feel over-heated . . .'

'It's a display,' said Katherine, 'not a panel. Humans call it a display.'

'Ah, quite so. Interesting concept. Lit up from . . .'

'Behind,' said Katherine. 'Do not press anything else.'

But he did, unable to stop himself.

A new display appeared, this time on a screen, moving all the time, its contents lines of different colours like snakes. Numbers too.

'What . . . ?'

A disembodied voice said: *Turn around when possible!*

'It's the Satnav, a human navigation device,' explained Katherine. '*Turn it off!*'

'I can't seem to . . .'

Keep in the right-hand lane.

'I can't concentrate,' said Katherine, 'and that's . . . there's . . .'

'What?' asked Stort more urgently than before, hearing the crisis in her voice.

But she did not need to reply.

Coming towards them were the two white lights of another vehicle, on their side of the dual carriageway and, they saw as it got closer still, in the same lane.

'What shall I do?'

Her voice was tense, eyes focused and the green light from the dashboard showed her jaws were clenched.

As quickly as he had engaged the Satnav Stort now turned it off and gave his attention to the approaching lights. There were alarmed murmurings from the others and the beginnings of conflicting advice . . .

'Swerve,' suggested Barklice.

Terce raised his hand to indicate the need to stop.

'Stop!' said Blut.

But Sinistral said calmly, 'Keep straight on and don't deviate. The Empire did not get built on a foundation of doubt and hesitation.'

'But supposing he . . . doesn't . . . sto—'

'He will stop or he'll swerve.'

'Accelerate,' said Stort suddenly.

'A hydden after my own heart!' murmured Sinistral.

The approaching vehicle was almost on them, its lights getting bigger and brighter, which gave Katherine an idea.

She turned the beam full on and, her voice strong and determined, said, 'Here we *go!*'

The vehicle ahead of them suddenly lit up and they saw everything. It was bull-nosed and painted in khaki camouflage, the wheelbase high, and the whole thing larger and more robust than their own vehicle. It was coming directly at them.

'Do not deviate,' repeated Sinistral quietly in Katherine's ear, 'I have always found it the best policy.'

She answered by accelerating even more and flashing the full beam on and off.

A large male human was driving, another two next to him, and all three had their hands in front of their eyes, blinded by the beam.

One of them, and it did not look like the driver, lost his nerve, leaned over and jerked the wheel sideways. The vehicle slewed to their left and there was a jolt and loud bang as their own vehicle hit its offside rear end.

Katherine clung to the wheel, Stort helping to hold it steady, and then they were past, skidding briefly before they were back into darkness and still on the road – just. The vehicle swayed violently as Katherine struggled to get it on course again and there was a sudden thump somewhere at the rear and then another. Neither affected the steering or speed but an airy roaring sound now filled the cab.

'Can anyone see what's happening behind?' called out Katherine, above the new noise, signalling to the still-deaf Terce what she meant.

He immediately indicated that the side mirror gave a view behind.

'It looks like the vehicle you hit just exploded,' said Stort matter-of-factly.

Katherine ignored this and said, 'I mean behind in our *own* vehicle?'

The bangings continued.

Until then those on the bunk had been too pre-occupied with the road ahead to bother examining the rear of the horsebox through the window at the back of the cab. Blut now did so and found a small curtain. He pulled it aside and found himself staring at very close quarters into a malevolent human face.

He cried out involuntarily and explained what he had seen. Katherine turned the steering wheel sharply to one side. The face disappeared and there was a thud and muffled shout. She righted the vehicle again and the face reappeared briefly before going the opposite way.

'We have a passenger in the rear,' Blut announced, coolly closing the curtain, 'and he or she is having trouble keeping balance.'

'In the rear, you say?' said Stort, resuming his interest in the panel of instruments before him.

'Must be one of those humans chasing us, who was able to climb aboard in some way as we escaped.'

'Is the rear in darkness?' said Stort.

Blut confirmed it was.

'And now?' asked Stort, pressing a button.

'A light has come on and . . .'

Blut peered through the window cautiously, briefly examining the rear before abruptly pulling the curtain to.

'. . . and it's a man. The two rear doors of the box are open, swinging about in the wind. That's what has been making that banging sound.'

'Is the light off again?'

Blut confirmed that it was.

'Ah!' cried Stort, turning on other switches and turning various knobs. A sudden cacophony of music came and went; the Satnav sprang briefly back to life; the seat they were on tilted slowly forward.

'Ah, ah!' cried Stort once more.

Above their heads, turned towards the driver's seat, a small television monitor came on. It glared white-grey for a moment before changing into a dark grey-green image in which a ghost-like figure of a man stood.

Katherine immediately understood what they were looking at.

'It's so the driver can monitor the horses in the box. It's also night-vision so they don't get startled by sudden lights. That's our passenger!'

There were two stalls near the cab, the window being centred on one of them. The man was now further off, standing up with some difficulty by holding on to the partition that divided the stalls. The area beyond, by the open doors, was unencumbered but for a ramp that made the floor slope towards the rear.

'What's he doing?' asked Katherine.

'Trying to reach out to one of the doors, maybe to close it,' said Barklice.

'Is he really!' said Katherine purposefully. 'We'll see about that!'

'He can't quite reach it,' Barklice said, starting a running commentary. 'He's pulled back, repositioned his right hand to a strap on the side, edged a bit nearer the door and he can al . . . most . . .'

'Hold tight!' cried Katherine.

She braked quite hard.

'He's shot forward from the door, towards the stall!'

'And again . . . !'

She accelerated hard and fast.

'He's swung back towards the doors. He's let go the strap and he's clinging on . . .'

'Hold fast!'

She braked very briefly and then shot the horsebox forward again.

'And now he's . . . he's . . . oops!'

'What?'

'He's gone. He fell out of the back.'

'Good result,' said Katherine pitilessly. Her control over the vehicle and herself was getting better by the minute. 'I'm going to get us as far towards Brum as fast as I can,' she said, 'but first we'd better sort those doors.'

She waited ten minutes, when she was sure they were well clear of the intruder, assuming he had survived his fall, before pulling over. Terce and Barklice got out to close the rear doors.

'Gentlemen and lady,' called out the verderer, 'if anyone wants to relieve themselves, this is the moment!'

Everyone but Stort tumbled out and Katherine disappeared to the far side of the vehicle.

'Not too far!' cried Barklice, worriedly.

The horsebox had given them a dangerous sense of comfort and invulnerability. Back outside on solid ground, standing in a cold wind with a starry sky above and shadows all about, was a salutary reminder that they were advancing through unknown territory where dangers of all kinds must lurk. They found the side door was also partly open and they closed that too, guessing the intruder had managed to clamber aboard that way.

Stort remained in the cab, playing with the instruments. He noticed that a red light with a door icon on the dashboard had gone out.

'Which was telling us that the doors were open,' he pronounced.

He turned on the Satnav once more, worked out how to lower its volume, and he engaged in a conversation with the female voice, admonishing her for giving warnings that were not needed and directions that were not relevant.

'She reminds me somewhat of Goodwife Cluckett, my housekeeper,' he observed, 'though *her* voice is rather less pleasant at times than this charming female's, now I am attuned to it.'

Barklice and Blut took a careful look round from the carriageway, which was raised over the fields below. There were almost no lights, near or far. There was a dim glow on the road far behind, which they guessed might be the vehicle they forced off the road. Ahead, across the night horizon, was a wider glimmer of light beneath a dark shadow that looked like an advancing bank of cloud.

It was time to move on.

'But before we do,' said Barklice, 'we should accept that it is unlikely our good fortune will continue. If there was one vehicle coming our way, there may be another. We too might be forced off the road or stopped. We should therefore have an exit strategy so that we are not taken by surprise.'

It was agreed they would vacate the vehicle in an orderly way with Arnold watching over them as they went. Barklice would lead them to safety.

'Better than wandering round looking for each other in unknown and probably dangerous terrain,' he said.

The 'sacs were placed ready for such an emergency exit and their various staves and other items stacked in an orderly way.

'There is one other matter,' said Barklice gravely, 'and it is one I would ask Emperor Blut to arbitrate on.'

He touched Terce's arm to get his attention and nodded, saying, 'He's going to show you something we found in the rear.'

The chorister went to the nearside wheel and removed something dark and metallic from its shadow. It was a weapon, a machine pistol, the first such firearm most of them had ever seen.

'Does it work?' someone asked.

'We don't know,' said Barklice, 'but this is not the time to find out.'

Blut stared at it uneasily. They had been fired on earlier and it might well happen again. But the debate about the use of human weapons such as this was a very familiar one in the Imperial court. Their use by hydden had never been sanctioned by Sinistral, *ever*. The closest thing the Fyrd had to such weapons were crossbows and they had been sufficient to win an Empire.

'Put it somewhere safe,' said Blut cautiously, 'and we can debate the issue as we go. Times are changing, I fear, changing fast, and now humans are attacking us. Something profound is happening across the Hyddenworld . . . I should perhaps say, across the *mortal* world.'

New times called for new ideas.

'We'll take it with us then,' said Blut, and Terce, who understood, hugged the great thing to his body.

They sombrely climbed aboard once more, the weapon placed behind Terce's seat.

'Now, let's try and continue without interruption,' said Katherine. 'Everyone comfortable?'

They were physically but not mentally so. To some the vehicle felt like a prison.

'I'll give it half an hour more,' said Katherine, 'and we can see where we've got to and decide what next. Agreed?'

The vote was a silent one and it was unanimous.

But the engine sounded good, the wind roar turned into just an occasional whine and they settled down to the prospect of a steady run along the still-empty road.

Their silence deepened, with fatigue and concern.

Only Stort appeared unaffected by either, showing increasing excitement as he played with the Satnav.

'Would someone be kind enough to ask me how far we are from the centre of Old Brum, or Birmingham, as humans call it?'

Katherine obliged.

'Would you like the answer in kilometres or miles?'

'Kilometres.'

'One hundred and sixty three,' he replied at once. 'And our ETA?'

'Okay, Stort,' she said heavily, guessing he had worked out how to use the Satnav, 'what's our estimated time of arrival then?'

'At our present speed and assuming for the moment that we were able to continue the whole way without let or hindrance, then I can safely say that we would arrive home in Brum at exactly . . .'

There was a loud bang, then another and their vehicle slewed left and came to an abrupt halt.

'Out! *Now!*' commanded Barklice. 'You all know what to do.'

A broken arc of beautiful orange light, accompanied by the crackle of a gun, swung inexorably towards them from fields on their right-hand side. They were being fired on.

They got out and away fast, their feet slipping on fuel spilling across the road from beneath the horsebox. Terce helped lift out Sinistral, followed by Blut, and the others hurried after Barklice into the shadows.

Moments later, tracer fire hit the cab in a shower of sparks and exploding metal. They dived down the embankment on the far side as ominous new flames licked the horsebox's bonnet and sides.

Terce followed almost at once, shoved by Arnold. They were brief silhouettes against the bright light of explosion and drifting orange smoke and Terce held the fearsome weapon, dark and ugly, under an arm.

They had barely crossed the field away from the road to the safety of the hedge on the far side before the tank of the horsebox blew up and the whole thing burst into flames. A short while later several humans appeared in the orange smoky light, some looking in their direction. They stayed still and low and there was no attempt by those on the road to pursue them. One turned his weapon towards the darkness and sprayed the field with bullets, but none came near the hydden.

'Time to move,' announced Barklice, taking the lead once more. He took them unerringly to a gap in the hedge beyond which they found themselves in safe and welcome darkness.

'Time to return to the Hyddenworld,' he said with relief. 'Stay close, Arnold to the rear, all within touching distance of the one ahead. No talking, no stopping, no dawdling. Nice and steady as we go . . .'

'Aye, aye, Cap'n,' sang out Arnold when he was in place, 'and what be our destination?'

'A place your kind of people know well, Arnold. The Bilgesnipe are well established in these parts. We are now within easy reach of the Quantock Hills.'

'Never nor nary heard on 'em,' said Arnold.

'You'll have heard of what it is they rise on the north side of.'

'Which be?'

'The Levels.'

Arnold let out a gasp of surprise and pleasure.

'The famed watery Levels o' the fairy shire o' Zummerset? You mean we be onnat way there?'

'I do.'

'Then off'n we start and away'n we go, me hearties, along the old ways, like what Mister Barklice be happiest with. The Levels be as much water as land and my ma said there's no place in all Englalond as misty dreamy as that grand place.'

'Just so,' murmured Barklice happily, '*exactly* so!'

15
CASUALTY OF WAR

Whatever or whoever it was had guided them over the Goodwins to the safer, calmer sea roads beyond, they never quite knew.

Riff and Deap were of the opinion that they – and Jack – had seen the light of the Mirror-of-All itself and this was what saved them.

'When we'm say "light" we mean reflection, for that be what all things *be* and nowt else,' observed Deap.

To which Riff added, 'Aye, t'was in your wyrd, Jack, that we should see that light when you'm took the helm like you did, bold as brass, movin' and heavin' and swayin' wi' the craft like you were born to it, which you were. Eh, Leetha? Which he was!'

Jack did not mention the White Horse and its Rider again, nor speak Judith's name, but for his part, though he believed in the Mirror, he was certain she had been there all along, showing herself only when she needed to. But was she, too, a reflection?

Slew kept his mouth shut, even when asked.

'Aye, I saw this and that,' he said, 'but what it was I do not know.'

As for Leetha, she stayed below deck most of the time.

'I danced,' she claimed.

'How'd you do that down there?' challenged Slew.

'I danced in my mind, my love,' she said, 'I danced time on.'

Slew could only shake his head.

Arguing with Leetha was hard. Her smile melted the bleakest heart, her beauty, barely faded, softened daylight and the stars.

'You danced time on?' wondered Jack.

She nodded.

'How else do you think we found time to heal your injuries, and Slew's leg and foot, and Deap's shoulder and arm? That takes time and I danced it to us.'

Jack frowned, puzzled. There was no denying these healings had been fast, impossibly so. Yet there the three of them were, healed.

But of what, of what?

The words were a voice in his ear, carried over the North Sea waves, ravelled into the rigging above their heads, punctuated by a tap of a comma and a rattle of a question mark, the block and the tackle on the deck.

It was, he knew, Judith's voice, and she was there, with them, hurt and angry and ageing and terrible in her distress, yet healing them all, saving them, journeying their thousand deaths and saving their lives each time.

'We got through, my lads, but 'tis all bad what be happenin',' said Riff, shaking his head, 'and I mean nobbut the truth when I say it feels like the end o' things.'

'The End of Days?' said Jack.

'You could say that, aye.'

'Aye . . .' growled Deap.

Slew said nothing and did nothing until Jack, catching his eye, seeing that there was no sense in making a landfall without making peace first, grinned.

Slew stared at him and, though it wasn't very much to look at, there was a brief wrinkle around his eyes, and a nod of acknowledgement. Finally they sat bobbing about in the calm after the storm, saying very little, the two craft lashed together, sharing their food, their brew, their thoughts, their words, and they shared a time of peace.

That time felt like everything to Jack. It was family.

Jack slept awhile after the craft were made fast, out on deck, a plaid for his bed and another to cover him, his family murmuring shadows all about.

'He makes a sound pottage, he does,' he heard Deap say.

'Shoves seaweed in,' said Slew.

'Seaweed, bindweed, any bloody weed's better'n our Lady's mess,' muttered Riff, whose hand was on Leetha's thigh, his shoulder to hers. There was a happiness in her eyes not seen in years, for she'd known a clutch of days and nights she never thought would come to pass.

A hawser clinked against a mast, water lapped, and the surf they heard was on another, safer, bank and and it slowly faded behind them as the wind, a south-westerly and warm, began to blow and take them on.

'Good enough for the last leg,' murmured Riff, stirring gently because he thought his Leetha was asleep. 'Look about, lads, set the sail and leave Jack be. He'm earned it.'

Then louder: 'Look about! Wind's up and we'm off!'

'Where bound, Pa?' cried Deap, separating the craft and crossing to his own.

'Maldon,' Riff sang back, his strong self again, 'and may Mirror grant we see some lights or else we're sailing to a fallen land.'

The northern reaches of the Thames Estuary and the Essex coast lay west but they hadn't seen a light on land since passing the North Foreland.

A fallen land!

It was the sailor's dread, worse than death itself, to end a passage 'cross the seas to find all life on land had died. For what is a mariner's journey worth, and the cargo that he carries, if he can't be sure that when he sets sail and leaves life behind, he'll find it again at landfall?

'We'll see lights soon enough,' growled Slew, who worried about the dark.

The craft ran steadily along together and when Jack woke he crossed over to be with Deap again because he had taken the warp and weft of his cutter to his heart and mind.

'Set oh!' sang Riff and he and Deap let their tops'ls out with a satisfactory wump of filling air and a pleasing lean of the craft as they went along, hissing through the water for a time before the wind rose a shade more and it was the rigging and the sails they heard.

Nor'rard they went, running clear of the Skullion Brake and hearing at last the bell buoys ringing softly, which is music to the ears of those who've made passage up the Channel from the south.

'But still no lights anywhere,' said Riff grimly, reading the last of the stars before they were gone and carping the wheel off a couple of points easterly, 'not a damn one.'

Maldon is the best known of the hydden ports along the eastern shore and the once-favoured destination of generations of sailors from the Continent, from Beornamund's time and on. It is connected to the mainland by a tidal causeway, and shifting sand and mud had made landfall easier on the north-east side. Riff favoured that point and he knew the longshorefolk who eked out a life there, from boy to man to muddy grave, as his pa and grandpa before him knew.

The island is little used by humans, and that on its higher north-west end. There are creeks aplenty on the eastern shore, and mergent flats and all sorts of moorings.

Riff knew it like he knew his own hand and if he was troubled before to see no lights he was filled with dread to see none at all now in that good place. Not for fear of grounding, just the worry that his mates on Maldon had had a mischief done to them and had fled or, worse, were no more.

They dropped anchor silently two hundred yards from shore, the swell and hustling breeze wanting to drive them in. Dawn had not broken so the light was bad. The clouds had thickened down, slight mist rolled in, the feeling was eerie.

Riff got his lantern, lit it low, slipped in the reddening glass and green, and said, 'It's worth a try but Mirror knows, if there's nowt showing onshore for a goodly tide like this, there bain't likely to be a soul about, not even 'in.'

He said it heavily, for the hydden he referred to he had known since a boy, and Baggy had seemed old then.

Riff swung his lantern back and forth towards the shore, several times.

There was no response. Just murky pre-dawn darkness and the slop of waves against spars and jetty and the scent of mud and seaweed. But no answering light, no call, no soft whistle.

'I like it not,' said Riff. 'I was never here before but that Mister Baggywrinkle was pottering about the place giving a hand, telling a tale, warning us on or off, as the case might be.'

'Maybe he died,' said Deap.

'He warn't *that* old, lad, he just looked it.'

He raised his lantern again, swung it slow and low, the soft red-and-green light not much at all.

'Maybe we should try something brighter?' suggested Jack.

Leetha shook her head warningly, for Riff was standing facing the land, not so much looking as smelling and sensing, obviously puzzled and distressed. She raised a hand to indicate to leave him be.

In any case, since their first coming the sun had begun to rise and its rays were bringing light to the shadowy shore before them.

'There's something . . .' said Riff quietly, 'I can hear 'in, like breathing, like a-tapping . . .'

He signalled that the anchor be raised silently. This done, he took up an oar and swung the craft round to shore and then, with no more than the occasional creak of wood on wood, he caressed her forward between spars and obstructions.

'There!' whispered Jack, whose sight bettered them all, 'under that jetty.'

He pointed a finger. There, among the mud and seaweed, in the shadowed wooden uprights of a jetty where it touched the land, was a ragged old hydden, searching about the wet seaweed on his hands and knees.

They went closer.

'That's Baggywrinkle!' said Riff, his voice low, since something didn't feel right and who knew what the muddy shadows of Maldon might turn into? 'He looks like a bleedin' bearded crab scrabbling around like that! What can he be about?'

The old hydden was muttering in a low voice, oblivious of their approach. He was moving painfully and searching for something which, when he finally found it among the filth, they saw was a whelk. Since he was turned away from them they could not see his face but they could tell he was sniffing it, maybe licking it.

Finally he pulled a curved knife from his belt and levered the creature from its shell. This done, and after a curious period when he breathed rapidly and deeply as if in preparation for a special effort of some kind, he dabbed with it at his face, or more specifically, though it was too shadowy to be sure, at one eye and then another. As he did so he uttered pathetic cries of pain.

He then began searching for another whelk and went through this strange process again.

'If he were eating the salty things,' said Deap, ''twould make a peck o' sense, tho' whelks is better stewed than raw, say I!'

Having dealt with the second whelk to his evident satisfaction, again with the same cries, he took a piece of cloth from his pocket, tore a strip from it with some difficulty and then, with one hand to his head and the other to the cloth, he attempted to wrap it around his head, a feat too hard to accomplish in one go. He tried again, contorting himself to achieve the difficult task before he finally did, turning at last towards them and looking as if he were playing blind man's buff, but alone and miserably.

Then, stranger still, he felt around for the whelk meat and, yet odder, stuffed each of them under the cloth and over his eyes one after another. This done, he pressed them again and whimpered before feeling his way from underneath the staging to the sandy shore a few steps away.

Riff moved and slipped, wood knocked on wood.

Baggy froze, turned, and peered blindly their way. As he did so the cloth undid itself and fell away and the whelks stayed stuck to his eyelids in a horrible semblance of eyes. Then, just as the sun shone brighter still and fell full upon his face, first one whelk dropped away and then the other, revealing not eyes but the bloody, empty orbits where his eyes had been.

'For Mirror's sake,' gasped Riff in horror.

But that was not quite all.

The old hydden's nose was bloodied and smashed; his lips were split and hanging open and showing fresh-broken teeth that were no better than filthy, jagged fangs.

As Riff spoke, Baggy stilled and blindly thrust his knife forward.

'Who be there?' he cried out in a cracked, frightened voice. 'Leave Baggywrinkle be now, he bain't never goin' to hurt a soul. Who's that? Who's there?'

His terror was so pitiable, and his condition so inexplicable, that for a moment they stayed still and silent themselves.

Then Riff spoke.

'It be Borkum Riff! Baggy it be Riff a-comin' ashore and Deap . . .'

'Borkum Riff,' Baggy whispered to himself as if trying to remember the name, still holding the knife aloft and waving it about in a pitiful attempt to keep imagined enemies at bay. 'Good Borkum hisself? Borkum . . .'

He said this last softly, unbelievingly, as if after a very long journey through horrors dark and unimaginable he had come to light and safety once again. He remembered and knew it was a friend, a good friend, someone who would not harm him.

He dropped his knife and, kneeling on the shore, the desolate muddied spars rising about him, in the shadows of the landing stage that had been his place, his home, his whole life since the day he was born, he reached out his hands as a child might who has fallen and seeks out his parent for help. Then he cried out a cry of grief and despair as great as any child's could be, his broken mouth bleeding, the sockets where his eyes had been mute testimony to the savage cruelty of those who had tortured him.

Riff leapt from the craft and waded to shore.

He knelt as Baggy knelt and, carefully taking him in his great arms, he said, 'You'm home now, Baggywrinkle, you'm come to port, you'm in a safe haven, my old friend, who ne'er not once nor never hurt a fly, you'm safe now.'

Baggy cried, and shook, and broke down in his arms.

A good while later he managed at last to speak.

'You'm come to a poor sort o' place, Borkum Riff, and there bain't not a thing, not a single thing worth having more in Englalond. She'm wasted, she'm ended, she'm fallen now.'

16

On Polden Hills

In the week since they had escaped so narrowly with their lives from human attack, Mister Barklice had had to use all his hyddening skills to keep his group from further harm.

Katherine's impulsive decision to use a vehicle to bring them north up the A30 onto the M5 motorway had brought them a great deal nearer Brum. According to Stort's examination of the vehicle's Satnav they had covered nearly one hundred and thirty miles since they left Veryan a month before, most of it in a very few hours in the horsebox. They had barely another hundred miles to go and, despite the unnerving end to the latest stage of their journey, hijacking another vehicle remained a reasonable option.

Meanwhile, however, they had a serious problem.

The unceremonious end to their ride had dumped them in the middle of a human battle zone. It soon became clear that the group who initially attacked them were not the only armed faction roaming the Somerset countryside.

'They are surely not targeting us,' said Blut, allaying their fears, 'we just happen to have run into them. The humans, it would seem, are more concerned about attacking each other than the hydden, even if they knew we existed, which they probably don't. If they did then the peace that has reigned so long between humans and hydden – unwitting on their part – would be over and our world a very different place.'

Sinistral and Stort looked at each other meaningfully but it was Sinistral who spoke.

'My dear Blut, I, and I think Stort here, think that it may not be long before the hydden are not hidden from humans any more. Since they have an infinite capacity for destroying all they see, especially if it lives and moves in the same space as they do, I will be surprised if, in all this turmoil in Englalond, and probably elsewhere in the Hyddenworld, the humans do not finally discover us. When they do . . .'

'When they do, my Lord, we will be dead,' said Blut.

Barklice insisted they lay low until the fighting all around them subsided, which five days later it did.

He then led them northward once more, keeping the embankments of the motorway in view, but steering well clear of any sign of mortal life that they came across.

The ground was generally low-lying, with no good opportunity of seeing far ahead until they reached the tower of a deserted church. While Barklice ventured up its spiral stone staircase, the rest of them kept watch amongst the mossy, leaning gravestones and yew trees. It was a moment of rest and calm and though the day was no brighter than any of the days past, at least they had left the driving rains and winds of Bodmin Moor behind.

The grass between the graves had been mowed before winter set in and was lush and green though covered in fallen leaves. These had scattered across a wide, flagstoned path, its borders weeded. It sloped down slightly to an ancient, roofed lychgate, red-tiled and open beamed, with horizontals on which to rest a coffin in former times, when humans too took a lot more time over burials, respecting such ancient proprieties. Beyond the gate, and beautifully framed by it, was a small village square, in the centre of which rose an ancient stone village cross.

At its base, scattered at random, were fifteen or twenty dead, mown down by gunfire, yellow-grey of face, rigid, bloated. A dog, a thin, mangy thing, wandered among them with indifference.

They were glad when Barklice returned with a positive report.

'Five or six miles north-east of here, on the far side of the motorway, is a low-lying rise of hills,' he said. 'These are the Polden Hills, are they not, Stort?'

'Ah yes!' he said. 'The human town of Bridgwater at one end and the famed hydden community of Glastonbury at the other. It might be tempting to visit—'

'But we are not going to be tempted . . .' continued Barklice firmly.

'No, of course not. Though . . . no, no . . .'

Stort stopped himself launching into an account of the Tor of Glastonbury and refocused on the journey in hand.

He screwed up his brow, pointed his nose in the direction they needed to go and said, 'There is or was a railway line that will take us up into these hills. The Poldens will give us a vantage point over the famous Levels from which we will be better able to decide how to continue our onward journey – by road, by dyke and river or by crawling on our hands and knees like penitent pilgrims, as Mister Barklice would have us do.'

'For your safety.'

'Humph!'

Stort had been subdued and quiet in the past days, no doubt fretting about love and gems and topographic history, so this intervention was welcome.

'Mind you, Barklice, I very much doubt that we'll be the only ones heading for the hills. The humans and hydden who have deserted these parts have to have gone somewhere! Maybe they have fled up there before us. Much good will that do us if they have!'

'I do hope they have,' replied Barklice, 'for we might gain some intelligence from them. I have never in my life journeyed so far without meeting other hydden. It is very strange. Something has put a deep fear into them.'

'Of course it has,' cried Stort, pointing at the nearby human corpses. 'The world is coming to an end, for Mirror's sake. If you can't say something useful best to say nothing at all!'

'Well,' replied Barklice coolly, used as he was to Stort's impatience with others when he himself was feeling stress, 'it would take a very large resident population indeed to inhabit the Poldens to the point of crowding us out of it!'

Stort scowled again, dug around inside his pack as if to find something to occupy himself with and, having failed in that, he eyed the weapon Terce had been carrying ever since they fled the horsebox.

'Hang on to that,' he said tartly, 'we may have need of it, given the circumstances in which we find ourselves. I confess I have examined guns in my laboratory and they are dangerous and destructive things which do no credit to the humans who invented them. Whether or not we use this one needs discussion does it not? Meanwhile, please make sure it's pointing the right way when you pull the trigger!'

Terce smiled gently, still totally deaf, but nodded as if he had understood. But he had not. He had mistaken Stort's words for an invitation to demonstrate the weapon. He picked it up and pointed it at Stort.

'It might be loaded!' said Katherine in alarm and disbelief. Surely Terce could not be so idiotic as to have loaded it. She pushed it to one side and gestured to indicate that it was dangerous.

Terce hesitated before making it horribly plain that he *had* loaded the weapon. Stort stood up, suddenly furious, and tore it from Terce's grasp.

'Let's find out what it can do,' he said very ominously.

He was able to hold it horizontally for only a few seconds before its weight grew too much for him and the barrel began to sink inexorably downward. Very unfortunately, to counter its weight and not topple forward, he had to lean backwards. This happened in such a way and put him in such a position that his eyes and the sight were suddenly perfectly lined up on Terce's cannikin, a medieval one of wood that had been passed down the generations of the ancient choir of which he was the last surviving member.

That errant impulse that so often led Stort astray overtook him now and he pulled the trigger. There was a loud and violent report, a brief flame and a drift of smoke that smelt of cordite. It was as well his aim was so poor for, had it not been, the old artefact might have exploded into splinters and caused them harm. The shot succeeded only in toppling the vessel over and Terce thankfully retrieved it.

The dog in the square looked up, its ears pricked, and he eyed them uneasily. First one paw extended, then another, and then it turned and fled for its life.

'It seems it was loaded,' said Stort matter-of-factly in the stunned silence that followed, ignoring the look of stupefaction on the chorister's face.

Incredibly, Stort heaved the gun up again, swung unsteadily round and pointed it at the foot of a nearby wooden cross, which marked a grave. He fired again. The post shattered at its base and slumped sideways.

'The thing about machines is that it's best to know how they work. I suggest we either throw this infernal thing away or learn how to use it safely.'

'Thank you for that demonstration of foolhardiness, Stort,' said Barklice very tetchily. 'Since the whole of the mortal world will now know from sound alone exactly where we are, I suggest we leave at once, weapons or no weapons.'

It was a chastened group that moved on, silent and uneasy for the most part. Barklice took them east and north, crossing the railway line Stort had mentioned and aiming for the higher stretch of the hills, which could soon be clearly seen.

He grew more cautious as they approached the motorway once more, over which they would have to go. It was exposed and he was aware that if humans were patrolling it then they might all be seen. But that was forgotten when the quiet of the afternoon was interrupted by a second sighting of a white horse. This one galloped towards them; black chunks of debris rose behind it from its flying hoofs.

A madness overtook them, an eagerness to see it better, a yearning to reach and touch and know something of such a horse for themselves.

They ran over the field, scrambled up the embankment, and though the horse raced fast and ever faster, time slowed and stilled. They arrived, panting, on the hard shoulder of the road it was on, now in the shadow of the hills themselves. It raced by, white and magnificent, its mane flowing, its head proud, its nostrils and ears beautiful.

But what they saw, more than all these things, and that very clearly, was that its flank was slashed wide open, from its stomach up to its great haunch, and that from this wound its blood sprayed, red as a deep and dying sunset.

They watched after it, appalled.

It turned up onto the motorway, which they saw for the first time was the site of tens, perhaps hundreds, of abandoned vehicles, some on the hard shoulder, some slewed into the crash barrier, but most simply stopped in their tracks by others in front.

Many had been burnt, their shells already rusting.

No people, no life, not even the flutter of carrion crows.

The horse, slowing too, picked its way amidst the fugitive detritus before, frightened perhaps, it leapt over one barrier and then the next, half-tumbled down the far embankment and took off upslope into the hills. They did the same, determined to rise above the flatlands at last.

There were no words adequate to speak of the fears and despair this terrible sight put into them, and no one tried to find them. But later Stort, who had taken the lead, turned and looked back at them and the vale of death from which they had come, tears in his eyes. Then he turned and climbed on, wanting to be alone.

It was Sinistral who broke the silence that fell among them, but only very much later.

'Stort is a very remarkable hydden,' he said quietly.

'Always was and will be,' observed Festoon.

'They all are,' said Blut, 'every one of them.'

'Well then, if we can judge a hydden by his friends,' said Sinistral, 'Stort emerges well from the scrutiny.'

Blut nodded and Festoon quietly smiled, for Sinistral too might be counted as blessed by the quality of those who loved him.

The green paths they found in the Poldens were over-worn and muddy with the recent passage of hydden, while the human roads were littered once more with the detritus of their own fleeing population: discarded bags, boxes, chairs and pots and pans.

There were human bodies too, most half-eaten by animals, only a few untouched. They avoided those areas as much as they could, just as they resisted their natural inclination to try to find and make contact with the hydden who had gone on ahead.

'Nary would it be a-trouble findin' 'em,' announced Arnold, 'but these days hydden and humans are best left abiding by themselves.'

'Why?' wondered Blut.

'Got the clangies and the dipplers judgin' fro smell and bell of what they spewed,' he said quietly, a kerchief to his nose, 'and they'm not disaffections you'n want nor need to catch, trust me on that! My nan died o' dipple cough. It racked her lungs right out of her thin chest into the festive sops! That were a Samhain best forgot!'

Taking over the lead once more, Barklice led them from the green roads altogether but did not crest the rise, preferring to find a woody, protected spot which caught the setting sun and from which a spring of good water flowed.

They sat hidden in among a stand of old willow herb and nettles grown soft and rank with rain and decay.

'We'll rest out the night and take our brot and brew and that right here,' decided Barklice. 'We . . . we . . .'

He stood staring at them, his lined face suddenly pale, his lean, rangy body drooping.

'What is it, Mister Barklice?' said Katherine.

'Tired,' said Barklice.

'Get Stort,' she said. 'Sit,' she ordered.

Barklice sat.

'You've led us too long without a break,' said Katherine.

Stort arrived, took one look and began scrabbling in his portersac. 'I do believe I have a recuperative remedy for just such an occasion as . . .'

'We all have,' said Katherine, 'and it's called sleep. You too, Stort. All of us. Time to stop . . .'

'Is it?' wondered Stort.

'It is, my dear fellow,' said Mister Barklice, 'I believe it is.'

Terce and Katherine did the honours as they often did, working the fires and cooking together, their pottage good, the brew just heady enough, and a pudding of spiced crab-apple crumble as good as any more high-flown fare.

'Sleep now,' said Katherine, and Barklice, then Stort, then one by one all of them, slept.

Morning brought a hazy mist to the vale below and they decided to stay where they were and recover awhile from a journey that had stretched them all to breaking point. As the day wore on the wind died, the sun appeared and the day dried out. The layer of haze and smoke hung below the high cloud, evidence of the fires they had seen so frequently through the many days past. Woods were ablaze off to the west while far to the east an oil installation of some kind sent thick black clouds into the sky, which drifted eastward.

They saw the movement of furtive humans on the hill and even, briefly, thought they glimpsed hydden. There was a sudden burst of gunfire in the vale beneath them and they went briefly on alert. But Barklice had chosen their campsite well and they stayed where they were, undisturbed, travel-weary and content to rest and sleep through the day.

As the sun faded and the afternoon waned towards a better evening, they gained new communal energy and talked a little, each in turn. It was as if, having travelled together for so many days without much said, they felt a need to know some more about each other before moving on. This time Stort prepared the food, a task he did a great deal less methodically than Katherine and Terce.

Yet his pottage was nutritious, while the brew he made, fortified with a fermentation of nettles and columbine and dashed with the peppers of hip and mustard seed dust, proved more intoxicating than any of them at first expected.

'Stort, old fellow,' cried Barklice, who had soon recovered from his brief collapse and was partial to Stort's alcoholic inventions and susceptible too, 'you have redeemed yourself! To your good health!'

'Redeemed from what?' asked Stort.

'Grumpiness in general and growsliness in particular in recent days, dear chap. Not to mention that untried medicine inflicted upon me at Pendower.'

'Ah!' said Stort.

'Sit down and join in the discussion. Tell us something edifying.'

'Or instructive,' suggested Festoon.

'And perhaps personal,' added Blut, 'for really we have not had circumstance or chance to learn about your early life.'

'Be bold, hearty Mister Stort,' called out Arnold Mallarkhi, who was on watch duty, 'like what a bilgyboy must be when he'm offered the command of his own craft.'

'That would be good,' said Sinistral, 'very good.'

Stort was silent a long time, the wintry evening closing in fast and growing chill; the dried and husky vegetation scratching and sawing lightly with the breeze that came up the hill. From time to time the sharp call of a kite came to them and in among the bushes the scuffle of moles and hedgehogs and smaller mammals still readying their winter tunnels and nests against the coming frosts.

As night fell, a light mist began to form a few feet above the vales they had crossed and the long, curving southward line of the motorway disappeared from sight beneath it. Taller trees poked out of the mist and, far to their right, to the west, beyond the motorway, a church tower rose up stocky and dark. Nearer to, over the fields in the lowland beneath them, the mist had turned to a blanket of white fog, hiding the very Earth Herself from sight. The fog turned dark blue, then darker still, before nothing but darkness itself could be seen and night was upon them.

Stort did not speak at all that night, despite their requests.

But a little later, when they were beginning to be drowsy, Terce stirred and stood up.

He cupped his right hand to his right ear and seemed to be listening. A pigeon fluttered its wings in the trees above them and he turned and looked up towards it. A muntjac barked on the slopes below and he smiled. The fire crackled briefly and he heard it.

A tear rolled down Katherine's cheek, but that made no sound at all. Yet even that, which was an expression of relief, he seemed to know, for he turned in the dark and smiled, his eyes alight with the last flames of the fire.

Then, with a quiet exploratory hum that came from the back of his throat, a brief, resonant sort of sound, he tried his voice. What had been tuneless before was more tuneful now. Though it wasn't much and seemed to give him pain to try to sing, the ability to do so had returned to him. Though the sound that came out was frail and cracked it carried within it something of what it had once been and might yet be again.

It was enough to make them stir and sit up.

'Try again, Terce . . .' called out Katherine.

'Help me,' he replied.

Then, one by one, they lent their untrained voices to his and he tried to sing as he had been taught to. Their voices swelled in the night, not very much at all, nor especially tuneful, yet together they sounded as folk who have been to the dark place and the void beyond and were now trying to find the way back again. They sang from the hills to the stars above, a still-broken song grounded in the invisible Earth below, which spoke of a white horse dying and mortals too. They sang to the Universe and they heard it begin to sing with them.

They sang of their hard task and all mortals' tasks and of those they missed, for whom they yearned. They sang until the night air cooled and winter rustled at their feet and in the boughs of the trees nearby and their eyes closed where they lay; until only Terce's voice was heard, a poor thing still. But it strove for a song of a better morrow and found a lullaby to grant them the sleep they needed if they were to find the strength in the days ahead to reach their goal.

17
THE FALLEN LAND

But that was not the song Jack heard.
There was no music of that kind along the Maldon shore. For several days after their landfall they subsisted quietly, focusing on Baggy's recovery from the torture he had suffered.

Not that his recovery could be very complete. He was so shaken and traumatized that it was more a question of finding some stability and inner peace for the immediate future than expecting him to live normally again.

At least he had been able, after a few days, to begin to give a sufficiently coherent account of what had happened to him for them to get a better picture of the extraordinary events that had overtaken the human and hydden worlds of Englalond.

But it had not been easy.

'Aye, 'twas four Fyrd did this to me,' Baggy explained, 'retreating from Brum, a-taking craft and anxious to get away and across the sea, angry with defeat, liquored, stupefied. Fourteen days ago, before the storm. When I warned them not to sail they took it into their heads I was trying to delay their departure so the humans could kill 'em . . . but o' course that was stupid talk because . . .'

'Humans?' repeated Jack, not understanding.

The blinded hydden inclined his head slightly – to nod was evidently painful – repeating very ominously, 'Aye, humans.'

'But no hydden can tell a human what to do!' said Deap disbelievingly.

'That's what I told them, that's what *I* thought. But they seemed to think that humans did hydden bidding in Brum and turned their weapons on Fyrd, which was why they had to flee. When they got here they thought I was guilty of working with or for the humans too, which I weren't. Even if I knew how to, which I don't. But they wouldn't listen. They were fleeing for their lives and they blinded me because they thought I was with the humans, or with hydden who were.'

'And who were *they*?' asked Jack.

'The Brummies. They who got the humans to kick the Fyrd out o' their great city and send 'em packing.'

'But the Brummies can't get humans to do things!' cried Jack, even more confused. 'And anyway . . .' his face changed from confusion to puzzlement, 'why did you say just now that they did this *fourteen* days ago, just before the storm? Didn't Maldon get hit by a more recent storm, the one we sailed through five days ago?'

Baggy shook his head, wincing as he did so.

'Fourteen days,' he said, 'and one storm. I can smell 'em coming like I can smell far worse yet to come. I bain't smelled more 'n one.'

He stood up, questing towards the sea and very troubled.

They looked at each other, not able to make sense of his ramblings.

'But I be tired,' said the old wharfinger, feeling about for somewhere to sit down again, 'and I bain't slept much o' late. Borkum Riff, old mate, I be tired as I've ever been and I don't have strength no more to face what's coming with the wind. I be all washed up. Show me a berth where I can lay my head . . .'

But Jack was having none of it.

There was danger in the air and, if Baggy was right, there was worse to come.

'You can sleep all you like later,' he said brusquely, 'but right now we need the information you have, however difficult it may be to give it. It may save our lives.'

Baggy began sobbing, little coughy sobs.

'Let him sleep,' grunted Riff, 'he'll be more clear-headed when he wakens and not talking daft like he is now.'

'No,' said Jack firmly.

Riff looked at him in surprise, used as he was to being in command, and the others did as well. Since they had landed Jack had changed. He had grown in confidence and command and the land under his feet gave him a new solidity. He held his stave of office with a strong hand and it shone and glimmered more than before.

'Give him more food, make him a warming brew, sit him by a fire, and let's get to grips with all that he's been saying so we can make proper sense of it!'

It took a long time to do so, but a combination of Jack's coercion, Riff's gruff companionship and a modicum of rum poured into his cannikin finally got a clearer picture of how things in Englalond had been since Stort, Jack and the others had left Brum for the South-West in their quest for the gem of Autumn.

It was a strange and disturbing tale. Combined with what they already knew, it finally caused each of them to rethink what they should do next.

The Fyrd, under General Quatremayne, had begun their invasion of Englalond across the Channel from Westphalia the previous September. Their objectives were twofold: to recover the gems of Spring and Summer stolen from the Imperial stronghold in Bochum by Jack and Stort and to suppress rebellious Brum on behalf of the Empire once and for all.

Niklas Blut, who as Emperor was their unwilling accomplice in this violent, vengeful strategy, escaped Quatremayne's house arrest and defected to Brum. The vital intelligence he brought enabled the Brummie forces, led by Lord Festoon and Igor Brunte, to mount a defence while the city was evacuated.

By the time the Fyrd reached the city's Main Square, Brum was all but deserted and Quatremayne's forces were harassed by an unseen guerrilla enemy who knew the city far better than they did, led by the city's Chief Staverman, the formidable Mister Pike.

Jack and the others were able to escape to the South-West to complete their quest for the gem of Autumn and appease the Shield Maiden, bearing witness on the way to the Earth's swallowing of the human town of Half Steeple on the River Severn.

Cut off as they were in the furthermost south-western tip of the Hyddenworld, they had no way of knowing what the impact of Half Steeple had been in the wider human world of England or, as a result, in the Hyddenworld as well. It was more than just another in the sequence of natural events and disasters of increasing severity that had created a sense of growing communal dread and alarm. It was the final straw.

Human alarm turned overnight to panic, law and order broke down and, as chaos ensued, hundreds of thousands of people, and finally millions, came to believe that the Earth was targeting them, beginning in the South-West. They began fleeing north and, inevitably, in the rush of cars, or trains, planes and any mode of transport that would get them away, fighting broke out.

Martial law was imposed but lasted only a few days.

Unknown to Jack, it was into this lethal unrest in which the military broke ranks, that Mister Barklice had unwittingly led Katherine and the others only a day or two before. But what Jack did now understand was why, as he and the others had rounded the North Foreland, the lights had gone out. Parts of the National Grid must have failed, and it seemed likely that the internet had slowed or broken down. The human world, as Jack had known it nine months before when he and Katherine returned to Woolstone for the birth of the Shield Maiden, was no more. It became fugitive from its own imagined fears, fleeing northward even as winter began, in mounting waves of violence and despair as city after city fell to the chaos of the hordes.

This much he was able to piece together from the things Baggy was able to say he heard and saw in and around Maldon as the humans fled to west and north and the Fyrd, believing their best chance was back across the North Sea in the Imperial headquarters in Bochum, came east in ever-growing numbers.

'They wanted to get away, the same who had disembarked two months before under General Quatremayne for the assault on Brum. It was from them we heard what had happened in Brum . . .'

Jack and Blut had left Mister Pike in charge of the forces there after the Fyrd occupation. They were to harry the Fyrd as best they could in the hope they might tire of occupying a deserted city and being attacked and killed for the privilege.

In the event, what happened was as unforeseen by Pike as it had remained unimagined by the absent Jack, Katherine and their friends. The panicking human refugees entered the city from the south and were soon fighting for increasingly limited resources with the indigenous human population. In some way or other the unspeakable happened: hydden were discovered after fifteen hundred years of staying unnoticed and unseen and the humans turned their wrath and rage, and soon their dogs and weaponry, upon them.

But ironically these were not the Brummies, who had evacuated the city on the orders of Festoon and Blut prior to the Fyrd invasion, but the Fyrd themselves. Order broke down among them, officers were killed, and they fled eastward in an effort to get out of Englalond and back to the Continent.

'They gathered here and at other hydden ports, I heard, and took any craft they could, including human ones,' explained Baggy. 'I tried to warn them of the approaching storm. The four who got me couldn't seem to find a craft, though Mirror knows there are plenty about if you know where to look. They turned on me and gouged out my eyes and kicked me about and then off they went. Like them who went before I'll warrant they were without proper mariners aboard to show 'em what to do. Borkum, you know better than most the dangers these waters hold – and that's when they're calm!

'Whole shoals of craft set off as the wind was rising, with barely more'n a sail among 'em, and many overloaded; and ill-found paddles and oars and all sorts! I warned 'em! It didn't help that the wind was easterly, for that took 'em off shore fast, made 'em feel good but gave 'em no hope of getting back any easy way. You'd best be a mariner born and bred like Deap and Riff afore him to know how to handle such a wind – *and* it was veering northerly. Hard in a well-found craft, nigh impossible in a scrabblied, makeshift one.'

He fell silent. Then: 'Not seen 'em since and never will because e'ym dead and drownded, the whole lot of 'em and washed ashore, Mirror knows where, bloached and puffed and swolled right up, mostly. I say mostly 'cos a few fetched up along this way. I dragged 'em outerways to get rid o' the stench.'

The question of when the storm had happened remained. There had been only one, of that Baggy was certain, but it seemed not to have taken place at the same time as the one they had sailed through. The difference was the time: he said fourteen days since, they knew six, so where had eight days gone?

Jack said finally: 'Bedwyn Stort always said that we'd know the Mirror was beginning to crack when time began to shift and break. I think we lost some days across the Goodwins and it's now later in November than we think. Which is maybe why the lights suddenly went out and folk were gone – we sailed across a time-boundary, as Stort called it, during which the Grid went down.'

'A boundary?'

Jack nodded and murmured, 'Of time not space. The Mirror's surely cracked.'

'But we survived,' whispered Leetha, who appeared to understand better than Riff the seriousness of what Jack was saying.

'Mayhap you did all survive,' said Baggy, 'but I be fetched up and finished now.'

'No yer not . . .' said Riff.

But the old hydden replied, 'T'would kill me to leave this place o' mine and in the short time I've left I don't need eyes to find my way around. I know it by smell, by touch and the sound and ways the gulls cut down through the skies and skulk about feeding and chattering on the shore. They're my day and night. Take me away fro' here and I'll be lost. I'll live here and I'll die here and that now soon enough!'

He cackled wildly, cheered by the company, the good brew and the food they made him.

'You'll never die,' said Borkum.

'Tomorrow's the day, first thing, with the tide. But you'll not be here to see it,' he declared with absolute conviction.

He was suddenly happy, laughing aloud and even getting to his feet and dancing a few steps, except that shook up the wounds in his head so he stopped.

'You're coming with us when we leave to cross the sea,' said Riff. 'You'm ready now, I'd say.'

'You bain't going nowhere seaward for a while, Borkum. Best go inland to be safe. Nor is that lad Deap . . . where is he . . . ?'

He reached an old hand out.

'Here,' said Deap.

'Drag yer pa inland, like I say. The sea's no place awhile. That storm, about which we disagree, has got ugly sisters and they's coming to pay a visit. Tomorrow. Maybe tonight. They'm already on the way.'

He prattled on, or seemed to prattle and they fell asleep that night to the sound of it, his voice being a whisper at one with the wind and sea about them.

It was Leetha who first took him seriously.

Leetha who understood he spoke truth.

For she woke up, stirred by a new wind, and rose to dance on the shore as she loved to do, off into the high ground, down by the creeks, drumming her feet on the old hulks, the dented oil drums, and twanging the rusted wires of the outbuildings; until, recovered, she stood in the fading dark and listened on the longshore and heard and felt what Baggy meant.

She hurried back and woke them up. Dawn was rising and there was no time.

'We have to go, Borkum. He's right, there's something coming. We have to go before full light . . .'

They argued in their rough, passionate way, as they always had. They made Slew annoyed, Jack amused, Deap silent.

Leetha won and Riff decided.

'We go inland, where I do not wish to go,' said Riff finally. 'Haul up the craft.'

'Won't do no good,' said Baggy matter-of-factly, 'unless you've time and strength to get 'em far enough, which you ain't.'

He sniffed the air, which was definitely freshening.

'Get going, up Totham Hill way north of Maldon, there's high ground there . . . Get going and be gone!' cried Baggy.

Still they hesitated and Jack saw they were nervous of the land, uneasy to head away from the sea.

'Come on,' he said, 'follow me . . .'

'We don't want to leave him . . .'

'Bugger off,' said Baggy, the wind freshening more, 'afore your dawdlin's the death of you all as well.'

Maldon was a human town, utterly deserted but for dogs, which ran away at the sight of them.

The place stank of death, and the corpses of the animals and humans lay like grey staring lumps across street and field, in creeks and on the far side of fences.

The wind came ever harder off the sea and as they climbed the steep street from the waterfront they saw the riverine lands spread before them and that the creeks round Northsey Island shone like twisting, turning eels with the light of the new day. The far sea horizon was a razor-thin wall of dark grey.

'Higher! Hurry! *Move!*' commanded Leetha, impatient at their dull, reluctant pace.

They saw a tower, a mock-Tudor folly, in the town centre and looking behind them realized that the thin black line which stretched the full length of the horizon was nearer now and bigger and blacker too.

That was the moment Riff felt real alarm. He had never seen a tsunami before but he thought he knew what one looked like now.

They bashed the door of the tower open, climbed the stairs inside and went right up, emerging on the false battlements on top.

Even in that short time the approaching black wave had grown bigger, its top steaming with spray, which caught the light of the rising sun.

'If that's a wave,' said Riff, 'it be the biggest there ever was.'

It was a wave and as the wind rose to gale force the wall it made got inexorably bigger, nearer and more fearsome. Then, quite suddenly, the eel-like courses of shining water in the myriad creeks writhed, moved, slid away towards the advancing sea, as if to welcome it. All that was left behind was mud and sand, flat fish flapping and crabs scurrying for shelter in the few shadows and shallow pools remaining.

The seabirds rose as one, panicking into great uncertain flocks which circled and filled the sky with their dark-white-shining shapes, in their hundreds and thousands, near and far, wheeling in the wailing, horrid wind as the roar of the great solitary wall of water was finally heard.

How slow it had seemed out there, but when it finally struck the outer banks and then the first floating derricks and the concrete islands, which made up the beginnings of the outlying human shore, they could gauge its true height and power and awful speed.

On it drove, on ever faster, crashing onto land and breaking up whatever it hit and driving itself forward through everything, *over* everything, an utter and entire overwhelming of all in its path. As it

came on its front part turned from thick sea water to something toxic
and never seen before by any of them: a driving, soup of noxious black
flotsam and jetsam.

They watched as the island of Maldon, where Baggy was, was
submerged in moments. Then, as the water drove up the creeks, on and
on past them, out of sight, horror filled them. The rushing water began
moving towards them, swilling and filling and racing and drowning
everything below them, right up the route they had taken, up the steep
street from the wharfs, which had all disappeared beneath it, right to
the tower where they stood, in through the door they had used, crashing
up the stairs they had hurried up.

And into houses opposite, whose windows thrust open like bursting
boils of bile, whose walls fell, whose roofs down onto which they looked
shivered, wobbled and then burst upward. Up and up and up, things
collapsing and the tower shaking, uneasy, creaking, shuddering, the
battlements themselves embattled and water spewing over the last step
to where they stood, and rising still.

Above them the sky darkened as the sun was blotted out by clouds
and circling birds and soon after by phenomena of filthy steam and
smoke rising through the swirling water like an exhalation of the Earth's
bad breath.

They clung on to the shaking battlements and on to each other, their
eyes cast upward in supplication to the Mirror itself.

The rising slowed and stopped, the grey-brown spread of sea stirred
and rushed about them, with only the highest modern human buildings
clear, and their tower, as the winds whined and hissed over the surface
of that unnatural sea; and birds shrieked across a seascape they did not
know; and the flotsam of human bodies, of vehicles, of broken roof
timbers and smashed branches, of tables, of coloured hoardings and a
roll of white, half-sunken cloth, unwinding as the water flowed through,
like a shroud over a dead body.

They stood atop their trembling sanctuary, they stared, they said no
word and nothing as far off across the inland vale of Maldon valley a
swilling chaos reigned.

Then, hearing a series of soft explosions behind them, they turned to
see the windows of even the modern buildings bursting open with the
water and debris that had risen inside and was forcing its way out.

The debris sent great waves in their direction, one after another, so high they went right over the roof on which they stood, so strong they several times nearly lost their grip on each other.

Then the last wave passed, the water subsided a foot or two and all they saw of Englalond was nothing but a fallen land.

18

DREAMYGIRL

The blanket of fog that had been settling around the Polden Hills when they first arrived grew so thick that, the morning after Terce recovered his hearing, Barklice decreed they should stay where they were until it cleared.

The air grew deathly still and the smoke and soot of their fire hung about their heads, moving only when they did, grey-blue wraiths that shadowed and entwined them.

The sky above cleared steadily, making the nights colder still, bitterly so. They kept the fire going and laid their plaids around it, drawing to themselves what warmth they could.

Yet they did not complain. The stresses of their journey, and the growing sense of how troubled the world had become, along with Terce's song, had put into all their hearts a desire for quiet and contemplation. What had begun as a journey of enquiry and return was becoming something more akin to a pilgrimage. The greatest catalyst for this was Terce's now nightly singing, which had the effect of melding day and night into one and taking them separately and together to places where memory was rich and time uncertain.

Stort's ill-humour disappeared and he, Blut and Sinistral engaged in discussions and debate about matters cosmological and metaphysical which by turns enthralled and bored the others. They could agree that the End of Days had come and, too, that the gem of Winter held the key, but how the world as they knew it could possibly survive they had no idea.

'Can we be so sure,' wondered Blut, 'that when the Mirror cracks it is really the end of things?'

'The end of things as we know it,' said Sinistral.

'Yet who is to say, as I observed once to Barklice, that there is only one Mirror?' added Stort. 'It too may be a reflection which when lost is simply replaced by another, or others plural.'

'In which case we ourselves may reappear, or rather be already there, or here,' said Blut.

'It is, I think, only the *musica* which is real and ever present, though its flow is so variable,' said Sinistral. 'I have heard it, I have lived it; it informs all things. I am inclined to think that it is the *musica* which holds the key to the truth of the End of Days.'

Their conversation was often less philosophical, and in time each told something of the stories of their lives.

It was when Katherine was describing her childhood, the saving of her life by Jack from her parents' burning car, that Arthur Foale came into the conversation.

'He and his wife Margaret adopted me and, in a way, my mother, who never fully recovered from the accident and died when I was sixteen. By then Jack had come back into my life.'

'So quite recently?' suggested Blut.

'Several lifetimes ago,' replied Katherine drolly.

The fog stayed put. So much so that such few sounds as they heard from the lowlands were muted and garbled, impossible to interpret. Nearer to, among the hedges and copses they could not see, and the fields they imagined must be beyond these known features, they heard sounds of a different, more disconcerting kind: dragging, moanings, whispered roars, talons on bark, the quiet flap of birds, pigeons or corvids most like.

Occasionally, too, the soft run of paws across the earth and just once the now familiar, disorientating race of a horse's hoofs. In the small hours of what proved to be the last night in that eerie camp they were woken by the wild, sickening breathy scream of a horse in agony.

Each one of them sat up, mouth open in alarm, eyes staring into the clammy night, the same thought in their minds and phrase on their lips: *the End of Days . . .*

But with the morning the mist around them brightened and began to thin at last. As they busied themselves about the camp, it burned off and on top of the hill at least was gone. They could see the world again, or that part of it up to which they had climbed.

Leafless trees, hedges full of red berries now bright with sunlight, sloes mauve and blooming amidst the blackthorn and the pale-green straggly fronds of dodder and old man's beard, a few last leaves, and rooks circling northward of where they were before flying off cawing in the direction they too needed to go.

They moved off with barely a word, remembering the horse's scream, which had filled their hearts with an existential dread. Each of them now, in their own way, truly understood the source and nature of Bedwyn Stort's general and personal concerns.

The End of Days was nearer and any one of them might have said, *It is time to get back to Brum and decide what I myself can do to speed the search for the gem of Winter.* As it was, they walked after Barklice in silence, their 'sacs heavy on their backs and staves awkward in their hands, not yet seeing anew the beauty of the world all about.

Until, that is, having crested the high point of the hills and begun to drop down the gentle slope on the other side, the fields on either side stretching away, they saw a wondrous view. The mist that side lay thick, white and shining with sun across the vast flat vale below, reaching away towards the horizon, where, a dramatic hazy blue, a high range of hills rose up.

'The Levels are under the fog beneath us, the Mendip Hills are those that rise before us.'

But it was not these hills that finally caught their eye and took their breath away but something to the north-west, which rose almost as high as they did. It was a solitary hill, a great hump of ground, as misty blue as the Mendips. Rising from the white sea that engulfed its base, it had a grandeur and mystery all its own.

'Mysterious indeed,' said Barklice. 'Its name is Brent Knoll and I know from the only visit I ever paid there that its hydden folk are proud and protective of their realm. They are, of course, Bilgesnipe, as are those who live here on the Polden Hills. But Stort will know more of its history, which is, I believe, a very mixed one.'

'Indeed it is,' he concurred, 'a history of trouble and treachery, born of the intense rivalry between those who live here, who believe they have prior rights to the hidden riches of the Levels below – which I am sure we will see soon enough when the mist has cleared – and those on the Knoll, who absolutely deny such rights. What is more . . .'

He looked set to continue his lecture but they were hungry and needed refreshment. Even as all their eyes were still fixed upon it there was a sudden flare of yellow-orange light on the Knoll, like an early counterpoint to the sun that was now rising ever more clearly above their heads against the cold, blue sky.

'It's a beacon!' said Blut in considerable surprise and not a little awe.

Weeks before, their own lives had been saved by the lighting of such a beacon above Pendower, which had been a signal to local hydden to answer a call to arms against the Fyrd and hurry to their aid.

Stort immediately drew out his monocular and surveyed the Knoll and the fire. He handed the glass to Barklice who did the same before handing it to Katherine.

'Yes,' she pronounced, 'I think we can take it that the Bilgesnipe there are calling for help!'

'A call we must answer,' said Blut and Sinistral as one.

They might well have done so then and there by impulsively setting off downslope to try to cross the Levels had not they heard angry cries from out of the fog below and shots, loud and clear and horrible. Then cries once more.

They did not have to wait long to see where they came from and what was afoot. The easterly breeze and the warm rays of the sun began to thin the fog, which turned to a rapidly dissipating mist as suddenly insubstantial and fleeting as a ruffle of wind on clear water before it stills again.

Then there before them in their entirety were the Somerset Levels, an intricate and nearly geometric patchwork of fields and hedges, dykes and canals, disappearing eastward into haze and to westward, nearer than they could have guessed, the winding estuaries of rivers flowing into the Bristol Channel, in which a few low islands lay and beyond which the mysterious land of Wales rose majestically.

But no sooner had this near-magical vision of Englalond's western watery borderland with Wales, Bedwyn Stort's homeland, appeared than the cause of the shots and ruckus they had heard became painfully clear.

A Bilgesnipe figure, a young female in colourful garb and a very athletic one from the way she moved, was fleeing rapidly towards them over the fields immediately below, pursued by three humans with guns. Her progress was made difficult by the dykes and hedges she had to navigate. It seemed she was trying to reach the shelter of some rough ground at the bottom of the field they themselves had just reached, though from their viewpoint it seemed unlikely to be able to offer her the lasting protection she would need.

The men came on, evidently beginning to tire as well, which was why, perhaps, when they paused to fire at her, their shots went wide. Far beyond this small and murderous scenario the beacon flared on Brent Knoll as if it too was an actor in this play.

'She needs our help – and fast,' said Katherine, her eyes gauging distances and directions as her mind ran through possibilities and options. 'Is this a moment we might use Terce's gun?'

She looked enquiringly at Barklice and the others.

Barklice said, 'If we can get her up here we might take her safely away with us along the top. The humans will not know which way we've gone or where to look. But whether we can do so without such an extreme measure as using human weaponry . . . ?'

'What do *you* think, Lord Festoon?' said Katherine, who did not want to set such a dangerous precedent without proper authority.

'I believe it *may* be justified,' he said cautiously.

'Lord Blut?'

'I am . . . I think . . .'

Blut was undecided. So too was Sinistral.

'For Mirror's sake,' ejaculated Barklice, carried away by the scene unfolding below, 'if we can get her to safety she'll have up-to-date information about the Levels which we can use. We need her.'

Katherine nodded. She too was getting carried away. As for Terce, he had boldly made up his own mind. He adopted a comfortable position on the ground and was sighting his weapon towards the humans.

'Too far,' said Katherine decisively. 'Let's go nearer . . . while Mister Barklice leads the others to the safety of that copse above, which edges the top of this field.'

They set off downslope, Katherine unbuckling her crossbow as they went so she could give additional cover while Barklice and the others headed upslope to the trees.

Only one of them objected to this course of action and that was Arnold Mallarkhi. He said not a word and had barely moved a muscle since the fleeing figure below had appeared. But his eyes were narrowed, his turbaned head thrust forward, and he was staring at her intensely as if trying to make his own decision.

'Lordy Sinistral,' he cried suddenly, 'can this 'ere boatyboy be a-borrowing your stave, it being the tallest and whippiest amongst those we have?'

Sinistral handed it to him, perhaps having a glimmering of Arnold's intent.

'Thank 'ee Lord of All as was! Now, I may not have a boat hereabout, but some skills cross water onto land. Off'n 'n upp'n we go!'

With that, he turned back after Katherine and the other two and, using the stave as he might the pole of a boat, he swung it forward, leaned his weight onto it, and proceed to vault downslope at astonishing speed.

He arrived just in time to stop Katherine's command to Terce to fire, bravely placing himself right in danger's way with the words: 'Nary you do'n that, my lad, for I seen another way!'

Katherine got Terce to lay down his weapon and, in a spectacular series of leaps, jumps and vaults, Arnold continued on down the hill and landed next to the fleeing hydden.

It was too far off for either group watching to hear their words, but they were having an argument and it was as brief as its end was resolute.

Arnold, who was taller than the other, simply heaved her bodily onto his shoulder, ignoring her protests. Then, with amazing strength and skill, he proceeded to contour the slope by leaps and vaults to get out of the line of fire up towards where Barklice had led the others.

Katherine and Terce followed upslope themselves and in almost no time at all they were out of sight and too far up for the humans to even consider following them over such exposed ground. A couple of shots whizzed through the trees above their heads. A short while later, with angry, impotent shouts, the humans were gone.

It was only then, when he had recovered his breath from his impulsive act of heroism that Arnold himself fully understood the nature of the female whose life they had saved. He was the first to do so.

His eyes widened, his breathing grew rapid and he said in a low, wary voice, 'Nary, nary, friends o' mine, ask not her name, nor her trade, nor anything more about her! She be a Bilgesnipe true and a dreamygirl who talks to fishes and flies with fowl! She'm knows the windy way of things and sniffles the air like a stoat in heat and'll freeze your toes as soon as look at you!'

This tirade astonished them all but seemed to have the opposite effect on the newcomer than that intended.

She reached a muddy hand towards Arnold and, grasping the strings of his jerkin between her fingers, pulled the cord through them caressingly, grinning as she did so, before laughing in evident delight.

'Dang me but it's a bilgyboy and one o' 'em that hails from Brum, if my nadders hear right!' she cried, her voice mellifluous. 'You'm mine now, Brummielad, by ancient right o' Level-lore. Wilst thou plight thy troth to me?'

'No,' said Arnold, without hesitation. 'I may be follerkins for wot I done but this boy bain't bannerkins as well!'

She laughed aloud, even more delighted than before.

'Which in Level-lore is the brighty, best-well-made response could be done to a proposal, for it means "yes"!'

'Oh no it don't!' cried Arnold, eyes widening in horror at what, it seemed, he'd unwittingly done. 'I may want a lass but not so fast!'

But she ignored him.

'My dreams is made true this day as witnessed by you all!' she cried, launching herself at him before anyone, least of all Arnold himself, could stop her.

The two fell into a desperate tangle of arms and legs, ribbons and turbans enriched by the myriad shine of the tiny mirrors sewn into the rich embroideries of fey though muddied attire from which, briefly, she emerged to declare, her ample bosom heaving, her lithe thighs commanding, 'sealed one folk 'n all with the bestest, grandest, most shimmering kiss a dreamygirl could ever ask for!'

She disappeared again into the melee that was them both and very soon Arnold gave up the struggle and lay still.

19

PREMONITION

The floods along the coast to the north and south of Maldon and far inland up the rivers and creeks to the edges of higher ground drained away only slowly.

It was two days before Riff, Jack and the others could even contemplate escape from their sanctuary. Even then they saw that the process might be a tricky one, for as the water level dropped the full extent of the damage to the ancient structure beneath them began to be revealed. The original flintwork and later brick repairs had been stripped away in many places, leaving no more than rubble to support the building that had given them sanctuary. The tower continued to suffer tremors along with a disquieting sloping of the roof, which gradually increased.

The option of immediate escape by going down the spiral stairs to a point where the windows were at the level of the water remained too dangerous. The water itself was turbulent, and though its retreat was steady overall, the incoming tides forced sporadic rises and strange flows up and down the flooded streets.

But to call them 'streets' was now a misnomer. Almost all the buildings of Maldon were gone, damaged by the initial rush of the incoming waves and subsequently undermined by the flood and put in such a state of ruin that in the hours and days afterwards they collapsed. This caused mini tidal waves, themselves destructive of the little that remained.

In these circumstances, and since the old tower had remained in place when so much else was destroyed, they took their chances and stayed right where they were, readying themselves for a hasty exit, if necessary straight over the battlements into the water below. Meanwhile they hoped that the retreat of the water would reach a point where escape down the stairs through the door became the better option.

This moment came on the third morning, by when the water had dropped back to the steps at the bottom of the tower and the way down the stairs, though cluttered with debris, was just about passable. When the tower shuddered again, this time with a deep, guttural groan, it was time to leave.

Jack went first, and Riff last, as a captain does from a sinking ship. The tower shifted again when Jack was halfway down, wet plaster falling on his head, and by the time he reached the steps outside, the surface of the water swilling there was roughening with the shaking of the ground beneath. When he saw cracks appearing in the façade he hurried the others out as fast as he could.

'Over here!' he cried, leading the first of them across what had been Market Street to a patch of ground that was a little higher and seemed clear of any obvious danger.

They saw the cracks in the tower begin to widen.

'Over *here*!' he shouted again.

'Riff!' screamed Leetha.

The tower began to roar, as if in despair that its usefulness to mortal kind was finally over. With parts of the battlements above crashing down into the water about him, Borkum Riff finally emerged and began wading towards the others. He lost his footing twice but managed to rise again and flounder on. As the tower began collapsing down into itself the debris drove a wave towards him but Jack was able to grab his arm and heave him onto their slightly higher ground.

The water swirled about them and spray carrying grit and stones drove into them, stinging and bruising their heads and shoulders.

Then it was over and the last building in Maldon, and one of its oldest, was down.

In their time in the tower they had reluctantly agreed what they were going to do if they got out safely.

Riff's loyalties were to the families of his other children and dependants in the hydden port of Den Helder on the Dutch seaboard, where they lived together amidst the dunes. Few humans went that way and their humbles and hovels formed an interlocking community close by the shore.

Since the storm and what had followed he said little about them, but a frown of worry now rarely left his face and they all knew he wanted to sail home across the North Sea in the hope of finding them safe and sound.

'They be hardy enough and can read wind and tide as well as any hydden on this Earth but, by my soul, I dread to think what has happened to them these days past, for no one could have foretold such a storm! Will't come with us, Jack, and meet your other kin?'

He might have before but now he shook his head. Their original plan had been that he, Slew and one other would make their way to Brum, Riff staying at Maldon in case he was needed as transport after Sinistral and Blut had taken stock in Brum. All that had changed and Slew's injury, though largely healed by Leetha, still meant he could yet be a liability to Jack and it was better he returned to Holland with Riff, his friends with him. When his leg was healed he might then accompany their mother Leetha, as he had before, to her home in Thuringia.

'It sounds a long way,' said Jack worriedly.

'It is and it isn't,' replied Leetha, 'and anyway it is too long since I saw the Modor and I need to.'

The Modor was the wise female who was said to live in the Harz Mountains with the Wita or Wise One. Leetha counted the Modor as her friend.

'And the Wita?' wondered Jack, who had a dim memory of the Modor helping him onto the back of the White Horse when he was six and spirited away to safety and a human life in Englalond.

Leetha shrugged.

'He comes and goes, mainly goes, and she misses him, which is why she likes to see me. Wisdom is not always accompanied by happiness, Jack. She misses the Wita as Katherine misses you.'

'And I her,' Jack said firmly.

'That too,' said Leetha, glancing briefly at Riff, who had always understood that Leetha was too free a spirit to stay with him for long.

'Aye, she comes and goes, which can be hard on others,' growled Riff, eyes crinkling to a rare and loving smile.

'You and Leetha, Katherine and I, the Modor and the Wita . . . and, come to think of it, Stort and Judith my . . . my . . .' muttered Jack.

'Our granddaughter,' murmured Leetha, finishing his sentence a different way than he intended and adding: 'There are many ways to look at things. Come with us, Jack!'

He was tempted but still he shook his head. As Stavemeister of Brum his first duty was to get back to that city and give its remaining citizens what assistance and leadership he could.

But Katherine's fate was also greatly on his mind and until he had found out what had happened to her there was no prospect of him leaving Englalond. Meanwhile, as soon as he was satisfied that Riff and the others had found a serviceable craft from the hundreds that were washed up everywhere about them he would head home to Brum . . .

It did not take long for the waters to recede after the tower collapsed and with Jack's help they found a vintage clinker-built craft of the kind Riff preferred to sail. It had been slightly holed, had mud below-decks, and the sails needed drying. But, working together, they had her back on the water and ready to sail within a day, provisioned with supplies scavenged from some human houses inland which had escaped the flooding.

Jack's goodbyes with Riff and his siblings were rough and ready but they were warm: an embrace, a handshake, words of pleasure to have met, assurances that they would try to meet again soon enough and the hope that what they found at their different destinations was joy not tragedy.

Leetha held Jack close, so tight it was as if she feared she would never see him again.

His goodbyes over, he left them awaiting a favourable wind and headed back up past the fallen tower, its footings now exposed, and on along the westward road to make his trek to Brum. By what route or means he would reach the city, and against what obstacles, he had no idea, but reach it he intended to.

He turned round and they waved back.

The second time he turned they were out of sight. All he could see was the wide stretch of the still-flooded creeks and estuaries and from there the far horizon of the North Sea.

✳

It was mid-afternoon before he got fully into his stride, his 'sac not too heavy, his carved stave good in his hand and, surprisingly, soon giving him a blister where he held it.

'I have been on a boat too long,' he told himself, 'far too long . . .'

A feeling of relief and spaciousness had come over him after living at such close quarters with so many people. Now he needed time to make sense of what had happened and come to terms with the warm familial feelings that had been aroused: a sense of belonging, a sense of need and all the confusions of attachment to one thing and desire for another.

Katherine had made the decision for him to go with them and she had been right. He had got to know, even to love, his father and mother and his siblings – Deap certainly, Slew not yet. It was hard to forgive the person who had killed Master Brief.

With this thought resurfaced the dread he felt after the explosion they had seen inland near Pendower, when he was sure he had lost Katherine forever. Even if she and Barklice and the others were all together in the vicinity of the explosion, as he had instinctively felt they were, surely one or other of them had survived? Their joint wyrd could not be so cruel for them all to have been killed.

If one and perhaps another had survived – and maybe even Katherine herself, with the Mirror's grace – then news about such a celebrated and important group of hydden as they were would have travelled ahead of them and to all points of the compass. That was the hydden way.

So now he walked steadily along the high road, not a mortal in sight, with evidence of the great flood having reached the vales to north and south, and the birds wheeling and screeching in the skies or huddling in the wet abandoned fields.

He didn't know it but he looked good. Thinner than before but healthy and with that confidence and shine that comes to one who has known a healing deep inside. He knew who he was at last and that made it easier for him to know where he wanted to go. Free to dwell less on himself any longer and more on the world about him. So his eyes were restless as he went, as restless as his thoughts, searching to right and left for signs of life, any life, but most especially hydden.

Where had they and the humans gone, and why?

What did poor Baggywrinkle's report of fleeing Fyrd signify?

And why, the further he travelled with night drawing in, did he feel such a desperate need to continue, to press on, to not stop until . . .

'What?' he muttered, the wind cold and spitting flecks of rain, clouds roiling on the far horizon. '*What?*'

Bedwyn Stort had once tried to describe to Jack a talent he had which others held in awe but which Stort himself said was unwelcome and generally troubling.

'When it descends upon me it is like an itch so low on the back of the calf it slows a walker down, or a splinter in a finger which suddenly gets in the way of everything,' he had explained.

'If my insights help others including yourself, Jack, you may have very good reason to be grateful for this so-called talent of mine. But for myself I have generally seen it as an affliction. I do not recommend that you encourage it in yourself! It is often wrong, or leads you astray! Be warned. Suppress it! Mention it not, even to yourself. Sing, hum, eat, drink, do *anything* to make you forget such thoughts when they hustle their irritating way into your mind!'

The talent or affliction Stort had been talking about was his powerful gift of premonition.

That day, for the first time in his life, Jack now understood exactly what Stort had meant and why it so disturbed him. Because, with the dusk, came a premonition he found hard to ignore.

Stort had talked about itches and splinters, Jack likened the unpleasant feeling he now had to a stinging insect buzzing about his head which would not go away however hard he tried to make it do so.

It came first as an image. He saw, or seemed to see, Woolstone House in Berkshire, the rambling old pile where Katherine had been brought up by Arthur and Margaret Foale, her adoptive parents.

Jack had been invited there for a visit when he was sixteen and ended up living there and, in time, falling in love with Katherine and journeying to the Hyddenworld with her. It was a voyage of discovery that Arthur had made long before, aided by the henge of living trees he created in their great garden within sight of the ancient White Horse, carved into the steep chalk slope of Uffington Hill that stood guardian over Woolstone.

It was no special surprise to Jack that these memories and this image should come into his mind that day. But with it came an inexplicable and urgent need to divert from his course to Brum and go to Woolstone then and there.

He knew he could not do so. His task now was to get to where his duty lay, which, in any case, was surely the best place to find Katherine, or from which to go and help her if that was what she needed. But, as Stort said of his premonitions, Jack could not rid himself of the feeling that it was Woolstone where he should be. The sense of it became so strong and disquieting that when he finally made camp, dog-tired though he was, he could not sleep.

He tossed and turned, wrestling with a thousand disconnected thoughts, images, memories, all in some way imbued with the feeling that something was wrong at Woolstone and that he must attend to it.

Stort, Katherine, Barklice . . . their names came to him again and again, all jumbled up, as did that of Judith.

Judith . . .

His feelings about her were confused, for she had grown so fast, been so angry, felt so alien. Even now, when he might have got used to the fact and so much else that was extraordinary had happened, the idea that Judith was the Shield Maiden and so the agent of Mother Earth Herself was almost beyond him.

Their troubled daughter was born in the henge at Woolstone and raised there. The house and garden were as much her home as Katherine's. When he was summoned back into the Hyddenworld and had to leave Judith behind, it felt like he was abandoning her to a fate worse than any hurt or loneliness he himself had ever known.

Jack did finally sleep, but only as a new dawn showed, his sleep an escape from wrestling with an impulse to return to where he did not wish to go. It was Brum that needed him.

Brum, Brum, Brum . . .

Drum, Drum, Drum . . .

When he was woken it was very suddenly, by a sound that drummed through his mind but which he could not quite identify.

He chewed brot while he heated a nut pottage, a gritty, poor creation which Barklice, an excellent camp cook, would have shaken his head at and munched in an exaggeratedly miserable way.

Jack struck camp without motive or desire to do so, or not do so. His mood had changed. He moved on listlessly, which for him was unusual, and found himself locked into a day of strange transportations which did not improve his spirits.

First feet; then a vast bicycle whose pedals he could not reach but which he freewheeled down a hill; then feet again until he spied a canoe by a river. He tried that for a time, gave it up, and then found an abandoned car with the keys still in.

The engine turned briefly, sputtered and stopped and he realized it had been abandoned because the fuel had run out.

On and on he went, on foot again, westward by the half-hidden sun, his suppressed premonition concerning Woolstone finally returning even stronger than the day before, while all about him, near and far, was the deserted land, the fallen land. Houses empty with doors wide open; more cars abandoned with keys still in; the bloated, stinking bodies of cattle in pens in a shed, left to die without food or water.

A goose, its wings clipped, waddling fast across a field, looking back towards him. The last survivor of a whole flock of them, which lay scattered across their field, killed by a fox which had spared just one. A burnt-out church, its medieval arches smoky black eyes on a broken world, their wooden frames charred, their window glass cracked and nearly gone.

'No!' he heard himself say aloud.

No, he decided, he would not deviate from his original intention to go straight to Brum.

The day drifted into another sleepless night, then back to a better day with a clearer head, the nagging thoughts behind him, Brum somewhere ahead and he and his stave and the Earth beneath a trinity of purpose that drove him stolidly on, a lonely figure in a landscape of despair.

But eventually his pace steadied and strengthened, his body swung with the rhythm of his steps, his stave, the Earth beneath and he was content, at peace, purposeful and . . . and . . .

The drumming again, a waking nightmare, real now because the ground shook beneath his feet, destroying all sense of peace.

Jack stopped still, defeated, and he knew by whom.

He scowled and muttered her name: *Judith, damn Judith.*

He looked northward along the ancient hydden way he had not even seen until he was in the act of crossing it.

Oh yes, Judith, I know it well.

Eastward was behind him, where Riff and Leetha had gone.

Westward was Brum, to where he was trying to get.

But you don't want me to, do you?

The ground shook with the pounding of hoofs and he swore, he cursed and then he looked southward along the old green road, the deeply rutted way, which was the oldest in Europe, maybe the world.

Southward, a direction he did not turn, southward on this damn road which he and Katherine had stood upon and sworn one day they would take together to . . . to

Here, where I stand, stave in hand, 'sac on my back, in the wrong moment in time and the ground's shaking and the hoofs are pounding and damn Judith . . . Jack told himself.

He had reached the Ridgeway, far to the north of White Horse Hill, to which it led and his wyrd led, as it always had, always must.

Jack could feel it, like his spine, his ribs, his past and his present and his future right here and now.

You want me to turn south along it and I'm damned if I'm going to. You want me in Woolstone and I'm damned . . .

They came suddenly along the westward road, the way he wanted to go, great dogs ridden by Mirror knew what. Shadows with teeth; shadows with claws; beings with burning eyes which rode the snarling dogs, all mangy and diseased but powerful. The beings laughing at Jack, they charged at him, circling him so fast that one blended to another before they spiralled away and came back, the dogs' teeth bared, to attack him then and there, from west and north and east and south.

He swore at them and raised his hand to hurl his stave, but there was no need for that. It knew its job. It tore itself from his grip, turning, twirling in the air, its carvings dazzling with the light of the sky, its indentations reverberating with that light, making the dogs and their cowardly riders scatter, turning to stare back, whining, cursing, spitting drool, hating him before taking their second wind and turning on him so fast his stave was lost in the melee of its own myriad shards of light and sound.

'Stop!'

The voice of the Rider, his daughter Judith, preceded her, a thunderous command that froze them all around him as shadows whose snarls retreated into their mouths and stayed there, venomously mute.

The White Horse and Judith bore down on him, went right over him, their vast shadow a chill, dark thing upon him.

'I won't,' he cried, turning after them, southward, 'I won't go the way you say.'

The Horse stopped, turned and Jack looked into Judith's eyes.

Oh dear God, the human in him said.

The Horse bent its front legs to let her down and there she was, before him on the path, fearsome and horrible.

Oh dear God.

His daughter, whose little hand he once held, who was so rarely able to forget her pain and laugh, his once-beloved whom it was his wyrd to have to leave behind when she most needed him, *oh dear God.*

Judith was grey-haired now, her face lined, her body beginning to sag and distort.

His daughter, born that spring, was now three times his age or more.

'Why the hell are you resisting all common sense?' she snarled.

Once she had called him Dad; now she might call him Jack; as it was she called him nothing at all but just looked angry and contemptuous.

'You know where you have to go!'

'I . . .'

'Yes you do. You're needed.'

'Katherine . . . ?'

'I have no idea how she is or whether she's dead or alive,' she said. 'Get on the bloody Horse . . .'

'Where . . . ? Why . . . ?'

'Woolstone, if you're not too late. Dallying across the bloody sea, trying to keep from getting wet on towers, swanning along the green roads of these drear parts. What the hell are you doing?'

He wasn't Stort but he loved her and felt and saw her dreadful pain, which was the Earth's.

'Take me to Woolstone, I need to find something there,' he heard himself say, looking at her in the hope she'd tell him what because he had absolutely no idea.

'Isn't that your job to find out not mine to tell you?' she grumbled, reading his mind. 'Can't do everything for everybody, can I?'

They stared at each other, irritated.

'Anyway,' she added, 'I don't know either!'

Their frowns turned to rueful grins and suddenly, briefly, they were father and daughter again.

Then, laughing, Judith put her great hands to his waist and heaved him on the Horse, climbing back on herself and taking up the reins.

'Hold on tight!' she called out into the icy wind that struck them in the face as they rose towards the sky, the Ridgeway soon far beneath.

She muttered and cursed as they went, a hundred thousand times, and only one short sentence did he understand.

'Bloody Stort,' she said, 'what's taking him so long?'

20

THE PLIGHTING

The scintillating mirrors that shone from the dreamygirl's bodice and skirts as she overwhelmed Arnold Mallarkhi with her startling and unexpected presence quite blinded him to all else for a time, as it did his friends.

It seemed to them all that the whole world shimmered with the wild magic of youth, of love and (it must be said) lust, and the utter abandonment of their worries and doubts to the positive flow and force of life itself.

As they emerged back to a sense of reality of where they were and the straits they were in, they understood that the delightful interlude created by the girl's arrival lasted but a minute or two.

If that were so for the rest of them it was not the case with Bedwyn Stort. Attuned as he now was to the different drifts of time that the cracking of the Mirror-of-All was inflicting on the Hyddenworld, he suspected that those 'moments' lasted rather longer than the rest of them immediately realized.

Thinking this might be so, and having the unwelcome feeling that time itself had shifted once again, he turned away, rubbed his eyes, shook his head as if to rid himself of errant thoughts and said, with a conviction he did not understand, 'My good friends, enough! Time has moved on and we are in some way urgently needed!'

It was a strange appeal and stranger still that it was made before and not after what happened next, as if he was in some mysterious way already in a time zone marginally ahead of theirs.

For even as he uttered that cry the deep boom of a distress rocket was heard, which drew their attention to the bright white light of a rocket that was drifting over the round summit of Brent Knoll.

'That looks to me like a further call for help!' said Katherine.

As she said this the girl disentangled herself from Arnold, turned to look towards Brent Knoll and, nodding her head, declared, 'You'm not enough to help them Knoller Folk so we've work to do if we'm to save lives! Where do you natters think I come fro' if not fro' they desperate souls? Aye, 'tis to get help I've a-come this way n'all. They be in more trouble on the Knoll than tadpoles in drying puddles and'll all be dead in no time if we don't get 'em help . . .'

The hydden gazed at her, whose eyes were as shiny brown and feral as a fox's.

Then she sighed and shook her head, saying, 'This be a local matter and t'would be wrong and gangry bad if the Knollers were saved by strangers when there's folk hereabout should risk their lives forrard.'

'We bain't seen nary a soul but ourseln,' said Arnold, stepping back from her as if for the first time and marvelling at the errant beauty he saw.

She stared back at him and for a moment her eyes softened, her fingers caressed each other as if in preparation for another delicious assault upon him. But duty called and she held back, though her voice was breathless.

'My bilgyboy, my love,' she said, words being a prudent substitute for action, 'you baint's seen 'em all about here because they'm sneaky clever at a-hiding away fro' danger and responsibility. But there them curs be!'

She pointed through the trees of the copse and they saw emerging from the shadows as motley a group of Bilgesnipe as they had ever seen.

'Aye, I mean them layabouts, my larkin' love, I mean these dreggy ones!'

The group that had appeared grew before their eyes into a whole army, all armed with rough-made weapons, males, females and kinder alike.

The dreamygirl, who despite her better intentions had reached and grasped Arnold's hand very fiercely, now let it go and boldly advanced on the approaching hydden.

'The Beacon be burning for the first time in more'n six hundred years and I've come to claim the right of the Knollers to the near-forgotten fealty of life and arms you owe 'em. It may go hard to hear them words, Poldyfolk, but so it be. The Knollers are besieged by human foe and demand your help! So light a fierybright with smoke to catch the wind. It'll let 'em know that help's on the way.'

The hostile Bilgesnipe did not move or say a word. They just stared, frowned and muttered to themselves. But Arnold understood at least a part of what was meant and set to at once to get a fire going with dry leaves from the edge of the copse. A task which Barklice helped him with.

They had no sooner got a fire alight than they began placing damp leaves on top to create smoke, which drifted upward through the trees and out towards the clear sky beyond. It was as clear a signal that help was on the way as they could make.

'It'll not be hard to see on a day like this,' he said, breathing heavily from his efforts and standing tall beside his dreamygirl, before eyeing the hydden army with mild contempt.

'My love, these lazy folk you'm kin and mates?'

'Useless cowry folks more like but . . . but . . .'

For the first time her courage seemed to fail her and self-doubt set in. Then a fiery anger took over.

'. . . but *all right!* All right, bilgyboy, don't lay me low for wot's no fault o'mine. *Yes, it be so!* Them's are wot you think they'm be but I be not like 'em even if them blood 'n mine have commonalities. Yes!'

'Yes what?' demanded Arnold, mystified and bewildered by her sudden temper, at him as it seemed.

'Yes, they be my blood,' she said, 'and they be my shame!'

She stepped towards them.

'You villens all!' she shouted. 'You'm gone and lost my bilgyboy for 'e won't love me more! You should have answered the Knollers' call yestermorn when 'twas first made instead of headin' to this wood to chat up your doubts and do nowt.'

She turned back to Arnold as if to apologize for them all and accept the blame herself. Never had a Bilgesnipe lass looked so piteous and vulnerable as she did then, all the more so for the solitary tear, all fat and shiny, that emerged from the corner of one of her beautiful eyes and coursed its slow and appealing way down her plump cheek.

Arnold was not taken in by this. Love may have struck him very suddenly that morning, out of the blue of the sky, and he might have been blinded for a time, but now he saw things more clearly, as a true bilgyboy must if he is to navigate the treacherous seas of love to safety, whether they be the palpable seas of the Earth or the uncharted seas of the heart.

'Dreamygirl, I know not your name as yettern, but I know this. You don't need the appeal of tears, or the look of a lost soul, to get my help. Indeed, my own true lass, that be the way to lose me from your heart. You just say it like it truly be and I'll answer like I truly should. Where I come from 'tis courage to say outright what you want, and cowardice to hide among the confusing undercurrents beneath the watery surface of us all. So state true for now and allers what you want.'

She stared at him, and again the world stood still.

He was tall, strong, no longer the bilgyboy Katherine had first met two or three years before.

'That tear *was* false,' the dreamygirl said, 'and that be so. But these tears now, they be true as love itself. What does I and all o' me want? I want 'em to follow us o'er the Levels. When that duty be done then you and I can say what we want.'

'Be we plighted or no?' demanded Arnold. 'I bain't a reader o' minds.'

'You say,' she said. 'I began it, you end it.'

He smiled a slow, big, toothy smile and said as soft as water flowing through a sun-swept meadow, 'You and I be plighted fair and square! Now, let's sort out your worthless kin, here and right now. We'm noxious, knock-kneed folk like you where I come from as well,' said Arnold, eyeing the array of weapons in the hands of the Poldyfolk with indifference.

'Pile 'em wet leaves on the fire!' he ordered Barklice, stepping towards them, 'and get a ferrylight ablazin' brighter still to give heart to the Knollers over yon!'

One of the Poldyfolk, their leader it seemed, stepped forward threateningly. He was hairy and a mess, with a straggly, ill-kempt beard, a pot-belly that sought to burst beyond his food-stained jerkin and a pair of thin, white shanks besmirched with the dust and detritus of the fields, as if he had been trying to rid himself of fleas. His teeth were stained brown with beetlechaw and he had about him a cunning, suspicious, belligerent air.

'Who'm you think you be, lad, to order us about? As for your'n dreamygirl she can go and jump off them Mendip peaks o'er there for all we care for her and her hoity-toity Knoller friends, pesky, rabbit, flea-ridden uppity bunch as they be!'

'You addressing them badly words to *me*?' said Arnold, his smile fading.

'You, that girl, and anyone else who's minded to interfere with us . . . including that rabble of folk you've 'n with you,' came the reply.

Arnold contrived to look outraged while Katherine and the others looked at each other uncertainly. Hands flexed on the shafts of weapons, tongues licked lips, eyes narrowed. They all readied for a fight but Arnold stilled them with a slight movement of his hand, as masterful of the moment as if he were skippering a craft in difficult water beyond which none but he could spy the destination.

'I bain't swift to anger on my own behalf,' he said, 'but where I come from dreamygirls are left in peace and nary made to suffer insult and words foul and unbecoming! Especially . . .' he continued looking at the girl enquiringly, for he did not yet know her name, 'one such as . . . like . . . *as* . . . ?'

'Madder,' said the girl promptly.

If Arnold was surprised at this strange name he did not show it, but rather blinked for a moment or two before asking in a reasonable way, 'You so named fro' a troubled noddle in't family or dyeing?'

Madder seemed pleased at this response, laughed and, raising her skirts, showed that her petticoat was a deep, natural red, like a sunset at the end of a troubled day, when peace and harmony has been found once more, and replied, 'Fro' madder the plant o' course!'

'Dyeing then,' said Arnold faintly, 'nary did I doubt it but these be strange times. My ma wouldn't want me spousing madness but dyeing's good.'

He turned back to the Poldy leader with a frown and took up a position closer still to his impulsive other.

'As I said, I ain't swiftly narktious on my own account but any that insults one such as Madder here, goodly as she is, comely too and braver than the whole pesky pack o' you, has me to answer to! And not just me!'

'Mayhap and mayhap not!' cried the other, suddenly furious, 'but we be many and you be motley and no match for us.'

Arnold's face reddened and now he really did begin to look furious.

'First you sully me, then you bander Madder here and now you'm stupid o' the subject of my bold friends and companions o' the road. And we bain't all! There's shadows o' my blood looming near, for my folks don't take kindly to girtly fools like you, so you'm facing a whole army which makes the Fyrdie ones look like drowned gnats.'

'Gnats! Girtly! Stupid!' cried the Poldy one, hopping about from foot to foot, his face puce with rage. 'We don't care if your blood be the finest ever made, provided we spill it on this'n sward here and now and rightaway. Eh, lads? Eh, lassies?'

'That's right,' responded his followers.

'Afore you start and make a fool of yerselves maybe I should tell you who I be and what I be,' Arnold called out, advancing on the one questioning him. 'I be of Brum born and Bilgesnipe bred and my name be one should make your throttle dry up and disintegrate.'

The Poldyfolk leader grinned unpleasantly and looked round at what seemed his mate, who was something else entirely. A fulsome female, of bright looks and bold intelligent eyes, who looked like she'd been spoused beneath herself. But she, loyal as Bilgesnipe are to their kith and kin, nodded in agreement with him.

'You speak, my dearest,' said he.

'There be only one name weighs heavy with us'n folk,' she said calmly, 'and you'm too willowy and slight to be of that great bloodline of Brum. No, lad, go thee home and stop orderin' your'n betters about! And take that sluttish wench and her dandy airy-fairy ways with you.'

'Aye!' said her spouse, rearing himself up taller than a slouch so that some semblance of the fine young hydden he might once have been, just about, showed itself, 'and we'm both a-saying, willowboy, that there be only one name does my throttle in and I'm guessin' you know it well enough.'

'Fools you certainly be,' said Arnold very menacingly, 'but even such filchy fools as thee 'ave heard o' Muggy Duck, I take it, even in these dim parts?'

They looked at each other gravely, while their followers all nodded, wondering what he was driving at.

'We have heard of it and we respect it.'

'You've heard of he who founded it?'

''Twas Pa Mallarkhi.'

'So it was,' said Arnold. 'I take it that be the family name you hold in reverence and awe, like wot you just declared?'

'Natural-most we do. And especially that famed and famous Ma'Shuqa, Pa Mallarkhi's daughter, who runs the place we've heard, Mirror praise her.'

'Well then, twatty ones,' cried Arnold, 'she'm not one to take disrespect a-sitting on her butt. She'd rise up and strike you dead with a frying pan if she thought you were less than polite to one of her own.'

'Like who, for example, bilgyboy?'

'Like me,' said Arnold coldly.

They laughed derisively.

'What be you, her scullery boy?' said the female.

'Scullery maid more like,' said her spouse, laughing aloud and looking at his supporters so that they laughed too.

Arnold shook his head.

'No, I bain't scullery-nothing nor any maid that I know of. Ma'Shuqa's my ma and Pa Mallarkhi is my grandpa and my names is Arnold Mallarkhi and you'm and your crew just made me mad . . .'

'And me!' cried Madder suddenly, 'and that be no lie! I bring a Mallarkhi into the fold and allers you do is like you allers done, trash 'im and them I've a liking for and like me.'

'Who be this spousled pair of idiots?' asked Arnold, turning to her in disbelief that they could be so rude.

'I was tryin' to say afore I grew briefly ashamed,' Madder replied. 'They be my pa and ma, Mirror help me!'

'Then it be time to teach 'em what you really be, my lass!'

'You 'n me both!' she replied.

With that, and to the astonishment of them all, Arnold threw aside Sinistral's great stave and Madder hauled up the hems of her skirts and petticoats and tucked them into her belt, revealing her sturdy legs and lacy drawers, for ease of movement, it seemed. Then, without pause for further verbal insults, they launched themselves at the Poldyfolk together. With kicks and punches, bites and pokes, kneeings and elbowing and gougings and a good many other tricks he had learnt in the backwaters of Brum, Arnold attacked his putative father-in-law and anyone else he could get his hands on before sheer weight of numbers subdued him, swearing, foaming at the mouth and generally looking terrifying.

As for Madder, she attacked a trio of smug-looking females, her older sisters it seemed, and might have killed them all had not four muddy males, seemingly kin of hers as well, hauled her off her screaming quarry and with difficulty subdued her.

But no sooner had they relaxed and elicited promises from Arnold and Madder to be still than the former cried, 'Boddle to that, we Brummies don't yield to snipey folk like you!' and he rushed over to Madder, freed her too, and the mayhem resumed.

Barklice and the others stared in astonishment and, initially, some alarm. But it very soon became apparent that the Bilgesnipes' approach to fighting was very different from that of ordinary hydden. For one thing, the weapons they had been carrying had been cast aside, as if they were a hindrance to the main action. For another, the blows they dealt each other were nothing more dangerous than biffs and buffets to ears and nose, and stomach, with occasional kicks to their shins and posteriors.

It soon looked once more as if Arnold and Madder didn't stand a chance. But after a further two or three minutes, with Arnold down again and Madder winded, her immediate family members suddenly became their friends against the wider group.

'The lad be hurt and t'bain't fair to set upon he when him grounded, so take that'm there and this'm here!'

'Come on, lass,' Madder's pa cried, 'upp'n you get and bide by me while I knicker out that snitchywitch your cousin once and fer all time, she didn't never play fair, not since she'm a wee spikey thing o' a girl!'

Mayhem reigned again, with Arnold and Madder lost to sight until at last, honour satisfied, the Poldyfolk fell one way and another and only the two lovers-to-be remained standing, back to back, jabbing at thin air as if at foes imaginary, or perhaps foes remembered. Finally they sank down together and sat on the sward still back to back, with the beaten Poldyfolk scattered all around.

To the astonishment of the bemused onlookers, these combatants rose up, apparently unharmed, and the females went to Madder and praised her while the males did the same to Arnold, reaching a hand to each and helping them to their feet.

Madder's father emerged from the crowd.

'My name be Donard, lad. Take my hand, for you be worthy of thy name and of my lass's hand 'n more.'

He stood bruised and bloodied but evidently bore no ill-will.

'What you say, Ma?' he cried to Madder's mother.

'I say this and then let it be. I say she'm been the dreamiest, driftiest, irritatingist, willow-the-way girl o' mine as I was ever cursed with and if I was angry at her ways and means it was disappointment made me so for never did I love one as I loved her, except o' course for my other kinder, curse 'em all. But Madder's got a maddening way with her, that squeezes a hug out o' me every time, eh, Pa?'

'She always had that, Ma, she always did, but that was then and now is now. I'm that proud o' her spirit and the wild way she be in spite of all we allers said that my heart and head are bursting with it. I love 'er now more than I ever did and that was much and a lot.'

They fell silent and came together and looked at Madder and Arnold, one after another.

'Shall I say it, Ma, or you?'

'You,' said Ma.

'So here and now I freely say that you was a girl once, Madder, and now you're a stirtly, brightly, wondrous bilgywenchy woman.'

'One o' those will do, Pa, and it bain't "wenchy".'

'I take that back. Now, Madder, what can we do by way of recompense?'

'Make me proud, Pa, make me proud to see you shake Pa Mallarkhi's hand if that day should ever come. Make me proud, Ma, to embrace his ma, as one equal to another, which I allers said we all should be, of whatever age or name or kin or spirit. Will you strive to that for me?'

'We will.'

'Even if you don't and he's right and you'm girtly, cowardly fools the lot o' you I still . . . well . . . you been brave and he said truth's best out.

Oh then I love you and that be true whatever you done: allers did and allers will.'

Chaos had reigned before but now a great group hug, which was the Bilgesnipe way at the end of fighting, came up and embraced them all, reaching its warm hands and touch and firm grip even to Sinistral himself, who might have expired of suffocation had not Terce pulled him clear just in time.

Only then, and as the breeze stirred the trees above their heads and smoke from the now dying fire reminded them all of their duty, did Donard say, 'We'm cowards no more. We'm all off to help the Knollers out. Which reminds me, Madder, who be 'is friends?'

Madder gazed at Barklice and the rest, as if she had seen them for the first time, which was almost true. Arnold had had the bulk of her attention.

Arnold was about to introduce them one by one when Donard raised a hand and said, 'Now don't go and tell some tomfool story to make bigger idiots of us folk than we are already. I'm ready to accept you'm the Mallarkhi heir but don't make false claims for your friends. You'll be telling me next that the tall one with the hoary hair is the Emperor hisself.'

'Not me, but him,' said Sinistral, pointing at Blut.

At which Blut took off his spectacles and wiped them, as if to pause for thought and see matters more clearly.

'Dang me and the Mirror if I ain't heard the Emperor's got specs,' said one of Madder's sisters.

A look of awe had come over them all as they began to think that Arnold was actually telling the truth.

'So next you'll be saying that he'm with the red hair and dandly legs is Mister Stort and t'other shorter old one is Mister Barklice, best hyddener alive?'

'The very same,' said Barklice amicably.

The awe deepened.

'So you'd be the Lady Katherine, troubled ma of the Shield Maiden, Mirror help you?' said Madder's ma.

'I am,' said Katherine, introducing Terce in his turn.

'Dang me but this be weird wyrd indeed,' said Pa Donard.

'Now, we better get on and do our duty by the Knollers. Follow us, one and all, for we may be slow off the mark to 'elp our enemies, which is only natural, but we got a plan and it'll be easier to see through under cover of the mist.'

As they all trooped off downslope towards the Levels, Pa and Ma turned to Katherine and said, as if in a final moment of doubt that any of what they had been told was true, 'If you be all you say you are, why's that famed Stavemeister Jack not here?'

There was something reassuring in the question which Katherine, who had missed him so much in the troubled days past, very much liked.

'He's otherwise engaged,' she said, going quiet as she sent Jack a silent prayer that he might know she was well and for the moment, just like him, 'otherwise engaged'.

21

BOHR

From twenty thousand feet the little known US airbase of RAF Croughton in the Northamptonshire countryside of the English Midlands looked like an oasis of light in a land of darkness.

Dr Erich Bohr, one of only two civilian passengers on the C40 Clipper out of Scott Airbase, Illinois, USA, peered down at the landing lights with apprehension mixed with grim determination, as the crew began their final descent. His present mission was difficult, dangerous and very important. He doubted that he could save the world from the extraordinary cosmic stress it was now under; probably no one could. But he reckoned he had a better chance than most.

The more so, perhaps, because he had Ingrid Hansen with him, his assistant and fellow researcher and the only other civilian passenger. She was his fresh pair of eyes and had a habit of solving problems others couldn't.

'Three minutes.'

The captain's words were a whisper in his ear.

He settled back in his seat, hands and elbows on the rests, shoeless feet relaxed, and he stopped looking outside. That's what he always did. He always had believed that if a plane was going to crash and he was going to die he would prefer not to watch the process.

He had last made this landing three months before, in August, also in the small hours. Then, the surrounding countryside of villages, towns and roads between had been well lit, with very few pockets of real dark. Now darkness predominated, as it had for the whole of the approach since crossing the south coast. What few points of light he had seen were real fires, not artificial light.

England was shut down, its population fled north, the various arms of its government bunkered, its communications now reliant on the specialist American equipment and personnel of RAF Croughton.

'One minute . . .'

The voice trailed and another crew member took over final instructions. Bohr closed his eyes and readied his body. Croughton was not the most modern of landing strips. Sheep grazed across its grass, or had when he was last there. Half the on-site buildings were non-functional, but that was a blind. From this airbase one-third of Europe's military communications were run, or used to be until a few weeks before. Now everything was shutting down, military and civilian. God alone knew what percentage of communications now ran from this base.

The rest of the personnel were military. Six were crew of the aircraft itself, from 932D Airlift Wing. Twenty-three were personnel from two different US Special Mission Units: ten from DEVGRU or Naval Special Warfare Development Group; thirteen from ISC, the United States Army Intelligence and Security Command.

The mission was a joint command with Colonel P. Reece, a tough US Army officer with considerable experience in covert operations in alien and unusual territory. They were tasked with entering the Hyddenworld to establish if the cause of the present natural disasters besetting the Earth derived from that realm and if so what the cure might be.

It was unusual but not unknown for the command of a complex intelligence mission, one that might involve considerable physical danger to some of its personnel, to be shared between a civilian and a member of the military in this way. Naturally, everyone hoped that the force and assets of the DEVGRU operatives would not be needed. But if they were, then their fast, highly skilled and well-honed, few-questions-asked approach to almost any situation the mission might face could save all their lives.

Erich Bohr was exceptional for a civilian in that he had the respect of every man and woman there, except Reece who trusted no one. He was a physicist and a former NASA astronaut, meaning that he too had been through some very special training. That part of his career over, his academic and corporate political skills enabled him to rise to the post of director of one of the Agency's research teams, with a special interest in cosmology and the science of the environment of space. He was also Special Adviser to the President of the United States.

But all that, including even his two trips into space, paled into insignificance compared to the potential importance of the mission he was now on and for which he was uniquely qualified. For Bohr was one of Arthur Foale's former pupils and second only to him in his knowledge of the Hyddenworld.

The plane touched down and twenty-five minutes later Bohr, Reece, Hansen and their team were in one of the airbase's briefing rooms. It was the same room in which Arthur Foale had also been briefed – and his skills and knowledge partially shared – in August, during Bohr's previous visit.

On that occasion Arthur had been keen to leave before pressure was put on him to divulge what he knew of the Hyddenworld and in particular how to enter it. He had realized that if he did not comply it was unlikely he would be allowed to leave.

The purpose of the meeting then, which brought together a range of world experts and specialists on natural disasters from seismic events to climatological phenomena, was to try to develop a strategy for the Western international community following a series of cataclysmic disasters worldwide.

As the brilliant but irascible former Professor of Astral Archaeology at Cambridge University, Arthur knew perfectly well what Bohr, one of his most original students, was likely to want. Arthur had foolishly let slip the fact that, after years of seemingly off-the-wall research into something he called the Hyddenworld, he had found a way of entering it.

Unlike most other cosmologists, Bohr was prepared to take Arthur's unfortunate claim seriously. But the more Bohr pressed him on the subject, the vaguer Arthur became, until relations between the two broke down. In any case, Bohr returned to the USA, where his career took off. But when the world entered a phase of natural disasters that might have a cosmological explanation, Bohr contacted Arthur again. Equally naturally, Arthur knew why.

His sudden removal from Woolstone to Croughton under military guard in August confirmed his worst fears. He had no doubt that the base had been chosen for the conference precisely because it was near his home. What Bohr did not know was that his former professor had very specialist knowledge of Croughton as a prehistoric site and that, in particular, there were two henges close to its south-west boundary.

Nor did Bohr imagine that an unfit, overweight academic in his seventies would be able to escape what was effectively military detention and disappear. He did not realize, as Arthur did, that perimeter fences are designed to keep people out, not keep them in. Once Arthur was certain that his brains would be picked, by force if necessary, he escaped through the fence and made his way to the second of the henges, of which no more remained than discoloration in the grass growing there, caused by differential soil in old post-holes, and a very slight raising of the ground. But it still functioned as a henge.

Arthur made his escape under the noses, literally, of the guards in charge of him. One moment he was there, the next he had gone.

But he did leave more of a clue than he would have wished to do. The Croughton fences were covered by cameras and one of these was angled such that it got footage of Arthur's escape. This, combined with Bohr's single memory of Arthur's much earlier revelation, that to use the henges as portals required some kind of systematic physical movement which could unlock a henge's power and turn it into a portal into the Hyddenworld, was enough to make him realize that he too might be able to work out how it was done.

Bohr himself had searched Arthur's house, including his library and research papers, while specialists had been through his computers and electronic mail. A great deal about his theories was found but nothing very specific about his travels into the Hyddenworld, where he began from and where he went when he was there. Also, Bohr's own people and the British authorities had searched for Arthur himself. All without result.

Meanwhile, the natural disasters besetting the Earth, and the Cosmos of which it was a tiny part, continued. Three weeks earlier, in October, the Earth had opened up beneath a town called Half Steeple on the River Severn in the county of Gloucestershire. Thousands of lives were lost. Such events had been happening with increasing frequency but this one, in England, was a tipping point both nationally and internationally.

Countries had reacted to these events in many different ways: some barely at all, others extremely violently. In the undeveloped regions of the world, used as they were historically to natural disaster, poverty and famine, it had been, until very recently, business as usual. In the West, where there were expectations that standards of living would remain good and where reliance on the utilities and the internet was universal, the systematic breakdown of communications, food supplies and transport produced escalating civil unrest. It was a doomsday scenario in the making but to most observers' surprise it was in the southern half of England that a general panic first took hold.

The tragedy of Half Steeple put into people's minds the idea that more was coming – and it had come, in hurricanes, early winter weather and the rapid breakdown of two things Britain was most famous for: law and order.

Matters were not much better in the United States. Panic set in at national and state level and an unparalleled state of civil unrest soon took over. Faced by such a crisis, Bohr might have expected to remain very low on the list of Presidential advisers needed at such a time. But then he had felt himself to have been sidelined, along with his agency NASA itself, for months and years before the present situation had arisen. He knew that if anyone in the Pentagon had ever got as far as even considering the possibilities of finding a solution in the cosmological field they would have rejected it. It was too far out and not obviously applicable to what was actually going on globally.

As for any notion of exploring a solution around something as nebulous and strange as the Hyddenworld, Bohr was too experienced an operator not to know that it would be a lost cause from the moment it was mentioned. Even if such a world existed, how could it possibly help the present situation to explore it? For Bohr the answer lay in Arthur's notes and some of the things he had revealed elsewhere about the Hyddenworld.

Far-fetched as it might seem, Foale had found a way of using one or other of the many henge monuments near where he had lived for fifty years in Woolstone, Berkshire, to access the Hyddenworld. He also seemed to offer evidence that people in that world might have ways of controlling natural events and disasters, and the descent into chaos, which all the scientists and funds available to America had signally failed to do.

In the previous months of escalating natural disasters and earth events Bohr had made it his business to read and research everything he could about the henges. Of the many theories about why they had been built and by whom, Arthur's seemed as good as anybody's and better than some. He believed they had been built over the centuries by two distinct groups of 'folk', each with different and well-defined roles: the human and the hydden, the giants and the little people.

Arthur argued, and Bohr had come to agree with him, that the humans were good at the mechanics of building – the sourcing of the raw materials, their transport, their shaping, alignment and erection. The hydden gave the spiritual direction, particularly in making the connection between the henges and the Earth below and the Universe 'above'. They were responsible for the henges' primary function which was as portals between different worlds, both spiritual and physical.

Centuries before, when the humans became too destructive of the Earth the hydden had retreated and become 'invisible'. It was natural that they should take with them the secret of how to use the henges as portals between the hydden and human worlds.

Bohr was convinced that any henge, of whatever material, even if newly made and temporary too, could be used in this way as a portal. In that sense they were like vehicles; almost any model or design, if it follows a few basic principles of construction, can be used to transport someone from 'A' to 'B'. So it was with henges.

The problem was, how exactly was it done? What turned a henge into a portal and how was it used? Bohr was certain the secret lay in Arthur's working notes and in a visit to Woolstone. But it was a project for which he needed funding and some specialist input. In addition he would need some kind of security and protection in the form of special forces military support if he was to visit the Hyddenworld and return from it safely.

But until three days before no one had been interested. Then everything changed.

First, not a single one of the many solutions and policies discussed and enacted in Washington and the White House had seemed to have relevance or effect on the rapidly evolving and changing real-world situation the politicians and military now faced. The disasters and the dangerous perception that politicians were impotent in their defence of citizens and corporations were escalating each day. In consequence the decision-makers knew they were losing their grip and had begun to open their minds to alternatives, however much they might have been discounted only weeks before.

It was the perfect moment for one of Bohr's researchers to come in with a blindingly obvious result to anyone who studied aerial views of Woolstone taken at sunrise or sunset: Foale's large, wild garden had, at its bottom end, its very own arboreal henge.

'Goddammit,' Bohr had exclaimed when he saw this, 'he could enter the Hyddenworld virtually from his own house, and he probably did.'

Secondly, a wider search in the grounds of his property had uncovered papers, maps and notebooks not discovered before.

Bohr saw a chance to resurrect his long-held wish to uncover Arthur's secret and persuaded the White House to make the funds and personnel available. Colonel Reece was not his first choice as a fellow head of mission – he was humourless, hawkish, monosyllabic and uneasy with civilians – but Bohr had no choice. They were tasked with the mission together.

Bohr had little doubt that Reece's view of him was unfavourable and that he saw him as being soft, out of date with current military techniques, systems and technology, and likely to be indecisive in the face of real and present danger. Certainly he had filled out since the days he was an astronaut and too many years of deals, compromise and the politicking that went with high-end scientific research had jaded him. Maybe he seemed lacklustre to a high-profile serving army officer.

But there he was, and here they were, in Croughton, with work to do together.

Now in the field and faced by the team, Bohr did not need to present yet again the evidence for the existence of the Hyddenworld. That had already been done in Illinois at the Scott Air Force Base. Naturally, most were incredulous that such a world might exist of which they had never heard. But when it came to the planning and logistics their combined years of training kicked in. All missions were hypothetical until they happened in real time.

Arthur's notes on the Hyddenworld left no doubt that planning would need to include kit, weaponry, technology and supplies suitable to a world half the size they knew. It was no more extraordinary than many scenarios they had planned for.

If they thought it crazy they did not say so openly.

Less easy was the question of how those remaining in the human world would communicate with those who made it – if they did – to the Hyddenworld. Every conceivable option had been covered and provided for.

Bohr was still a clever enough tactician to save the best evidence till last, or rather until their arrival at Croughton and the necessary brief acclimatization to the place, the mission, the likely locales and each other. It was some security footage taken in Birmingham three weeks previously. It had been temporarily lost when that city went into a state of panic and civil strife, but recovered since by his own people here at Croughton.

'We know that our first objective is to enter the Hyddenworld,' he said, 'and find Arthur Foale. Since his escape from this base in August he has not been seen, despite every imaginable search for him. However . . .' Bohr indicated that the lights needed lowering. '. . . the following clips show what he currently looks like and where he may be . . . and they confirm that the Hyddenworld is real and not the imaginings of a future-world cosmologist . . .'

The meeting fell utterly silent as film was shown of recent scenes in Brum, caught both by day and night on two security cameras near the city centre. One had originally been directed towards public buildings but had been dislodged and covered ground deep in the interstices between buildings.

It showed a group of small, strangely dressed people and brief action around one of them.

'We have enhanced this footage. It shows an individual, a hydden as I prefer to call him, being kicked and beaten . . .'

They watched the sickening footage.

When it was ended, Bohr simply said, 'A positive identification has been made – by me. That's my former professor. That's Arthur Foale.'

The second lot of clips were night-vision shots of a railway terminal and a train jolting about and nearly derailing.

'Now watch what took place seconds before . . .'

Two hydden were seen placing an obstruction on the line, which clearly caused the incident.

'Now watch the aftermath . . .' said Bohr quietly.

The next clip showed bodies and parts of bodies spewing out from beneath the train as it ground to a halt after being derailed.

'And these clips as well . . .'

Footage from security cameras located at different positions all over central Birmingham followed. The clips showed a maelstrom of fighting, destruction of property and death.

'We are looking at a war zone,' said Bohr, 'right in the heart of Birmingham, which we humans did not even know existed until now.'

'How do we know Foale's still alive, sir?' someone asked.

'We don't,' said Bohr.

'But sure as hell we intend to find out,' added Reece. 'Foale is an asset we need and we'll do what it takes to get him back.'

He turned to Bohr.

'Agreed?'

Bohr nodded but said nothing, nothing at all. If Arthur was dead then all kinds of disasters might be waiting to happen.

'To work,' said Reece to his people.

'To work,' echoed Bohr to himself.

22

WOOLSTONE

The Vale of the White Horse, to which Jack was now returning, was one of the most verdant and beautiful in all of Englalond. It was fifteen miles wide from the Cotswold Hills in the north to the scarp face of the steep chalk hills of Marlborough Downs in the south. The River Thames rises between these two ranges, its source being near Cheltenham, from where it meanders eastward for nearly forty miles before entering the flatter landscape of Oxfordshire and flowing on to London and thence out into the North Sea. The Vale is an area of ancient villages and old churches, of pastures and stone-built granaries, of medieval fisheries and modern gravel pits.

The oldest of the early settlements in and about the Vale lay up on the chalk downlands to the south, which were drier, safer and easiest to clear of forest and shrub by early mortal life, be it human or hydden. Humans have forgotten that part of their history but the hydden version is recoverable in the proto-runic script of indigenous antler folk and the surviving oral traditions of green road and campfire. These leave no doubt that, at that distant time, before blessed Beornamund's day, hydden lived alongside humans in harmony right across the Downs. They helped each other build the roundhouse settlements, henges, the old ways, farm terraces and the first defensive forts, of which many traces survive. Some of these sites remain and are rather more than traces, as hydden who visit the stone circles of Stonehenge and Avebury know well, for their power and majesty are a continuing testimony to the spirit and faith in Earth and Cosmos.

But it is the White Horse itself, which still gives its name to the great

Vale before it, which is the greatest testimony of all. Sitting as it does above the spring-line villages of Uffington and Woolstone, carved in a place where the chalk forms a veritable wall, hydden remember well its origin, of which humans have no idea.

It is said that strife had broken out between the humans and hydden living together on the downland. Wishing to avoid division and war, the ealdors of both communities set their weapons aside and gathered at a location very near the highest point of what is now called Uffington Hill. It had been a hard winter and the folk living in those parts wished to put their differences behind them, so that the start of a new spring might be an auspicious one. But, though their fires burnt late night after night, no resolution was found. Then, as darkness fell on the last day of February, which is the end of winter, and all hope seemed gone, a light was seen approaching across the Vale below. The nearer it got the brighter it seemed, as if it had about it something of the Fires of the Universe.

The bearer of the light rode a great white horse but whether he or she was human or hydden, adult or child, none could tell. They watched in awe as the bearer dismounted and thrust the torch in the ground behind the horse so that its shadow was cast across the face of the hill where the mortals stood. It played over the steep sward, sinewy and strange, shifting with the breeze such that it looked as if its legs were stretched back and fore in a gallop and its head and single eye knew what they were about and where they were going.

The ealdors began to argue again among themselves, this time about the meaning of the great shadow that played at their feet. Until one came among them who they had not seen before. Without a single word he took up a piece of flint and began to cut the shallow sward so that the shadow outlines of the horse might be revealed by the chalk beneath. Soon others joined their labour to his until all were working in harmony once more.

It is said that they began the hindquarters of the White Horse in winter and finished the front quarters in spring and that the head and finally the eye were cut into the chalk as the sun rose.

When they looked up from their finished work they saw the white horse and its rider had gone with the light of day. So too had the one who began carving the horse.

When someone asked, 'Who were they?' no one knew.

'But they were wise,' they said, 'wiser than us all for they brought harmony and shared purpose back into our lives.'

It was at this spot, this place of legend, which Jack knew well, that Judith and the White Horse, having picked him up along the Ridgeway after his departure from Maldon, now dumped him unceremoniously, as if he should have known he had to go there all along.

There was no explanation, nor any farewell.

One moment he was flying through the air, holding on to Judith's waist for all he was worth, the next she heaved him off onto the grass below right on the edge of the escarpment itself.

He stood up cautiously.

Take a wrong step and fall forwards just there and a hydden, or a human, might tumble three hundred feet to the ancient farmlands far below.

Fall back and the thick sward embraces a traveller, cushioning him so comfortably that it seems the best and only way to take in the great wide expanse of the sky above. Nothing much darkens that vast space in the day, but for skylarks in summer and wandering rooks in winter.

But at night, lying in the grass when the cloud cover is thin or non-existent, there are too many stars to count, too much of a moon not to feel awe, too much of a depth and wonder to things not to believe that the Mirror-of-All and the White Horse exist.

Jack lay there in the night, icy wind whispering in the cold grass at his ears, Judith's laughter disappearing with the soft drum of the Horse's hoofs into the night sky above. He lay there awhile, not cold, not yet, though he knew that would come soon enough if he stayed too long.

He remembered the time he lay with Katherine on the same spot. He remembered her kisses and her hands to his neck and face and, with a smile, the taste of dry grass and earth in his mouth as they pleasured each other with all the urgent passion of youth, as if nothing else mattered, which it did not.

He sat up, suffused with the warmth of the memory, and stared down at the Vale. It was shocking for the lifeless, pitch-black spread it made beneath him. Not a light in sight. He looked at his feet, or tried to, but he could barely see them.

No matter, he knew the ways off the hill like the back of his hand, even in that dark. He knew them by the sound of the wind along the lynchets below, and in the trees at the bottom of their old garden half a mile away, and the hiss of the breeze up the steep Iron Age earthworks to Uffington Fort behind.

But Jack was not so sure where to find his 'sac and stave, which, disobligingly, Judith had dumped some way off. Her dogs and their riders, the Reivers, had worried at them for a time, mock-killing them, until his stave, growing weary with their futile play, hardened its heart, blunted their teeth, whirled about above their heads and thwacked them one by one, the whole lot of them and sent them packing after Judith like the curs they were.

His stave, taking pity on him, looped itself through the strap of his far-off 'sac and portered it right to his hand and let him heave it on before, rushing high up into the sky, it whirred back down, fearsome of sound, and he caught it in his outstretched hand, blindly, it being too dark to see.

He set off downslope, happy to be home, there being nowhere else in the world other than Woolstone that came near to having that name and meaning for him. The scarp face was steep and slippery and he tumbled a few times, cracked his head on the road halfway down, swore, somersaulted in the air at the next steep bit, used his stave to break his fall and bring him upright until he arrived by the fence at the foot of the garden of Woolstone House.

He ducked under it and a short while later reached the safe sanctuary of the henge Arthur had begun to make fifty years before. He had just decided that he might as well sleep right where he was and explore the house and garden in the morning when he realized he was not alone.

A human was standing in the dark, on round the henge, no more than twenty feet from him. Jack pulled back further into the night-shadow of the tree from which he had nearly emerged before he turned his head to stare. The figure was standing by a tree as he was, for the same reason, which was that trees are safe havens for the wary.

Jack could smell him, the sharp, acidic scent of garb washed in detergent. A scent, not an odour, but not quite pleasant. Jack relaxed and took in the human's other scents. Oil, very slight, no more than the wraith of a smell in the air which he recognized. It was waterproofing used on boots.

The figure moved, very slightly, and Jack was able to see that he had raised a weapon to take aim towards something in the garden. He was looking through what Jack guessed was a night 'scope on the barrel. Whatever he was aiming at was obscured by a tree.

There was the short phut! of a silencer and moments later a form arced backwards into Jack's line of sight and fell onto the grass. The weapon had an infra-red beam and this now caught the two eyes of the creature the man had shot. It was a fox and it stared unblinking and unmoving, helpless, its body broken underneath.

Now, dying, terrified, the fox stared at the human until, slowly, one eye began to dim in the red light, to dim with the coming of death.

The soldier fired a second time and the fox's head exploded in the dark, its mass scattering away into the night.

'Bastard,' said the human.

Yes, bastard, Jack murmured to himself, disgusted and grieving. But he stilled an impulse to retaliate on behalf of the fox. Rolling his back round the tree trunk and away, his movements slow as a snail's, retreating inside his own form so there was no lateral or vertical movement away from the shape he already was from the other's viewpoint. Just a retreat, a diminishing and finally a waiting until the human went back up to the house.

Jack eased around the trees he knew so well, scenting where he had to, staring where he could. Briefly his body aligned itself with the trees to dexter of the physical entry to the henge, which was formed by two great conifers, from which began the portal 'dance', as Arthur and Stort had sometimes called it: the subtle dance by which hydden and humans, if they knew what they were about, could weave the lines of power into a portal and move between the realms. He had not thought to move into the human realm and did not now, but the feeling of being but a few steps of mind and body from his other, bigger self made him feel nostalgic.

He moved on, spotted several guards and decided to leave further exploration until the next day. He left the garden to sleep in another down the lane. It would be safer there.

He woke after dawn but before the sunrise, stretching where he lay;

listening; feeling the wind and light rain flurry about him while he tried to locate any guards nearby by sound.

He sat up, drank water, chewed brot and pondered what else he had found out the night before. In addition to the guards he had found some CCTV cameras, which were inadequate to cover such a place. There would be more. And dogs probably, which hydden never like, since they can scent and hear and sense what humans cannot.

He hid his 'sac but took his stave and did again what he had done the night before. Four humans outside now, more inside. Eight cameras found so far and probably more among the trees. No dogs.

The house was a great pile of a building, built around a very ancient structure, a pilgrim hospice, Arthur claimed, whose three remaining arches were internal now. From the outside it was unkempt Victorian, with heavy casement windows on the ground floor and a red-tiled roof, that was always too expensive for the Foales to repair and for Margaret's parents before that, when the last servant died, who was never replaced. An Edwardian conservatory was added with some legacy money, and a patio and dressed stone steps as well, but these were cracked now and so full of thick invasive weeds that they were unrecoverable.

At the front, which always felt like the rear to Jack, because the family had spent most of their time in the conservatory and garden, the door and its steps were hemmed in by the lane a few yards away. It was occupied now by a US airbase truck, from which cables ran into the house, the open front door being guarded, the perimeter patrolled.

The day was dull and wet, which made things easy for Jack. The human hyddening skills were so poor and Jack's so practised that he barely thought about what he was doing. It was, almost literally, a walk in the park, dancing along with the welcome movement of the shrub- bery, sliding with the infinite shift of subtle shadow and exploiting the light between the trees, whose brightness a hydden knew how to use.

Jack stood studying the different elevations of a house he loved, all the richer in memory for knowing that Margaret and Arthur Foale would never now return. Nor would Katherine and he, probably, not to live. The world had changed and it felt as if time had passed the old place by.

The rain eased and the wind freshened and he heard the sound of the Chimes, the strange shards of crystal and glass that hung in their tens and maybe hundreds in the shrubbery down by the tree henge. It was there that Arthur used to sit and watch his tomatoes grow, as he liked to put it.

'Should be in the kitchen garden!' Margaret used to complain.

But Arthur ignored that, sitting with a drink, enjoying the sharp smell of the leaves and ripening fruit, popping them into his mouth and, for the short period she was young enough, into Judith's too. The Chimes never stopped making their sound, whether loud, or soft, and they did so now. There was a wealth of meaning in the music they made and now . . . Jack stilled, heart racing. Now they were sounding a warning, an urgent one.

He retreated into the kitchen garden and from there to the shrubberies, the Chimes nearby to his right, the dead fox's congealed and shattered body obscene upon the lawn. He moved on by it, his sense of outrage at such gratuitous destructiveness still strong, and went on past the henge to the area of copse beyond.

He saw something more.

It was a muntjac, unnaturally curled up on the edge of the lawn. Its odour was of death but not yet decay. He went closer and saw that its legs were tangled in the fine, nearly invisible mesh of a net. There was no damage to its body and where its brown-grey fur poked through the net the breeze caught it and it trembled as if alive.

Jack felt his stave tremble in his right hand too, a warning that something was wrong. He froze and began easing himself into deep shadow.

Phut!

The soft sound came from the shadow of the nearest tree and as he heard it his stave shot away from him. Only as he felt himself struggle and fall did he realize he had triggered a new trap meant for an animal. It enclosed him at once, sticky and elastic, tightening as he struggled.

He stilled, his face into the ground and his vision confined to just a close-up, angled view of it. Then he caught the same odour of waterproofing on leather as he had the night before. Stupid. A booted foot, a hand and a human voice.

'What the *hell* are you?'

He felt himself bodily picked up, the world swinging round, and then he heard a shout.

'Shit,' said the man.

Jack felt himself tossed into the darkness of the undergrowth and heard the man say, 'Later!'

He lay still and immobile, knowing without trying that there was no way he was going to be able to free himself and that in this situation his stave was not going to be able to help except as back-up if he could find his way out of the mess into which he had got himself. He swore, unreservedly, inside his head, words of the kind he would not dream of speaking aloud.

Eventually he did say something, though it was mumbled, since his face was flattened by the netting, just like the rest of him.

'Stupid!' he mumbled. 'Very, very, stupid!'

He heard a clatter and that, at least, offered a measure of reassurance. His stave had reacted faster than he had, twisted free of the net and had fled to the darkness of the trees. It now lay where it fell, its ancient carvings catching the light of day, and later that of night, awaiting a command from its master.

Only later did Jack roll over, which was all he could do, catch the glimmer of his waiting stave, and whisper, 'Help!'

The word tumbled through the vegetation, found the stave, made its way into its dark, reflective carvings, where it reverberated softly.

'Help!' said Jack again, more loudly this time. '*Help!*'

The stave heard it, considered it and transformed it in its ancient depths to something new, something urgent. Dark and desperate shards of light appeared, multiplying all the time until they sped out in their thousands, spiralling forth like a vast flock of starlings through the tree canopy above and out into the Hyddenworld beyond.

23

ON TO STANTON DREW

It was very obvious to Katherine and the others as they followed the Poldyfolk up Brent Knoll to rescue their brethren atop the hill, that they had no clear plan of action, knowledge of tactics or any conception that in Slaeke Sinistral and Niklas Blut they had among their number two of the foremost exponents of modern Imperial warfare.

Seeing which, and aware of the chaos that was likely to ensue following the unruly charge up the Knoll towards the humans laying siege to it, Katherine made sure that the elderly Sinistral was well protected and far from the action.

The truth was that the threat to the Bilgesnipe on the Knoll was more imagined than real. When the Poldyfolk charged the scattering of ill-disciplined humans they upped and fled around the sides of the Knoll and thence towards the distant shoreline to the west. There was a token resistance and a noisy, flamboyant second charge. A few minor injuries were sustained on both sides, Arnold was conspicuous by the lead he gave the others and his dreamygirl by the oaths she hurled after the fugitive humans.

'There is no need for us to linger,' said Barklice, 'and I have no intention of climbing this steep hill for a Bilgesnipe celebration that is likely to go on for several days!'

That much agreed, and Arnold left behind to cement his relationship with his future in-laws ahead of a spousal that must surely take place in Brum in the near future, they determined to journey on that same day, using one of the many abandoned army vehicles they found to do so.

They were happy to let Katherine drive and she to drive them, at least initially for that day and the next.

But it was not long before she needed a rest and decided that someone else could help with the driving.

'My Lord Blut,' said Katherine very suddenly and rather formally, 'I think it's time *you* learned to drive.'

'Me?' he replied, visibly alarmed. 'But I have never touched a human machine in my life nor ever desired to! Especially one which moves!'

But no wonder Katherine was tired. Their progress up the motorway had been slow, principally because Katherine had to pick her way through innumerable abandoned vehicles. It had been cautious too, for there was much evidence of violence and brutality on the road and not far off it, and the first sightings of humans in daylight.

From the way these people wandered unseeing in nearby urban gardens and along railway lines, or squatted by fences in lanes, it was plain that they posed no great threat to a moving vehicle. Indeed, more often than not the sight and sound of their approach sent these vagrants scurrying away to hide themselves.

It was now a frightened, beaten kind of human world they were travelling into, and the motorway, raised above the landscape or separated by barriers, embankments, concrete bridges and high fences, gave them a welcome feeling of security.

'How far before the next exit, Terce?'

She had thought at first that Blut would be the best of them at navigating with the road atlas they found in the vehicle, but his sight was against it. He could see the road ahead clearly enough, and read the signs, but close map work needed him to remove his spectacles and then to adjust his eyes to the small print. Added to which, his spatial awareness was not good.

But Terce, whose sight was perfect and who was used to reading musical notation at the same time as following his Kappelmeister's conducting, took to navigation easily. Or rather, enjoyed sitting in the front seat, with Blut next to him, pointing out such features and names of places as the atlas showed and their view allowed.

So when Katherine asked him about the next exit his reply was prompt.

'Half a mile,' he said, 'and I believe I can already see the sign with three white lines which is indicative of the approach of an exit.'

'Where does it go to?'

'Bath,' sang out Barklice, whose methods of route-finding were entirely different and more intuitive than humans ones.

'That's right,' concurred Terce.

Katherine's earlier request that Blut might drive had pricked the bubble of easy comfort and complacency that had overtaken the group for the past hour and a half. Within a few minutes of climbing aboard another vehicle they seemed to have forgotten the hardships and realities of pedestrian travel and begun to believe that all they had to do was to sit back and idly watch the road go by. Then, without further effort or thought, they would soon be safely back in Brum.

As they approached the first exit warning Katherine slowed right down. The road was a mess of crashed vehicles and the barriers along the central reservation had been flattened.

Katherine was suddenly forced to brake sharply. Two hundred yards ahead the motorway was blocked by two trucks on their sides and burnt-out vehicles in front. It looked like some kind of deliberate barrier. They had stopped just before the stippled line marking the start of the slip road off the motorway.

A human appeared ahead, next to the roadblock, staring and apparently surprised.

'He was not expecting us,' said Blut.

Another human appeared and they saw that both were armed.

There being no possibility of speeding past them, and since turning round was difficult with so many obstructions on the road, Katherine eased the vehicle to the left to the beginning of the slip road. It went gently upward, towards some kind of roundabout, built above the motorway to feed traffic to either side of it.

She stopped again.

'Is it blocked as well?' she asked urgently.

Terce, who had a better view, shook his head.

'One of the lanes is clear,' he said, 'but I think I can see another human.'

Katherine strained up to get a better view, looked towards the barrier again and said decisively, 'It's a trap! Hold tight!'

She crashed the gears into reverse, peered into the side mirror, and accelerated backwards. They hit vehicles, shots were fired, the noise was deafening, the jolting sudden and violent. Then, on her right-hand side, the central reservation opened up where the metal barriers had been smashed.

She pushed the gear into first, turned the wheel, revved the engine and drove the vehicle bumpety bump over the remnants of the barrier and right across the two lanes to the far side of the motorway. She accelerated forward, forced a crashed vehicle out of the way and drove up the other slip road, the one intended for vehicles coming down from the roundabout above.

Up it they went, the road that side unobstructed but for a solitary human guard, who ran out and then dived sideways to avoid being hit. At the top Katherine turned right into what would normally have been oncoming traffic and jolted away down the road to Bath, finally regaining the correct side of the road a few hundred yards later.

Soon the houses gave way to countryside, Katherine slowed, breathing heavily, and they trundled along at a slower pace once more.

Then, the strangest of things, a snow-white bird, starling-like, fluttered against the windscreen, its black shining eyes briefly peering in before it recovered itself, ducked and weaved away ahead of them and was joined by a few others which twisted and turned together before disappearing west into the mottled grey sky.

Katherine was so shaken by this, for reasons she could not understand, that she stopped the vehicle the moment they next crested a hill, to give themselves a view in all directions and herself a break.

'Do you know where the nearest henge is to where we now are?' she asked Barklice. 'I mean, is it *close*, because for some reason I feel it might be.'

She barely gave him time to think before adding impatiently, '*Well?*'

This might normally have seemed a very odd thing to ask but ever since she began driving that day, perhaps even before, Katherine had been restless and slightly irritable. She had kept glancing from one side of the road to the other as if on the lookout for something specific; she ignored questions; and, as now, having asked one of her own, she expected an instant reply.

Stort, who had been somnolent, stirred and peered expectantly at

Barklice and raised his eyebrows. Barklice looked at him, nodding slightly.

'Let me see, we're on the Bath road,' he said quietly. 'Then I suppose the nearest henge would be Stanton Drew, eh, Stort?'

'I concur,' murmured Stort.

Slaeke Sinistral, also slumbering as it had seemed, opened his eyes, suddenly alert. He too seemed to have something on his mind.

'How far off is it?' asked Katherine,

'Ten miles ahead or so,' said Barklice, 'more or less.'

'Terce, can you see it on the map?'

After a short pause he nodded and, using his fingers to measure distance, announced, 'It's less than ten miles.'

This seemed to satisfy her and she fell silent once more, enjoying the quiet and stillness, as they all were. The sky above was pale blue, the air very chill, the northern sky a rolling, broiling, pink-grey. The slight north wind was bitter to the taste and the trees of hedge and copse leafless and still. Such vegetation as there was beneath them was drooped and slightly frosted.

Their breath condensed in the cold air and they pulled their jerkins tighter and got out their jackets. But it was good to feel the ground again and stretch.

'It looks like snow is on the way,' said Barklice, eyeing the sky.

Katherine ignored him, pacing about, as unhappy as they had seen her.

She turned to Stort and said abruptly, 'I have been oppressed by a general feeling of unease . . . and that white bird . . .'

'Tell me how you feel,' said Sinistral.

'As if . . . as if I am standing by a river into which I should put myself.'

'But you don't want to?'

'The feeling hasn't been strong enough until now and anyway we are heading for Brum and not where that river might have taken me . . .'

'And that seemed . . . ?'

'Brum seemed more important. But . . . earlier . . . I mean on the road this morning . . .'

'At about the time we said farewell to the Poldyfolk and took this vehicle?'

She looked surprised.

'How did you know it was then?'

Sinistral raised a hand as if to say that he would explain in a moment and said softly, 'Please . . . please continue.'

'I felt on Bodmin what I feel even more strongly now that . . . that . . .' But she shook her head and frowned, unable to put into words what it was she had felt.

'You felt something was wrong?'

She shook her head.

'No, I felt that flow again, the same as up on the moor, but stronger.'

'A compulsion?' suggested Stort, glancing at Sinistral.

'Yes.'

'About . . . ?'

Again, the hesitation. Then: 'You're trying to get me to say it. You both are. And I don't want to.'

'Are we?' said Sinistral matter-of-factly.

'If I do it might come true . . .'

'What might?'

'Whatever it is,' she said feebly.

'But then again,' said Stort, suddenly impatient, 'if you don't say it, *whatever it is*, it might *also* come true. Katherine, we cannot use the power of the henge, not accurately, unless the person most affected knows and says what they are affected by. Otherwise we could end up anywhere at any time as I tried to explain when we were at the Stripple Stones.'

'Who's talking about using the henges?' called out Barklice, uneasily. He did not like this kind of talk. That way lay all kinds of uncertainty and danger. Dancing the henge portals was a lost art only recovered in recent years by Arthur Foale in the human world and Bedwyn Stort for the hydden. Katherine and Jack had learnt the art but it was not a thing to be lightly used. So the idea of the whole lot of them dancing about a henge trying to turn it into a portal to satisfy a craving Katherine suddenly felt filled Barklice with apprehension.

But it was not in Stort's impulsive nature to be cautious about such things. 'Who is talking about the portals, my dear fellow?' he asked rhetorically. 'Well, Katherine is! *Obviously.*' In fact it was not obvious to her, nor anyone else there except perhaps Sinistral. 'So? *Well?*'

persisted Stort, now almost hopping about with that special impatience he felt when others seemed not to see what was very obvious to him. 'What was the compulsion you felt about? Say it, for Mirror's sake, and then we can get on our way and sort it out.'

Katherine stared at him belligerently.

'You know what it is!'

'Do I?' said Stort ingenuously.

'Yes, you damn well do. It's *Jack*, he's in some kind of trouble . . .'

The sky darkened, the clouds broiled and up there, high against them, the shining white birds which had been one, and then become a few, now burgeoned to thousands, high and far away, wheeling and turning, fluttering and shining, across the sky ahead of them. But Katherine was barely looking, lost as she was in her own discomfort and unease.

'I've been feeling worse and worse about it all morning and I'm sure . . . that . . . we . . . should try to go and help Jack as quickly as we can.'

'Thank you!' cried Stort, 'we have finally got there! You mean, I take it, that we will attempt to use the portal of Stanton Drew to find our way to Jack?'

'Yes,' said Katherine, 'I suppose I do.'

'Excellent!' said Stort. 'My Lord Blut, you'll now be driving, I believe. Good luck with that! Terce, you're still navigating. Destination? The stone circles, plural, of Stanton Drew. The party travelling? Katherine and myself. The party continuing on to Brum? Mister Barklice, my Lords Blut and Sinistral and Festoon and Terce. Any questions? No . . . ?'

There were several but Stort ignored them, trying instead to hurry them, protesting, back into the vehicle.

But Sinistral did not move.

'I too have felt what Katherine has called the flow, the need, the call to travel by way of the stones. I am therefore coming with *you*, Mister Stort . . .'

'But my Lord . . .' protested Blut.

'That would be very unwise . . .' said Barklice.

Slaeke Sinistral shrugged. 'I appreciate your concern but Katherine has put it more elegantly than I. I, like her, feel a need.'

'To help Jack?' she said.

'I think that may be it. So that is how it will be, eh, Mister Stort?'

The light of excitement was in Sinistral's old, wise eyes.

'Agreed,' said Stort.

'But I . . . *my Lord*!' Blut tried to say once more.

'I am retired, Blut, and I think I may choose to do what I want and go where I wish!'

The decision was made, and Katherine, purposeful and happy once more, told the startled and wrong-footed Blut, 'Get in and drive, my Lord, you might actually enjoy it!'

Blut started badly, finding the gears had an irritable mind of their own and that controlling the acceleration was nearly impossible. But, after crashing the gears many times, braking too abruptly almost as often, running off the road twice and rolling into a barrier once, he began to get the hang of it. His shaken passengers were greatly relieved when his driving finally settled down to something nearly comfortable. Not long after that, and aided by Terce calling out which way to turn so well that he might almost have been to Stanton Drew before, they all began to relax and enjoy the journey.

The last few miles were by a steep and twisting road and Katherine was right: Blut began to enjoy driving. By the time they reached the village that had given its name to the stones he had gained such confidence that he was almost slap-happy at the wheel, skidding finally to a pleasing stop with a cry of satisfaction.

The stone circles, of which there were three close together, were easy to find: they were near a square-towered church, and human notices pointed out the lane that led to them. They, like the village itself, were deserted. The afternoon was drawing in and the temperature dropping fast. Ice crystals had begun to form on fallen leaves along the wires of the fences.

'It would be as well,' said Katherine, looking at the threatening sky, 'for you others to get back to the main road.'

'It's only two miles,' said Terce, 'if we continue the way we were going. The A37 north.'

'But . . .' said Blut, speaking for them all.

'But nothing,' said Katherine. 'If you can drive eight miles as well as you just have, you can drive eighty without mishap. Terce is now a master at reading a map and Mister Barklice will keep an eye on your general safety.'

A fleck of snow drifted down among them, and then another.

'Off you go!' ordered Katherine. 'You have work to do and so do we . . .'

Without saying more, she led Sinistral and Stort towards the stone circles. The largest and easiest to see was nearest them. The others were across the field and from their low viewpoint one merged into the other.

'Which one, Stort?' she asked, walking into the first and at once feeling their good power all about her.

'This is your journey, your need,' said Stort softly, also as happy as he had been for weeks. 'Simply ask yourself where you wish to be, and walk or dance the portal into life in the way Arthur taught you.'

'Dance,' she whispered, 'dance for Jack, feel his need, know his call, turn dexter towards him . . .'

She reached her hand to Stort and he took it in his and then he took Slaeke Sinistral's as they turned and turned, from one henge to another, the stones beginning to encircle them, to dance them, to welcome them in.

While out of the village and up on the road, Barklice put a hand on Blut's arms and said, 'Slow, just for a moment, slow down . . .'

Blut stopped the vehicle gently and they looked down across the fields where the circles were, all three as clear as anything from their viewpoint, and as the first snows of winter came, utterly exquisite, drifting with the last grey light of day, they saw their friends winding in among the stones with light steps, a following of trust and friendship and a swirl of shadow in the flurries all about them.

'See!' whispered Barklice as they saw ten hundred thousand tiny white flakes turn and turn within themselves, weaving and interweaving like the starlings, or reflective shards perhaps, they had seemed to see before, weaving the flow of life itself.

Then their myriad mirror wings stopped as one, still in the air, no movement at all, a cessation of everything.

How long did it last? No time at all perhaps, or maybe an eternity.

When they looked again the stones of the circles across the whitened fields below were covered in snow and their friends were seen no more.

24

DANCING MASTER

Erich Bohr's instinct when he arrived at RAF Croughton was to travel the forty miles to Woolstone early the next morning and immediately examine Arthur Foale's house and garden. But he held himself back, knowing there were things he could do better at the airbase, starting with some desk research.

If he had not already been to the house it might have been different. But there had been social visits over the years when he was working in England and he had been to Woolstone only three months before, after Arthur fled from Croughton into the Hyddenworld. At the time Bohr had hoped that all Arthur had wanted was to get home. Bohr could have understood that. Maybe they had been heavy-handed dragging him off to an airbase; maybe they should do things differently.

It wasn't to be.

Arthur wasn't home and he had not been seen again and Bohr was sure he was not in the human world as humans knew it. The security footage of Arthur Foale showed him 'dancing' in the henge adjacent to RAF Croughton. If only they could work out from that exactly what he had been doing and why, then they might have had a basis for going forward with their own research. What irritated Bohr so much was that, if they had had another day or two with him, they could have got what they needed to know out of him and no harm done.

No harm done.

Bohr wanted to believe that but the more time he spent in the presence of Colonel Reece, the more he began to doubt it. Highly decorated he might be but he was rigid, unsmiling and vengeful towards the 'enemy' in a way that boded ill for a mission that might need some delicate handling.

I shall see that no harm is done . . . Bohr told himself, hopefully.

The immediate need was to go through any new Arthur Foale material that his researchers had found at the house and brought on to Croughton for analysis. In addition there was a collection of photos, some digital, but most old fashioned prints, which had been collated and, as far as possible, set up in chronological order ready for Bohr to examine. There might be a clue somewhere there about how to follow Arthur's footsteps into a henge and beyond it.

There were a few old Kodak snaps taken just before the war, and some prints taken with a better camera after 1945. There were images taken by Arthur's former students, and a surprising quantity of group shots taken at the many international academic conferences he had attended, including some of Bohr as well.

In more recent times there were images of Foale's adoptive daughter Katherine, her chronically ill mother Clare, and a family friend called Jack. In normal circumstances Bohr's people could have learnt a lot more about some of these images and the people in them but the recent collapse of the UK infrastructure, the failure of the internet, the breakdown of society and, as US intelligence had reported, the covert devolution of power to a government that had moved to Newcastle, had made that kind of research nearly impossible.

As with most collections of personal photos Bohr found there were more of some subjects and some periods than others. Arthur's early life was poorly represented, as were the later, academic years, except for the formal photos. Most of the images were obviously irrelevant to his research but Bohr, like any former student, had a natural curiosity about his professor. He was fascinated by the images of Arthur's wedding to Margaret in the late forties. It was over-represented with posed group monochrome shots but interesting all the same: very charming and bucolic with dancing on a temporary stage set up in the garden in Woolstone, with the guests dressed in eighteenth-century costume. It seemed that when they were younger, Arthur and Margaret had a shared interest in dancing of that time and formed a university society to revive lost dances of the period. Bohr dallied too long with these images, deciding finally that maybe there were some things that former students did not need to know about their teachers. He consigned the wedding and the dancers back to their buff envelopes.

Bohr had hoped that Arthur had carried a camera into the Hyddenworld and kept a record, as an anthropologist might, but in that he was disappointed. There was nothing at all.

Turning from these images, Bohr began going through the mountain of recent geophysical and cosmological 'disaster' data already collated and catalogued by his people, comparing it with Arthur's notes and papers in that period. Again, nothing. It seemed that Arthur had lost interest in his subject when he retired.

Meanwhile, over this same intensive period of two days, Colonel Reece assessed and re-assigned what he called his personnel and military assets. He rarely used the word 'our', though the mission was meant to be shared. He sent some of his people on ahead to Woolstone, to liaise with the limited security already placed there by Bohr himself weeks earlier and established a field command centre. He reported at once that he was not impressed with what he found.

'Lax, undisciplined idiots,' he called them. He had neither command nor jurisdiction over them but that did not worry him.

'I'm dumping 'em,' he pronounced after twenty-four hours.

For the time being he was focusing on improving covert surveillance in Birmingham, where the last known sighting of Foale had been made. Satellite and airborne facilities had been so degraded by recent global events that a group of Reece's operatives were dropped at Birmingham on the second night after their arrival, tasked with securing a second field centre, making a rapid survey and sending situation reports.

'We are not at war,' Bohr said.

'I wouldn't call this being at peace!' responded Reece.

It had become horribly clear to Bohr that Reece had attitudinal problems. He could not hold the man's personal appearance against him, but his belligerent face, which was badly scarred by a wound above the right eye, now slightly sunken, made him unappealing. He was full of a barely controlled anger, which in combat situations might have its uses, but for a delicate operation of the kind they were engaged in Bohr was sure he was the wrong person.

After two days Reece's work was done, Bohr's nearly so.

Arthur's handwritten working notes and computer files were untidy, inconsistent and voluminous, and they too did not yield anything of interest. His considerable working library, covering a wide range of interrelated archaeological, astronomical and cosmological subjects, remained in situ in the house, as Arthur had left it. The books had been gone through, listed in their entirety and replaced as found.

Again, Bohr found plenty that gave him a handle on Arthur and his renaissance character and interests but nothing, or almost nothing, about the Hyddenworld or how to get into it. It was all too apparent from the gaps in the papers, especially in the recent years when Bohr was sure he had been researching the Hyddenworld and possibly visiting it, that Arthur had systematically destroyed his own material to leave no clues. But Bohr knew that few people can excise everything that matters most from their lives. They cannot help but leave tiny clues.

One such was the plan of the tree henge at Woolstone, drawn to scale and with the Linnaean names of the different trees given. There were lines in pencil between the trees marked on it, some rubbed out as if Arthur was trying different things. Also the very odd sentence Bohr found written on the plan, in Arthur's familiar handwriting: *Charles Haddon attacked Charlotte on the north north east.*

Bohr knew both the people mentioned, one of them being a Cambridge contemporary of his, and the other, probably, being Charlotte Soutier, who had worked with Arthur on various pieces of research. Was it a clue? Maybe.

Reece appeared on the afternoon of the third day to announce that the live cameras were now all up and running at Woolstone, inside and out, every corner of the property covered. The place was being monitored 24/7.

'In case there are intruders, or visitors, whether human or . . .' Reece smiled dismissively, he had yet to be convinced, 'er, hydden. Let me show you.'

They sat down in one of the base's communication rooms to look at a big screen linked to Woolstone.

'We see things differently this way than on the ground,' said Reece. 'The facility includes head cameras used by the patrols. If it moves we'll pick it up.'

They worked through some of the cameras, room by room, starting with the outside of the building and then in through the front door.

'Untidy place,' said Reece.

'Always was,' said Bohr. 'Arthur needed what he called a "creative mess" to function. Margaret . . .'

'Margaret?'

'His wife. Deceased a few months ago. Margaret wasn't much better. They worked facing each other in the library . . . his desk, her desk. His books and hers.'

'Sweet,' said Reece.

There were three cameras in the library. Bohr stared at images of shelves, books, desks, waste bins, computers and chairs. There was not much else.

'Found anything?' wondered Reece.

Bohr shook his head.

'And in that material you've been through?'

'He sanitized the lot,' he said.

'Books are hell,' said Reece. 'Too many of 'em, too many pages, too damn obvious. You checked them out?'

'My people have been through them,' said Bohr. 'I ordered them to after Professor Foale disappeared.'

'Just checking,' said Reece. 'No offence, but your guys were local.'

'Were?'

'We took full command this afternoon. Left them to guarding duties. Back-up to our technology.'

'Like these cameras?'

'They work continuously and detect movement, heat, change. Men can't do that, not all of it – and there are always lapses in concentration . . .'

Bohr shrugged. He was content to leave the practicalities to Reece so he was free to focus on the other stuff, whatever that was. As of now he had no idea.

They moved with the cameras down a corridor to a scullery, then the kitchen, a lower store area with the ancient arches of which Arthur was proud, and finally the dilapidated conservatory. All in colour and sound.

One of the men on the stairs saw the camera move at Reece's distant touch, and saluted.

'First floor?'

They did a virtual tour upstairs, turning this way and that.

One of the corridors showed an untidy pile of dirty washing.

'Marines!' grunted Bohr.

'Your lot,' responded Reece, meaning the personnel put in place immediately after Arthur's disappearance. 'Mine are better disciplined.'

It was a huge house in which almost anything might be hidden anywhere. But Bohr knew that Arthur didn't work that way. If there were clues to find they would be in a logical place – but what? And where?

They continued their virtual tour into the garden.

'What the hell's that?' said Bohr, pointing at what seemed interference on the screen. Thousands of randomly moving white dots were obscuring the image. 'Birds?'

'Snow,' said Reece, tracking the camera back to focus on two large conifers in the distance, the rough lawn in between and the snow.

'Just flurries. The worst is yet to come according to the Army forecasters. They're doing it the old-fashioned way, by calculation. A lot of the relevant satellites are down.'

'Jesus,' said Bohr. 'We're running out of time. We're done here. Time to get to Woolstone. I've ordered a car.'

He said it wryly, without much hope Reece would buy it. He fancied forty miles of gentle English countryside.

'That's a no-go,' said Reece predictably. 'Too dangerous. The roads are not secure. Some are blocked and there are vagrants roaming the countryside. Forget it.'

An old Huey UH-IN helicopter got them to Woolstone in just over twenty-five minutes, flying over the blocked roads, burnt-out housing and empty countryside Reece was wary of. They saw no one and little movement but for rooks and gulls circling over a reservoir and a herd of horses stampeding round a soccer pitch, as if chasing their own tails. They skirted Oxford, whose medieval towers and colleges, narrow streets and wan gardens looked like the abandoned set of a film that never got finished.

The pilot, at Bohr's request, took them along the line of the Ridgeway, hovering briefly over the White Horse before turning north towards Woolstone itself. The house was easily recognizable and, from the air, as his researcher had said, the henge was easy to see. The trees formed a circle of sorts, with two distinctly taller conifers marking an entrance facing the house itself. They landed three hundred yards away on a landing pad in another property. Reece's people had had it repainted yellow and white.

They had decided to sleep at the house, which was large enough to accommodate all of them, the patrols establishing billets on the ground floor, while Reece, Bohr and his assistant Ingrid Hansen commandeered rooms upstairs. The conservatory was converted into a command centre-cum-office and housed the computers.

Bohr left Reece to his people, to make a swift tour of the garden, starting with the henge itself.

The trees towered above him. He pulled out the plan of them Arthur had sketched long before but it looked nothing like the real thing.

'"*Charles Haddon . . .*"' he read out aloud. 'What the hell have you got to do with all this?'

The Woolstone henge was impressive and its majesty and endless wind sound high above stilled something in Bohr's soul.

'Arthur, how the hell did you work out how to use a place like this?' he muttered. 'How did you even think it could be done?'

A tinkling of sound made him go back out onto the lawn to some shrubs, where what he took to be wind bells and charms hung. Bohr remembered Margaret Foale showing him the Chimes, as she had called them. The sound, she said, never stopped. It was hypnotic and it still was, but Bohr was not yet ready to be hypnotized and he turned up towards the house.

The sight of a dead fox at his feet in the grass, head blown apart, stopped him short. He knew that kind of bullet wound when he saw one. Had one of the security personnel he had put in place or one of Reece's done it? He had no idea, but either way, not good.

The study was bigger than he remembered it and a lot bigger than it appeared on screen.

There were two desks: a big one and a bigger one. Margaret's and Arthur's faced each other with barely a gap between. Hers was turned to face the room, so she sat with her back to a big casement window.

His faced hers, with the window beyond her and the door, a big wide one, to his left, her right. Behind his chair was a wall of books, and to his left and right as well

Her library was much smaller, confined to the area between the window and the corner of the room, and then the return towards where Arthur's shelves began. Unlike Arthur's, her shelves were uniform and the books neatly ordered by subject and author. Mainly literature, most of it old – Old Norse, Old English, Old German, Icelandic – and dictionaries, a dozen of them in different languages, on different literary and etymological subjects. A few journals, but nothing recent, and some historical fiction.

It was obvious from the way the books had been put back, without being quite tidied properly, that someone had been through the lot for inserts. A few of the books in both collections were smudged grey-white with powder for finger-printing.

Right on cue Reece's forensic specialist, an ex-military policeman, whom Bohr had asked to see, appeared. He stood relaxed, as special forces often did. They were comfortable in their own bodies. Bohr never ceased to be impressed by these men and women. He had been fit himself once, but these were fitter than in his day, or more honed. They could do more too, apart from killing people with one finger and having reactions as fast as wild animals. Well, maybe.

'Sir,' he said neutrally.

'You went through them?'

The man nodded. 'We went through the lot, sir, every page of every one.'

'Hers as well?'

'Them too. Sorry, but your people missed stuff. Found receipts, a few notes, a Christmas card used as a bookmark . . .'

'Signed?'

'From her to him. It's all on her desk, along with what we found in which books.'

'And you dusted them for prints?'

The ex-MP nodded his head.

'Wanted to see who accessed which book. A library like this is old stuff, shelved and rarely looked at again. The quickest way to find out where something is hidden is with dust and infrared. We can date the access too, more or less. She accessed twelve of his, mainly journals. We marked them with small yellow stickers. He accessed a good few of hers, marked with red dot stickers. Question marks mean a long time ago. It's hard to see the stickers . . . shall I . . . ?'

Bohr shook his head. 'If something's there I'll find it,' he said.

When he was gone, Bohr began looking along Margaret's shelves at the marked books the ex-MP had mentioned. He was surprised at their number and variety. It took longer than he expected to work his way through each one, seeking for clues.

Sometimes he got diverted. One that interested him was a collection of translations of Anglo-Saxon poetry, made by Margaret herself. Touching that Arthur had looked at it. Forensics had even marked the page he had recently opened. It meant nothing to Bohr.

After a while, dispirited, he took a break.

When he came back he stumbled almost at once on a title that was promising. It was an old book, *very* old, and had been re-bound and gold-stamped with its original title, *Orchesography 1706*. The author was Anthony L'Abbé. The ex-MP had question-marked it, meaning Arthur had not accessed it in a while. It was quite thin, the pages greyish, the print old-fashioned and beautiful, and there were sketchy illustrations, each with music at the top and a title in the middle and the sketch, which was asymmetrical, around it.

It was a book of dances. Obviously the book went back to the days when Margaret and Arthur danced together. He noticed that the title of several included the word 'Chaconne' but nothing more. He closed the book and was about to put it back on the shelf when he felt a sudden chill down his spine that came with a moment of revelation.

Bohr liked crosswords and knew a mnemonic when he saw one, or rather one that had been spelt out.

Charles Haddon Attacked Charlotte On North North East.

The penny dropped.

'*Chaconne!*' he said aloud.

He opened the book again and it did not take him long to work out that a chaconne was a dance and the pages were eighteenth-century notations of different ones. Bohr's heart beat faster as he turned to the beginning of the book and began working his way through. Some of the stuck-in pages were of vintage paper, probably from another book. This was a codex, a collection. Some of the pages were modern, the dances sketched in the same form as the eighteenth-century originals. There were seventy-eight pages, consisting of twenty pages of text and fifty-eight different dances, each with a line of music and a title: 'The Favourite: A Chaconne Danced by Her Majesty', 'Galathee', 'Mistress Isabel's Chaconne'. They showed paired mirror-symmetric steps, most of them clearly beginning and ending in the same place.

But for a few, which at first glance appeared printed but, Bohr saw, were handwritten using Indian ink. Bohr's facility with numbers and patterns kicked in and he began looking for differences. For one thing these were not symmetrical and for another there was only one odd man out: this alone showed movement from the bottom of the page to the right . . .

'To the right, or dexter, as Arthur would have said,' murmured Bohr.

It showed large dots and small, unpatterned, which Bohr's mind instantly related to each other and something else he had seen that day: Arthur's sketch plan of the henge. The distribution of the big dots showed a third of the trees on the right-hand side and three to the left. Lines between them in pencil, very faint and lost among the arrows and a single bigger arrow, north. And a three-digit number.

The page showed not just any dance, it was surely *the* dance. A spiral that ceased to be a spiral; a confluence that broke into three parts; a roundel that repeated itself; a chain whose links turned over, interlocked, unravelled and finally broke free.

Bohr's ability to read music was not great but he knew enough to work out the score at the top of the page whose predominant notes were A and F. Arthur Foale.

'And the title!' Bohr exclaimed aloud, *'The Dancing Master's Favourite!'*

It was pure Arthur, simple and clever. Of course he had to leave a record. He was a scientist, an explorer, whose life work lay in things verifiable, not things forgotten. It was a record expressed in a medium of love for Margaret and himself.

Bohr felt both satisfaction and apprehension. It was one thing to explore Arthur's work, a very different thing to now embark on replicating it by actually going to the henge and trying the dance for himself.

His mobile buzzed in his pocket. It was Reece.

'Where are you?'

'In the library.'

'You better get outside. Down by the two conifers, to the left . . . I'll meet you.'

Reece was grim-faced, puzzled, alarmed. His cool seemed shattered.

'We found it by the smell.'

'The fox? I saw it earlier. I meant to . . .'

'Not the fox.'

He led Bohr past the remains on the lawn to a creature by the edge of the wood. It was tight-bound with netting and it was dead.

'What the hell's that?'

'It's what's called a muntjac. That's the smell but it's not what I wanted you to see.'

Some of Reece's other men were there, but they were standing off on the lawn, guarding the location uneasily. Odd, thought Bohr, for men as tough as them.

Reece led him into the wood away from the group. Reece pointed at something on the ground. It was strangely shadowy and hard to make out. 'Another muntjac?'

He wanted to peer closer but Reece shook his head and shone a torch. Still Bohr could not make it out. It was . . . it seemed . . . it . . .

'What is it?' he asked with a mixture of horror and bewilderment in his voice.

Then: 'Jesus, Reece, is this a *child*?'

He said it with something more than horror in his voice because it was trussed up horribly, mesh cutting into skin, fingers stuck through here and there, clothes flattened and patterned with the net, and a head and hair.

Reece shook his head.

'It's a dwarf,' he said quietly, 'a bloody dwarf.'

'Is it dead?'

Bohr moved a shade closer to get a better look.

It looked dead, very dead.

Reece kicked it, first with one boot, then another.

It was time, Jack decided, to open his eyes.

25

A WELCOME

Very wise was the Modor and very old.

Old as the Earth some said, therefore old as time.

Wizened, eaten up, lined, existing in dank shadows, dressed in Mirror-knew-what for garb, though some said – and still say – she could morph into something beautiful.

But no one living ever saw that happen, nor seemed likely to.

Age was her habitat, all bent and crooked she was, with arthritic fingers like the exposed roots of an ancient tree.

Modor was female once, but was she still? Did she have a vestige left of that soft form? She shuffled and grumbled and muttered when folk came to see her, keeping them waiting in the cold while she peered suspiciously through her bothy window, or round its rotten doorpost, peered at them and the world.

But it was worth making the effort of getting there.

The few who did didn't leave the same, but better. Once she had heaved her rackety door open and smiled her smile of welcome, they felt they'd come home at last after a long time wandering alone.

Her visitors would enter and, sitting by her fire, they wondered how her skinny arms clung on to her skewed frame and how it was that the last few of her straggly hairs managed to hang on to her scabby skull. But then she smiled and none of that mattered any more, because she made them understand what it was that really *did* matter.

'You look tired,' she would say, 'so rest a little. No need to talk, just sit and be still awhile.'

She would look into their eyes and they knew again what it felt like to be loved.

'Tell me,' she would whisper, pouring them a steamy brew of heady herbs, 'what's happening out there in the world I left behind?'

'The same as always, Modor. Nothing changes.'

'Yes it does,' she would chide them gently, 'if only you wish it so. Now, tell me, why is it you have come to see me . . . ?'

Then they would talk and she would listen so well that they knew they were heard.

At the end, when she grew tired and they knew they must leave, she would ask, 'Have you seen my consort, the Wita?'

At that they had to shake their heads, feeling it was best to say nothing. Everyone knew that the Wita was gone and not likely to come back. In all their lives they never saw him.

'Being wise,' she would say, reading their thoughts, 'and loving others does not mean you cease to yearn for another's touch. I miss him. Tell him, if you see him, it must be time he came home to me.'

The Modor's domain lay high up in the Harzgebirge of Germany, where, whatever she sometimes implied, she really did live with the Wise One, her beloved consort, the Wita. He was just errant, that was all, absent without leave, away too long, and that was why she complained about him to visitors, but most especially to those she called her friends.

One of these few, the very few, who had an affinity with her and loved her and was not afraid was the Lady Leetha, mother of Jack, and, through him, grandmother of Judith the Shield Maiden. Leetha often visited the area nearby and used, when she was younger and nimbler than when she sailed to Englalond and back, to dance all the way up through the forests to the top of the hill and say hello. But time catches up with everyone, even Leetha, who . . . who had been thinking of the Modor.

'When we get to shore, Borkum,' said Leetha very impatiently when they were three weeks out of Maldon and still not home, 'I'm not hanging round. I'm going home to Thuringia and on my way there, or shortly afterward, I'll climb up among the pines, stumble over the rocks, and take food for her who eats nearly nothing, so I can tell her my news.'

Borkum Riff scowled.

'I mean the Modor.'

Riff spat tobacco. He did not believe in such things. If that old hag was really wise she would not live up a mountain in the cold eating nothing.

The journey back to Den Helder from Maldon was not normally difficult but the recent hurricane had disturbed the currents and displaced the shingle and sandbanks all along the west European shore, from Skagerrak to Biscay. It had been a hard, long voyage since they left and *still* they had not landed.

Riff was thinking that too much of Lady Leetha at close quarters on a sailing craft might drive a hydden mad.

Leetha liked to dance, she liked to sing, she liked to laugh and she hated all that stopped her doing those things, which was confinement. Like Jack, a long spell in a boat was far too long and it made her cranky.

'Where's the shore, Riff? Where's landfall? I'm tired of ropes and sails and being damp and eating fish. I can't dance far on a boat, on *your* boat . . .'

'It's a craft, a cutter, not a boat.'

'I can't dance far on your boat without stubbing my toe and my toe is not what it was. These days it hurts and it aches. Like the Modor my toe is getting old. I miss the Modor and she misses me.'

Riff growled and said, 'We got blown off course. Deap'll tell you. Tell her again, Deap, for Mirror's sake.'

They were hove to off the shore and able to talk well enough against the wind, screwing eyes up against the cold, hands cupped to blowing mouth to keep them warm.

'Tell 'er, lad.'

'Got blown off course, Ma,' said Deap, eyes twinkling at his parents' mutual impatience. She hated the repetition, she loathed being called 'Ma', but he knew she loved the smile in his eyes and voice.

'"Blown off course", for Mirror's sake, and you two meant to be the best mariners in all the North Sea,' she said. Then she screamed, enough to make the sails shiver, and added, 'That's why you both drive me mad. I need the Modor.'

'And she needs you,' said Slew grudgingly. The old jealousy was still there but since his time aboard with Jack he had lightened up, the old anger diluted by the respect his half-brother had gained among them.

Leetha stretched her still-lithe body, her greying hair streaked and shiny with spray and foam, her skin magnificent, and said, 'So then, all that being so, since no one here will say when we get back to shore, I'll cook.'

It was a threat and they groaned.

'Jack cooked and used seaweed as a herb, which I can do. What have we to put with it?'

'Cod, skate, a pollock, a few mackerel and pouting.'

'Tope, conger and some ling,' added Deap.

'In other words, *fish*,' said Leetha acidly.

Riff growled defensively and said, 'Cows don't graze on North Sea waves. Sheep don't nibble straiths. Pigs prefer swill, not swell. So yes, Leetha, it be fish.'

Leetha laughed as only she could and, going below, called out again, 'I miss the Modor.'

After a while Riff called after her gently, in a rough voice filled with abiding love, 'We'll get you to shore just as soon as we can.'

And Deap added, 'Ma . . . we'll get you home.'

In the dark privacy of the galley, Leetha wrapped her arms around her breasts and smiled.

Above them, the wind finally shifted, they heaved in the anchor and the craft made points to north and was able at last to tack and begin the long run through the surfy shallows towards Den Helder, sending up two rockets made for the purpose by humans, to say they were safe and were finally coming home.

The Modor, stuck alone in the fastness of her retreat high up in the crystalline Harz, might have been wise, but that morning she had woken up lonely. She needed touch, if not of the Wita, who wasn't around and hadn't been in many a year, then of a mortal.

I miss Leetha, she said, smiling with pleasure at the memory of the one she loved almost more than any other, the kind of love, she was aware, she was lucky to know.

I miss . . .

She had no sooner said it the second time than thunder clattered across the snowy peaks so loud it shook the snow off the pines and conifers all around her home.

Oh, but she loved that, the powdery snow forced to fall a second time, swirling down amidst the green pine needles, turning around the thick-set trunks, settling on paths untouched for weeks by the feet of humans or hydden.

'I miss you, Leetha,' she whispered at her open door.

The thunder grew louder and the Modor went outside and waited.

The Horse's hoofs were bigger than her, and its head high in the clouds, its nostrils all flaring and steamy.

'Where is he?' she cried out. 'Where's he gone? Why's he taking so long? I *miss* him.'

For a moment the Modor truly looked her age. A dried-up, lost, withered thing, untouched for too long, unloved for decades, missing her Wita so much.

'He's taken a lifetime,' she whispered, her voice cracked and old, her eyes so sad, her crooked fingers intertwined as if it was only with each other they could find the comfort they missed in the holding of his hand.

I miss him, and her voice was the shrill of the wind in among the bitter trees, the dark of the wind on the lake below, the rasp of the wind among the cones, *I miss my love*.

The White Horse, whether indifferent or not, ignored her words: it always did. Instead it dropped down to its knees to let her grasp its mane and mount its broad back.

As it galloped away she bent forward to its strength, holding her old, thin thighs to its flanks so tight that they became strong again, as when she was young. She laid her gaunt cheek on its neck and her face grew plump again and roseate with health.

'If you won't tell me where he is,' she whispered happily to its ear, the bleak moment over, 'tell me where Leetha is.'

The White Horse flew through the wintry clouds, its hoofs galloping on thin air yet making so much sound that mortals below watching the clouds above wondered what went by.

Leetha, mollified to be on land, pleased with the attention she was getting from Riff's happy kin, was content to take the credit for their safe return.

'Oh yes,' she said, 'without me they would all be deep down in their nightmare watery graves.'

'You'm told'm where and why and what to do, Lady Leetha? You'm done that?'

'Oh!' she sighed mock-wearily, 'how slow these mariners were, how much in need of all I knew! On top of which I had to cook for them, loathsome fish, day after day, night after night. They would eat nothing else. Would you like me to cook for *you*?'

They stared at each other, eyes widening, not sure if she was serious. Not sure, come to think of it, if any of them were really there. Not sure of anything, they were so happy to have Riff and Deap safe home. They liked Leetha's loving game, but cook? That was serious and Leetha's reputation preceded her.

'Cook? For *us*?' they whispered uneasily.

They glanced at Riff and he at them, shaking his head almost imperceptibly.

Pretending to mistake their politeness for possibility, she asked, 'What have you got that I can cook?'

'Fish, my lady, only fish but . . .'

Leetha laughed and put a hand to ruffle Riff's hair and beard.

'I'm a terrible cook and that's the truth,' she said good-humouredly, 'so it's better that you do it. Oh, but I'm glad to be here again. Borkum and Herde and Witold and Jack saved my life a hundred times each! I saved no one's.'

'Tell us 'bout Jack,' they said while they prepared the feast, 'tell us about Deap's other half, tell us how he made it good with Slew, for we'm sure he did. Slew's got colour in his pallid cheeks and that'll be the other's doin'. Tell us.'

So while they cooked and readied their homes along Den Helder's wildest shore for a feast that would begin in one humble, continue in another, and travel wherever the festive candles flamed, so that all Borkum's kin would share in familial fare, she told them about the weeks past with dance and song and her many Leetha ways, which had lit the paths of others all her life.

'But wait!' she cried, interrupting herself, 'this looks like a feast beyond feasts! Is this how you always welcome Riff home?'

'It b'aint,' they said. 'But you'm forgetting what night it w'or four nights past when you were on the high seas and we'm stuck here worried sick 'n thinking he'm and our'n'll not be home no more 'cos they'm drownded deep like you described before. Deep down in the watery grave.'

'What night was that?' wondered Leetha.

'T'was Solstice night, the longest there is, when we folk have a special feast. Nobbut we couldn't, could us, while we thought they'm dead? We ate brot and water and prayed. This night be the twenty-fourth, which some folks celebrate wi' tinsel and bells and song, so we've borrowed that celebration for this night o' your return.'

'Its name?' asked Leetha.

'Yuletide,' they said.

'Yuletide,' repeated Leetha, considering the strange word. 'What do you think of that, then, Riff?'

He considered it.

'You'm here, they'm here, we'm all here together and at one,' he said eventually, 'and that's just how it should be, whate'er name you give it.'

Leetha was asked to inspect each of the humbles before Riff saw them, the decorations being wyfkin and kinder work.

'They've made a special place for you in every humble along the shore,' Leetha reported, 'all garlanded and candle-lit.'

'That bain't for me,' he said, 'that be for she!'

'You mean me?' said Leetha misunderstanding and utterly delighted.

He shook his head.

'Not for thee, Leetha! But for she who never comes.'

'But on the day it matters then she will,' they said with certainty.

Leetha liked this mystery, which those shore dwellers acted out at Solstice time but had delayed this year until the night of the twenty-fourth. The truth was that no one knew who 'she' was at all but they set a place of honour for her every time in the hope they'd find out in the end.

'How long have you been waiting for her to come?' she asked them, when the feast was set, the candles lit and the festivities in the first humble just begun.

'Since afore anyone remembers,' they replied, 'even Old Riff, Borkum's pa, never saw her come, or if he did he wasn't telling.'

Nor did the mystery guest come to that first humble, or the second, or the third, and each time the empty place stayed empty, though its platter was full, its decorations undisturbed. Each time they moved on, the night deeper, folk madder or happier or more inclined towards dance and singing and merriment. The kinder asked seriously, their eyes wider, 'Why bain't she here who'm a'coming and *now* can we eat her sweetmeats and her caggletoff?'

They didn't know the adults took these things to each humble as they went and laid that food in the empty place anew, not in expectation she would come at all but to mark a beginning in that home and to say to all present, and the kinder especially, that if there's a knock on a door at whatever time of night, however things might be, if you're a Riff you open right up and you smile and you say, 'Welcome, stranger! You'm honouring us! Come on in, your place is laid!'

Which words the kinder practised, just in case, and if a sweetmeat or 'toff slipped their way when they got it right, who'd be worried just by one? Not them!

Oh, but it got hot as the night went on! The candles, the driftwood fires, the fierce and heady brews, the feasty food and the chattery laugh all made it so.

Until, by the time they reached the last of those humbles, made of ships' timbers all holed and copper-nailed and tarred, over and across the dunes, where Riff-kin lived, who had near nothing at all but the warmth of their good hearts and the few scraps they'd put together with the help of the other wyfkin earlier on . . . by then no one cared for food much at all. As for the platter for she who never came, why, the kinder eyed its cheery contents with relish, having worked out that this time, before the end of the night, it would be theirs.

Outside, the surf roared far off and the wind blew near and candles guttered until the door was closed and everybody warm within.

'You'm welcome all, as you'm always be,' their poorest kin said loud, 'and what we bain't got in food we make up in good cheer and the fire's the brightest you'll e'er see!'

Which it was, for the tar flared well and the copper nails shone copper-blue and the brew was good and by then they were bursting stomach-wise and a teaspoonful of this and that was all they needed.

'Ma?'

'Pa?'

Kinders' voices don't count for much against adult hubbub of that kind.

'Ma!'

'Pa!'

They counted for nothing at all, hardly audible above the noise the Riffs can make at the end of things.

'*MAAAA!*'

And those two kinder, peering out, shouting at the top of their voices, stopped the whole lot of 'em short.

'Pa, there's someone at the door.'

A hush fell, deep as time.

'Then open it, my love,' their ma said, her voice trembling.

It crashed open with the wind and there they saw, white and wild, the Horse's mane.

The adults stared like they were terrified.

So did most of the kinder.

But those two by the door, who'd been waiting all night long because they were the last to believe she who never came finally would, knew what to do, scared and awed though they were. They held each other's hand for courage and went outside into the windy night, while candles and fire blew all over the place inside, and they looked up and then up and then up some more to where she rode among the Yuletide stars.

The White Horse, seeing them, knelt down and its Rider dismounted as best she could, which wasn't much, and she turned and looked at the two waiting for her, who shivered to see one so old.

But the moment she smiled it seemed to them, as to all who saw her then, or ever saw her past, that the light within was without age.

'W . . . w . . . welcome . . . st . . . stranger! You'm . . . you'm . . . you'm *honouring* us! Come on in, your place is laid.'

The Modor took their hands and entered in and she declared that *never* had a place been better laid.

Riff grinned, which he did not often do, to see his Leetha's face.

Leetha laughed to see the Modor's.

'Welcome,' Leetha said holding old Modor tight, very tight indeed, 'welcome! I've missed you.'

'And I you, my dear.'

✻

'Have you seen him?' whispered the Modor, much later, when dawn approached and the White Horse was snorting and it was time to go.

'Who?' asked Leetha.

'That consort of mine, of course. I've been missing him this terrible winter.'

'No!' said Leetha, 'I haven't. Have a sweetmeat, but don't eat them all . . . and did I say I've missed you? '

'Come and see me.'

'I am already on my way, Modor. I have things to ask, things to know, things to learn.'

'Come soon,' said the Modor, giving the kinder the sweets and caggletoff, her eyes filled with the same light as theirs, 'come soon. For the Earth is weak now and this winter long.'

'I will,' said Leetha.'

'Dance for us, my love!'

Leetha did, and while they watched, the Modor slipped away, nearly unseen. Back outside she went, as beautiful again as when she was young, grasping the Horse's mane and mounting up, her thighs to its flanks, her cheek to its neck, as she whispered, 'Tell him to come soon,' in the Horse's ear that the one she loved might soon return and she too could say, 'Welcome, stranger, welcome!'

Welcome home.

26

RESCUE

Jack woke to Colonel Reece's kicking in a state of confusion and discomfort, with something shining so close to his eyes that at first he could not focus on it. It was moving, it was bright, and it was . . . *the blade of a serrated hunting knife.*

Adrenalin cleared his mind fast and his senses moved to overdrive. Since his range of vision was so restricted he had to still himself and listen hard to get a picture of what was going on around him.

One and two . . . two people very nearby. Three further off. Five in all. They were quiet and disciplined, so probably military.

The knife retreated and something round but not too hard pushed under his shoulder and heaved him onto his back. A boot, that's what it was.

Light from the sky temporarily blinded him.

When he could see again, through screwed-up eyes, he was looking at two foreshortened, uniformed legs, then at a flat, khaki-shirted stomach, and beyond that to a face looking down at him. The sky was so bright and the angle so acute that it was almost a silhouette and he could not make its features out. Jack swivelled his eyes, rolled slightly and was able to see two more legs, these ones in the dark material of a suit. Both humans obviously.

Where's my stave?

He sensed where it was but did not look in the direction in which he had thrown it before being caught by the net. He had been stupid once, he was not going to be again. The stave was capable of looking after itself and he was not going to risk revealing that it mattered to him by staring at it. Hopefully, if they saw it and were able to get hold of it, which he very much doubted, since the stave had a mind of its own and was loyal only to him, they would have no idea what it was.

He waited, trying to work out what to do if, as he now thought, they were going to use the knife to cut him free. His initial fear had gone. Even humans were not so unintelligent that they would kill him without trying to find out something about him first.

What can I do when I'm free? he asked himself. *Not a lot immediately because I'm going to find it hard even to sit up, let alone fight.*

That was because he had been unable to move for so long that he had cramped up. He would have to stretch, to go through the agony of sudden blood flow to areas deprived, of muscles strained and waking and having no sense of balance for a time.

Between the ages of six and eleven, when he was subjected to a series of skin grafts following his rescue of Katherine from her parents' burning car, he had sometimes spent days in bandages, unable to move. It had been a kind of torture then and was again now. The sudden itches which he was unable to scratch, the pins and needles, the throbbing aches and pains, the horrible need to pee and defecate and the nearly equal desire not to do so in his own clothes.

As for moving again once he was freed, it would take him an hour to even start to move properly and a day or more to fully recover.

The worst moment had been during the night, when the man who netted him, who was the same who shot the fox, judging from his scent, came looking for him. Jack heard him before he saw him.

'Where . . . are . . . you . . . ?'

Then he had heard feet in the grass approaching near, then getting more distant.

'I'm coming to get you . . . !' came a mocking voice.

The feet came near again.

'Where . . . are . . . you . . . ?' and laughter as the cruel game of mock hide and seek was played.

Bastard.

Jack had not moved, hoping he would miss him. He saw the torchlight dart here and here, heard the man's tread and winced when a powerful beam was directed straight into his eyes.

'Oh! There you are . . .'

Bastard.

The man had kicked him hard in the small of the back, first on one side and then on the other.

'We don't like shitty little kids trespassing in here . . .'

Jack had no doubt that his life was in danger but at least the guard did not know he was a hydden.

A shout from afar, no, a command.

The man's third kick had halted in thin air and he had sworn. Summoned by a superior, it seemed. He put out his light, half turned, aimed a parting kick in the dark that glanced off Jack's head and was gone. He never came back.

Others did, different ones, cleaner by the smell, but they missed where he lay.

He slept, had one pee into his pants, which was warm and then cold and finally stingy and unpleasant, and slept again.

He had woken sometimes, flexing and relaxing his muscles to try to keep them from stiffening. He used the cover of night to roll back and forth. He stilled when he heard or smelt the patrols go by.

One of them had eaten processed meat of some kind. He could smell salty preservatives and flavourings and that scent, which made him thirsty more than hungry, made for the worst moment of all.

Thirst would kill him before hunger so he hoped it would rain. It did not.

At least it was cold which meant there were few insects about. Moths troubled him briefly, as did a grey squirrel which nibbled at his feet. He kept coming back, touching and nibbling at Jack's shoe and then his ankle. Jack rolled about a little and finally, chattering, the squirrel left him alone.

Foxes and dogs would have worried him, but none came by, put off probably by the stench of the dead one. A magpie landed on him, its claws surprisingly sharp but in the end more ticklish than painful. He kept his eyes shut for fear of having them pecked out.

Then sleep again and now, *this.*

The men. The knife. The cutting-free, he hoped.

Or maybe not.

The one in the uniform knelt over him, produced the serrated knife again, and rolled him sideways.

He's going to cut my throat, Jack told himself and he called out to his stave: 'Help!'

The stave, if it was still there and could hear him, did not respond.

Katherine was still holding Stort's hand when, falling from what felt a vast distance and simultaneously shifting from a sleeping to a waking state, her legs left far behind her and her free hand way, way ahead, she came to on grass in a state of extreme alarm.

In the last few waking seconds shards of sound and light had played and melded all around her, conveying a three-dimensional sense that Jack needed help *now*.

But where?

Stort, mumbling, thumped into the ground at her side and Slaeke Sinistral a short time after. In fact, they were all holding each other's hand.

She let go of Stort's, sat up, looked round and saw the glint of the knife before anything else, in among the trees, beyond the henge, just there. She glanced around again to confirm that they had arrived, as she first thought, in the Woolstone tree henge. The clear intention she put into her mind at Stanton Drew was to find Jack because she had no doubt he was in real danger. That feeling redoubled now.

'Leave this to me,' she said, clear and cold. 'Be ready.'

'Where are we?' asked Sinistral and Stort together.

'Woolstone,' murmured Katherine.

She rose up knowing as she did so the importance of what Jack had always said: *surprise*.

'Stay there, Stort, and keep Sinistral with you. Be ready.'

'For what?'

'For *leaving*, of course. I don't think we'll be hanging around.'

'But we've only just . . .' he began, stopping when he saw humans in grey-khaki through the trees in the long grass next to the lawn.

'Stay!' she commanded.

The humans had not seen them, but that was not surprising. They did not expect to, for one thing, and the hydden had tumbled to the ground at the edge of the henge, so the view through it to that knife and those men was angled between trees and through thin vegetation. Also, there was something about opening henge portals that lent a shimmer to the air and to those travelling through it, as if being between worlds rendered them for a few seconds, perhaps even longer, hard for others to see clearly.

She felt absolutely in control and she felt no fear, like a mother whose child is threatened, who knows exactly what to do.

'No . . .' she cried out, aware that her voice was a hydden's, to them more like a bird's, 'no . . .'

She controlled her impulse to run.

Surprise was her only weapon and there was never going to be a surprise like a hydden appearing among humans. She ran straight into the open where they stood.

The knife stilled, the man stood up, two giants looming over . . . what. *What?*

The wyf in her turned into a raging demon.

What had they done to him?

She didn't give a damn how big they were or what they might do or anything.

She reached him, knelt down and said, '*What have they done to you?*'

Jack stared at her, baffled.

He opened his mouth but the net tightened more and what he said was slurred, as if he was in pain or had been beaten.

'What have they done to you?' she said.

If he could have answered he might have tried but as he couldn't he stared at her with mute appeal.

For Mirror's sake get me out of here. Katherine . . .

Her initial anger had changed to rage when she first saw him, now it became fury, total and complete, but icily controlled. Surprise had been essential, now speed was of the essence.

She reached down to the net and found it impossible to grasp. She turned and looked at the knife but that didn't seem an option. They had not seen the others apparently, but stood staring open-mouthed at her, rubbing their eyes as if they could not quite see what was happening.

She turned back to Jack, bent down and grabbed the easiest bit of him that was graspable, his left ankle.

Katherine . . .

She heaved at him in her fury and he began sliding along on his back over the humus and dry leaves.

'*Stort!*' she shouted. 'Help me! My Lord Sinistral, please stay where you are.'

She knew they had very limited time before the humans recovered from the shock of seeing them and, she now suspected, the aversion to touching what must seem to them alien, strange and perhaps repulsive figures. Then, too, the shimmer in the air induced by a portal being opened, was still helping.

'Stort, *now!*'

He came and managed to wrest Jack's other foot from the net and joined his strength and greater leverage to Katherine's. They gained momentum, Jack bumped over a branch and then went bumpety-bump over some roots.

Katherine!

The bedazzled and bewildered men were finally moving, shouting and turning in slow motion, as humans did, reaching out.

Katherine, behind you! Jack tried to say.

They reached the henge trees and began pulling Jack into the sanctuary of their circle as the first man reached forward to grab her.

Jack tried to speak again, twisted his head, got his mouth free and shouted, '*Stave!*'

There in the dark of wet vegetation where it had lain waiting, it stirred to action. Trembling, gathering light again, shaking itself as if sloughing off a tiredness. Then it was up and out and a stream of stars behind it as it rushed from the dark, turning over and over on itself as it came straight at them, slid sideways, and bashed the first man's hand; then the barrel of a gun and someone's head, then another and a third . . .

As it did so, and the men fell back and two fell down, Jack was pulled into the henge and Stort was already turning, turning dexter, round and round, Katherine following, with Jack bumping along the ground and swearing and hurting because the net was torn now and his arm, which he could not move himself, was caught behind him, the muscles stretching to breaking point, the sinews cracking and the bones deep-hurting as bumpety-bump . . .

'Oh God it feels like I'm going to die!'

The fateful, ill-timed words came out at the same moment Katherine called, 'Sinistral!' and reached for his hand with her free one so they could all make the dance together as she turned dexter after Stort, 'Oh yes . . . yes . . .'

Dancing away, the stave dancing too, the men in confusion at the edge, staggering about as Stort turned and danced back into the henge, and its spiralling darkness, turning far away, and away, until they were nearly gone.

I'm going to die, Jack had said and his unfortunate words hung like dark, sharp shards, blocking their safer way, forcing them towards the dark vale, beginning to jab at them with their points of death, trying to take them down to the void.

Sinistral heard these words and his eyes widened in alarm and recognition of the mortal danger they created. As he felt Katherine's hand beginning to grasp his he knew such words must not be the last thing said if his friends were to be portalled to safety. No, not the thought of dying, because the henge would deliver them to the place they thought of last. That included death itself, a subject about which Sinistral knew more than any mortal alive, having fought off death for so many decades past. He was ready, they were not.

'Oh God . . .' screamed Jack in the agony of his tearing limbs, 'oh . . .'

Slaeke Sinistral slowed his feet, he stopped his dance, he leaned forward and gently steered Jack the way he needed to go, not to death but towards life . . .

'*Sinistral* . . .' screamed Katherine, feeling his fingers letting her go and guessing what he was doing and the nature of his sacrifice, 'you must come with us . . .'

All stilled, all moved at a pace beyond speed.

'It is all right, my dear, I shall go instead to where Jack was going, I shall dance that way . . . listen! Listen! I hear the *musica* and that is enough for me but you all . . . you must live to save the world . . .'

Then they were gone one way and Sinistral another and all that was left in the henge was Katherine's cry before it was lost within the siren sound of the Chimes outside.

'What the hell was *that*!?' gasped Reece, his head throbbing from the thump it had had from a flying stick.

Bohr stared up into the heights of the trees, lost for words.

'What was it?' said one of them a few minutes later.

'Hydden,' said Bohr, unutterably awed by what they had seen and what had happened, 'they were *hydden*! But we lost them, they were so fast we have no way of knowing how and where they came in and what they did to get out.'

Reece smiled a knowing and unpleasant smile and pointed up into one of the trees. There was a tiny camera there.

'Put it up this morning. And another over there. What were they *doing* before they . . . er . . . left?'

'Dancing . . .' said Bohr, stopping himself saying more because he did not like the belligerent look in Reece's eyes.

'Right,' said Reece dismissively.

'Well, it looked like that,' said Bohr, sounding as doubtful and uncertain as he could.

'Freaks!' said Reece, 'that's what *they* were.'

They came to at dusk in wide, open grassland, scattered like leaves, with no henge nearby that they could see. But the grey, drizzly day was already too dark to see far and they stirred only slowly, as if from a very long sleep.

Jack found himself almost free again, the net in tatters about his feet, pulled nearly clear by Katherine when she hauled him into the henge. But his arm was painful and he winced as he tried to kick his feet free of the net. His throat was so parched he could not say clearly what he was trying to get out.

Sinistral . . . he . . .

Stort sat up, bemused.

Katherine crawled over to Jack and gave him a drink.

Sinistral . . .

'Where's Sinistral?' asked Stort suddenly. 'He's nowhere to be seen!'

But Katherine already knew, or rather had guessed.

'He chose to stay behind,' she said quietly.

'Not good,' said Stort.

'No, not good,' she replied, adding, 'and yet . . .'

'And yet?' asked Jack, frowning, stretching very cautiously.

'What was the last thing you heard?' she asked.

They thought back and tried to remember but as they did and the light dimmed the strangeness of where they were bore into them. A vast, undulating landscape, as it felt, and everywhere they turned the sense that they were not quite alone, nor quite in company. As if they had landed in a place where people had just that moment gone, or might at any moment arrive. The silence of these thoughts was interrupted only slowly by a sound above the breeze.

Running water, not far off.

'Come,' said Katherine, helping Jack to his feet, 'but carefully.'

Stort supported him on the other side.

'The last thing I heard,' he said, 'was the sound of the Chimes.'

'Sinistral has gone to them,' said Katherine, her blank tone hiding the grief she dared not yet feel.

'The last thing I heard was my own voice, speaking of pain and death.'

She shook her head. 'The last thing was his voice calling after us to say that we must live.'

They stumbled on, not yet knowing where they were but in the certain knowledge that to save their lives Sinistral had finally given up his own.

27

BACK TO BRUM

The hundred-mile stretch between the stone circles of Stanton Drew and the city of Brum was a two-and-a-half-hour drive, three hours at most – for a human in normal conditions when there was no civil strife and the Earth had not gone mad. But it took Niklas Blut, Lord Festoon, Mister Barklice and Terce more than three exhausting days.

Blut had to steer the large, awkward military truck through winding, hilly roads and territory unknown. Many a time, the roads being blocked by abandoned vehicles, or seeing signs of vagrant and troublesome human life ahead which they naturally wished to avoid, Terce was obliged to pore over the road atlas and direct Blut to alternative routes.

Even *in extremis*, when they grew confused by conflicts between the map and roadside fingerposts, they did not stop to call upon Barklice's expert aid until they were quite sure it was safe to do so. For it was not enough that the road ahead seemed clear, and the route behind had revealed no obvious danger. If Blut was to stop, it had to be on a crest of some kind, where they could see they were safe all around and, which was important, that if they had to flee they had an alternative to simply going forward or back.

They began taking precautions early on, after they had stopped at what seemed a safe place. They climbed out of the vehicle to take the air, relieve themselves and stretch, when four humans emerged from a nearby wood, holding metal rods as clubs, and charged at them with shouts and threats.

The truck was parked facing uphill and it was with the greatest difficulty that they clambered back into the cab, got the engine started and gained enough speed to throw off their pursuers. Had Terce not used his strength and feet to ward off the humans at the last moment, suffering severe bruising to his thighs and shins in the process, they would have been lost almost before they began.

As it was, one of those chasing them managed to hurl his metal bar through the passenger window and another to grasp on to the vehicle's side and very nearly open the door. Blut had stayed characteristically calm, swerving and braking violently almost as naturally as Katherine had done with the horsebox, and so dislodged the human that he was left hanging from the side between the wheels. A few seconds later Blut swerved hard enough to throw their attacker under the rear wheels.

'Needs must,' was his tersely grim comment.

After that, when they lost their way and it needed Barklice to get out and look around, Blut always chose his spot with great care.

'I wish I could stay within the cab itself,' said Barklice apologetically, 'but I lose all sense of where I am relative to the landscape about me in such a noisy, confined space as this!'

They would watch in wonder as Barklice wandered about, sniffing the air, feeling the wind with wetted finger, humming and hawing. Then kicking the ground and closing his eyes, he swung about until, with absolute confidence, he pointed the way in which they should proceed once more. He was almost invariably right.

Their route ran north and east, broadly following the line of the Cotswolds some way below the level of the steep west scarp face of that great line of hills, which faces across the wide and verdant valley of the River Severn. They felt safer on the eastern side of the hills, where the shallow slopes formed an undulating landscape of small fields, woods and streams, interspersed by village houses of honey-coloured stone.

Here the alternative routes were many and after their unpleasant early encounter with humans, the towns and villages proved devoid of life. Once or twice their diversions did take them west to the top of the escarpment and they were able to see, in the vale below, the motorway they had been following before turning off towards Bath and Stanton Drew.

'Would it were that way was clear and safe!' cried Terce, the atlas on his knee. 'I could guide us home to Brum in almost no time at all!'

But it was neither. The many lanes of the motorway were littered with the vehicles of refugees from the south and they saw and heard sporadic fighting down there too; by whom and for what they had no idea. Then, too, in the fields far below, between the foot of the escarpment and the motorway itself, they saw at least two bands of vagrant scavengers.

One of the groups, fifty individuals in all, spitted flesh across metal frames over foul-smelling, smoky-orange fires. They drank and danced and whooped obscenely as they did so. At first the oily smoke obscured what they thought was a pen holding cattle beyond. When the wind direction changed and the smoke drifted another way they saw it held humans. They were shackled, hunched and beaten. It was only when one of these was hauled from the rest that their initial curiosity turned to horror and disgust as they realized that what they were witness to was the murder, butchering, cooking and festive eating of human flesh.

Little wonder that they turned thankfully, if fearfully, back to the more obscure route they were taking, happy that, though their progress was very slow, they were spared such sights again and the map confirmed that little by little they were getting nearer to Brum.

They had already agreed their strategy for when they reached Brum. It was, after all, the city of which Festoon was High Ealdor and it seemed right that he should take charge even in the presence of Blut. So it was that when they began to see the road signs indicating that the city was near, Blut made clear that, as far as he was concerned, Festoon was now in charge. Surely few Emperors stood less on their dignity than Niklas Blut.

During the afternoon of the third day of their journey, by when they had reached the village of Alvechurch on the outskirts of Brum, where they stopped for a break, the air temperature began to drop rapidly. They noticed it was colder the moment they got out, but within fifteen minutes of their halt they were stamping their feet and rubbing their hands in response to the persistent chill. The sky was not clear, nor the day still, as often happens with such temperature falls. Rather, the cloud cover was very high, and strangely stippled, like skin too long submerged in water. Whether or not more snow was on the way it did not look as if it would be safe to drive much longer.

Even before they had left Brum two months before, Barklice had

agreed with Mister Pike, the city's Chief Staverman, that when they
returned they should go first to Waseley Hill, west of the city. It was a
spot well known to locals, which the invading Fyrd, if they were still
about, would be unlikely to patrol. The River Rea rose there and could
be easily found by day or night.

'If we can, Barklice,' Pike had said, 'we'll set up a system whereby
someone or other will always be about the hill, watching out for returning travellers, however long it may be before you and the rest of
our friends are able to get back.'

It was therefore towards Waseley Hill that they now decided to
turn.

'It'll be dark by the time we get there,' said Barklice, 'but better that
than another night's camping in this cold.'

Blut started up the truck once more and they rolled slowly down a
lane that would take them under the M42 motorway, across the official
boundary of the city. The last phase of their journey began. Not that
they could yet see anything of it at all. The human city of which Brum
was the hydden part lay on mainly low, undulating ground, spread
across tens of square miles. It was heavily built up and the approach
from the south failed to give much of a view at all. That would have to
wait until they climbed up to the source of the Rea.

'Ah, but it is good to be back!' sighed Festoon, who, like Barklice,
was Brum born and bred. 'I may be biased, my friends, but I believe
this to be the greatest city in the Hyddenworld!'

It was a claim many had made before and was easily justified. Brum
was very ancient, having been first colonized by humans, and soon after
by hydden, after Beornamund's death fifteen hundred years before. His
service as CraftLord to Mercian royalty, and the fact that his famous
forge was located on the Rea, attracted craft-folk of all kinds. The river
ran for only twelve miles before it was subsumed by the River Tame. It
was along this short watercourse that the human city grew.

Old Brum was the most ancient part of the hydden city within
Birmingham, being tucked away deep in the interstices between river
and canal, sewer and drain, railway and road, where no human could
easily go. With the coming of the railways in the mid-nineteenth century

the hydden city expanded from this base, attracted to the footings, basements and arches beneath the railway lines. Here there were rich pickings for hydden traders from the industrial wastage of the humans.

This became New Brum, a mile to the north of Old. It was here that new hydden dynasties built their fortunes. Emperor Sinistral and Lord Festoon were both scions of these families – the first leaving Englalond to make his fortune in Europe and create the Empire, the second becoming Brum's much-loved High Ealdor.

Niklas Blut had no blood connection with either, or with anyone from Brum, but three months before he had been brought into Englalond, the reluctant prisoner of General Quatremayne, head of the Fyrd or Imperial army. Blut had defected to Brum, taking with him vital secrets of the Fyrd invasion plan. Along with Festoon, he had been instrumental in the successful resistance to the Fyrd, enabling an orderly evacuation of citizens before the invasion took place. The Brum forces were left under the control of Igor Brunte, a former Fyrd and formidable opponent of the Empire.

When Blut and the others had left the city under their control ten weeks before, to help Stort find the gem of Autumn, the evacuation was all but complete and the guerrilla war against the Fyrd about to begin.

Only Terce spoke as the truck rumbled west and north through the suburbs of Barnt Green and Marlbrook, up to rough Rubery and through suburbs broken and razed, giving directions as best he could: right and right again, forward and left, no . . . yes . . . straight ahead then oops and down! *Left*, my Lord, and right and then . . . then . . .

On they went as darkness came, the cold now so intense that they had to stuff a jacket in the broken passenger window to try to stop the cold coming in. They continued long after their normal stopping time, carried forward by a need to arrive.

'Not far, my friends, not far,' cried Barklice eagerly. 'Soon, soon . . . this is Gannor Green and here, yes . . . *left* . . . *left* . . . *le* . . . to Waseley Hill!'

But the final stretch was not as orderly as Blut would have liked. The road was narrow, its camber difficult and its surface covered in black ice they could not see. The wheels began to spin, the truck to slew sideways and they were suddenly sliding backwards . . . back . . . and back . . . as with a screech of brakes they slid into bushes and a shallow ditch, the offside wheels spinning in thin air. They could go no further.

A panic overtook them as if, the truck having been for so long their sanctuary, it had turned by virtue of its sudden uselessness into a gaol. One that would make them vulnerable to any lurking and malevolent eyes in the darkness beyond.

'Turn off the lights!' cried Festoon.

'Sshh . . . keep quiet,' whispered Blut.

'Terce is on top of me!' rasped Barklice.

It took a few minutes for their eyes to adjust to the dark and to disentangle themselves from each other, clear the glass from the broken window and heave themselves out of the cab to the road below. Terce was last, throwing down one 'sac after another.

They needed no telling to don warm garb quickly, for the temperature had plummeted still lower and in less than ten minutes had their ears tingling. The darkness was almost absolute.

'Do you know where we are, Barklice?' asked Blut.

'I do,' said the verderer very happily, 'indeed I do! But stay close and advance in single file, a hand on each other's belt, with you, Terce, at the rear!'

Of the following moments even the most clear-thinking and analytic of them, namely Niklas Blut, afterward had little accurate recall. The ground was icy, the air viciously cold, and they proceeded, as it seemed, by fits and starts, in such darkness and across such treacherous, slippery, sloping ground that their feet stumbled one over another.

They went uphill, that was certain.

They stopped twice to listen, the first time after heaving themselves through a prickly hedge, when they heard nothing; and the second on a contouring path, which rose steeply on their right and dropped more steeply, as it felt, to their left.

'We should be able to see the city from here,' said Festoon, 'or rather its lights! But there is only darkness!'

'Sssshhh!' hissed Barklice.

They listened, hearing nothing at first because of their puffing and panting. But as they got that under control and they felt their feet more secure on the path, they heard, as Blut remembered it, the gentlest of rippling, the first watery whisper of the Rea's source.

'That is the sound of the Rea I wanted to hear! Gentlemen, we have reached our destination!'

They might have celebrated then and there but that a warning voice cried out from a little way ahead, 'Don't move an inch more if you value your lives!'

They stilled.

The voice was youthful and Brummish.

'We're friends!' said Barklice.

'How many of you?'

'Four.'

'Well, there's an army of us and we will harm you if you don't answer true! What are your names?'

'I am Mister Barklice! I have with me . . .'

'If you're Mister Barklice give us the name of your son!'

'Bratfire,' said Barklice.

'What colour's his hair?'

'Red. Now, for Mirror's sake . . .'

A lantern appeared ahead of them, too bright for them to see who held it. It advanced upon them, taking a path a little upslope to keep the advantage. The shutter opened wider and they were scrutinized.

'Blimey! It *is* Mister Barklice. And Lord Festoon himself! And wait a minute, I know you from your specs.'

'Blut,' said Blut pleasantly, 'Emperor of the Hyddenworld.'

'Humph! Who's this last one then?' the voice behind the lantern said.

'Terce.'

'And what do you do when you're not wandering about in the dark?'

'Sing,' said Terce.

The lantern was lowered and its shutters all opened wide. It was indeed a great army that stood before them, in heart at least. It was a small boy whom Barklice recognized as one of Bratfire's friends.

He gave them that bold, defiant, streetwise Brummie gaze that held such great good humour and friendliness that it always defied definition, but which so many visitors to Brum through centuries past had commented on.

'Where are the rest of you?' asked Barklice.

'There aren't none up here in the freezin', bleedin' cold. We ain't daft! But there soon will be, especially when they hear who's come home!'

He whistled shrilly, twice and then three times, and there was an answering whistle from far below. Then a whistle again as news of their arrival was sent post-haste by sound alone to Mister Pike in the city.

'He'll fall off his seat with surprise when he hears!' said the boy. 'There's only one person in all of Brum thinks you're still alive, Mister Barklice, and that isn't Mister Pike, though he's the one kept us going all this long and horrible time. Just one of us thought you'd make it back.'

He led them along the path, round the hill a little way to a fire that smouldered by the source of the Rea itself.

'And who would that be, who had such faith in my friend here?' asked Festoon as they sat down and warmed themselves by the fire, his eyes twinkling in the light and his great hand patting Barklice on the back.

'Bratfire,' said the lad. 'He never stopped saying, "My pa's the best at finding routes in all the Hyddenworld and getting folk back safely to where they should be." He never once doubted it! But hold it, I'm forgetting what we're meant to do if you ever got back!'

He moved off a few yards into the murk, took something from a plastic bag, stuck it in a receptacle of some kind, came back and took an ember from the fire.

He went back into the dark, the ember danced about in the air, there was a sudden fizz and shoot of sparks, followed by a roar, and up went a rocket, up and up, to explode with a powerful bang high over Waseley Hill, red and green stars floating down.

'Hold it, friends,' the boy cried again, 'I got to send a second up!'

Which, moments later he did, the rocket whooshing up into the air to make an even more powerful bang and burst of light than before.

'What does it mean?' murmured Terce.

Barklice smiled, the stars making his face as bright as the fire that was now beginning to warm them, because he knew what it meant. He had given the rockets to Bratfire for this very purpose.

'It's to tell my lad that his pa's come home,' said Barklice.

28
PERFECT MATCH

The brief yet illuminating encounter with hydden in the garden of Woolstone House brought out the best in Erich Bohr and the worst in Colonel Reece.

The scientist in Bohr saw it as a triumph: he had managed to meet the hydden and record their method of entry and exit from a henge – and probably in the very same location where Arthur Foale had achieved the same thing. Bohr felt he now had a solid basis from which to move forward very rapidly towards the Hyddenworld.

But the soldier in Reece saw it as a defeat. If he had had doubts about the existence of the hydden he did not have them any longer. He had seen them with his own eyes and his life-long training had taught him to think of any living being which did not fall into line with his expectations of what was reasonable, as suspect. That disgusting dwarf of a thing had a chance to be an ally. Not now. Allies do not attack but enemies do – and this one had. Allies are open and comprehensible but enemies are sly and underhand – and this one was. Allies cooperate but enemies do not. Yes, Reece was able to label what he was dealing with.

'Which means,' he said, 'that until they prove themselves deserving of the trust of myself and my force we shall – we *must* – treat them as an enemy.'

'But Colonel Reece,' said Bohr, 'we cannot know . . .'

'We know what they are not. They are not allies, they are not friendly, they attack without good reason and we will treat them as they now deserve until I am satisfied that they will not abuse the trust we put in them.'

It was all too horribly clear to Bohr that Reece saw what had happened as a humiliation and a disaster. They had lost an asset which would have given him a great deal of intelligence about the 'enemy' and his personal authority had been undermined with his troops.

Bohr was grateful for one thing at least. This early mistake had confirmed what he had feared from the moment Reece was forced upon him. He was the very last kind of officer needed for such an unusual and delicate operation. The hydden were not and probably never had been 'the enemy'. Human beings were.

He could now see better why Arthur had retreated so rapidly into silence about his work and he decided that when it came to attempting a journey into the Hyddenworld he would try to give Reece and his men the slip.

The positive aspect of what had happened was that they had valuable footage from two different cameras, one in the henge and one just outside it. Bohr and Reece might have different takes on the incident but they could at least agree that what they had was real, it was important and it might show them the best way forward.

In fact, what it actually showed was not immediately clear. The clips of hydden Bohr had obtained from Birmingham, and those other clips that Arthur had gathered from wartime news and military cinematographers, were a lot clearer than what they had now obtained. The light in the henge had been shimmery and odd, resulting in curiously broken images whose timeline was disrupted. Neither Bohr nor Reece had ever seen anything like it from state-of-the-art cameras, and differed about the causes.

But at least the basics were undeniable. Three figures had appeared out of nowhere in the henge. 'A' appeared female from the clothes she wore and her hair. 'B' and 'C' were males, 'C' being the oldest, judging from his white hair and the stiff, slow way he moved.

All were carrying stick-like objects which might be weapons. Reece was convinced they were, and likely to be firearms of some kind. Bohr thought they looked like medieval staves. The first two were carrying backpacks, but 'C', the old one, was not.

What happened after their arrival was undisputed except for the final seconds. 'A' moved at an angle across the henge, from where she appeared to look in the direction of Bohr and the others at the moment

Reece had knelt down, taken out his knife and was about to proceed to cut 'D', the hydden they had found, free of his net. 'A' then moved rapidly between the trees and out of the henge and boldly went to 'D'. After a brief pause and without any apparent communication with Reece or anyone else, she grabbed 'D's' foot and dragged him back into the henge, 'B' coming to help her.

Reece and his men were, in Bohr's view, very slow to react. When they finally did, something or somebody attacked them, keeping them out of the henge while the next phase of the hydden rescue took place. The images were especially poor regarding the attack on Reece and the others since there came from the attacker, or attacking object, a startling diffusion of light which affected the cameras.

Although the personnel from Reece's force were not seriously wounded, he and four of his men were very rapidly put out of action and two suffered concussion.

Meanwhile, and this was the part which fascinated Bohr, the hydden in the henge began what he recognized from the moment he saw the footage as the same dance Arthur Foale had inscribed in the book he found in the library. Its movement, its orientation, its steps, its whole pattern, were the same. The figures followed each other, almost like identical shadows. But the last few seconds before they were gone was obscured by that same breaking light which made the earlier moments of attack so hard to read.

It was only when they examined footage from a second camera higher up the garden that they noticed something else. The timings showed it happened during the 'lost' final few seconds. Something, maybe someone, emerged from between the two great conifers. It looked like 'C' but the image was unstable and very hard to read, like a piece of transparent tissue blown helter-skelter by a fickle wind.

'Odd,' observed Bohr, who watched these few seconds many times. As it exited the henge the shape turned left and disappeared into the shrubbery on the right.

'That's where those damn wind chimes are,' said Reece.

'Yes, it is,' said Bohr, 'let's go and take a look.'

They found nothing and nobody, not a trace of anything. Nothing but the 'damn' chimes, which seemed to tinkle away in the lightest of winds.

It was only later that evening, when Bohr was watching the footage by himself, that he realized the soundtrack revealed something interesting: the chimes fell silent during the visit by the hydden and only started again when 'C' exited the henge. What this meant he had no idea but it suggested that the chimes might have significance. He decided that was not something he was going to talk with Reece about.

Nor were the implications of a conversation he had late that evening with Ingrid Hansen, who had jumped at the chance to get back to the UK. Having a first degree in environmental sciences from Cambridge, she knew of Arthur's work and had an interest in British prehistory.

That night Bohr found her working late, running the images of the movement of the hydden through a programme of her own which rendered their footsteps as graphical lines in time and space. Effectively the dance could be seen as a series of lines in progression. Seen that way, as a single image, it matched Arthur's sketches and the dance Bohr had found in the eighteenth-century dancing master's book.

That evening Ingrid was tired, which made her look even more geekish than usual. Her glasses sat too tight to her eyes and she wore black leggings with holes in them, a baggy denim skirt, whose hem was loose, and a woollen black top that made her look shapeless from neck to hips.

In fact, on the rare occasion she had made an effort, she scrubbed up well: her figure was good, she had lovely warm eyes behind her glasses, and, as Bohr remembered it, good legs too. But all that was never uppermost in him, not because he did not notice it but rather because a long and uninspiring marriage which ended in his being left for a younger man had made Bohr feel dead inside. Work became everything, intimate relationships nothing.

Ostensibly he had taken Ingrid on out of a very talented field because she was incredibly quick, thought outside the box and had a quiet sense of humour that simply needed confidence to come right out. Also, which he liked and would have responded to if only he – and she – had found a way to make it so, Ingrid was still romantic about the cosmos.

But there was something more, and it was helped by the fact that Ingrid was tall while he, relatively, was short. For some this might have been a difficulty, but though they were not a couple, or had ever been intimate, Erich and Ingrid found a curious comfort in it which only increased their unspoken liking for each other. Over the years this sense of companionable friendship had grown ever stronger and it was a source of puzzlement and frustration to their colleagues that the two had never quite found opportunity or courage to say to each other what they obviously felt.

What got in the way was the gulf in status between them and that they were work colleagues. Bohr felt he must not make a move, Ingrid dared not. When, at different times, they had tried to say what they felt, the words dried up, shyness, false propriety and lack of confidence getting in the way. The years had passed until now they were older, greyer and settled into a kind of helplessness. Professionally brilliant together, personally a failure. Lately Bohr had begun to get irritable, which he never had before, and Ingrid Hansen had begun to stumble and stutter when she was close up and personal with him, almost lost for words. The more she tried to be indifferent the more she failed to be.

That evening he found her at her computers and asked what she had found.

'It may just be chance.'

Nothing was chance to Bohr, nearly everything had pattern and potential.

'Try me.'

'I ran a check of the dance pattern from the book you found against the cache of henge images taken from your old professor's computer and . . .'

'I'm not sure I understand.'

'Well, they're plans really, near enough. Many are based on Aubrey Burl's work . . .' he nodded – he knew it '. . . along with Ordnance Survey data and a lot of early twenty-first-century satellite digital imagery and, well, the point is . . .'

'Is what?'

'I think I've found a perfect match.'

Bohr stilled. His heart began thumping.

'You mean a match for these lines you've derived from our footage of the hydden in the henge here in Woolstone?'

'Sort of, not exactly, a bit different, actually . . . well . . . um . . . more interesting.'

'Go on.'

'Right, yes . . . I took these graphics, what you call the dance lines, and I correlated them with the eighteenth-century dance graphic you brought in yesterday and I created a mean, if you like, a sort of idealized version. And then I ran that version, which really is no more than a pattern through time, because of course one step comes before another or, if you like, each follows the one before . . .'

'What time sequence does it show?'

'I based it on the footage we have and assumed that, since that sequence produced a positive result, meaning the dancers did actually leave the henge, we can assume their timing was correct. Okay with that?'

'Yes.'

'So . . . I put mathematical values to the space-time sequence of patterned dance steps, digitalized them, and that enabled me to check the dance against the known post-hole or stone patterns we have for all the known henges in Western Europe. Of course, different henges have different patterns so presumably dancers must adapt the steps to the particular layout of a henge. What I was looking for was a henge, or henges, that matched this *particular* record of a dance.'

'How long did *that* take?'

Ingrid Hansen pushed her glasses even closer to her eyes, riffled through the printouts on her desk and said, 'Two minutes thirteen seconds.'

He laughed: stupid question. She grinned, a moment of ease.

'And you found some matches?'

'Three beyond reasonable probability. One in Wentnor, one in Scotland on the Isle of Lewis, and one perfect match quite near us here, in Wiltshire.'

'Where? There are dozens of henges in Wiltshire.'

'I think you'll know *this* one,' she said, retrieving another print, which showed more than a hundred black dots arranged in concentric circles.

He gazed at it in amazement.

'This is Woodhenge,' he said.

'Yes, Woodhenge,' she said softly, with that delicious sense of conspiracy that people enjoy when they have a shared interest and curiosity about something few others recognize or know. 'Look what happens,' she said with a growing confidence, 'when I superimpose a printout of this particular dance on these prehistoric post-holes, which of course is what the dots represent, as you know . . .'

He did know.

'Go on,' he said.

'They dance a sequence which takes them to a succession of particular posts or stones in the henge, much like you might go through a front door of a house, then into a hall, stop off in the lounge, head for the kitchen and exit through the yard door . . .'

He stared at the lines and dots, trying to make sense of what she had said.

'Of course, it's more complicated than that and maybe they intone words of invocation as well, I wouldn't know. But what seems to be taking place is a build-up of a quite complex but evident pattern of movement from one point to the next, starting *here* . . .'

She pointed to a spot to the east of north on the henge.

'Ah, yes, the prehistoric entrance to the henge . . .'

'Exactly! And leading finally to an exit point here . . .'

Again she pointed, this time to the south edge of the henge.

'You can see how the dance pattern makes a perfect match with these major post-hole points and appears to exit at a circular group of holes to the south . . .'

It was a stunning piece of spatial analysis.

'What about the other sites you mentioned?' asked Bohr.

She showed him two other printouts.

'Close, but not such a perfect match. But I reckon if I'm right that this page of the dance book relates specifically to Woodhenge then all that the dancers would do would be to adapt the dance to the posts or stones in situ, just as ballroom dancers adapt to the shape of a room and the other dancers. A waltz is a waltz even if its direction changes. It's the step sequence that defines it.'

Bohr shook his head in astonishment and finally said, 'Well then, Ingrid, I think it's obvious what we're going to have to do sometime in the next few days.'

She looked blank.

'We're going dancing in Woodhenge,' he said with a smile.

'Oh ... um ... thank you,' she said faintly as if she had been asked on a longed-for date. Which, in a way, she had.

'Thank *you*,' he replied, adding, 'and ... ah ... Ingrid ... I think that until we are sure of these results and have worked them through in the field we should keep them to ourselves.'

'You mean from Colonel Reece? Yes, well ... that seems sensible.'

'When did you last dance?'

'Pardon me?' she said, briefly confused, as if Bohr was about to lead her in a waltz about the conservatory and between the computers. 'Oh ... I see ... not for a long time. I mean I don't exactly ...'

They stood staring at each other.

'Well then, goodnight,' he said.

'Er, yes, um ... er ... Erich,' she finally said, colouring, to his departing back.

29

SILENCE

It is said that for the unquiet spirit the early hours are a dying time, especially in winter. Both physical and mental strength is low and the desire for the release of death very great. Even more may this be true for those trapped in a sick, hurting frame. The clock ticks more slowly through those cold, unyielding hours and the road to each new tick becomes an eternity of pain and of suffering for some. The clinging on to life becomes no longer worth the while. They slip back to the oblivion of the Mirror-of-All to discover that their pain was as illusory as they themselves once were, just fleeting reflections, shards of light that race on by so fast it is as if, in the greater Cosmic scheme, they never were.

But for other mortals, those whose life has been rich and fruitful, the early hours of a new day, before light comes, have a quiet peace, a slow satisfactoriness which allows for a smile of fond memory, or a shake of the head at some remembered foolishness when the self got a touch above itself; or the abiding pleasure of being where one is, unhurried, with each in-out of breath all that there needs to be as mind and body and spirit float between the Earth beneath and the Universe above before, turning lengthways, sideways and all ways at once, there is no direction at all, neither time, nor space any more.

This, or nearly this, was the state in which Slaeke Sinistral, former Emperor of the Hyddenworld, found himself that morning, in the garden in Woolstone, waiting for the sun to rise. He was quietly wondering whether one more day was really needed now; thinking that maybe he had had his share.

A hydden, even one as skilled as Mister Barklice, would have found it very hard to see him, sitting as he was among the tinkling Chimes. Sitting as he had been for hours past. Sitting, as he now began to hope, with no need of ever moving again, except involuntarily, carried by the sound of the Chimes themselves back into the universal world of the *musica*.

In the pre-dawn light his pale, exquisite head, his eyes so light and grey, were little more than the reflection of the dim sky above in the drops of condensation on the Chimes about him which, to his great gratification, were beginning at last to still and fall silent.

He was, he knew, finally beginning to die and he was at utter peace with that, as with the world. Or nearly so.

Well, not quite, perhaps.

For something had stirred in his awareness, far, far away, and it was gathering such pace that Slaeke Sinistral, not without good humour, could not but stir as well, frown a slight frown and scowl a very unconvincing scowl.

'Death,' he whispered with affection, 'is more preferable than . . . *you!*'

Judith's irritation, however, was very real, her anger palpable and her scream so loud the mountains shook.

'Noooo!'

No, you're not going to die, Sinistral, not yet, not after so long, not without me bloody well coming and . . .

'Not yet!'

The White Horse ignored these shouts at Sinistral, as all others she now made, telling it to hurry up, galloping for once from where they had been to where they must go with all the clumsy tardiness of a reluctant carthorse plodding up a muddy track, heaving a heavy load at the end of an unpleasant day.

'I'm *not* a heavy load, for Mirror's sake, I'm the Shield Maiden and I have a job to do and that Sinistral, always cunning, slippery as an eel, is trying to slide away back into the Mirror without a by-your-leave, let alone an affectionate bye bye bye.'

She kicked the Horse with her bare, calloused, filthy feet and, turning her torso southerly to where the Reivers skulked and grumbled in the jungles of the sea, she whistled them up.

'Go and wake that Slaeke what's-his-name from his slide towards death. Nip his ankles, bark in his ear, claw his chest, fart in his face but do *not let him die.*'

The Reivers liked a chase, they did, and their flea-ridden dogs, bored, fancied a chase as well.

'Mistress,' the Reivers said through their slimy yellow teeth, 'oh fine Mistress, we will . . .'

'Forget all that,' she snarled, 'just do it now, right now.'

'Yes, yes,' they said, cursing their great fearsome dogs as if the delay was the dogs' fault and not due to their own indolence, 'we will.'

Erich Bohr was woken that morning by such a storm of noise in the garden that he pulled on his dressing gown and padded down to the conservatory doors.

'What the hell is that noise? Sounds like dogs.'

He was joined by two of the patrol, by Reece, a few of his clipped hairs awry, and Ingrid Hansen, her pale cheeks pinched by the cold at the open door.

'Nothing out there, sir,' reported the patrol, 'but wind and what felt like rain; and cold, like cold I've never experienced, except in a Montana blizzard. That rain's going to turn to snow and ice.'

They stared into the sudden wilderness of a winter dawn wind, the rattling of branches and the Chimes making an unusual din.

'Drives me mad,' said Reece. 'Always did.'

'You've heard it before?' asked Bohr, wondering.

'In my nightmares,' growled Reece, with a momentary expression that told of a dark and shadowed life, 'in my frigging nightmares.'

'What the hell are you playing at, Sinistral?' cried Judith the Shield Maiden, leaping off the White Horse before it ceased its gallop, so she landed skidding on the lawn with a volition that took her to his side, hands raised among the roaring Chimes to slap him. Which she did, almost, but could not finally, her hand stopping in a near-caress of his old cheek, which she too needed then herself.

He reached a gentle, ancient hand to hers but she shook her head and said, 'You cannot, you must not, I am the Shield Maiden. Touch me and being mortal you will die.'

Slaeke Sinistral looked through the darkness of that early hour into the lonely light of her beautiful eyes and, smiling, said, 'You heard me, then?'

She stared, furious.

'I heard you dying.'

'So I am, so now I am.'

'You can't, not here, not now. He needs you, my beloved needs you. Stort needs you.'

'And my beloved Leetha needs me in her way too, but ... but ...' he saw something behind her, something which lightened his eyes and was about to remark on it, a puzzled frown of coming insight on his crazed-porcelain face, when he said, 'Those dogs of yours, they kept me awake unmentionably. Otherwise I would have gone before you got here.'

She laughed, the real laughter of one who has been alone too long and remembers suddenly the joy of company and good humour.

'I ordered them to do all sorts of things. Was it wrong of me?'

'No. No it wasn't, Judith.'

Her need to touch and be touched was nearly overwhelming. Not doing so was only made bearable by the abiding love for her she saw in his eyes.

'I had hoped to live long enough to see the gem of Winter,' he said. 'I've known the other three ...'

The gold chain of Beornamund's pendant round her neck was visible, but the pendant itself was covered by the rags she wore.

'Best not to even look, Sinistral, they'll make you yearn as painfully as they make me age. Do I look old?'

'Yes.'

'Very old?'

'Yes. Too old.'

'Will he always love me?'

'Stort loves you now, he loved you before, he will love you, Judith, to the end of time. Age has nothing to do with it.'

'But ...'

'You are beautiful . . .'

'You talk like Leetha, my grandmother, who loves *you* . . .'

They sighed together for the briefest of moments before laughing at the absurdity of it all, the wind dying, the morning advancing, their contact now as real and palpable as if they had actually touched.

'What did you see just now behind me?'

'I saw the White Horse, not the real thing which reaches up to the sky and stamps the ground impatiently, but the one on the hill, carved out by a hydden whose name is now forgotten and . . .'

'And . . . ? *And?*'

'I saw something, Judith, I saw where I must go now and why you've come . . .'

'If I touch you, Sinistral, you will die . . .'

He shook his head and whispered, weaker now, so weak she could hardly see him there among the Chimes, 'This version of me will die, this reflection, but what matters will go back into the Mirror, it will.'

She shook her head.

'The Mirror has cracked and with it all that has been in this reflection is all that you are. The other reflections are surely lost.'

He smiled.

'Leetha will understand my need to go. But Niklas Blut . . . tell him I thought of him and wished to say goodbye . . . teach him to grieve, for he'll be uncertain how, but Leetha, my beloved . . . what will she do?'

'Sinistral, don't leave us.'

'What will she do?'

'Dance, dammit, and creep and crawl up to see that damn Modor, two crones cackling together by then. Don't leave us . . .'

'I must, here where the Chimes are, amongst their sound, which, when I heard it over there in the henge, I knew was a call to me to reach an end. We reflections get tired, we are not eternal. In any case,' and here he smiled and put his hand over hers despite her warning, 'it's so . . . very, very elegant, the solution that Bedwyn Stort must find, if he does, which he'll never, not ever . . .'

'He never will?' she whispered, her hand in his, his frail leaf-on-the-wind life flying through her now he touched her, going onward with the Chimes' *musica* and up towards the White Horse on the hill.

'Don't leave us . . .'

But wise Slaeke Sinistral was doing so.

'Don't leave me alone.'

You have the strength, Shield Maiden, as I did, to continue to the end . . . his thin, lovely old voice whispered into her grey hair.

For a time her weeping was the only sound in the awful silence of her life. Then the Reivers and their dogs, reduced by her sadness to whimpers, surrounded her, as if to protect her from a world that with the loss of such a friend felt too harsh for any of them to bear.

30

THE RUINED CITY

Lord Festoon, Brum's much-loved High Ealdor, found his city a very different place than it was when he had so reluctantly left it two and a half months before to help with the search for the gem of Autumn. A fact which Blut, Barklice and Terce each commented on too. Its buildings were in ruins, its citizens scattered and desolate with loss, and those in charge now at the very limit of their authority and control. The once-peaceful, thriving city was in decline and there was an unpleasant feeling of violence and danger lurking beneath its shattered surface.

During Festoon's absence the safety of the city had been the responsibility of Marshal Igor Brunte, a former Fyrd who had wrested control from the Imperial forces years before. When the Fyrd had launched a long-expected assault on Englalond the previous autumn, subsequently attacking Brum, Brunte had taken measures to ensure there was time for an orderly evacuation of civilians to take place.

The eventual takeover of Brum by the Fyrd's much larger force had been inevitable, and Brunte had prudently withdrawn his forces to the suburbs, where they helped Brum's refugees. The city's stavermen, a civilian force under the control of the doughty Mister Pike, who knew every nook and cranny of Brum Old and New, had then moved in to harry the Fyrd invaders.

This had been the point when Lord Festoon and his friends had left on the quest for the gem of Autumn, and what had happened since in Brum was unknown to them, as Englalond had suffered a series of violent weather and seismic incidents, and communications among the hydden were all but lost.

It was therefore with surprise that, on their return, the travellers had discovered that the Fyrd were all gone. But in the days following, their initial relief had turned to mounting horror as they learnt the full scale of the problems left in the wake of the Fyrd's departure.

It was Brunte and Pike together, at a meeting in the now half-destroyed city Library in the Main Square, who explained what had happened and why they, along with surviving Brummies everywhere, were filled with apprehension about the future. They would have met in the building opposite, the High Ealdor's own residence, but it had been completely destroyed.

'But we are at least content,' said Brunte, a thickset, middle-aged hydden whose friendly bonhomie rapidly left him if he was crossed or did not get his way, 'to learn that in addition to yourself, Lord Festoon, Emperor Blut here is fit and well and, of course, Mister Barklice too. Not forgetting you, Brother Terce who . . . well . . . I was never quite sure what it is you do.'

'I am a chorister,' replied Terce.

'And useful in a fight,' added Barklice.

'Ah! Good . . . now . . . to business . . .'

He was about to continue when, somewhere in the city, they heard an explosion.

'What the Mirror was *that*!?' said the Marshal.

Pike signalled one of his stavermen over and whispered in his ear.

'We'll soon find out,' he said.

Brunte nodded approvingly and resumed what he had been saying.

'What we must now decide . . .'

But again he was interrupted, this time by Niklas Blut.

'Before we deal with the future,' he said, wiping his spectacles as was his habit before asserting his authority, 'it would be helpful to have a simple account of what actually happened in the immediate past. So far we have had very different and fragmented versions of events.'

There was a very slight edge to Blut's voice, though his grey eyes were impassive behind his spectacles. He might not look especially impressive but his natural charisma conveyed both an intelligence and command that others deferred to, as they did now.

'Well then,' said Brunte, 'the Fyrd took control of the city the same day as you others had to leave. They immediately set about destroying as much of it as they could, looting and pulling down some of our most ancient structures and burning such records and other moveables as they could find.'

'I believe we had removed a great deal from Brum already?'

'Yes, Emperor, we had. They proceeded to destroy the rest. This went on for three weeks or so when two different but related things happened. First we had a further series of seismic shocks in the city, a good deal worse than the ones we had earlier in the year. These had the effect of spreading fires set by the Fyrd and starting new ones, especially in Old Brum. It was at about then that we heard, as the humans must also have done, of the destruction of Half Steeple.'

Blut and the others looked at each other, thinking that 'destruction' was too mild a word.

'We were witness to it,' said Festoon quietly. 'Mother Earth swallowed that human town whole, before our eyes. It was most horrible.'

'Which explains,' continued Brunte, 'the panic among the humans. As those in Brum began to fight each other, the situation was made worse by the arrival from the south and west of Englalond of human refugees fleeing Earth's anger. What they thought was its cause I have no idea but we hydden know very well that the humans are reaping the harvest of abuse of the Earth which, for so long, we have been witness to. Mister Pike can take up the story of what happened next . . .'

Pike nodded his grizzled head, but did not immediately speak. Festoon and Barklice knew him very well, and his lined, grey face and wearied eyes spoke volumes for what he, and Brum, had been through.

'We stavermen began as agreed by harrying the Fyrd as much as we could, which was quite a lot. We killed, we maimed, we frightened them. We used those same messengers as we had when the fight began, a group of lads and lasses led very ably by young Bratfire, Mister Barklice's son. They did brave service, even after three of their number were caught by the Fyrd and put to death.

'Some of the stavermen were lost as well and I was beginning to think we had done enough, or as much as we could, and that the time had come to withdraw, when something unexpected happened. We do not know how but some of the humans, driven by the violence of their own kind to hide in the sewers and conduits, succeeded in first seeing and then capturing some of the Fyrd.

'For the first time in centuries in Englalond there was hydden–human interaction. It was savagery on savagery, for the humans burnt those Fyrd to death, whether as a warning or out of plain sadistic bloodlust we cannot know.

'Soon after that the Fyrd, no longer under the harsh leadership of General Quatremayne, who followed yourselves in search of the gem of Autumn, decided to leave Brum. Whether they were afraid of us, of Mother Earth or the humans, we do not know. Probably all three. Anyway, they left almost overnight and soon after, the wave of human refugees who had come up from the south left Brum for the north along with the humans who lived here, torching what they left behind.

'When they were gone Brum was ours once more, but it was ruined and its infrastructure broken, as you have seen. It was not a place for humans or hydden to live in without much repair and rebuilding . . .'

Such was the sorry tale the returning travellers heard and it fitted well with their own experiences on the way back to Brum, which they now shared.

'It is good to know that the others who were with you are, so far as you know, fit and well,' said Pike finally.

'Certainly Stort and Katherine were only a few days ago,' said Barklice, 'and we must hope they still are!'

'As for Jack,' said Festoon, 'who left us by sea, he is not one to be easily beaten, or distracted from his duty as Brum's Stavemeister. He will surely return to us soon.'

But such hopes did nothing to dispel the sombre mood and doubt that had descended on them all.

'We must do what we can to make Brum habitable for hydden once more!' declared Niklas Blut. 'So far I have seen but few folk about the place. A city is not a city without a population to make it thrive.'

'I'm afraid what you've seen, my Lord,' said Pike, 'are stragglers and ne'er-do-wells, hoping for some pickings from the ruins or to take over abandoned humbles or business premises not yet claimed back by their rightful owners . . .'

'But you have the situation under control between you, I think?'

'Just about, my Lord,' said Pike heavily, 'just about.'

Brunte looked dubious.

'Marshal Brunte, have you something to add?'

He got up and paced about restlessly.

'Pike mentioned stragglers. We have questioned some of them and found they are not all Brummie folk. It is true that a few hydden are still drifting in from the south, but the ones who concern me are hydden who have found their way here from the north, displaced by the flood of human refugees.

'What they have told me is worrying. They cannot understand why the humans have fled northward in the winter months. The weather deteriorates rapidly north of Brum once the higher ground of the Dark Peak, the Yorkshire Wolds and the grim Pennines is reached. These folk predict that if temperatures drop further still this savage winter then a return flight of humans must begin. Brum will be in the direct line of it and we can expect human strife on our streets once more, which hydden will find impossible to avoid.'

'What do you suggest?'

'Naturally we need to know more. A week ago I sent two of my senior people to investigate, one to the North-West, the other to the North-East. I expect their return any day now and their intelligence will be helpful in planning Brum's immediate future.'

Blut considered this.

'It seems to me,' he said finally, 'that we should assume the best, plan for it, but quietly put in place what fall-backs and safety measures we need to. We have evacuated the city once under pressure and very fast; we can easily do so again with far fewer hydden now in residence.

'We should also ask ourselves if there is anything we can do in the short term to improve the situation here and make Brum attractive enough to lure those citizens back who are hesitant about returning when things improve.'

They discussed several possibilities but all seemed problematic until Pike said casually, 'Things would be easier for us all if the Bilgesnipe came back!'

'Explain!' said Blut, his interest suddenly piqued.

'It wasn't until they were no longer here that I understood how much we rely on them for transport, control of water supplies and portage. I do not think we can get the place going again without their help. Even the Muggy Duck is closed!'

No hostelry was more loved in all of Brum, nor better known in all the Hyddenworld. More than once the very history of Brum had revolved around events at the alehouse established by Pa Mallarkhi.

'Closed is one word for it,' growled Brunte. 'Burnt down might be better.'

'Burnt down!' cried Barklice, who had not visited the Muggy Duck since his return.

'The inglenook is still there, the great drinking parlour remains with half a floor above it,' said Pike with feeling, 'and the beer-stained table we used to sit down at is charred but still standing. But Ma'Shuqa and her pa left with the rest of them, as Bilgesnipe do, suddenly, just like that. They entirely disappeared. It's a mystery. Brum is not the same without them.'

Barklice pondered this and suddenly said, 'I think I know a way to get them back! As you are all very well aware, my son Bratfire is, genetically speaking, a Bilgesnipe, though the circumstances were too shameful for me to say more of them here.'

He had no need to. All Brum had heard the tale of how Barklice had been seduced by a buxom, comely Bilgesnipe who had borne him a son who he did not even know until less than a year before. Since then he had taken full responsibility for the boy, who, despite his unsatisfactory origins, was a credit to both parents.

'Yes indeed,' said Barklice, 'since his mother is a Bilgesnipe, so is he! Added to which, he was raised by them and knows their habits. I believe he might know ways to find them even in the present difficult circumstances.'

Pike shook his head.

'That's all very well, but they'd need a very good reason to come back to Brum!'

'But there is one, a very good reason indeed,' rejoined Barklice cheerfully. 'Arnold Mallarkhi is affianced and wishes to get spoused in Brum! That news'll bring the Bilgesnipe back to town! They like nothing better than a party, and nothing worse than missing one!'

'How do you know when Arnold is coming home?'

'His birthday is in January and he will wish to get here in time to celebrate both events together. He will find a way.'

'But you'll not let Bratfire venture off alone in search of Bilgesnipe?' said Festoon.

'I will not,' declared Barklice. 'I was apart from him too long and I would not willingly be so again. In any case . . . when I come to think of it . . . there is a very good reason for me to go along with him, quite apart from keeping him safe. Yes . . . definitely . . . yes there is!'

More he would not say but this: 'Pike, my dear friend, I strongly advise you to gather together some of your sturdier stavermen for a task for which every one of them will be needed.'

'Which is?'

'To make the Muggy Duck habitable and usable and, as it were, potable once more. For if the mission Bratfire and I set out on this afternoon is successful I venture to suggest that, whatever else may be happening in Brum over the next few days, at the Duck it will very soon be business as usual!'

That same evening another meeting took place in the Library, this one between Festoon, Blut, Brunte and Pike, and no one else. Its tenor was very different from anything before.

Insofar as anyone formally took the chair on this occasion it was Niklas Blut, as he had so effectively back in September when the city was under threat from the Fyrd.

'Gentlemen, Mister Pike has spoken in confidence to me about something which I need to draw to your attention and about which we need a joint and I think unanimous decision. Mister Pike . . .'

Pike usually carried himself with a calm assurance, the same with which he first picked up a stave when a boy and turned himself into the best staverman in Brum. He was older now and less agile but maturity had given him such authority that it would have been a brave staverman who took serious issue with him. But that evening he looked uncertain and troubled.

'We have discovered a group of humans holed up in Deritend. They are armed. Under cover of darkness and the continuing chaos in Brum they have placed cameras and listening devices similar to those that were used by the human authorities toppermost in Birmingham, our shadow city, before its collapse. Like those, we have left these well alone.

'Naturally my stavermen have had the humans under surveillance. Their hyddening skills are not very good. We do not think they are even aware that we know of their existence here, always a good thing in our kind of business. The element of surprise is a powerful extra weapon.'

'How many of them are there?'

'Four, my Lord. But with human weapons four can do a lot of damage. I would not have troubled you with the matter, which so far is under control, but that yesterday they began readying some new devices, presumably for use in the city. I have one here.'

Pike heaved a 'sac onto the table and slid from it a saucer-shaped object two hands wide.

'It is what we understand humans call a landmine. Step on it, disturb it, and it explodes.'

He smiled briefly.

'Relax, it has been defused by one of Marshal Brunte's bombardiers.'

Brunte shrugged. He had not been told this but he was well aware that his people and Pike's worked together sometimes and he was inclined to turn a blind eye to it.

'We think that so far they have not distributed them. But what do we do if they start spreading explosive devices about the place, just when we want our people to return? We saw what some of the humans did to the Fyrd. If we are not careful it may soon be our turn.'

'You are sure they are not aware you are watching them?'

'We are. When it comes to hyddening these humans are little better than clumsy children. But their explosive devices are anything but childish. We therefore have to decide what to do about them.'

'Marshal?' said Blut.

'Eliminate them,' he said brusquely. 'We know from recent experience and from our history lessons what humans do. They destroy. We should strike first.'

'Festoon?'

'If we do that, more will come,' he said at once. 'If we do not, more will come anyway. I will not make such a decision myself but I will not stand in the way of what you others decide . . . this is an unhappy time for Brum and the presence of such humans raises the question of whether or not we should encourage our citizens back at all.'

'Pike, what's your view?'

'We should kill them.'

Blut remained silent, aware that, if he said no, Festoon would say no as well, creating a futile stalemate.

'Gentlemen, I agree, but not with any enthusiasm, or any hope that eliminating a few humans will make any difference to Brum in the short or long term. My apologies for this, Lord Festoon, and you others too . . . but I think Brum's days are done.

'Something has shifted. Times have changed. This now feels like, whether we like it or not, the End of Days. I am tempted to suggest that we exit Brum and leave these humans to it. Hydden, like humans, are at their best in nature, not among buildings. You have lived your lives in the interstices of buildings here that should never have been created in the first place. I have lived most of my days until very recently in a coal mine in Germany which is, in terms of nature, an abomination. It is time for change. But that will not happen overnight. Whatever I think or say, hydden will come back to this city whether or not it is safe to do so. Most have no other home and we have a duty of care towards them. Therefore, we should rid the city of these humans even if it is only putting off an evil day.

'Lord Sinistral would have argued for getting them out of Brum. Failing that he would have commanded the Fyrd to kill them. They failed; we must succeed.'

His spectacles flashed and he looked hard at Brunte and Pike.

'Gentlemen, do what you must. Lord Festoon and I leave the details to you!'

31
REALM OF THE LIVING

It took Jack three days to recover from his ordeal at Woolstone, which gave them all time to come to terms with Sinistral's death. For the fact surely was that Sinistral had chosen to stay behind to save their lives.

When Jack had cried out the words *I'm going to die* as they dragged him to safety and his cramped, trapped body was violently and agonizingly stretched, he unwittingly endangered all their lives.

Arthur had frequently warned that at such moments a portal traveller's expressed intention was everything and whatever it is invokes a solution that meets it. Whether this was because the portals tapped into *musica* or wyrd no one knew, but to talk of death, let alone predict it, risked death itself.

Sinistral had been so close to death so long, and understood *musica* so well, that he instantly saw the danger they were in and what he must do. He had literally pushed Jack the way he should go – towards life itself – and accepted to himself the fateful expression of the wish to die.

'It was courageous certainly,' observed Stort, 'but I think we would do better to praise his action for its clarity of thinking and acceptance of death. Such things are hard to us all, for when we return to the Mirror and are reflected anew, the life we had is annihilated forever, memories in those who knew us are short-lived and very soon it is as if we have never been.

'I do not say that Sinistral has died, for that I do not know, but I do think he felt he had done all he could in this life and could therefore accept death graciously. That would not be so easy if we felt there were things still left to do which we had left undone. Or . . . well.'

'Or what, Bedwyn Stort?' asked Katherine gently.

'Or, if we loved another and never found a way to see that love fully lived and requited, how agonizing would death be then?'

'I am sure you will find a way,' Katherine said, knowing very well that it was of his great love for Judith the Shield Maiden that he was thinking.

'I do not think I ever can,' he replied sombrely.

In this way and others they took time to come to terms with what they were certain had been the fact and nature of Slaeke Sinistral's final passing.

They made camp in the crook of a stream near where they had ended up. There was rough pasture on either side and the few sheep that grazed there gave them a welcome sense of normality.

Jack worked out physically, using his stave to stretch and turn, a thing it seemed to enjoy because it challenged him, spinning away and making him reach for it, coming back suddenly and forcing him to catch its end and hold it still.

They were all tired and what had happened had put them in a state of shock which felt like suspended animation. Even Stort was keeping his head down, venturing no more than a few yards from where they were, disinclined to explore. None of them was yet willing to face the fact that very soon they would have to decide what next to do.

'Assuming that Arthur's theories about using the henge portals are correct, and they certainly proved right when it came to getting us from Stanton Drew to where we needed to be, we must accept that once more we are where we need to be,' said Katherine. 'But where this place is and what we do now I don't know and for the moment don't want to think about it!'

What they did do was talk, sharing their different experiences over the long weeks past and trying to make sense of what they had seen and felt. Stort listened far more than he talked, processing the facts of Jack's narrative and in the light of it reviewing what had happened to them both and the others during their journey overland.

'We have been here before, my friends,' he suddenly announced, 'and by that I do not mean this place spatially – though something tells me it is not entirely unknown to Katherine . . . ?'

Perhaps it was but she did not rise to the bait. She wanted to rest.

'No, I mean we have been here before in terms of quest. We have less than four weeks to find the gem of Winter and I have absolutely no idea where it is or where to begin.'

'Which is much as it was with the gems of Summer and Autumn,' said Jack.

'Just so,' acknowledged Stort. 'Of course, the gem of Spring more or less fell into my lap or, more precisely, I fell on top of it on Waseley Hill!'

He grinned ruefully, remembering again that difficult and turbulent night when he found the first gem.

Jack and Katherine looked at each other, glad to see him smiling again, but said nothing. At least Stort seemed to have got over the raw sense of loss he felt at the end of October, after he had put the gem of Autumn into the Shield Maiden's pendant. Neither of them found it easy to say 'Judith' for a daughter who they felt had been taken from them in so many different ways – by wyrd, by the Mirror and by an angry Earth. 'Shield Maiden' was easier.

That Stort loved her and that that love was returned they had no doubt. But an impossible love like that, born of innocence and certain to die on the rock of harsh experience, seemed to them to get so much in the way of things that it had clouded their friend's judgement.

'All I do know,' continued Stort, 'is that before each finding of the previous gems one or other of us visited the Chamber of Seasons in Brum and found the spirit and purpose to open the relevant door and pass on through to a place which led us to the gem we sought.'

It had been so.

'Well then, since time is running out, I suggest we get back to Brum as quickly as we can and visit the Chamber once more. It seems the best starting point.'

'Getting back to Brum is exactly what we've been trying to do, Stort!' cried Jack, less patient than Katherine with their friend's occasional statements of the obvious. She understood better than he that this was the way the scrivener worked things out when the way forward remained unclear.

'So . . .' said Jack, turning to Katherine, 'Stort here seems to think you know where we are.'

'Well I do and I don't,' she responded reluctantly, 'but that's not what's worrying me. There's something about this place that presents us with an important choice but I just can't remember exactly what it was that Arthur told me.'

Jack stoked the fire, made a brew and handed them some brot and elder-cheese, all without a word.

Only when they had imbibed and eaten to their entire satisfaction did Katherine feel ready to tell them where they were. Or rather, show them.

They had been in no state to notice much beyond the immediate area of grassland near the stream they had arrived at. Since then they had been hunkered down, barely moving.

Katherine now walked them north away from the water, across rough pasture, slowly veering west as she did so. Only when she pointed it out did they notice the nearly imperceptible ridges on either side of their route, which suggested it had once been a green road of some kind.

She went slowly, breathing deeply, eyes half closed, engendering in them the sense that there was something very special about where they were.

'And very familiar,' murmured Jack.

'You could say that,' she said with a grin and such obvious irony that Jack turned to Stort and said, 'She obviously thinks we should recognize this place . . .'

At which moment Stort, taller than Jack and looking south-west, laughed and said, 'Ahh! Yes! I see it now! Does that structure not remind you of something!?'

Jack turned and stared, walked a few yards more, looked carefully again until suddenly the familiar became the very obvious indeed, like someone met out of context who becomes recognizable only when a name or a look prompts the memory.

Jack's eyes widened in astonishment and, feeling a fool, he said faintly, 'It looks like Stonehenge.'

'It *is* Stonehenge,' said Katherine laughing. 'That's where we are.'

The familiar, prehistoric megalithic structure sat stolidly in a slight depression and a few hundred yards from where they stood. It was not nearly as impressive as Jack might have expected, seeming dwarfed by the vast landscape about it. But there it was, grey and massive and, well, tempting.

'Let's go!' said Jack.

'I think not, Jack,' said Stort, shaking his head and immediately taking his arm. 'I believe that might be a very grave mistake. This is what you meant by making a choice, is it not, Katherine?'

She said that it was.

'Instead of doing the obvious, Jack, we should retreat at once, very quietly, very carefully, and without looking further at those alluring grey stones. Having done that, we should go the other way.'

But Jack wasn't having it.

'Stop being ridiculous, Stort. The stones are only a few hundred yards away and we could be there in no time . . .'

He walked a few steps towards them, the others not following. He continued on a few steps more and began to feel a lassitude, a weakening of will, the need to battle with a deeper instinct to turn back.

'But the portal brought us here,' Jack called back to them, 'so obviously Stonehenge is where we're meant to be!'

'Obviously it is *not*,' said Stort acidly. 'Would you not agree, Katherine?'

'I would,' she said, 'but I can't exactly say why. Really, Jack, it's not safe to go further. Please come back!'

Grumbling, Jack turned and followed them back to their camp.

'I was twelve when Arthur brought me here,' explained Katherine. 'I remember we explored the landscape all about while he expounded his theory about what it was for. The faint green path we were on runs from the river where we camped to Stonehenge and he explained that it had a use, but I can't remember what exactly.'

Jack was feeling better now he had retreated from Stonehenge and he looked questioningly at Stort for an explanation. But he was not yet ready to say what was on his mind. Instead, he said, 'You say you explored this landscape "all about". What exactly do you mean by that? Isn't this "all"?'

'Well, we didn't start by Stonehenge itself but two miles north of here at a place called . . . Damn! I can't remember its name though he mentioned it sometimes.'

She wrinkled her brow trying to remember.

'Doddington . . . ? No . . . Derrington . . . No . . .'

'Durrington?' said Stort.

'Yes! How did you know?'

'My mind retains useless information in case one day it might become useful. A waste of effort mostly, but once in a while it pays off. Do you remember what he showed you at Durrington?'

'Nothing as dramatic as Stonehenge, which is probably why I can't remember much about it.'

'Try.'

'Well . . . I felt disappointed about the place. I mean, I wanted to see Stonehenge not a crummy little . . . Durrington was just a depression in the ground, like a big football pitch.'

'Anything else?'

'There was another henge there. In fact he said there were a lot of henges and burial mounds and this cursus we've just walked . . . that's right! This old green road was part of a route all the way from Durrington to Stonehenge. He said the other henge was made of wood and that was the whole point, but . . .'

She petered out.

They turned to Stort, who, as so often when he had something to impart, was pacing around, eyes half shut, moving his hands about in the air as if trying to grab hold of his own thoughts and make them solid.

'There are many theories about these stone henges. One thing is certain, in those ancient times stone had a very different symbolic meaning than wood. The first is dead, the second is alive. Or, if you like, wood is the realm of the living and stone that of the dead.

'I have heard, from Barklice, I think, that within the orbit of Durrington is a henge of wood. It was this, I am sure, that Arthur showed you, Katherine. But your disappointment was natural enough: the wooden posts of which it was constructed obviously rotted away millennia ago, their holes all filled up with debris, leaving no more than a low circular earthen mound within which there can only be the merest trace of post-holes.

'But that was the realm of the living in ancient times and from it, when folk were dying or recently dead, they began their ritualistic journey to Stonehenge. First by water and then by the grassy way we walked along to Stonehenge.'

He fell silent and pensive.

'What is significant is where we ended up after escaping from the humans at Woolstone, which is halfway between these two realms,' he continued. 'No doubt that is because as we were leaving the Woolstone henge Jack unwittingly mentioned death. But for Sinistral's intervention we might very easily have emerged at Stonehenge itself, with fatal consequences. He understood the danger and saw a way to neutralize it.

'But by taking that intention to himself he chose to find death another way, leaving us to end up safer than we might have done but still only halfway there. I conclude the land of the living is where we should be and that we head for Woodhenge and see what happens when we get there!'

They struck camp and set off immediately, following the river upstream, Stort slow and pensive once more. But later his pace quickened and he began to hum.

'He's thought of something else,' Jack said quietly to Katherine as they walked along.

'I have indeed,' cried Stort. 'If this theory of realms be true then it answers a question of even greater importance than those surrounding Stonehenge, impressive though that grim and miserable monument might be to those of a mordant disposition!'

Stort was on form.

'The question I have in mind is simple,' he went on. 'Why was the White Horse carved into the particular place where it *was* carved? Goodness me, the possible answers are many, are they not?'

The afternoon was darkening, the going was heavy but they felt they had a destination and a purpose once more. It was a very long time since Jack and Katherine had found time and space to simply hold each other's hand and walk together in silence.

At first sight Woodhenge was a disappointment. The area was one of undulating chalk downland higher than Stonehenge. The henge itself comprised over one hundred posts set in concentric circles within a raised grass bank so flattened by time and human interference that it was barely visible.

The posts were round and made of concrete and except for a few slightly taller ones were half the size of a hydden. From a distance they appeared as a jumble of uprights, set close together without obvious pattern or meaning. But close-to they made sense, and interpretation was made easier because there was an explanatory noticeboard nearby for humans.

They were circles-within-circles, each painted in different colours to indicate successive stages of building and usage. Katherine remembered enough of what she had learnt from Arthur on different walks to similar sites to be able to make a stab at interpretation.

'These places were built successively over centuries by different groups of builders who probably had a whole range of beliefs. Sometimes, just like humans and hydden, they razed a site and started again.

'That makes the landscape in which they were set as important as the structures themselves. Without appreciating one it is hard to understand the other.'

Stort's first concern was that humans should have been so insensitive as to replace the wooden posts with concrete ones.

'They have missed the point and robbed the site of something of its power,' he said.

His bad mood was temporary for he found much of interest in the adjacent and much larger site of Durrington Walls. This was a vast semi-circular embankment immediately to the north of the henge and enclosing a rough grassy area the size of several football pitches.

'It seems plain enough to me,' he declared after two days' exploration, 'that this extraordinary site had several interrelated uses. I would suggest that its primary one was as a collecting point for hydden and human folk together, engaged in rituals of a hydden origin now all but forgotten. These "walls", as the humans insist on calling them, inclined as they are to think of defence and attack and enclosure, are nothing of the kind. They are no more nor less than comfortable seating for faithful and awe-inspired mortals, come to watch the greatest ritual of them all, which, as we have seen, takes us from the realm of the living to what ancient folk wrongly construed as the eternity of death.

'Quite obviously the concrete posts of Woodhenge mark out in a vestigial kind of way the ancient place or house or humble from which that journey started. Perhaps it was here that the remains of the recently dead were in some way consecrated *before* their spirits, as they were once called, were deemed to have left their mortal remains. Only then, and still living in a sense, did they begin their journey south and west, into the setting sun, to their final resting place.'

Stort spoke these words standing on a wooden table whose original purpose was as a picnic table for humans but which he now used as a soapbox for his learned oratory.

'Ah, thank you, Katherine, I *will* have more of this excellent brew if you please!'

'Stort,' said Jack, 'I know we've seen no humans about but you're making yourself very obvious from miles away . . .'

But Stort was in no mood to be stopped and at least in such open ground Jack was well able to see if any danger appeared. Meanwhile Stort stood suddenly taller, having had a new insight even as he spoke, and which seemed to him both revolutionary and important.

'I begin to see,' he cried out in a voice that might well have been heard by the deafest of his prehistoric listeners, were they assembled there, 'that these ancient hydden were seduced by the gloomy, death-loving humans into the false belief that death ends in that realm of the dead defined so darkly by the grey, stony, eternal and intransigent monstrosity which is Stonehenge. Whether they went by river or were carried I care not! They went the wrong way! We are fortunate, are we not, that later hydden saw the light and turned from the valley of death that lies before us, with its tumuli and dank sarsens and chambered graves, towards the stars, the Universe and that much greater symbol of transformation from life to supposed death. I refer, of course, to the White Horse! *That* is the great journey we embark on from Woodhenge!'

This was indeed a startling transformation of thought, at least in the minds of his captive audience. For Katherine, raised as she was within sight of the White Horse, it was a revelation to think that the Horse was a positive alternative to the great and mythic but negative edifice that was Stonehenge.

'It is surely not "an" alternative but *the* alternative!' she said.

'Exactly so, Katherine, you have grasped the point almost as swiftly as I myself! It tells us that the White Horse is our ultimate destination and in some way holds the clue to the meaning and location of the gem of Winter.'

Which was all very well to the ever-practical Jack, who was not sure if he grasped the point they were so excitedly making.

'Meanwhile,' he said prosaically, 'it is my job to get us all safely to Brum, so quite why we've ended up here I don't know. But there's a reason for it, no doubt, and here, for the time being, we shall stay. As for returning to the White Horse and Woolstone, where I so recently almost died, I've no intention to returning there any time soon!'

32

TAKE MY HAND

Two nights after Erich Bohr's discovery of the special importance of Woodhenge in Arthur's research in accessing the Hydden-world he was woken in the early hours by the soft but persistent thwump-thwump-thwump throb of a helicopter's rotors. He had been restless anyway, because he had arranged with Reece for a helicopter flight to Woodhenge later that morning. A military presence seemed prudent. He was surprised to hear the departure of a much earlier flight.

Bohr got up, opened his window wide and listened carefully. He was in time to see a dim silhouette against the night sky rising from the direction of the helipad on the adjacent property and moving over the henge trees and heading south. This was not a flight Reece had mentioned to him. Bohr had already come to the reluctant conclusion that he had him – had them all – under twenty-four-hour surveillance. He now guessed that he had been privy to his night-time discussion with Ingrid about Woodhenge and knew about the dance.

When he had subsequently explained that he intended to go to the site and to take Ingrid along with him to take notes, Reece had seemed unperturbed. He had even suggested that perhaps there would be no point in going along himself, unless Bohr intended to try to enter the Hyddenworld?

'I doubt I'll be able to do that,' said Bohr ambiguously.

'That's right,' Reece had replied heavily.

Bohr was now pretty certain that the dawn flight he had seen was to put in place some kind of observation team at Woodhenge to collect data for Reece's own use. He did not like the idea but he could see why Reece might think that way and maybe provide extra security and cover – he too had a job to do. Bohr had worked around the military long enough to know that, generally speaking, they were not such good liars as politicians, or even political academics like himself. If there were going to be others on the ground at Woodhenge he needed to know, and the best way to find out was to ask the question straight out.

Still in his pyjamas and dressing gown, he went to ask Reece if he had sent a flight ahead of his own.

'Sure,' was the frank, unrepentant, reply. 'I've sent people in ahead of your trip this morning. You got a problem with that, Doctor?'

'It might affect the outcome, having your people crawling all over the place. You could have discussed it.'

'Need to know,' said Reece bluntly. 'Have *you* told me everything you've found out?'

Bohr gazed at him.

Stags at bay.

'Need to know,' he replied, with an irony that passed straight over Reece's head and brought not a flicker of amusement or acknowledgement to his cold eyes.

Bohr was sure that by the time he got there Reece's people and their equipment would be discreetly in place, ready to keep an eye on all that happened. Maybe Reece thought he would learn more about Bohr's real intentions by lying low – either by actually not being there, or being there covertly. Either way, Bohr had no intention of trying to find out anything more, either before they left or on the site itself. No point. In situations like this, the business Reece and his people were in was to stay invisible and Bohr doubted he would spot any of them even if he tried.

But he was also certain that there was something Reece could not know and that was the one clue that Arthur Foale had let slip about travelling to the Hyddenworld on the single occasion, years before, he had talked about it.

'It's all about *intention*, Erich. That's the trick. To know where you're going.'

You dance, Erich told himself now again and again, *with a purpose or a destination which is really one and the same thing. And anyway, it isn't a dance exactly, it's just . . . a few steps.*

The thwumping throb from the helicopter that woke Bohr did the same to Jack thirty-five minutes later.

Katherine was asleep to his right and she stirred at his touch. Stort, always a heavy sleeper, lay further off and showed no sign of waking.

'What is it?' whispered Katherine.

'Humans are coming. I think that whatever it is we're meant to be waiting for here is now beginning to happen. I'll go and find out what they're up to. Only wake Stort if you have to; we're less likely to be seen if he stays still.'

Jack stayed on the far side of the river from the henge until he was certain that the approaching helicopter was going to land. Predictably, for a flight arriving at that site, it dropped down right in the centre of the space defined by the Durrington ramparts.

He got within reach of it in under a minute. It carried no external lights but he was near enough that when its side door was opened he could see the interior lights of cabin and flight-deck. The engine did not stop as four military men jumped onto the grass, each with a backpack. The Huey flew off at once.

The men moved fast, black shapes across the frosted ground, and went straight towards the henge. Jack was careful to keep a close eye on all four as they moved quickly and purposefully into what looked like pre-arranged positions. They seemed unaware they were being observed, Jack instinctively using the steep, east side of a rampart whose broken, rucked-up sward offered perfect cover. They walked single file across the grass, using each other's footprints in the frost until they reached the road between the walls and the henge.

Two of the men went and established themselves in a small group of trees a hundred yards from the henge. They faced towards it, meaning that their backs were to Jack's campsite two hundred yards away. The two others walked past the henge to the few trees that formed its southern boundary and established themselves there. Jack watched with interest as they set up cameras and some tiny directional microphones. It was done very fast and in total silence. Long before the sun rose the site looked deserted once more with only Jack to know who was there and where they were.

By then, Jack had returned to their camp.

'They're obviously expecting someone,' he said.

'You sleep,' said Katherine, 'and I'll take the watch. I'll wake you when I need to.'

That moment came two hours later when she heard the throb of the helicopter approaching once again.

Erich Bohr and Ingrid Hansen arrived just after nine in the same Huey as the covert force had done earlier and, though they did not immediately know it, in the same place.

Three of the six marines accompanying them climbed out before the rest, explaining they needed to secure the ground. They set off towards the henge and obliterated the prints made by the earlier contingent. When Bohr and Hansen got out they stood in pale sunlight, the whole area shining with frost and cold, stamping their feet and hitting their gloved hands together.

'Hardly dancing weather,' said Bohr, turning round slowly, eyeing the landscape near and far. He saw evidence of neither marines nor anyone else having visited the site but then he didn't expect to. Certainly no sign of Reece, who had not accompanied them.

Bohr's earlier excitement was replaced by an initial disappointment with the site itself. The so-called Durrington Walls were low earth mounds topped to the north-west by ordinary housing. The post-holes of the henge just south of the site had been picked out by dull-looking concrete posts, dozens of them.

'Over a hundred and thirty in all, apparently,' said Ingrid.

Bohr's conviction earlier that morning that their attempt to enter the henge portal might succeed, now waned. Standing there, the noise of the helicopter still reverberating in his ears and a combined security and communication team setting up positions, robbed the site of any sense of the past.

Why they were repeating the exercise, assuming a covert team was already in place, he could not imagine. This might be a prehistoric site, but with modern technology and military all over the place and with houses to one side, a road passing through and a car park with an information board for the public, it was hard to see it as such. The idea of 'dancing' the henge seemed absurd.

Yet, as Bohr stood there, unsure at first how to approach the place, he had to admit it held a certain power in a grim, strange way.

'Er . . . in which direction is Stonehenge?' wondered Ingrid.

'You have the file and the map,' he replied tersely. 'Work it out.'

She took his irritation calmly, glad to be given clear directions. As she stood there orientating the map to what she could see around her, Bohr walked slowly to the henge itself, ordering the marines to move back and give him space. Ingrid Hansen joined him and they worked out the map's orientation together.

'It's quite . . . spiritual,' she said, to his surprise.

'Is it?'

'Um . . . well . . . yes . . .'

'Yes,' he said more gently, annoyed at himself for denying what he was also beginning to feel, 'yes I think maybe it is.'

They approached nearer and suddenly it was, strongly so. The posts' interlocking concentric patterns pulling at his mind like thorny under-growth, catching his clothes and bare skin, some behind and some to one side, impeding forward movement, inviting the half-turn, the dis-connection . . . the dance.

'Maybe we should just try to see where to start . . .' he said, breaking the spell, or trying to.

Maybe we should be rational and scientific about this.

Or maybe we should not.

'I've found the starting point,' she said, looking at the sheet she had printed off and, again to his surprise, she reached a hand, half laughing, half embarrassed, for his.

'Ah, yes, right!' he said, aware of the troops looking, aware of his awkward body, of his feet, of the damn concrete posts. Aware of being overweight.

They took a few steps, Ingrid in the lead, until she stopped, dropped his hand and pored over the plan.

'I don't think so.'

The posts spiralled about him and he was glad she was taking charge, because the place made him feel dizzy and out of control. He turned and turned again, right where he stood, the sun in his eyes and then out of them, then in again.

'Here! Sir . . . oops, I mean Erich!'

Her voice light, her hand offering itself, 'I think maybe if we . . . yes you follow . . . that's right . . . I mean . . . um . . . ooo . . . ow!'

She banged a shin on one of the posts, a blue one, and sat down to rub it. She was laughing. She was transformed. She was his partner in dance and the marines were stiffening, watching, taking steps closer. It felt as if something was swirling round and round them.

'Let's try again,' he said, and this time he took her hand, led her back to where they had just started from, and began once more.

'Come on . . . yes . . . on . . .'

A wind which wasn't there before, nor surely had been earlier, whirled a tiny tornado of ice crystals towards them from the north-west end of the Durrington Walls, a few inches off the ground.

Jack saw it, watching closely as he was, Katherine to one side and Stort the other. Watching the two humans in the henge and the two marines lying amongst trees much nearer.

'Look!' whispered Jack pointing towards the minuscule swirl of white that showed the wind. '*Look!*'

At his insistence they had packed their 'sacs and had them on, ready to move fast if they needed to. He and Katherine had their crossbows set, loose at their belts along with their dirks. Stort was ready for a quick exit too, having picked up the same edgy, fragile feel of the day and the way the humans were, stiff as stones but for the two in the henge.

'The wind's getting up,' growled Jack, 'and those humans, what are they *doing?*'

'Messing about,' muttered Stort, 'which is not good in a henge, especially that one. Mirror knows where you'd end up!'

'They're not messing about,' said Katherine with a mixture of aston-ishment and alarm, '*they're trying to dance the portal!*'

They all watched, stunned. It was true: the two humans, hand in hand, who had seemed so awkward at first, so humanish inside the henge, were dancing free now, turning the step, leaning the slant and going dexter as they should except, *except.*

'Except they're doing it wrong,' said Stort.

The wind was whirling and swirling snow in its wake, rushing about, cracking the scene open, and the marines, up and alarmed, the two before them who had been so still, now restive, visible, forgetting themselves and the wind so strong up and down the walls and across Durrington way, stirring the blades of the helicopter, shaking the machine, and dry grass flattening right across the site, and yet where men stood, where they lay, nothing but cold, terrible cold.

'See that wind,' said Katherine, her own voice beginning to shriek as if against its sound, which they could see but not hear, which is impossible, except it was happening like that, it was.

'Everything's stirring,' said Stort, and it was, it was, the wind fractiously cutting the air into shards of cold that swirled above them all, threatening to come down, and ice dust combining to sharp points that flew like thin, invisible, shrapnel at *them* now, at their hands and eyes, their cheeks.

The marines were turned and turned again, discipline leaving them all but for the nearest two in front and those other two beyond the henge rising now, making themselves seen.

'Ingrid I cannot I cannot I cannot . . .'

Bohr whirled in his dance, almost there but lost at the last moment and she too, her hand in his, impossible to part, locked in a fall from the sky which was filled with ice, cold cold ice, and they heading where they did not want to go.

'Erich, I am dying, I am dying, dying . . .' she screamed, unable to pull him the way she wanted as she was pulled southward towards darkness, towards enveloping stone and he unable to pull her back but wanting to go with her, as if together they were bound to the wrong way, which was sinister, too sinister, all sinister now.

'Ingrid, let go of my hand, you're drowning me in stone.'

'Let go of mine, we're falling too fast towards the grey, the hard hard grey, we're falling and my feet can't get a grip to hold us back.'

Slowly, as it seemed, the marine a hundred yards in front of Jack raised his weapon to take aim, the madness of the landscape and the wind and the blizzard ice made incarnate by his killing act.

Jack rose at once and grabbed Katherine and she Stort, bound together in a certainty what would happen if they did not do what now they must.

'They . . .'

'Are . . .'

'Losing their way,' they said, beginning to run.

Jack raised his bow and shot the shooter in the shoulder, sending him spinning with the wind.

He heaved Katherine past him, she being the most adept and needing to lead, and Stort second, turning back towards one of the men near them who was now raising his weapon. Jack kicked him hard instead of using a weapon, sending him tumbling after the other, eyes wide in surprise. Then, catching a glimpse in his peripheral vision that one of the others was also levelling his weapon, Jack aimed at him without hesitation, watching the bolt slide away slow and slower still, flexing and turning slightly as it flew through the ice-filled air, just right, turning and flexing just, just so . . .

The bolt glanced across the turning head, cutting a flap of skin that flew down, the blood flowing, and the marine falling against his companion, down. Both down as well.

'Here!' screamed Katherine at Ingrid across the shards that cut through them with sound, 'take my hand!'

Oh and they caught each other in a breaking, whirling circle of dance, pulling back from the realm of death, choosing the light, forcing the turn to dexter once again.

'This way,' she said in that voice Jack loved, strong and purposeful, good as her cool hands upon his old burns, 'this way now . . .'

The portal opened and the henge took them, the dance continued on its meandering way, an echo of the Avon's death-flow faded and they were up and away and safe.

'Not down,' she said, 'up, follow, hold out hands, feel the flow, come on through . . .'

And Ingrid Hansen laughed and laughed, and Erich Bohr grinned as if he was young again, before the world of men began to eat his flesh and suck his mind, young as the day he first met Arthur Foale.

Then Stort next to last and Jack last of all, his stave enlivened more than ever it had been by the spirit of the ancient staves that once rose where it now flew, turning its glints and shimmers back on the ice wind's flow, as shots flew in, bullets as slow as armadillos, turning like the bolt had, slow and slower, as Jack's stave played ancient cricket with them all and sent them out across the sky, thudding through the thick, shady air, straight as arrows to land thud, thud, thud and harmless now, flattened, useless and spent, the frost on the ground steaming briefly where they lay in the distant shadows of Stonehenge.

'Where are we?' asked Jack later.

'Where we need to be, I expect,' said Stort, feeling more relieved than he cared to say.

'Safe, I'm sure,' said Katherine.

Erich Bohr and Ingrid Hansen, still holding each other's hand, said not a word as they slowly opened their eyes to gaze for the first time upon the Hyddenworld.

33

BILGESNIPE

The portal out of Woodhenge brought Jack and his party into nearly pitch-black night in what smelt and sounded like a wood. He used a lantern to check that the two humans were alive and well and in no way threatening, which they were not. In fact they were tired and subdued, which was hardly surprising considering what they had been through. He left Katherine in charge and briefly explored the location.

'It's a yew wood, and an old one,' he told them on his return from a reconnaissance. 'We're on a hill top with no obvious sign of life nearby at all.'

'Well . . .' said Katherine, 'I'm not so sure about that! I could have sworn I heard a snatch of singing and the high fluting sound of a bulpipe. But it stopped, suddenly.'

'Bilgesnipe,' said Jack. 'If they see or hear us they'll not harm us.'

He brightened his lantern to take a closer look at the strangers.

They were a male and female, eyes wide, and they sat with their backs against huge roots, looking both vulnerable and embarrassed. They also looked very cold, which was unsurprising considering they were capless, their shoulders bare, as were their legs, which protruded from beneath the voluminous wrappings which were all they appeared to have for garb.

Katherine grinned, opened her 'sac and offered the female a jerkin, underwear and trews.

'Jack . . .' she prompted, 'do the same for this gentleman. Their clothes have not shrunk with them.'

It was one of the mysteries of portal travel, about which Arthur had often warned, that while the mortal form may shrink or grow depending on which world it is arriving in, garb is not always so obliging. For newcomers especially.

Stort knew that because on the one occasion he had inadvertently travelled to the human world his clothes had torn and fallen in tatters about him, leaving him naked. As for Arthur, it had been his habit to take a suitable change of clothing with him for he liked his comforts and the Hyddenworld had not discovered the pleasures of corduroy trousers and shirts with breast pockets. Jack grinned and gave the man some of his clothes.

'You can have use of this plaid,' cried Stort in a friendly way for the two looked intelligent and he was intrigued to find out how they had first thought to dance the henge and then actually nearly succeeded in doing so. 'I am much impressed that you have found a way to dance the portal into the Hyddenworld. Though I fear you very nearly killed yourselves!'

'Are you . . . um . . . a hydden?' asked the female.

'I am, she isn't, and he's what's called a giant-born,' replied Stort.

'I'm Ingrid,' she said cheerfully, as if they were meeting at a tea party.

Jack scowled, preferring to leave the small talk until they were safe and set fair, but Stort persisted.

'A fine name of Nordic origin, I believe. For myself, please call me Stort. This is Jack and this Katherine.'

'Um, hello,' she said.

'And your friend?'

'He is Doctor Erich Bohr.'

Stort looked startled. Jack's eyes glistened and grew cold.

'The Erich Bohr who attempted to abduct Arthur Foale?' he said, grasping his stave and loosening his dirk in a threatening kind of way.

Bohr gulped. His throat went dry. It was bad enough that his head was still spinning and he felt sick but this hulk of a person talking with him – no, interrogating him – seemed to actually know who he was and not like the fact. Anything could happen!

'I wouldn't say we were trying to abduct him . . .'

'But you forced my adoptive father to flee an airbase and cut his way through the perimeter fence, which could easily have given him a heart attack, did you not?' said Katherine.

Bohr began to sweat, for this female was formidable and she talked of fathers and fences and . . . and she too had a dirk and crossbow. They had fallen among thieves and murderers.

'He was there of his own free will and we . . .'

Jack and Katherine exchanged a glance. Arthur had talked of Bohr and, if they remembered aright, rather admired him. That he should appear as he had at Woodhenge was not quite so surprising as it might at first seem, given the wyrd of the times. Bohr might be – no, probably was – unwittingly following in Arthur's footsteps to complete the work he had begun.

It was unfortunate that Jack and Katherine, lost in such musing, were holding their dirks and frowning.

'My dear friends,' cried Stort, misinterpreting what he saw, 'do not hurt or maim them! Or if you do, let me extract what information I can first. But really I see no need for violence or, at any rate, not unpleasant violence.'

'Stort,' said Jack, 'kindly stop talking.'

Bohr was now unsure whether to run in his unrobed state, taking Ingrid with him, like two nymphs in the wood, or remain silent, or talk more.

Not Ingrid. She felt suddenly enraged by what she imagined to be this attack upon them both. But she kept her temper.

'We come in the name of world peace and reconciliation,' she began, 'and I can tell you from the bottom of my heart that . . .'

'I would very strongly advise you to say no more,' said Katherine. 'Jack can get irritable and, trust me, he is getting so now. The introductions and suchlike can wait until later. Stay silent, follow orders and all will be well. Now, get that garb on!'

As she closed the shutter of the lantern to give Bohr and Ingrid a modicum of privacy, the sound of music and song she had heard earlier came up to them from the wood below. Its scales were exotic and the voices that accompanied them sensuous and not entirely female, for they bore within them a thread of the tenor and a touch of the treble.

'Bilgesnipe, indeed!' cried Katherine with delight.

'The last time I heard such a thing,' declared Stort, rising and peering in the direction from which the sound came, 'was with Mister Barklice on that famous occasion when we were wending our way towards Woolstone.'

He turned to the newcomers.

'You, sir, and you, madam, are lucky indeed to have stumbled into the Hyddenworld at such a time and in such a place. That, without question, is the sound of revelry of the kind usually only heard at Paley's Creek!'

'Which means,' said Jack, 'that they're not going very far very fast, so let's eat and join them later.'

They lit a fire and got hot refreshments sorted in no time at all, making sure their guests were fed first and respecting their now rather nervous silence.

'Which is understandable, considering,' whispered Katherine to Jack. Both remembered their first worrying journey into the Hyddenworld and how disconcerting it had been. 'Maybe it's as well it's dark! They can't actually see very much.'

But everyone was so hungry that soon all they wanted to do was eat – and to the sound of the music from below the hill, which was companionable and soothing.

'I hope they don't ask what Paley's Creek is,' Katherine whispered back. 'If they do, Stort can explain!'

The truth was that no one, not even the Bilgesnipe, knew exactly what Paley's Creek was, or where it was. It was a kind of happening and for decades, until only a few months before, most hydden had imagined it was a real place. That Bilgesnipe met 'there' was certainly true. That things went on there – things sensuous and strange, things magical, things transformative – was true too.

It had been at Paley's Creek, or an event that had that name, that Mister Barklice had fathered Bratfire by a bilgygirl, his one and only experience of carnal delight. Only years later, and with Stort's help, had he had the opportunity to return to Paley's Creek to accept responsibility for the son he had fathered, an event which raised respect for him very high among the Bilgesnipe and brought to Brum his excellent son and heir, Bratfire, who had all the natural hyddening skills of his father, though still so young.

Then again it was at Paley's Creek, on that same occasion, that the

Modor or Wise Woman had appeared to Stort, putting him in the way of wisdoms and grief which deepened his character and made his later quests for the gems possible.

Now, once more, it seemed that Paley's Creek was about and abroad, sending out its siren call, luring the hydden into its strange, heady and otherworldly embrace.

'I swear,' said Stort dreamily when his supper was finished, 'that I am catching an alluring scent from what is going on below us! But, of course, we cannot, we dare not, go there. Dare we?'

'No!' cried Katherine rather hysterically, 'we must not and will not, but oh, how wonderful that drifting scent of the Bilgesnipe female is!'

Jack frowned in the dark.

'Don't listen to 'em,' he told the newcomers, 'or you'll get into all kinds of trouble.'

To which Ingrid replied breathlessly, a touch eagerly, unable to stop herself thrusting her hand through the crook of Bohr's arm, 'No . . . I won't . . . we mustn't . . . Um . . . what is it these Bilgesnipe do at Paley's Creek? Is it quite harmless?'

The music swelled as she said this, as if it heard her and wished to lure her in its direction.

'It's *complicated*,' said Jack very firmly, 'and it . . .'

He stilled, for there was movement in the wood behind him, a dancing green and red light, soft laughter and the run of feet as of several does across the forest floor. And the scent grew stronger, exotic and as richly spicy as a souk in Araby, or like incense of the sort sold by traders along the Silk Road of Samarkand.

Jack stilled even more when a hand, soft and gentle, touched his shoulder and a voice – was it real? was it in his mind? – whispered, 'Jack, it bain't complexiting but it be befuddling, that's true enough, so come along fro' this dull place and join us where we be . . .'

Unable to help himself, he stood up and turned round, hoping for . . . for what? He knew not. He only heard more feet running, all around them, and the lights among the yews, round and soft as a fruit, dancing and playing where they hung, like the laughter that they heard.

'I think . . .' he said, giving his hand to Katherine.

'I think,' said she, helping Stort to his feet.

'Um, I think,' said Ingrid . . .

'I think we should,' said Bohr, his head lighter than it had been in years, his body dancing like it never had, her hand in his as if it truly, always, should have been and now would always be . . . no no no . . . *needed* to be.

'They seem all right,' murmured Jack, as they danced all together down the hill into the night that was Paley's Creek.

'They do,' said Katherine, 'eh, Stort?'

'Indeed!'

Then, because the mood took her and the moment seemed right, Katherine said to Bohr, 'If you've come in search of Arthur I am very sorry to tell you . . . he has returned to the Mirror.'

'You mean he is . . . ?'

'I mean he has died.'

'But how . . . ?'

She told him then, as they danced along, in a kind of way she did, so he visioned the pyre on which Arthur's body was burnt and how his ashes were blown up to the stars.

Later Bohr's grip on Ingrid's hand tightened, and hers on his, and he was silent.

'I feel . . . very . . . *sorry*,' he said.

'Of course,' she replied, or was it Katherine or Jack or maybe Stort who spoke, or the trees all about?

'No need to feel sorrow, my newly hyddeny one,' said a passing male. 'Sorrow be less useful than good intent!'

'And he'm not sorry for hisseln, is Arthur,' called out another, 'he'm only glad you'm come here now to help his friends.'

'I . . .' began Bohr, a firelight rising before them, dancers all about, 'I don't know what to think . . . I don't know *why* I'm here . . .'

'Your wyrd brought you here and now 'tis your own task to find out why and do what you must,' the female suddenly dancing with him said.

'Bain't so hard if you set your course in the right direction,' said the next.

'I . . . don't . . . think I understand,' said Bohr, battered by these voices from among the revellers, who seemed to see better into his heart than he did.

'Why do you think you'm here, my love?' said another, holding him tight.

'I was here to find Arthur but he's . . . passed . . . away.'

'You mean he's gone Mirror-ward. So you'll have to do what he would have in his stead, that's what they'm a-sayin', that be all. That's why you'm come.'

'I . . .'

'Who'm be this whose hand you hold?' another asked him. 'Be she thine?'

'Um . . . I . . .'

'Yes,' said Ingrid, 'she be.'

'Well, then, you'd best ask her about this and about that, she looks like she might know the answers!'

It was only much later, when the dancing had ceased and the Bilgesnipe sat down to eat by two great fires, that they were able to really see their hosts and get to know them. The wyfkin and kinder were plump and cheerful, dressed in colourful, many-layered silk dresses and petticoats, beribboned and bedecked with dry flowers, it being winter.

The males were large and well girthed and, being mariners and hardened by long hours of watery labour, strong, their forearms muscled, their necks thick, their calves solid. Most wore a kerchief around their necks, some had rings in their ears, a few dressed their hair in pigtails, shiny with a tincture of camomile and lint.

The teeth of all were white and big, their smiles enormous, their eyes crinkled in the firelight with good humour and the long-suffering patience of those who put the welfare of their kinder first and last and in the middle too and themselves a good way behind.

It was some hours before they learnt from the elusive Bilgesnipe where they were and where they were bound; and that the festivities of which they were now part were not in fact, or not exactly, Paley's Creek at all, but on the way to being.

'That be Wychbury Hill wher'm you were took and now 'tis Clent, this dried-up place! But why'm you askin'? A hydden who don't know where he is has got his navigation wrong!'

'We're portlers,' said Jack, remembering from before that this was a word used of folk who travelled by the henge.

'That be an ancient art and fearful. It bain't summat Bilgesnipe like to do. You'm clever folk then?'

'Not really,' said Katherine.

But a ripple of interest had gone through the crowd and candle lights were lofted near to appraise their faces.

'You'm *look* intelligent,' said one.

'Thank you,' said Katherine. 'We're trying to get to Brum.'

'Then you'm in the right place at the right time! Which proves it good and true!'

'Proves what?' asked Stort, puzzled for once.

'That you'm portlers, for who else would get where they need to be at the time they need to be there and know so little *where* they be. I doubt these bedazzled folk know the difference between their kneecaps and their arses!'

This provoked a good laugh and the evening continued happily thereafter and never seemed to reach its end.

But when morning came, they rose from the fog of deep sleep to a cold winter's day, to find the Bilgesnipe already on the move.

'Come on, lad!' said a passing Bilgesnipe. 'Be off 'n up and come along.'

'But . . . where . . . ?' began Katherine.

'Where are we . . . ?' demanded Jack.

Stort cut their questions short.

'My dear friends, I enquired last night.'

'So where are we going?'

'To the Muggy Duck.'

'Why?'

'Because the word is out and about that Arnold Mallarkhi is affianced and about to be spoused!'

So they set off too, all five of them as one, for sometime in the night Bohr and Ingrid had sloughed off the stresses of the human world. He had acquired a gold ring in his ear and she, though grateful to Katherine for the loan of garb, had acquired ribbon and flowers in her hair and brand-new flowing silks and petticoats that might have made a bird of paradise look dull.

'Come on,' she said, truly happy for the first time in her adult life, 'come on, my dear!'

34
RESPITE

The temperature continued to drop as Jack and the others entered Brum's low-lying western suburbs with their Bilgesnipe friends. The air was still and heavy, as if the whole metropolis was trapped beneath a pall of bitter cold.

'It's like nothing I've ever known,' said Katherine as the Bilgesnipe parents bundled up their kinder tight and warm and then themselves.

Slippery black ice was everywhere underfoot and the going got increasingly difficult. The often clumsy Bilgesnipe, always better on water than on land, clutched on to each other to stop themselves falling. After a painful slip or two, even the most agile of the youngsters began taking each step with extra care.

Jack and Stort led the final part of the route, which was the traditional one used for centuries by pilgrims to and from Waseley Hill, along the banks of the River Rea. The river itself was still flowing, but ice was building up at its edges and icicles were forming at the mouths of drains and pipes that fed into the river.

Everything was now covered with hoar frost, but not the kind that made fallen leaves look beautiful and turned the twigs on trees and each blade of grass all white and shining, imbued with the light of the sky above. The sky was a lowering and angry grey and it was this dour colour that the frost caught, making all seem dull and threatening.

The Bilgesnipe visitors, who in better weather might have expected their local kith and kin to ferry them on down the river to the canals and conduits that ran so plentifully and secretly to Old and New Brum from the western gate, stayed on the bank, eyeing the water without pleasure.

'It bain't good, one and all, it's got the whiff o' trouble and we'm thinking that city-ward is not the way we should be agoin' but backaways home to places we know to be safe. But needs must and this be an occasion which not a Bilgesnipe in all Englalond who can get here will want to miss.'

'You are,' suggested Ingrid, 'off to a party of some kind?'

'Party! That's a mingey kind of word for summat that needs a whole tome to set it fair!'

'So it's a very special occasion indeed?' tried Bohr. Ingrid had taken to the Hyddenworld and the vagaries of the Bilgesnipe with ease; so far Bohr was less comfortable.

'Bless'n you'm both!' cried one of the females, taking pity on them. 'You'm puzzled by our speech and bedaffed by what we say . . . !'

'Or don't say, Ma,' cried her spouse. 'Where have you two portled from? Same as them other ones?'

He naturally had no idea they were human but anyone could see they came from foreign parts, not least because they spoke a soft, long tongue not heard but on the mudflats of Bristol among the shrimpers there.

He did not wait for an answer, but looked meaningfully at Jack and Katherine instead, though it was finally at Stort he pointed.

'You'm know who'm that tall feller be?'

'Only his name,' said Bohr.

'That be enough for me!'

Bohr sensed it was best to say nothing more.

'And you'm tway,' continued the inquisitive Bilgesnipe, nodding at Jack and Katherine, 'whom look like dowdy doves in love, you'm got names azlewell?'

Jack laughed. He knew the game. The point of information exchange had been reached.

They identified themselves cheerfully and no one seemed much surprised. Their appearance was now too well known in Englalond, especially as a trio travelling together, for them not to be easily recognized.

'Well, that's no surprise! You'm comin' as guests of honour I daresay!'

'To Arnold's spousal?' said Katherine. 'We're coming, but just as ordinary guests I expect.'

'"Tis the greatest spousal of our lives ... Arnold Mallarkhi and his affianced!'

'It surely is,' agreed Katherine.

One of the Bilgesnipe females came near and grabbed the arms of Katherine and Ingrid very confidentially.

'They do say, as I've heard, and I had it from one who heard it good fro' another who knows such things, because he'm an ear as big as a cave that she'm ... she'm ... a dreamygirl. What do you say to that!?'

'I say it's true,' said Katherine, 'true as we're standing here!'

'Indeed, madam,' said Stort, 'a dreamygirl she is.'

'You speak very positive and very certain, Mister Stort,' came the reply, his name now being something they could say to his face.

'That's because we've met her.'

Nothing could have caused more surprise and delight than this startling announcement.

'Met her! With your very eyes? Talked to her with your very mouths?'

'Indeed!'

'Dang me, lads and lassies, we'm a tale to hear right now and here! Mister Stort and Katherine know the dreamygirl! Is she pretty?'

'Very,' said Jack who had never met her himself but felt it best to say she was.

'Be she fair and plumply like?'

'She is,' said Stort, more truthfully.

'Be they dimpled when together and like a brace of well-set craft afore a following wind on a course as clear and dandy as 'tis true?'

'They are,' said Katherine, understanding exactly what was meant, 'they *are* very much in love.'

'Give us yer kerchief, I think I'm a-goin' to cry!'

The party now arrived at the West Gate of the city, buzzing with this welcome first-hand account of Arnold's girl, and debating its many ramifications. The Bilgesnipe soon met some friends on the same mission as themselves and went off to take the watery route together to Old Brum, while Jack and the others threaded their way eastward through a city they barely recognized, to find their friends.

They soon saw, as Barklice and Festoon had a few days before, that Brum's streets and buildings were in a state of ruin and dereliction. It had been one thing to see the evidence of human civil strife occasionally and from a distance during their respective journeys from the south and east, but quite another to have to pick their way through it yard by yard.

There were burnt-out buildings, collapsed walls, broken tiles and glass across nearly every thoroughfare and down every lane and ginnel. A great deal of the litter, once sodden, was now grotesquely frozen where it lay.

Here and there the rubble was free of ice and frost, warmed by residual fires smouldering below in basements and sewers. From these depths too, especially where covers had been broken or removed, came the sickening smell of death: sweet, filthy, retch-making and once breathed in almost impossible to breathe out.

There were bodies of humans in the ruins and sometimes on the street, horrible green-black swollen things which to hydden looked like foul giants. Worse still were the rats, fat sleeky things that knew no fear until, when Jack stamped the ground or beat it with his stave, the creatures slunk away, heads low, their greasy grey-pink tails the last thing to disappear.

Or, more horrible still, those slippy animate tails sometimes stopped still in full view, showing in amongst the detritus of ruin, waving and wriggling in what seemed a kind of ecstasy as rats otherwise unseen came upon another rotten cadaver to eat.

No wonder they proceeded slowly, picking their way carefully and averting their eyes from the worst of the horrors. Yet even that precaution sometimes failed them. On one street, faced by the sight of a pile of mutilated corpses ahead, they turned away down a dark lane to find, halfway down, three severed human heads lying on cobbles by an open door from which protruded a pair of bare, blackened feet.

'Humans!' exclaimed Stort in disgust, '*humans!*'

Of them all Bohr was the most affected, the change in the scale of things and all else being a disorientating shock to himself and Ingrid, making it all seem worse. To the hydden the humans are giants, often slow and clumsy, unaware, sometimes grotesque and violent, very rarely beautiful. But that was a fact the hydden tended to forget, so used were they to the reality. For Bohr, who until the day before had only ever seen the human form as the norm in size, his own kind seemed grotesque now – violent, degraded ones.

'I cannot go on,' he said suddenly at the far end of the lane within which they had found the heads, 'I cannot face more of this.'

'Then stay,' said Jack brutally, for he felt as angry as Stort at the evidence of mindless human savagery that littered Brum's once beautiful streets.

He pressed on with Stort, with a cloth to his mouth and nose against the smell of putrefaction, leaving it to Katherine and Ingrid to urge Bohr on after them.

'We could try to find your humble, Stort,' suggested Katherine later, when they crossed a street they finally recognized near where the scrivener lived. 'There might be a message there . . .'

He shook his head.

'The Library in the Main Square is our best goal,' he said, 'for if it still stands I am sure that Festoon and Barklice, assuming they are now safely back in Brum, will have left a message there for us. Or they might be in Festoon's residence opposite, if *that* stands!'

The Main Square, like so much else of Brum, was nearly unrecognizable. Festoon's residence was no more than rubble, the Parlement building next to it much the same. The square was a mess of abandoned barricades of wood and vehicles, as if it had been a place of final confrontation between the humans, or worse, the humans and the hydden. Here too rats were scurrying, but of bodies there were none.

'The Library doors still stand!' cried Stort as they approached the building in which he had spent so much of his youth. 'Though . . . well . . .'

His gaze went up to the floor above, which was more or less intact, but for broken windows. But the floors above that were burnt out, the surviving blackened rafters serving no better purpose than as perches for rooks and seagulls, which squabbled among themselves, their plump breasts as sleek as those of the rats below.

The Library doors were stuck open wide enough for a hydden to slide in between them. Before they did so they paused to look across the Main Square to the pile of rusting steel and rubble, the broken fenestrations and rain-ruined furniture and fitments that were all that remained of the High Ealdor's Residence. Its topmost floor had contained one of Brum's greatest artistic achievements, the fabled Chamber of Seasons, upon whose octagonal walls, which told of seasonal change, were the images which contained the clues that enabled Stort to begin his quest for Beornamund's gems.

Between the panels of imagery had been four great doors, each named after one of the seasons. Until recent times none had been opened. When the first three finally were, they had taken Jack and Stort and others onward with their quests by way of unexpected and unpredictable destinations.

'Well, my friends,' said Stort, 'I regret to say that it looks as if the untried door of Winter will now remain forever closed, broken and lost beneath those ruins as it now must be. Which is a pity, for I confess I had hoped that there at least we might find some help in seeking out that last gem and averting the End of Days.'

'Which now begins to feel inevitable,' said Katherine, pulling her jacket tighter against the cold, 'unless we can find a way out of all this . . . this *mess*.'

Jack herded them inside, sensing some kind of danger perhaps, ever conscious of others' safety.

'I had thought that if the End of Days ever actually happened it would do so in the form of an escalation of the ever-worsening earthquakes and storms of recent months,' he said. 'I did not imagine we would be slowly overwhelmed by cold, against which even my stave has no defence!'

The interior of the Library was marginally warmer, perhaps because, very unexpectedly, its inner depths and recesses were lit by candles. These revealed row upon row of empty shelves and dusty desks and marked a route to some meeting place within.

Stort led the way forward and was gratified to find his earlier hunch was right. They walked by candlelight to the familiar spiral stone steps that led down to the stacks below, where he had often worked. The empty shelves were no surprise: most of the books and papers in the collection had been removed to a place of safe-keeping months before. What was a surprise was that in the arched room where Stort's own desk had been, and still remained, seat and all, straight and tidy as if someone had just left it so, a refectory table and chairs were set. On it, astonishingly, was fresh brot, flannigans of warmed pottage and soup, sweetmeats of a simple kind and a solitary jar of jam, sealed with oiled paper and an orange ribbon, labelled in a hand so beloved and familiar that it brought sentimental tears to Bedwyn Stort's eyes.

He picked it up in wonderment and read: 'Cluckett's Own Elder-flower Preserve'. Beneath it was a folded paper which Stort took up and read through rapidly and then aloud to them all:

'Mister Stort, sir, having heard of your return with joy and fearing that your first visitation would be to your ruined humble, but knowing your second would be here, I have done as best I can to provide vittles for your present needs. Eat, sir, partake, sir, and if them others are with you as I heard they might be, namely Master Jack and Mistress Katherine, apologize that I am able to find so little fare as yet! I shall return with more. Your bed is made up adjacently with toothbrush and mug as you like them.
    Faithfully Yours,
      Goodwife Cluckett.'

Nothing could have cheered them more than this missive from Stort's fearless and faithful housekeeper. It meant that in one heart at least the old virtues of Brum, of welcome, of care and of thoughtfulness, even if sometimes disguised in her case behind a stern façade, still survived.

It was only when they began to tuck in that Jack noticed a second note nearby, lost among some cutlery, cannikins and paper napkins. It read:

I am back, sir, briefly, but you not yet here. You will find serviceable ablutions through the arch marked Medieval Manuscripts and Lord Festoon's Quarters in the Librarian Thwart's Office. The others, from the Emperor down, occupy Rare Books and Manuscripts.
    Cluckett.

PS The Spousal is at eight tonight, as is traditional, at the M. Duck, to where I am returning to help as I can, guarded by Mister P's stavermen.

PPS Mister Barklice is informed of your coming as are their Lordships Blut and Festoon, who will come. Master Terce is in fine fettle but he does sing so!

Stort consulted his chronometer, as did Jack.

Dark and gloomy though it was outside, it was only a little past one o'clock. Plainly their best course of action was to stay right where they were, enjoy the refreshments provided and rest or even sleep awhile.

If Cluckett knew they were coming, or guessed they had arrived, news gleaned no doubt from the Bilgesnipe they had met, then others would know soon enough as well and come and join and bring them up to date.

'Meanwhile,' said Jack, 'if she talks of being guarded, that must mean that Brum is not entirely safe. I will patrol the building right now, Katherine can take over later. At least until our good friends come to see us. It would seem that Lord Festoon has adopted this building as his new headquarters. And we may take it that he and the others are out on some business or other and will soon join us.'

It was a reunion they greatly looked forward to and when they heard the unmistakable sound of footsteps above theirs, hopes were raised, but Jack warned them to stay still. He took up his stave and went to investigate, returning moments later.

'Four of Pike's stavermen were here already, half asleep by the look of them. We woke them up! They had a late night it seems, looking for folk who mean no good, who they didn't find. They say that Pike, Festoon and our other friends will be here later and will no doubt bring us up to date. For now we seem safe. I have a feeling another late night, of a different kind, is in store for us all! Bilgesnipe spousals are never modest affairs and if the Muggy Duck's involved we can take it we won't get sleep until tomorrow. Best to rest . . .'

They needed no further prompting. It had been a long and stressful twenty-four hours.

They ate, they drank and fell asleep by candlelight, just where they sat.

35

OPERATIONAL

The debacle at Woodhenge turned Colonel Reece's frustration
with the nature of his mission in England into smouldering
anger.

The fact of being taken by surprise and outmanoeuvred for a second
time by a small force of ill-equipped amateurs whom he and his men
barely saw and did not understand was bad enough. What made it
worse was that the 'enemy' had used only proportionate force to achieve
their objectives and caused relatively minor hurt and injury. But not so
minor that he did not have two men out of action with wounds from a
crossbow, a third with a broken jaw from a kick and two more still
suffering the effects of severe concussion from a flying object they
never really saw. In short, the so-called hydden had performed with an
exemplary professionalism that showed him and his own force in a bad
light and left him personally humiliated.

To this was added the fact that Erich Bohr had proceeded recklessly,
as it seemed to Reece, without the proper consultation and clearance
due to a joint commander and without subsequently following agreed
protocol. In other words, he had disappeared without 'permission' and
had made no attempt to make contact since.

Finally, other factors were now undermining Reece's sense of security in the mission's viability. Systems at RAF Croughton were down
because of the cold and ice, and the breakdown in civilian society
rendered communication with the base now nearly impossible. His
transports, both air and road, were suffering equipment failures for the
same reason. Fuel was low and its further provision out of Croughton

uncertain. Morale was understandably down at Woolstone, not least because the continuing value and relevance of that location as a command centre was in serious doubt.

Then things changed again – and for the worse.

On the morning after Bohr's disappearance at Woodhenge, Reece received a call from the unit in Birmingham. It was urgent and the signal was poor. Three more men were down, a fourth injured and the caller now on the move in alien territory and soon likely to be under attack again.

'What do you mean by "down"?'

'Non-operational. They are all dead, sir.'

'And the other one?'

'Bad,' his man said quietly, apparently for fear of being overheard. 'Field dressings on this one are inadequate . . . He's bleeding to death.'

'Jesus,' said Reece.

'We need to evacuate him now or bring in further medical aid and reinforcements.'

'Any sign of Foale?'

There was a short laugh.

'Any sign of Bohr, dammit? He has that assistant with him.'

Another unpleasant laugh.

'I have no idea, Colonel, what I'm seeing or who it is. The enemy is . . . elusive. The conditions are very bad. What little you see of them they all look the same.'

'We're coming in,' said Reece tersely. 'We'll assess the situation on the ground and get you out, or we'll stay put and sort it. I'm going operational. Give me coordinates.'

'We' consisted of four of the five fit men he had remaining. The rest, the injured ones, were staying behind with one who was fit. They had supplies, they had road transport and it was just a matter of getting back to Croughton. Not ideal, but nothing was ideal in the deteriorating situation in which Reece now found himself.

'Operational' was Reece's word for taking personal charge.

He called his force together, gave them the facts, listened to discussion, nodded his head and gave his decision in the form of clear commands.

By the time the force got to the Huey its blades were already beginning to turn.

'Going hunting, sir?' one of his men asked him, eyeing the familiar shape of the extra personal weapon he was carrying with a knowing grin.

Reece didn't respond, but he didn't need to. The carrying case was instantly recognizable to his men. He was taking along his AWM sniper's rifle with his initials on it – the weapon he used to kill vermin in his native Montana, and the one he favoured while on active service . . .

'Good for any vermin we find in Birmingham, England,' he said as he climbed aboard the Huey.

Moments later it was in the air and turning low past the tower of Woolstone church on a bearing towards Birmingham with an estimated time of arrival of 13.34 hours.

36

FIRE AND ICE

Erich Bohr woke after the meal in the Library feeling better than he had at any moment since his sudden arrival in the Hyddenworld.

Ingrid Hansen was asleep in the chair next to him, her spectacles awry. He gently removed them, marvelling that after so many years feeling alone in life something as seemingly simple as a dance had changed everything. He let her sleep.

The others were all there as well, in various modes and positions of slumber, with the exception of the tall hydden called Stort. The one who, if not exactly the leader of this disparate group, certainly seemed to have some kind of vision of where it was going.

Until now Bohr had been frankly nervous of separating himself from hydden he had so unexpectedly become allied with. After his initial doubts they represented the only security Ingrid and he had in the strange and alien world in which they found themselves.

But on waking he needed to stretch his legs and relieve himself. The place for ablutions, as they quaintly called it, was at 'Medieval Manuscripts', wherever that was. He set off upstairs to find out.

The candles that had been burning so brightly before were now beginning to gutter and the ground floor where they had come in was darker than it had been.

A voice said, 'Hold it, chum! Your name?'

'Bohr.'

'One of Mister Stort's party?'

'Er, yes . . . I think I am.'

'I think you are too. You'll find him toasting outside. Over there, through the main door.'

A hefty hydden with a stave appeared from the shadows. His presence was intimidating but his smile reassuring.

'I was hoping to . . . um . . . you know . . .'

'Do it outside. Mister Stort did.'

Toasting? Could that be a hydden word for 'abluting', whatever that was exactly?

Bohr squeezed himself out between the doors to find a great fire burning in the middle of the square, which brought cheer and activity to the late-afternoon scene. There were guards with staves about the place. Some were clearly on duty, standing around the square and stamping their feet on the icy cobbles to keep warm, their breath steamy in the cold air. Others were sorting things to burn among the ruins nearby, making piles of the heavier items like doors and hauling skirting boards, picture rails and broken window frames and suchlike straight to the fire.

In the midst of all this and apparently indifferent to it, Mister Stort sat alone by the fire, toasting crumpets.

'Ah! Doctor Bohr! Well timed! Sit down, it is tea time.'

The oddest thing of all for Erich Bohr was, as it seemed, that such a strange and surrealistic scene should feel normal so soon. He almost wondered if he was hallucinating and that what Arthur Foale had discovered was simply a world of illusion.

'Crumpet, Doctor?'

'Er . . . yes. Yes. Please call me Erich.'

'Rape butter?'

'Pardon me?'

'Rapeseed oil butter?'

'Um . . . well . . . yes . . .'

'And, of course, Cluckett's Own, of which there is no like.'

Bohr gave up trying to understand what Mister Stort was talking about. Whatever it was it looked and smelt good and he was hungry.

Stort dolloped the orange-red conserve onto the dripping crumpet and handed it over.

'This may very well be the last jar in existence. Perhaps the last that will ever be made if, as we all now fear, all is coming to an end, including the making of conserves by Goodwife Cluckett. Not that that need happen if, but only if, we can find the gem.'

'No,' said Bohr.

The hydden, who was red-haired and freckled and not nearly as old close-to as his words and behaviour sometimes suggested, looked down at Bohr, being gangly in the leg and elongated in the torso.

'So tell me,' Stort said, 'how you come to be here and the reason for it.'

'Well I . . .'

Bohr began to speak, his normal cool and rational way of being slipping from him most strangely. By the time he was into his third crumpet, and feeling warmed by the fire and the hot tea Stort provided, any hope he might have had of making scientific enquiries had deserted him. He simply talked, as he had rarely talked before, telling the extraordinary hydden who listened so amiably, about his life, his fears, his everything.

All the while stavermen went back and forth across the square, carrying wood and other combustibles from the ruins and feeding them to the fire. Occasionally they stopped for a brew and word, but mostly they got on with their work, giving Bohr the pleasant sense that he was in a far more friendly and supportive community than he was used to. A thought he happily expressed aloud.

'Which you are, my dear fellow,' said Stort, 'you most certainly are. Now . . . have you met the Emperor, Niklas Blut?'

A slight but curiously impressive figure had joined them by the fire. He wore old-fashioned round spectacles and had been listening with interest.

'Ah . . . yes . . .' said Bohr, shaking his hand. 'Um . . . Emperor of what?'

'The Hyddenworld,' said Blut matter-of-factly, 'but please continue . . .'

The sky had darkened, the shadows deepened, the fire grown ever bigger and hotter. Other hydden were lingering, apparently interested to hear what Bohr had to say. Some, including the one called Blut, seemed anxious for him to repeat what he had told Stort before they came.

'Now, please,' said Stort, 'I am not sure my friends fully grasp the direction we are now heading in our conversation, so perhaps you could explicate in a simpler way the thoughts you just now expressed to me, Doctor Bohr?'

'Yes,' added Blut, his spectacles red hypnotic orbs in the firelight. 'Go back to the start of things in a way I can make better sense of, if you will.'

'And have another crumpet as you do so!'

'Well I . . . if you insist I suppose . . .'

Wherever Bohr had begun, he began again, munching with pleasure between times, feeling for the first time in a very long time indeed that he was, as it were, simply sitting still and enjoying the company of others for no better reason than that it was a good and happy thing to do so.

Then, wherever his words might have been heading, they took a back step or three and headed somewhere different.

Wherever he had hoped to reach he made it to somewhere else entirely, beguiled by the place, the situation, the contradictory mix of extreme cold behind him and extreme heat immediately in front; and by Stort himself, who at times appeared asleep but who time and again asked the most astonishing and perspicacious questions imaginable.

It seemed to Bohr that engaging with him was not unlike having a tutorial with Professor Arthur Foale in his rooms in King's College, Cambridge.

'Ah! I hoped you might mention Arthur!'

Had Bohr mentioned him? He was not quite sure. Yes, of course he had.

'You do realize that Katherine . . .'

'Katherine?'

'. . . Jack's consort, companion and, as the hydden of Digbeth say, "is better two-thirds".'

'Yes,' said Bohr.

'She was raised by Arthur at Woolstone House, where, I think you said, you have lately been?'

Had he? Maybe he had. Of *course* he had.

'So what's gone wrong, Doctor Bohr? Why is the human world in the mess it is? You said you were a cosmologist, so I imagine you have a view?'

'I think I . . .'

'On what, Stort?' cried a rich and mellifluous voice. 'A view on what?'

Stort rose up to greet Festoon, whose hand he shook formally, more for the benefit of Bohr than anyone else.

'This impressive hydden is Lord Festoon, the High Ealdor of Brum.' They too shook hands.

'If I have not said it before,' cried Stort, 'I say it again – *this*, gentlemen, is Doctor Bohr, who as far as I can see has been sent to the Hyddenworld as a replacement for Professor Arthur Foale.'

'I . . . no . . . really . . .' Bohr tried to protest. But it fell on deaf ears, for both Blut and Festoon shook his hand and congratulated him on his arrival and, if he heard them right, his appointment.

'Gentlemen, I am not . . .'

But Stort cut across this further protest, saying, 'The Doctor was about to give me his view about why the human world is such a mess . . .'

The firelight danced, the edges of the square receded in the dark and began to feel infinite as Bohr had his hand shaken by others as well and found himself giving a view, a human view, of matters about which, the terrible truth was, he had very rarely in recent years had any chance to talk.

With an Emperor?

A High Ealdor?

With stavermen, whatever they were?

Not before, but now it seemed so.

And crumpets? Tea?

A feeling of homely warmth enveloped Bohr.

'Which is all very interesting and touching, my dear doctor,' cried Stort, 'but what I really had in mind, and frankly hoped you would enlighten us about as one who has come very recently from the human world, is whether or not what humans have done to our Mother Earth is reversible. Or is it too late?'

'Exactly,' said Niklas Blut.

'Because,' said Festoon looming over Bohr, his cheeks shiny and face ruby-red in the firelight, 'it may have a bearing on the search for the gem of Winter, which is a matter of very great concern to us all, since time is running out.'

Blut consulted his timepiece.

'Stort has a habit,' he said confidentially, as if Stort was not there, 'of losing track of time to such a degree that I swear he has forgotten that if he does not find that gem by the end of January, which is not very far off . . .'

Stort put his hands over his ears and began to hum as Blut continued in a louder voice, '. . . then the End of Days will be upon us!'

What Bohr could not quite adjust to was that in the Hyddenworld it seemed that there was a different and refreshing mixture of levity and seriousness, of pleasure and pain, of the imminence of life and death.

Of this nothing felt more emblematic just then than the fact that, whilst the fire was so intense, his back was freezing, his earlobes numb but his nose very hot, his knees about to burst into flame and the whole world more alive than he could quite cope with.

Now they wanted a pronouncement on the inevitability or otherwise of humankind's slide towards extinction.

Is that what I am proposing to talk about? Bohr asked himself. *If so, then it would be better if Ingrid . . . joined . . . me . . .*

She *did* join him, just then, as if she had heard his thoughts, giving Bohr the impression that this conversation by a fire with people he did not know, in a place to which he had never been, had a certain inevitability about it, as if his whole life had been leading to this moment. And it *was* better she was there, for it was Ingrid who had for so long, though usually too timidly, advanced views on this difficult subject, which he himself, for reasons of NASA politics and personal expediency, had been equivocal about with everyone, from his interns to the President himself. They had all been so, more or less: hedging their bets, avoiding being categorical, saying nothing that rocked the boat – not speaking truth.

'Generations,' Ingrid observed quietly, 'of doing absolutely nothing about anything!'

'How right you are, madam!' cried Festoon.

Blut nodded his agreement and said, 'I have certainly missed having Arthur Foale to talk to about such matters so it is good to have you both here, in place of him as it were.'

Bohr looked from one to another and opened his mouth to reply, but once more he was interrupted.

'Of course,' said Stort, 'Doctor Bohr represents a different, younger, generation than Arthur. But then it is in the nature of the Mirror-of-All that we often create the very thing we *need* to see!'

'And hear!' added Barklice, who had joined the company inconspicuously, as he often did.

For Ingrid and Bohr it was another name to remember and hand to shake but eventually silence fell, except for the bright crackling of the fire and the snapping of icicles falling from a nearby roof, the heat having got to the ice. And still the fire was fed by shadowy figures on its fringes.

But finally everyone was settled and attentive.

'Is it reversible?' Bohr found himself saying rhetorically to his audience, which now seemed as rapt as any he had ever addressed. 'Which begs the question whether or not our decline and fall was going to happen anyway! The lifetime of most species, according to research I have seen by earth scientists who know the geological record, is no more than three million years. For some it is much shorter, especially those who came into existence just before one of the five great mass extinctions.'

Did the fire burn briefly brighter as if remembering its different and much more catastrophic forebears?

'There is a view among some of my colleagues that to the latest "official" geological age, namely the Holocene, should now be added a new one, in which we are already immersed, the Anthropocene.'

His listeners looked blank, until Bedwyn Stort, understanding, cried out, 'Ah! A splendid conceit! "Anthropo" means "human" and of course "cene" means "age".'

Bohr continued. 'One of my friends proposed the name rather informally at a conference and it was soon taken up. If you look at the geological markers that are used to define any of the distinct geological ages, like biodiversity or the climatic signature, you will find that what humans have done in recent decades has been so dramatic, so nearly total, that geologists in ten million years will use them to define *our* age . . . except that there won't be any humans to do so!'

'Because it is irreversible?'

'Yes,' said Ingrid, not afraid to express that opinion, 'because it is now too late. Humans are a juggernaut that cannot be stopped. Slowed but not stopped. We . . .'

She talked more, as did Bohr, as did all of them, except for Stort, who had fallen silent and pensive, so much so that everyone began to want him to speak, which he seemed about to do when something caught his eye on the fire, as it caught Bohr's, something so extraordinary that he started back with a combination of astonishment and alarm. In fact, the more they saw it, the more astounded everybody became. For there was no doubt at all that what they saw in the flames was ice. As if the flames themselves, though clearly very hot, and flickering as flames do, and sending smoke and sparks up into the night air, had changed their colour and nature to a veritable storm of ice, a whole weather system of it, raging and terrible, which morphed right there in front of them to a great roundel of flaming blizzard snow, turning, struggling, forming and reforming in the centre of the fire.

They were so dazzled by this and the odd fact that ice could be so hot and not boil that they only slowly saw what it was that they really *did* see, which was not ice at all, but the semblance of it.

'Surely it's a film, or the illusion of one!' whispered Bohr to Ingrid.

'And what is more,' said Stort, 'if we look there . . . yes . . . to the left . . . yes . . . Can you not see through the smoke, some kind of ashy green . . . ?'

'And above it, my dear chap,' cried Festoon, 'I would say that looks like sky . . .'

'But surely . . .'

'There cannot be . . .'

But there were!

There were people on the frozen green pasture in the fire as it seemed, people near an icy river flowing, people blotted out by the wild returning blizzard and . . .

Bohr peered more closely.

What was it that loomed now out of the blizzard?

'Is it a white horse?' he asked. 'And an aged rider . . . there . . . *look!*'

A face, a hunched form, a cry of despair which was surely just the fire wheezing and exploding; the blizzard blowing, which it felt as if it might very soon, all around them.

Stort stood up and backed away from the image and the fire that held it in its flames. Then he turned to see where the stavermen who were feeding the fire had come from and came from still.

'Oh, look what they bring, my Lord Festoon, look what we burn!' he cried in horror and despair.

They had been taking material from the ruins of Festoon's official residence and what they had found, and Stort now recognized, were the last remaining strands and tatters of the painted panels from what had once been the Chamber of Seasons.

'No!' cried Stort. 'Not that . . . put it back . . . back . . .'

It was too late.

Nothing was left, and they had made of ã Faroün's fabled creation, lost and ruined in the debris of the official residence, no more than a brief conflagration by which to take tea and toast crumpets and make speculative conversation about the end of all things.

'Yet what did we see while it burnt?' said Stort, when he was a little recovered and back to being curious as ever, convinced that in what had been seen and was now finally burnt away there was a meaning or message he must try to understand.

'We saw Winter,' said Blut.

'And we saw the Shield Maiden in old age,' said Stort.

'And we saw Waseley Hill, Stort, and the White Horse,' added Barklice, 'just as you saw it before.'

Stort shook his head, not yet convinced.

'And I felt pain,' he said, 'here in my stomach, the pain of sickness and a loss, a loss in a blizzard greater than I could bear.'

'My dear fellow,' said Barklice, 'this was most unfortunate. If only we had known, we could have kept those scraps of the Winter painting and perhaps used them to help us find a way onward from here.'

Again the scrivener shook his head.

'No, dear Barklice, it was necessary. We saw what we needed to see, just as that great fraudster and genius ã Faroün, who created these images, no doubt intended. So, what did *you* see, Lord Festoon?'

'A blizzard.'

'And you, my Lord Emperor Blut?'

'Ice, grass, people trekking.'

'And you?' asked Stort, turning to Pike.

'A chase, a killer, someone there who . . . who . . .'

'Bohr?'

'An icy death I think.'

'And you, youngish madam?'

Ingrid replied, her voice breaking, 'I saw love found and lost.'

Silence then, the fire a little less than it had been.

'I saw,' said Jack, who had joined the company then, 'a henge, a grey, cold henge of what seemed to be stone.'

'*Stone*henge?' suggested one of them.

'Maybe,' said Jack.

'I saw it too,' said Katherine.

Silence again, the fire dying now.

'And you, Barklice, what did you see?' asked Jack.

The verderer stood up and turned about, restless and unhappy.

'I saw something I did not understand. I tried to but I couldn't. It . . . it shone like the flames, it rose like the flames, it was ice perhaps, just ice. Ice and fire. Maybe that's what I saw but . . . I . . . don't . . . know.'

He looked so unhappy and frustrated not to be able to work out what he had seen that he turned away from them and paced about in the shadows beyond the circle of flame.

'Well, then,' said Stort very confidently, 'we have all seen what we needed to see, or were most able to see. As for myself, I saw illusion. I saw reflection. I saw no more than what the Mirror shows. I saw an ending and a beginning, which may be found in all these things we saw, separately and together.'

He paused, thinking.

'And I saw an answer, or the beginnings of one, to that great question we asked of Doctor Bohr: is the End of Days reversible?'

Again he paused and Jack, always impatient with Stort's convolutions and stoppages, said, 'Well? What *is* the answer?'

They laughed sympathetically, for how could there be an answer to such a conundrum?'

But Stort did not laugh, he rarely did.

'Yes, Jack, there is a way, I believe there is. I felt it, as surely as I feel that impossible love for Judith the Shield Maiden, right here in my gut where I felt that pain. In that answer lies another to a different question:

will we find the gem of Winter? Well then, well then . . . I believe we will! It is simply a matter of replacing one reflection with another!'

'Meaning?' said the ever-persistent Jack.

'Yes, *meaning*?' challenged Katherine.

'I have no idea,' said Stort, exasperated. 'You always want specifics and they rarely exist until they're really needed. Now, I hate to break our party up, but I do believe we are all imminently expected at a Bilgesnipe spousal!'

Indeed, they were, consisting as they did of as fine a company of the great and the good of Brum as ever assembled in the Main Square, with new friends thrown in for good measure and stavermen all about, keeping an eye on things as Mister Pike had very carefully instructed.

Off they began to go, the warmth of the fire still within them, as they trekked through the cold, dark, broken streets down towards Deritend and from there into Digbeth.

'Do you know where we are going?' asked Erich Bohr and Ingrid.

'To the Muggy Duck,' they all replied.

But Jack stayed back for a moment, keeping Katherine with him.

'Pike is not going with the crowd,' he said quietly, pointing to where the Chief Staverman was talking with people whose faces he could not see, in the shadows of the square. There's something going on and I intend to find out what it is.'

She nodded.

'I noticed that too. It may be nothing much but we can't both not make an appearance at the start of Arnold's spousal. One of us needs to make an excuse for the other and you *are* the Stavemeister . . .'

Reluctantly it was agreed that she would go on to the wedding while he stayed behind to see if he could find out what else might be going on.

'I don't pretend I like it, Jack. Brum's not a place to stay in for very long just now. If only Stort could work out what we should do and where we should go to find the gem.'

Katherine had changed in recent weeks and months. Their journeying, their violent confrontation with both Fyrd and humans, her learning how to use a crossbow, which she now carried on her belt, had turned her into a fighter. She was no good with a stave, never had been, but in all else where an enemy or difficult situation was concerned she was cool, calm and decisive.

They embraced fiercely neither wanting to let the other go.

'Jack,' she whispered, 'I've not felt good about things since Pendower Beach. We got sucked into doing things the way humans do . . .'

He nodded and they kissed again, feeling bleak and unhappy, not with each other but with the times.

'Didn't Sinistral tell us once that taking a life is the thin end of the wedge? It may be justified or seem so but it eats into you . . .'

'It's eaten into me and yet I know I'd kill to save your life.'

'Me too, the same,' he said. 'But maybe we should have walked away at Pendower . . .'

'If we had we might have felt just as bad. Whatever happens now, take care, my love,' she said finally, their fingers entwined and lingering.

Then she was gone as Jack set off to talk with Pike.

37

CIVIC PRIDE

When Jack caught up with Mister Pike he was involved in a discussion with the Lords Blut and Festoon which appeared to be turning into an argument. The normally calm Pike looked flushed; the usually cheerful Festoon was frowning. As for Blut, a master of negotiation and compromise, his face was set and his arms folded across his chest.

For a moment Jack felt inclined to retreat and choose his moment better. But, as Katherine had said, he *was* Stavemeister of Brum, and in a city for which time seemed to be running out, there might never *be* a better moment.

'So . . . what's going on?' he said coolly.

They turned to him irritably.

'The situation's under control, Jack,' said Pike tersely.

'Well! I am very glad to hear that!' he responded. 'You three were having a conversation which is obviously important; Marshal Brunte is nowhere to be seen, and there are a lot of stavermen posted about the place who look to me as if they are on high alert . . . Added to all of that . . .'

He brought his great stave down on the cobbles in front of him, stern and straight.

'Added to that, gentlemen, my stave is feeling restive and troubled.'

The truth was that the role of the Stavemeister was an uncertain and undefined one. Under Chief Librarian Master Brief, its previous incumbent, it had been largely ceremonial, though once or twice he had felt it necessary to wield his ancient stave of office for real.

After Brief's death Jack had taken over the position and worked well with the city elders and officers on assignments of great importance which required individual courage and initiative. From these Jack had emerged, along with the fabled and magical stave that went with the office, as one of the greatest fighters in Brum – and perhaps outside it too.

'This great and ancient stave, which I verily believe was once Beornamund's own,' Brief had once told him, 'is loyal only to the Stavemeister and reflects in its actions and powers what he is, what he can be and what he dares become.'

As he stood there that evening Jack found himself reflecting on what service he might perform as Stavemeister that was most valuable to Brum. The answer was suddenly very clear.

They stared at him in silence, awed by the glints and silvery shadows, ominous and forbidding, that emanated from the carvings of his stave.

'Right now,' he declared, 'the first and most important task of my office is to ensure the safety of Bedwyn Stort and those around him, who, together, might help him find the gem of Winter. Which being so, I demand to know what it is that troubles you all.'

Festoon broke the silence.

'He's right, Pike, he needs to know, even if there's nothing more to be done by any of us just now.'

'*What* do I need to know?' said Jack very firmly.

Pike signalled them all to move into the shadows and to his stavermen to keep special watch. Two stavermen lingered behind the four, another in front.

'Some days ago,' began Pike, 'my stavermen discovered four humans hiding at the north end of Park Street Gardens, which is . . .'

'Not very far from where we now stand,' said Jack.

'Exactly. They were in rainwater sewers near Masshouse Lane and had established themselves very cleverly. They were well equipped and, as humans go, quite skilled in hyddening.'

'But not so skilled that your people were unable to find them?'

'They *are* humans,' said Pike dismissively, 'and therefore made mistakes. They gave themselves away by urinating into the water that flows south-westward from that point and which we monitor. We tracked them back to where they were and observed them. They also had some fearsome-looking weapons . . .'

'Machine pistols, explosives . . . ?' murmured Jack.

'That sort of thing. They also had cameras and listening equipment which they had begun to install in Old and New Brum. Again, they did it cleverly. In fact, we had found some of those earlier and first thought they were left behind two months ago after the period of civil strife when human fought human and then Fyrd as well and Brum was largely destroyed. But when new equipment appeared we realized that some humans were still here. As I say, it did not take long to find them. We thought it sensible to make ourselves obvious and mislead them into thinking we had no idea they were here.'

'And why do you think they *were*?'

'It seemed plain enough they wanted to observe us and perhaps even attack us, but . . .'

'Did you see any nets or suchlike?'

Pike grimaced.

'We not only saw them, two of our people were caught in them . . . but more of that in a moment. Marshal Brunte and I brought the matter to the attention of the Emperor here and my Lord Festoon. We pointed out, that, in addition to the cameras, they were beginning to distribute and plant explosive devices of the devastating kind we saw here in November, and we felt they should be stopped. The decision was taken, but only after a difficult debate . . .' Pike hesitated.

'It was decided that we should kill them,' said Niklas Blut, his spectacles flashing. 'Once you let humans through the door they do not go back out of it. Their nature is destructive. It is what they do. We felt it best to eliminate them while we could for Brum's sake. We . . .'

Festoon continued, making clear the decision was a shared one: 'We felt that, if they were allowed to spread explosives in Brum, even if we found most of them, we would never be sure there weren't more we had missed. Have you seen the effects of explosives on hydden, Jack?'

'No.'

'Well we have; some days ago we saw what happened when the humans deployed such weapons on the Fyrd. That was the reason they fled Brum so soon after taking it over. Please, carry on, Pike.'

Jack did not like the sound of this at all. It meant that the city he and the others had returned to with such difficulty was effectively still under siege. Worse, he had not been fully briefed, with the result that Katherine and Stort were now in personal danger.

'We therefore attacked the four humans and inflicted damage on them in our legitimate defence, some of it brutal,' said Pike. 'That was not so difficult. Surprise is everything. But . . . it is difficult to live with the kind of carnage that human weapons can inflict. Hard to get out of one's mind the people you kill, whether human or not.'

Jack nodded. 'Katherine and I know the truth of that. We killed humans to save life on Pendower Beach and we have not recovered either. I doubt we ever will. Killing others may be justified in self-defence or in defence of others, but even that I begin to doubt . . . So, you killed some but not all of them?'

'How did you know that?' asked Pike.

'Because you're still looking over your collective shoulders. What went wrong? What happened?'

'We made a mistake, a very serious one: we underestimated them,' continued Pike, his face now very grim. 'The decision having been made, I led seven stavermen in to kill the four humans. One went down immediately but the others fought back with such overwhelming fire power that we lost three of our force in moments.'

'Three?' repeated Jack, appalled.

Pike looked grimmer still.

'We retreated momentarily and then came in from a different angle, a tactic that worked well against the Fyrd. It worked again. We got two more before the remaining one brought his weapon to bear on us. And then . . . disaster. I knew we had lost three but only as we retreated did I see we had lost one more, shot from *behind* our position . . .'

'You mean there was a fifth human?'

Pike nodded.

'We had missed him completely and nor did we see him then at all. Our retreat was difficult and I lost two more, by which time I was by myself and outnumbered, with the last one of the four we attacked still firing, though wounded, and the one I could not locate. It was a rout. I was lucky to get out alive and in some ways I wish . . .'

Jack raised a hand. There were some things best left unsaid.

Pike's face and eyes expressed his terrible despair and guilt. It was obvious that he wished he had been one of those killed.

'What weapons did you have?'

'My stave, my crossbow, my dirk . . .'

'Against human weapons,' said Jack softly, 'the outcome is no surprise.'

'It was a decision born of ignorance.'

'You said two of your stavermen had been netted,' observed Jack.

'They were. We got to them before the humans did and were able to set them free.'

'And the remaining humans?'

'The one we wounded has died today. The one we never saw we think we may have wounded too and have been following a blood trail in and around the sidings and footings of Moor Street Station.'

A staverman emerged from the darkness and whispered in Pike's ear. He asked a question in a low voice, got the answer and then turned to them.

'We have just tracked him to the Corporation Wharf.'

'He can't be that badly wounded then, unless the trail was left to confuse you,' said Jack. 'The Wharf is a long way from Moor Street. Which end is he?'

'He's at the crossing. We think he's trying to get to the surface, which, if he succeeds, will . . .'

'Will be easier for him, more difficult for us,' said Jack who knew the ground well.

The Wharf occupied a large triangle of ground south and east of Curzon Street Station. The 'crossing' was not a level crossing for rail tracks but where the Warwick and Birmingham canal ran in an aqueduct above the River Rea. It was a maze of rail lines, embankments and storage facilities and less than half a mile from where they now stood.

'Igor Brunte is there in the field and thinks he has our quarry pinned down. He will not make a move until I get there,' said Pike.

'I'm coming too,' said Jack. 'I won't get involved but I want to assess the risk from the point of view of Stort. At some point, as we all know, he will come to a conclusion about the likely whereabouts of the gem of Winter and I want to be sure to get him, and anyone else we need, out of Brum, assuming it will be out of the city we need to go.'

Pike seemed to want to resist Jack coming but said nothing. Jack looked as formidable as any of his stavermen. He was not going to be denied.

'My Lords,' said Pike calling two of his people over and turning to Blut and Festoon, 'these staverman will see you safely to the Muggy Duck, where your presence is probably already being missed. We'll go to Corporation Wharf and decide then what we are going to do . . .'

Blut did not like vagueness and ambiguity.

'And if you find this human, Mister Pike?'

'We kill him,' said Pike unequivocally. 'One should not be beyond our capability.'

Jack was not so sure.

But minutes later they arrived at the point where Fazeley Street bridges the Rea. The crossing was a hundred yards away to the east. Igor Brunte appeared.

'He is on the wharf side,' he said in a low voice, 'in a conduit and . . . he's good. Clever. He leaves the routes behind him mined and booby-trapped. The surface thereabout is now lethal. We think he is trying to escape eastward into the railway sidings and then to Lawley Street but he has not tried to move on for ten minutes. Maybe he wants a fight! If so he'll get it. But we proceed with caution, this one knows what he's doing.'

The way it was said, the way Pike withered a little, told Jack that confidence had been lost between the two. Which was not surprising.

He was about to ask some detailed questions of Brunte when they all fell silent, listening.

A low and urgent thwump-thump-thwump filled their ears. It was coming very fast, from the south, and rapidly grew so loud that they instinctively ducked. The Huey helicopter that Jack had seen landing at Woodhenge the day before flew over their heads, banked east and went in the direction of the sidings.

'What the Mirror's that?' said Pike as a great shadow went by.

'Reinforcements,' replied Jack. 'Our problem just grew exponentially.'

The helicopter landed three hundred yards away beyond some

railway buildings. The throb of the engine and thwump-thwump of the blades quietened and stopped.

Silence fell.

It was then that Jack understood for the first time the real quality of Brunte's skills and leadership for, despite the recent loss of confidence, he was still willing to put his trust in Pike.

'Mister Pike,' he said quietly, 'the ground beyond the Wharf is tricky, is it not?'

'It is.'

'I know lives were lost to the humans,' growled Brunte, 'but I have not forgotten how many lives of my troops were saved by your stavermen before the humans came, and after they arrived. I have ten of my people hereabout. Your force is also ten.

'You know this ground better than anyone alive. I am putting my people at your disposal. You're now in command. Good luck!'

They shook hands.

Pike had a second chance and he grew in stature before their eyes. He was Brum born and bred and he had served it well all his life. And there was a mistake to rectify.

He whistled twice and a staverman appeared.

'Mister Pike?'

'Are any of the young lads here?'

'At the spousal, sir, serving and that.'

'Pity,' said Pike, 'this is a situation where messengers are needed. If we just had one . . .'

They heard the sound of running feet and, as if he had heard the summons, Bratfire appeared, grinning.

'What the Mirror are *you* doing here?' exclaimed Pike. 'I thought you were meant to be at Arnold's spousal doing useful things like serving sweetmeats and brew?'

'Pa sent me,' said Bratfire.

'You mean Barklice sent you to tell us to come to the spousal?' said Jack.

The lad shook his head.

'He'm said things smelt bad and nobbut is good outside the Duck and you'm and Mister Jack might be needing us messengers. So here I be. Others are on the way. If there'm trouble again, we'm your boys!'

Pike smiled, but very seriously.

'Here's what I want you to do . . .' he finally began, as Bratfire's friends began to arrive in ones and twos and more stavermen appeared as well.

Jack relaxed and saw that Brunte did too.

The city had been invaded by Fyrd, nearly destroyed by humans, and come under siege by the very Earth Herself. A great deal was wrong that could now probably never be put right. But here before their eyes was proof that the ancient, bold and plucky spirit of the citizenry of Brum was living still. This was a folk who had always accepted to its heart all those who came with the right intention and defended liberty. A folk who, in the end, however great the odds, would surely always find ways to get rid of the invader and make Brum, Old and New, live again.

38

INTERLUDE

Katherine arrived at the Muggy Duck in time to witness the arrival of the groom and his close family, headed by Arnold's grandfather Old Mallarkhi, and Ma'Shuqa, his mother.

Naturally they arrived by boat, helmed by the groom himself, dressed from top to bottom – from turban to curly schuhe – in a fabric shot through with gold thread, made sparkly by diamonds of the highest quality. As Old Mallarkhi was eager to point out to all and sundry.

'An' if you'm say different, any o' you layabouts who'm came for a free sup and crumble, I'll knock yer nose!' he cried, scrambling up onto the wharf next to the now ruinous Duck.

'Diamonds, my arse,' whispered one of the guests, 'they'm broken glass by any other name! He's an ol' skinflint.'

'Which be why, you drunken nannerkins, he be rich and well content and you be poor and miserable!'

True or not, Arnold looked a splendid and sparkly sight. A happy one too, for his grin went from ear to ear.

He steered his craft to its mooring with such finesse, such elegance, that even the hangers-on clapped him home. He was, all agreed, after his adventures with Mister Stort in the South-West, the very greatest and most courageous Bilgesnipe mariner of his age.

''Tis said,' stated another guest with confidence, as Arnold roped up his craft and joined them on solid ground, 'that our lad here had a race to shore with that crafty cove Borkum Riff of Den Helder, who'm not a Bilgesnipe but bain't narf bad wi' boats o' the sea.'

'And?'

'Our Arnold won and Riff crawled on his pesky hands and knees and licked the lad's boots by way of sayin' thankee for teaching 'im how to sail better.'

'You'm talking nonsensical!'

'Maybe I am, maybe I'm not.'

Such and similar were merely the start of one of the last and greatest spousals held at the Muggy Duck.

The Duck's shattered kitchen and great drinking parlour had been cleared and repaired so that they were serviceable. A temporary tarpaulin roof had been erected and extended onto the wharf itself. The main wooden table and some smaller ones, which had served so many generations of drinkers, had been hauled out onto the wharf, leaving only three smaller tables inside for those who wanted quieter conversations.

Great braziers, some lofty, some low, were set up to give cheerful light and that smoky, pleasant warmth to the outside air that winter demands. Their orange flames were complemented by the many candles set on the tables, the mooring pins, the cobbles, the nearby warehouse windows and walls and across the wide water where Old Lamley's Abattoir still stood. A hundred more candles had been placed on its many window sills, the glass reflecting them many times more.

The water beneath did the same, so it looked like a cloth of gold, in amongst which, when the light breeze flurried up a wave or two – which also made the candles flare and show more brightly – pinpoints of reflected stars were seen.

Across the waterway, to the western side, from which direction it was traditional for brides to come, arches of bamboo had been set, supported by thin metal struts which flexed and moved gently as if they were alive. Along the length of these arches short swatches of wet cloth had been attached, beneath which lights hung in jars. As the evening had progressed these cloths began to freeze and ice to form, making the arches look like a vast, fantastical receding cave of ice, lit with flickering light, paved with icy gold.

Everyone kept looking that way, for that was where Madder, Arnold's dreamygirl, would appear, and few had yet seen her.

A small group of guests and revellers formed around Katherine, including Barklice, Bohr and Ingrid. They sat at one of the smaller tables, Old Mallarkhi nearby and Ma'Shuqa at the larger one. Ma was sitting down for once, for the feast itself had been arranged and managed by a host of sisters, sisters-in-law and aunts no one even knew she had.

Asked why Jack was not yet there, and not wishing to alarm anyone, Katherine said no more than that she expected he would be with them soon.

Stort took a seat next to her but was in such demand that he was up and down, saying hello, giving advice, eating cakes, until he went off by himself to a corner, where he ignored everyone and began muttering and gesticulating to himself.

'What's he doing?' Katherine asked.

'I believe he is very much worried,' offered Barklice, 'by the fact that he has as yet no idea where to find the gem of Winter but is not saying so.'

Ma'Shuqa heard this and shook her head.

'Mister Barklice, you'm a good sort but stick to route-finding. Mister Stort bain't give two figs right now about that gem. No, what he be about is readying hisself for his great task, seein' as Arnold's pa, who I have not seen since the day our lad was born, is not present and correct,' said Ma'Shuqa. 'He's to make the speech.'

'Which one?' asked Katherine, who knew that at Bilgesnipe spousals there were many speeches.

'The ninth, which be important if you don't count the six that follow and the last.'

'Who makes that?'

'My pa, his grandpa, Old M.'

Ma'Shuqa was in her best, which meant that she had so many silken layers of gossamer-thin frocks and petticoats, plus assorted jewels upon her vast bosoms, rings and bracelets on hands and fingers, ankles and toes, as well as earrings, necklaces and ribbons of so many hues in her hair, that she looked like a rainbow.

By contrast, Old Mallarkhi, who had lingered near death's door for many years and was normally pale and cadaverous and dressed in a torn nightshirt, had been scrubbed up. He was very neat and sober-looking in shiny trews and jerkin of sail-cloth. Ma'Shuqa had rouged his gaunt cheeks with essence of dog-rose, which made him look and smell like a cheerful corpse just risen from a bier of rose petals.

'I don't mind aught else for Arnold,' he said, 'but that he'm as happy in his girl as I was with mine right up until the day she drownded.'

'No need to natter on about Ma's unseemly death, Pa. She wor lookin' for love, that's all.'

'Didn't I give her love, dang me?!'

'Yes, Pa.'

'Well, there you is, and there you be, Katherine. Happiness is not predictable.'

'No, Mister Mallarkhi.'

'In fact, it's a pesky nuisance is happiness, but I had it then and I have it again now. That's all I'd ask for Arnold. But . . . where's this girl o' his?'

'She'm comin', Pa.'

Stort joined them, still muttering.

'Ready?' said Katherine.

'I shall make an oration like no other ever made!' he said.

'Just keep it short, Mister Stort,' said Ma. 'That's all we ask.'

'Humph!' said Stort.

A few minutes later a hush fell and word got about that the bride was on her way. But before she came Lord Festoon and Emperor Blut appeared. Their health was generally toasted, their backs slapped and the seating changed such that Katherine's table was brought adjacent to the bigger one, so their Lordships could sit with the family as well as Katherine and the others.

Moments later the cry went up that Madder the dreamygirl was about to hove to in sight and they all rose up to watch her arrive.

The night was dark but the sky clear, so those stars seen earlier and now the rising moon shone bright over the canal waters and ruins of Digbeth and the Muggy Duck, turning them from gold to silver.

The arched bride's route was within and without so bright and beautiful that it was inconceivable that anything, even the sun and moon combined, could have outshone it and made it brighter.

Yet as the guests hushed and the Bilgesnipe music lulled into something soft and lyrical, a vision appeared. It was a boat, painted white as snow, and bedecked with flowers of paper and cloth, tinsel and mirror, in the form of pink hearts and red roses, which glowed with love and life and seemed to leap forth and shine beyond all else.

There in its midst, standing, not seated, was an apparition so beautiful, so fulsome, so overflowing with youthful joy that there was not a single person there who did not stop and stare in awe. Males murmured and sighed, females shed a tear.

When the bride smiled and waved and blew kisses to them all, as she did, the crowd murmured its appreciation and many wept again.

Then, when what had been a nearly non-existent breeze strengthened a shade and turned her dark, thick hair to streaming tresses, her ribbons to streamers and her silky white and cream frock and underskirts to fields of windblown carnations, the crowd could do nothing less than cheer and laugh with pleasure once again.

Arnold stood tall on the wharf, ready to receive his nearly-bride, his swarthy face and hair catching the braziers' light.

Behind this craft, which seemed to be all but sinking beneath its many decorations and Madder's wild, excessive, exuberant and out-of-control skirts, were three more boats containing her family and friends. They were in milder garb, though the females were beribboned and the males in brand-new suits of jet fustian, grobbled with white silk and hemmed in pinks and reds to match the bride's flowers.

'My, but she'm bootiful!' cried Ma'Shuqa. 'Pa, double that dowry at once!'

It was the Bilgesnipe's custom for the groom's family to pay the dowry and not one the Mallarkhis much liked, but the bride was exceptional.

'She'm got a smile to 'er like ten roses thrown into a summer sky!' said Pa. 'I'll treble it!'

As Madder came under the last arch, Arnold went forth to the wharf's edge to greet her and utter the vows the simple Bilgesnipe way.

'You'm my dreamygirl, Madder, and you were fro' the moment I clapped eyes on thee! Be mine!'

To which Madder replied, as she had to if the union was to be legal, 'And you'm my spousal love, which you'm were fro' the moment you held me tight and whispered words that be our secret forever and a day!'

This got a great cheer, and the spousal truly began. Rings were exchanged, the story of their meeting told and retold, the telling by

Katherine being judged the best. Then Ma told of Arnold when young, which got laughter; and Madder's ma did the same, which got sighs of sympathy, for dreamygirls be never easy ones to raise. Then the speeches started . . .

It might be thought that by the time it got to Stort's turn to speak, which was a long way down the list, that there was very little left to say about the history of young Arnold, the present beauty and charm of his bride or the wonderful future which their spousal promised, and that was possibly true. But Stort was popular and the estimation of his wit and wisdom very high and his rising was greeted by cheers and clapping and the imminent prospect of his utterance with a sudden and respectful silence, full of hope and expectation.

Stort was never daunted at such moments.

'My dear friends,' he cried, 'it was my great privilege as it was that of several people here, to be present at that never-to-be-forgotten moment when our bride and groom met for the first time!

'Those who shared that witnessing with me will agree . . . most certainly . . .' They nodded that they would and did, even though they had no idea what Stort was about to say, '. . . that in those magical moments the very air itself was filled with the music and perfume of love! We who were there, acting, I suppose, *in loco parentis* in the absence of Arnold's esteemed mother and wider family . . .' Stort waved importantly at Ma'Shuqa and Old Mallarkhi. '. . . remember that it seemed as if in these dark and troubled times in Englalond a great light was suddenly turned on, an ethereal lantern flared, and the birds in the trees sang as one . . .'

Stort continued in this florid vein for some time, each new phrase, each soaring cadenza, each increasingly expansive gesture and each pregnant pause, being greeted by cries and whoops of delight and admiration. Until Stort barely had to continue but that his audience continued for him, cheering and clapping and in absolute agreement – when he finally sat down – that none had yet spoken as well or with such erudition as he had. Until, a natural break occurring before any further speeches, with the arrival of more food and a swelling of the music, the dancing began and every word he had spoken, and sentiment he had expressed, was lost and forgotten in the heady excitement of the latest moment.

39

IRREVERSIBLE

The moment the formal part of the spousal was complete and the Bilgesnipe began the festivities in earnest, Blut, Festoon and Bohr, wanting some quiet and warmth, moved thankfully inside. The old inglenook had proved indestructible and a merry fire was burning there, though much of the chimney above it was gone.

Their mood being sombre and their foreboding great, there was a general inclination for more serious conversation. With this Katherine and Barklice concurred. As too did Ingrid when, flushed from dancing, and bright-eyed from the strong brew, she came to be with Bohr.

Niklas Blut, his hands stretched out towards the fire, said, 'It is not since I was with the late and very much missed Arthur Foale that I have had an opportunity of talking with humans, and never with three at once, that is including you as one, Katherine, if I may for this purpose. I count you, Doctors Bohr and Hansen . . .'

'Please call me Ingrid.'

'. . . as the other two. Let us be honest. Tonight is but a respite from reality, is it not?'

They all conceded that it was.

He took off his spectacles, wiped them and clamped them back on his face, the orbs of glass as bright as ever, the eyes behind them as sharp.

'We cannot know what our wyrd and the future hold,' he began, 'except that, according to hydden tradition and belief, if the gem of Winter is not found and returned to the pendant on or before the night when this dark season gives way to spring . . .'

'You mean the pagan spring, which starts on the first day of February?' queried Bohr. 'That feels early and odd to humans!'

'Which Arthur also often remarked,' said Stort. 'My Lord Blut is not saying that spring begins at the stroke of midnight: there is some latitude. But what hydden scholars of myth and legend all agree is that at the seasons' turn, between the hours that run from sunset to sunrise of the day in question, the gem must be returned to the Shield Maiden . . .'

His voice faded and he looked despairing – and they all knew why.

'My dear chap,' said Festoon, 'I will not ask if you have yet found the gem . . .'

'I have not,' said Stort.

'. . . or whether you know where it is . . .'

'I do not.'

'. . . or even if you have some idea . . .'

'No idea at all, my Lord. My mind on that subject is a void and I would rather not talk about it.'

'I was trying to say,' continued Festoon sympathetically, 'that I will not ask those questions, natural though they are, but I *will* make this observation. Time is running out!'

'Thank you for the reminder, my Lord,' said Stort tartly. 'Now I would much prefer we spoke of something else!'

'Certainly,' added Barklice ingenuously, quite missing Stort's desire not to be reminded of the pressures on him and so confident in his friend's abilities that it did not occur to him that he might be in a state of self-doubt. 'It does seem as if there's no time left! Why, by my chronometer' – and here he foolishly pulled the instrument out – 'you have only – why, goodness me, where has the time gone? Only . . .'

Katherine kicked him on the shin.

'Really, Barklice, I don't think it's helpful to talk of it,' she hissed.

But Stort's nature was such that, stressed though he was, where his good friend the verderer was concerned he was inclined to forgive anything. He knew there was no hydden so good-natured yet canny as Barklice, nor one who *in extremis*, when it came to helping his friends find the right ways and routes forward, would go the extra mile to help them.

With a shake of his head and an exasperated smile he said resignedly,

'Mister Barklice is quite right to point out that we have barely a few days left. He knows very well I have been avoiding the issue.'

'Ah!' said Blut, who had wished to raise the same point himself but had not been quite sure how.

They waited in expectation of a response from Stort.

'The truth?' he finally said in a low voice. 'The truth is I do not know where to begin, even though we have so little time left. It was the same with the gem of Autumn, but on this occasion much more is at stake, since we may all soon cease to be – and there is even less time *this* time, I believe. In fact, how much time *is* left, Barklice? Tell me the truth.'

'Less than a week, Stort, and that's assuming the time runs its normal course, but as you very well know it has not been doing that these past weeks and months. Like a glass pitcher full of water which gets broken, it could run out rather quicker than we expect.'

Barklice could hardly have put the situation better.

'Yes, time moves in fits and starts just now,' agreed Stort. 'Why? Because the Mirror is cracked and time messed up. If I look despondent, I am. When we finally got back to Brum, I had hoped I might start, as I did with the other gems, with the Chamber of Seasons at my Lord's Residence. The images of the seasons there were filled with clues. But that is all gone, lost in the ruins of the Residence. And we were witness to the burning of the imagery of Winter itself on the fire this evening. If only I had realized it earlier, that great work of genius, or the part we needed, might have been rescued. How much I might have learnt studying it, even in its ruined state. But I realized all that too late.

'That is a loss that may be fatal, for there lay the only hope we had of finding the clue that is so sorely needed. Now the end feels as if it is drawing near and I feel quite oppressed and unable to think with any clarity just when I need most to be able to do so. So yes, I would be much obliged if we might talk of other things!'

He turned to the Emperor.

'My Lord Blut, you said just now that you have missed the opportunity of talking to, and learning from, humans since Arthur's death?'

'I have. He often stated the opinion that the End of Days, which is what we now fear so much, is the result of human interference with the Earth and, perhaps, the Universe. His view was that the situation was irreversible.'

Bohr nodded and said, 'And I can assure you all that he was not the only one. Many of us humans have long believed that to be the case. Even assuming we knew what to do to save the Earth, which I'm not sure we do, it was always going to be too little, too late. The die was cast and the will was not there to try to change the result. In the end it came down to two simple truths: humans are too selfish and greedy to think beyond the short-term.'

'Quite so,' said Blut, who seemed rather less gloomy than some, as if he sensed that somewhere there might be a way forward if only they could help Stort to see what it was, 'which gives rise to two very different questions. It is these I would now like to ask, if it is not too inappropriate to do so on an occasion such as this. After all, the opportunity may not arise again.'

But outside on the wharf it seemed the moment was fast approaching when the bride and groom were to depart. Katherine got up to investigate and came back at once and said with a smile, 'Pa Mallarkhi is about to make the final speech, which gives us a little time . . .'

'The first question, then,' continued Blut, 'is if we believe that the position is irreversible and the End of Days is nigh, why do we even hope the quest can possibly have a positive outcome, even assuming Stort finds the gem?'

'Because . . .' said one, his voice petering out.

'Because . . .' began another, with nowhere else to go.

'Because we *believe* it,' a voice said from behind them, 'and we must believe it, even to the very end.'

It was Jack, come to the wedding at last. He looked tired and in need of a rest and a drink and he wouldn't sit down.

Instead, glancing meaningfully at Katherine, he signalled that he needed a discreet but urgent word with her.

'Because we believe it,' Blut repeated quietly as she got up with the excuse of ordering more drinks, 'Yes, I think that is the answer I wanted to hear. I think there can be no better one. Good! Now for my second question . . .'

'What is it, Jack, what's wrong?' whispered Katherine, slipping over to him.

'We need to leave, *now*,' he said.

'But . . .'

'*Now*. But I don't want to cause a panic which I will if I try to gather together those who are leaving with us. So who have we got here . . . ?'

'I don't understand, Jack.'

'It's now, Katherine, *now*, but there's no time to tell you why. We *have* to go.'

He looked pale and shocked but only because she knew him so well did she gauge the real depth of his concern.

'Who do you want to come with us . . . ?'

'Stort, of course, and Barklice will be needed. Emperor Blut, Terce . . . where the hell's Terce? We need him. Bohr as well, though Mirror knows why.'

'Ingrid?'

'I suppose so but we have no time to argue about it.'

'Who else . . . ?' he muttered, looking around.

'You, of course,' she said.

He hesitated and half shook his head.

'*You*, Jack, you're coming to wherever it is.'

'I may not be able to . . .'

'*Jack . . . !*'

'Ah Jack!' called out Blut, the drinks having come and the conversation resuming. 'I have a second question!'

'Find Terce,' Jack said in a low voice. 'Have him ready but out of sight . . . I'll bring these others.'

Then, turning to Blut, Jack said, 'Your question is, my Lord?'

Blut turned to Erich Bohr as Katherine went outside unseen.

'Doctor, I daresay you have a better grasp of human history than most of us, so I shall direct this one at you: at what moment in the historic past of human history might what we hydden call the End of Days have still been reversible? Ten years ago? Twenty? One hundred? Perhaps back at the start of what you call the Industrial Revolution?'

Bohr stared at him, seeking an answer to a question he had never been asked before.

'You mean a general period of history or a specific one moment in time?'

'I mean the question as I ask it and you wish to interpret it.'

'Well . . . I would have to think if . . .' said Bohr uncertainly.

'It must depend on all sorts of things and how you define "reversible",' added Ingrid.

'Jack?'

'A very long time ago,' said Jack, his voice tense. 'Probably you'd have to go back two hundred years to before the Industrial Revolution to be certain that, if humanity had taken a different direction, then . . .'

'Humans being human,' said Bohr cynically, 'you'd have to go back whole millennia! They have always been on a road to self-destruction. It's just we seem to be its final witnesses.'

'Stort?'

'I have and can have no answer to such a hypothetical question, my Lord Emperor. Did you ask it of Arthur himself?'

'Ah! I wondered who would ask that!' said Blut. 'Yes I did.'

'Did he give you an answer?'

'Not one that I understood. I thought he might answer it as we seem to be trying to do, broadly, or in terms of inevitability, as Jack has. He said something very different.'

The noise outside swelled, there was clapping; the moment of departure was almost on them.

'Well?' said Stort.

'He said that it wasn't a question of history so much as human will. He put it as Bohr seems to be doing: suggesting that as a species Homo Sapiens is innately self-destructive and will never find a solution. In those terms, he said, the end is indeed irreversible. But his time in the Hyddenworld had taught Arthur a different way of seeing things. We are, he said, part of the *musica* and the *musica* is positive, always finally positive.

'It needs, Arthur suggested, but one individual in the whole world to sing a different song and if it can only be heard, all can change. Naturally I asked him if he thought there had been a moment when that "song" might have been sung. Or, in other words, had there been a moment when the intervention of a single mortal might have made the difference needed to reverse it all. He thought a long time and said that maybe there had been many such moments, but in his lifetime only one and that, probably, a final one.'

'And what moment was that?' asked Bohr, very curious.

'He gave me a date, indeed a precise date and time, but since I am a hydden and he was talking about human history it meant nothing to me. I asked him to explain. But very soon after that we were rescued by Jack and I'm afraid the opportunity to ask him again for an explanation of what precisely he meant slipped away.'

'A specific date,' exclaimed Stort, 'how interesting! But what might that possibly be?'

Just then their deliberations were interrupted by the fizz and roar of a rocket. At the same moment Jack saw Katherine outside, hurrying a bemused Terce behind the crowd to the street-side of the Duck.

Jack rose impressively and said in a low, commanding voice, 'Gentlemen and lady, I need your attention and I need you to trust me. There is no time for argument or for discussion. It is necessary, in fact essential, that we all leave now. We need to do so singly and discreetly, starting with you, Emperor . . . You will find Katherine on the street outside with Terce . . . follow them . . . tell her not to hurry . . . and please, "now" means *now*.'

Blut knew Jack well enough that a full explanation would come later but that meanwhile they should do as he said. He slipped out, and since the crowd was facing the other way no one noticed.

'Lord Festoon and Stort, you're next,' said Jack.

When they had gone Jack turned to Barklice: 'Now you, Barklice . . .'

'I'm not going anywhere without Bratfire.'

'He's fine, he's waiting for you already I'm sure . . . *Go!* And finally Doctors Bohr and Hansen . . .'

As they left Jack turned towards the crowd to make sure no one was looking, gratified to see that most were Bilgesnipe. They, more than most, knew how to look after themselves.

Over their heads he glimpsed Arnold leaping nimbly to the helm of the white wedding craft, and paused a second more to say a mute goodbye. He raised his hand in salutation as more rockets and fireworks began to go off and Arnold turned the craft expertly beneath a shower of golden sparks until, with a wave and a shout, they were gone.

'Goodbye, my friend,' said Jack, 'good luck . . .'

Then he too was gone, after the others, to try to find a way to save their lives.

40

HUNTER AND HUNTED

The encounters of Colonel Reece and his men with the hydden had been little short of disastrous.

First, the captive inadvertently netted at Woolstone had escaped from under their noses. At Woodhenge his best men had been left injured and bewildered by hydden they hardly saw. In Birmingham they had lost several men without really knowing how it happened.

Now, the greatest disaster of all, which overshadowed all the others. The Huey UH-IN helicopter which was his main asset and only realistic means of escape from the city had exploded two hundred yards behind him, which had seemed inexplicable until he realized that once more the hydden had got the better of him.

Colonel Reece's rage turned toxic and his need for revenge overrode all reason and training. It was a moment that had been a long time coming – not for minutes and hours, nor days and weeks, but for years and decades, back to his teens, long before he ever heard of the Hyddenworld.

Back then, when he was sixteen, someone – he knew who – tried to shoot him out in the open, from behind. It was a very good shot, from a great distance, but not a fatal one. It nicked his ear and nearly took his eye, burying itself explosively in the rock and soil in front of him.

A month later, one afternoon in winter, in the Montana snow and supposedly shooting for elk, Reece set off to hunt down his would-be-killer. He did it slowly, methodically, like their dead father had taught him: he was hunting his own brother.

The shot that nearly killed him was the remaining proof he needed to confirm his suspicions that it had been his brother who had killed their father. Fearing that Reece knew, he had also tried to kill him.

Bastard.

Now Reece wanted to enjoy the process of hunting him as prey, so he did it cruelly, shooting first to frighten, then to graze a leg and next to shatter a hand. Not the right but the left, so his brother could still shoot.

When his brother shouted Reece's name in the dark, *Phil Phil Phil*, it was the beginning of the fearful pleading of one who knows he cannot win and likely will soon die. Philip Reece began to feel alive for the first time since his father died.

Bastard.

Reece spent that afternoon and far into the night, right until first light, hunting his kin-prey, hating him, loving it, his blood racing with anticipation of the penultimate, perfect, shot. The one that was going to slice his temple and nick his ear and bury itself right in front of him to mirror what happened before. To lull him into thinking that was all he intended.

Phil . . .

The sound of hope in that last cry was sadistic bliss to Reece. Two minutes later, as the sun rose slanting across Flathead Lake, lying in the blood trail he had been following, Reece aimed a final time, his hands rock-steady, his eyes alight with sunlight, his sense of power absolute until, pulling the trigger, he watched his brother's head explode.

That was then.

But revenge was bitter and left a bitter taste.

Killers do not escape their killing.

Hate never left Reece, though he held it in check. Training turned the poison into a drive to be better, better than better, better than the best. He used the hate to rise higher through the ranks. But hate and anger, held inside, show outside: they make a mouth thin, make eyes dead, make a life withered and bleak as frozen water in a dyke. Yet this was what steadied his hand, stilled his breath, cleared his mind and enabled him to take his time and shoot his sniper shots.

But fratricide and ice inside twist a man's mind so much that one day he breaks and the poison spews. It all caught up with Reece that day in Birmingham, England, when a little bastard hydden, dwarf filth he didn't even see, crawled round him and blew up his Huey. Even that he might have held in control but for something more. As the Huey blew up behind him, a bolt from a crossbow fired from one side of them passed straight through the neck of the marine at his side, the last one he had, and he fell at Reece's feet, spouting blood, gurgling in death.

So Reece was suddenly alone, with no way out, and it was beginning to snow, and that was the moment he felt he was right back there in Montana, intent on his first human prey.

These latest kills he had in mind were going to be his last and he intended to make them good – very good.

He had all he wanted to do the job right: his favoured AMW sniper rifle, enough .338 Lapua Magnums, no one to answer to, or for, any more . . . and prey. Because they were going to come back and this time he was going to finally take them out.

'Bastards,' he murmured as he threw a grenade to kill the shooter of the bolt and readied himself to roll away with the explosion.

Bang!

Then he was off, unseen, running so fast, swerving so low, turning just where he needed to be to get the one who got his Huey.

Which, to his astonishment, he failed to do. Found the tracks, traced them to a canal and there lost them for good.

Clever bastard had climbed in and waded away.

No matter. Reece retreated to take up a new position. As soon as he went he felt he might as well have been one of the shadows themselves, or the landscape, or the ground and the concrete and the filth and the rising ruins of the world and the blizzard wind. He felt he was all of it. That was the way it was done.

Then he slowed, stopped, lay down, put his eye to his night 'scope, swept the terrain, saw nothing, and began his wait.

He gathered enough snow and ice to put in his mouth to reduce its temperature and take away the giveaway condensation of his out-breath.

Then he breathed easy, breathed good, knowing one way or another he was going to die but not until he had got them all.

The blizzard drove high above his head, across the open space he had made his killing ground, the place they had made the fire and had been seen and most likely would be again. They used the building nearby and that was where one of his men swore they had seen Bohr, or the runt-version of him, so far as anyone normal could see hydden at all. Still, that's where Reece counted on them coming back to. If he saw dwarf-Bohr he'd take him out with pleasure. He lay very still, which he knew how to do, breathed his icy breath and very soon he looked like nothing more than another undulation on the frosty ground.

Jack hurried them away from the Duck, up through Digbeth to Deritend, past the bombed-out stores, through the lanes off New Canal Street, on and on.

The sky above the wharves and old factories around the Duck had been clear earlier on, the stars showing. Now, when it was still lit by the occasional rocket and fireworks from the wedding, they saw it was livid and that the clouds raced by like an angry, muddy stream filled with ice.

But at ground level the air was unearthly still, the wind's roar being high above their heads, above the highest buildings. The lights of the festivities faded further behind them, the air grew ever colder and the night darker. Yet the sky above and the clouds there made their presence felt: ominous, raging, a growing threat.

Suddenly the air was sharp with flecks of ice that pricked their cheeks and forehead and which sometimes shone as a brief wink of sharp light.

The lanes north from Old Brum were criss-crossed with waterways, on which the Bilgesnipe had moored their crafts.

Katherine was surprised to see that they were not the only ones hurrying. Here and there, down along the waterways, silent as they themselves, whole families of Bilgesnipe hurried too, with but a single light to show the way. They climbed in boats and poled off fast into the darkness, the icy water crackling as they went. The helms, standing tall, sometimes knocked icicles, which fell and skittered onto their crafts' cold sterns.

'They're trying to get away to more open water,' said Jack when they paused briefly for a rest, 'or to where the waterways run underground.'

'Explain what's happening,' said Katherine, 'Jack . . .'

'Come *on*,' was his reply, 'we've little time.'

There was something in his voice she had never heard before in all the years she had known him. It was not alarm or fear. It was a rising and terrible sense of panic, or helplessness, perhaps even of despair.

'Jack . . .'

Terce hurried them on from the front, a lantern in his hand, Jack followed behind with another.

Only when they finally stopped, just before the entrance into the Main Square, and she saw his face in the dim and flickering light, pinched now with the bitter cold, as the others' were, did she see what it was his voice expressed. Jack was a protector of others, it was what he did. He would overturn every obstacle to save any one of them, or lay down his life if he must. That was what defined Jack.

But now, standing there, breathing heavily from the exertions of their flight, he looked like a parent who is beginning to lose faith that he can save his own children from harm. Jack, she guessed, was running out of options.

But why?

She did not have time to ask the question because he barked an order at them to stay together while he checked the Main Square.

He gave his lantern to Katherine and crept forward and did so, as best he could. What he was looking for was a line of safe retreat into the Library.

The fire they had lit outside the Library steps still smouldered, a red glow in the middle of an icy wasteland. The smoke drifted across the path and against the Library wall. Then it rose up, past the first floor and beyond the second, ruined one. Jack followed its passage and could just see that two floors up it was whipped violently away into the night by the icy river of air that drove over their heads.

'What is it?' asked Katherine of Barklice. 'Have you ever seen the like?'

'I've heard if it but never wanted to see it,' he replied. 'It's a cold front of air overreaching itself, held back by its own power but getting lower all the time. Like a wave before it crashes down. When it reaches us at ground level it'll be a killing kind of cold.'

Jack returned.

'Listen,' he said. 'We face two enemies, not one: the cold and the humans. You've seen the blizzard blowing above . . . ?'

They nodded.

'We heard today that it was coming our way.'

'Who from?'

'One of the officers sent north by Igor Brunte who returned yesterday. He had black hands.'

They didn't understand.

'Frostbite,' said Jack. 'We tried to warm him up. He died. The bitter winter winds have devastated the refugees in the north, human and hydden alike and are coming our way.'

As if in confirmation of this warning, a blast of icy wind drove down into them; the ice it carried like shards of glass in their eyes.

'I'll explain fully when we get into the Library. Barklice, you go first . . . and the rest follow at short intervals. I'll touch your arm to indicate when to go. When you do, run fast but without panic.

'My Lord Festoon will follow with me . . . Do not bunch together, it's too dangerous. Use the smoke as cover as much as you can and then run up the steps and right through the doors. It's that last bit where we'll be most vulnerable if any humans with guns are watching . . .'

'Now, go, Barklice . . . go.'

'Is Bratfire in there?'

'He may be,' said Jack evasively. '*Go!*'

Reece sensed their arrival moments before he saw their feet underneath the drifting smoke. He was tempted to fire in among where they were obviously standing but he did not do so. They would be heading for the doors of the Library and he liked the idea of having them in his sights on the steps, where they would be slow and pleasing targets.

Even as these thoughts went through his mind the first started running and moments later cleared the smoke, ran the final yards and mounted the steps. Reece had him nicely in his sights and was about to fire when a second appeared, then a third . . .

'Perfect,' he murmured as, at last they continued to appear, before one by one disappearing inside the building, 'once inside they're trapped.'

This appealed to his hunting instinct much more than simply shooting a few of them where they were. Instead, he decided to count them as they went . . . four . . . five . . .

'Godammit, how many of the bastards are there?'

The final count was nine and the last most interesting of all.

The image in his 'scope was monochrome, like an X-ray, and heat sensitive. That made the smoke blowing across blur and double the image of the hydden. Reece thought he knew the final one from the jizz of him: stolid, head thrust forward, carrying a stick. He was that same bastard who escaped the net in Woolstone, the one he saw next on the footage from Woodhenge, shooting some of his men with a crossbow before dancing out of sight with Bohr. *That* one.

He waited, ready to squeeze the trigger moments before he reached the last few steps.

'No,' murmured Reece unpleasantly, 'I prefer to kill this one later, with my knife.'

But the hydden paused, slowed by one in front, and Reece changed his mind. Stilling his breath, getting the cross-hairs of the sight plumb on the centre of the hydden's back, he fired as sweet a shot as ever he had.

And stared in amazement.

The hydden continued running up the steps and pulling sideways as he did so as if he knew the shot was coming.

Impossible, but it happened right before his eyes.

He fired again, but this time at thin air.

Jack passed through the smoke, into the relative light, and felt exposed. He also felt the urgent trembling of his stave, felt it wreak from out of its depths its shards of light, brighter than moon, brighter than sun, a terrible warning.

'Run, Festoon,' he shouted, rolling sideways, '*run!*'

The stave's glints and glitter brightened into a brief blinding flash and Jack fled up the steps after Festoon, heaving him onward through the door, following so fast that they tumbled inside together and landed before the others in a heap.

A rifle shot whizzed in above their heads and glass broke, but they were all safe, every one of them.

For now, thought Jack.

41

INTO THE BLIZZARD

Bratfire saw it all and waited.

He had watched the human for a full hour past, since he had tried to catch him after the explosion. Bratfire had stared up at his boots protruding over the canal edge, seen the hand that scooped water out and threw it on his coat and trews, heard the slight crunch of feet on ground as he left, heavy like the noise humans make even when they try to be quiet.

Watched him go, watched him crawl, watched him secrete himself, hydden-like, until, lying still enough for the canal water he had thrown so oddly onto his garb to freeze and turn grey-white, he was harder to see. Clever!

Then the puffs of breath fading, fading, after he put ice in his mouth.

Oh yes, Bratfire told himself, he was clever, this human, but not as good as him and his pa. He had chosen the wrong spot to make his lair, for one thing, because from the place that Bratfire had finally reached, which was just thirty yards away, he could watch his every move. Three yards to the right and it would have been harder.

But that didn't matter. What did was the agony, the terrible decision Bratfire had to make, when his pa and Jack's friends appeared one by one from the far corner of the square and the human had his rifle on them, moving it slightly, sighting them. That was agony.

Bratfire had hoped that after the helicopter exploded the human would be long gone and he, Bratfire, free to go down to the Library to wait for them.

Now, if he shouted a warning someone got shot for sure. And so did he. If he kept quiet then maybe the human would let them be. Maybe. Maybe his pa would get shot. Maybe. Bratfire didn't know. He didn't know what to do.

It was then, for the first time since his pa began looking after him, a tear coursed down his cheek because he felt alone and wasn't sure what to do. He wanted to stand up and shout, 'Shoot me, just me not my pa!'

But he didn't have the courage and once the solitary tear froze common sense told him that wasn't an option either.

It was wyrd that saved them, Jack's wyrd.

When the shots began and Jack's stave shone as bright as suns, blinding the human and him as well, Bratfire knew it was all right.

Jack rolled and ran, straight up the steps, bashing into Lord Festoon so they crashed through the door together.

That made Bratfire laugh, and as he did he knew what the human was going to do and why he hadn't shot before; and what *he* was going to do. His eyes swivelled right, towards where the High Ealdor's Residence had been, and beyond it in the direction of St Bartholomew's Church. He would take them there.

Meanwhile Bratfire shivered and waited for the human to get up. Which Reece did almost immediately, not entirely displeased. The shot had missed, maybe because he was momentarily blinded by the light that shone from the hydden's whirling stick. But that Reece doubted, because his aim had been good and he had anticipated the hydden's sideways roll. No, it was the light itself, it deflected the bullet.

Can't tell with these bastards, he told himself. They're using technology real people have never heard of.

So no, he was not displeased with what had happened so far. Getting them into the building meant that they would not come out again in a hurry for fear of him, which meant they were trapped inside.

He got up and headed fast towards the side of the building, intending to go from there to the back, where, he knew from his own reconnaissance, he could get inside.

Now he had them where he wanted he was going hunting again, but this time out of the cold. Buildings, half-derelict ones, had a certain charm. The challenge of several of them made it even better. Reece took pleasure in the prospect of herding them, frightening them, hurting them.

Freaks, the whole lot of them!

'*Freaks* . . .' he muttered, licking his lips.

When he was done and they were dead he was going to go outside to the fire again and pile on some of the surviving furniture he had seen, shelves and old doors that had been stacked and ready for that purpose. If the blizzard got bad, and it looked ready to come down finally, he could sneak back inside again.

Reece laughed, happy to be alive, and began his fresh advance.

'What happened, Jack?'

'Nothing.'

'We thought we heard a shot.'

'*Nothing.*'

No point in frightening them.

A shadow at the door, and a violent rattle, and they all turned in alarm. It was the wind. The blizzard had begun.

'So now,' said Katherine, 'what happened before you came for us?'

'We have to defend this place, we need . . .' he began evasively.

But this time they were doing nothing before they knew. His face said much, his silence more.

'Where are Pike and the others who were with him, Jack?'

He breathed deeply, moving a little inside to get away from the rush of the wind, the swirl-around of ice and dust. A filing card slid across the floor as if pushed by an unseen hand. Windows rattled. And the humans were still after them.

'We made a mistake,' said Jack, 'a terrible mistake. We thought that the forces of Pike and Brunte combined would be enough to stop a solitary survivor, but . . . it was not. He was clever, almost as good as you, Barklice, but he had something you don't have: a radio. He summoned help.'

They stared at him in horror.

'More came?'

'Five more. With that number, staves and crossbows were no match for the weapons they deployed. They killed Brunte and three of his people just after Pike had begun to move in with his stavermen. It was as sudden and quick as breaking glass. I know, they died next to where I stood, without time even to know what hit them, or from where. A rattle of thunderous noise and they were gone.

'We didn't hear it. Maybe because of the fireworks.'

Jack shook his head.

'We were underground by then and this wind carries sound away from Old Brum.'

'And then?'

'We heard Pike and his people move in, using all the knowledge and skills of a lifetime in this city. We didn't know they were being herded towards the tricks and traps laid down earlier by the survivor. They were going to their deaths. But before that . . .'

'Where is Bratfire . . . ?' asked Barklice, the deepest of fears in his kind voice. 'He isn't here, is he?'

'He set off round where the humans were, right round, intending to use explosives they had left.'

'*Explosives!*' cried Barklice most terribly.

'His idea and he was not stoppable, Barklice. He was going to try to destroy their craft . . .'

'But Jack, he's only . . .' whispered Katherine.

'The Huey,' whispered Bohr, 'without which they wouldn't be able to get away . . .'

'They can use their damn feet,' said Katherine. 'This has got to stop. Why are we fighting them anyway?'

'I shall go and find him,' cried Barklice. 'I must find him . . .'

'He'll get back,' said Jack. 'Like father, like son . . . Barklice. He said, "Glad Pa's not here because he wouldn't let me do it but I'm doing it anyway." He said he'd find his own way back and there was something about him, the light in his eyes . . . something made me agree. Seconds later the real firefight began and where he had been standing, on my other side, took a direct hit. If he hadn't gone he'd be dead. There is wyrd in this, Barklice, there is a purpose to it, though Mirror knows what it is . . .'

He stopped, Stort's face making him do so.

A look, a kind of astonished look of someone who has glimpsed something through a fog – or maybe a blizzard.

'There is a way,' he said, 'there *is* a way but Mirror knows if it is where the gem might be.'

'A way to what, Stort?'

'To find the gem or rather to make things . . . ah, yes . . . hmmm.'

'To make things *what*?'

'Reversible,' he said. 'There *is* a way! But it would be dangerous.'

'How?'

'How? How is the question. It would be tricky, complicated and complex and very, very unpredictable, but there *is* a way.'

'What must we do?'

He shrugged. 'Ah, now there you have me and on a night like this with a blizzard blowing and humans after us and Bratfire lost and not yet found who can tell? Not me! Except . . .'

'What?'

'I think it would be wise to get us out of here.'

'I don't think so,' said Katherine. Then, turning to Jack, she said, 'Tell us the rest. What happened to Pike?'

'He and his people killed some of them but then . . . they suffered the same overwhelming force that Brunte did. I'm sorry, but Pike is dead. I'm sorry, Barklice.'

'Pike,' murmured the verderer softly, 'poor Pike!'

He went to Stort and put a hand on his shoulder. The scrivener had known Pike since a boy when he had personally travelled to Wales to bring him in safety to study under Master Brief in the Library. En route, the youthful Stort's quick mind and inventiveness had saved Pike's life and this reversal of roles had bonded the two closely together.

'Dead,' muttered Stort, 'Mister Pike . . . dead.'

In normal circumstances they might both have been able to grieve for their much loved and respected friend properly, but that could not be, and Jack knew it.

'We think,' he continued quietly, 'there was only one more human, maybe two. We don't know for sure. One certainly!'

A figure loomed behind them all and Jack spun, his crossbow raised.

'Mirror help us!' said the staverman. 'You got them safely here, Master Jack!'

'Where's Bratfire?' demanded Barklice.

'He got the helicopter and I got the last but one, through the neck. Bratfire will be on his way back and there's only one left. Just one.'

'He shot at me,' said Jack.

'I heard that. Until we find out where he is we can't go out front or back. Which is just as well, seeing that it's so damn cold outside, beggin' your pardon, my Lords, that it would freeze your ears off, so to speak.'

'Time to sort out our defences and patrols,' said Jack. 'Here's how we're going to do it . . .'

The moment the human was out of sight Bratfire began to run downslope towards the Library doors to warn those inside what was happening. It was a distance of no more than one hundred and fifty yards, but even before he had covered half the distance, the blizzard wind rode down on him.

Its strength and extreme cold nearly stopped him in his tracks, like running into an enveloping wall of ice. The wind had swept in from the north to West Bromwich and Sandwell Hall, down the Elder Road to Hawthorns, across to Handsworth, the windows there shattering and the trees in Victoria Park bending, bending and bending more as it drove on. It froze them as it went. Branches sheared off, trunks gave way, the cold was a tsunami made visible by the fragments of snow and ice it carried on to Winston Green.

The first buffet of that wind, the sign that it had arrived, ripping along the ground into Main Square ahead of Bratfire, tumbling him several times before he hooked his arm around a bollard.

'Pa!' he cried, his voice carried on across the square and out the other side before he finished uttering it.

A pause, a moment, and he was up, running to reach the steps up to the great doors, shouting through the gap between them, 'Pa!'

Barklice heard it first, heard it like a pa would hear it, heard it as he had to hear it.

'Bratfire,' they cried and Festoon hauled the young lad in. He was shivering so violently that he couldn't speak, try as he might, so desperate was he to inform them of the danger they were in.

'You c–c–can't stay here, M–M–Master Jack,' he eventually gasped. 'Human's coming.'

'Which way?'

'From the b–b–back,' said Bratfire pointing.

But it was too late.

A shot rang out, and as it did the staverman staggered back and fell dead at their feet.

'He'm set to kill you all,' shouted Bratfire. 'Follow me . . .'

The main doors, stuck so fast, blew open with a bang.

Another shot, from Mirror knew where, and Jack knew that Bratfire was right, and so did Stort.

'How many are there?' said Jack, fearing that if they went out others would fire.

'He'm one alone. Come *on*, Pa! We can get 'em to Bartholomew.'

Jack nodded.

So did Stort, wondering, thinking, working something out.

'My Lord Blut,' he said, grasping the surprised Emperor by his collar, 'if you can just remember . . .'

But Jack barked orders to Barklice to follow Bratfire's lead and get them out and Stort's moment with Blut was lost.

They heard steps on the floor above, which meant they had a little time.

'He's going across to the other stairs . . .' said Jack, watching the ceiling as if to follow the steps but seeing instead something odd and smelling something odder. It was the sharp smell of petrol and what he saw was the ceiling at the far side of the hall begin to stain with it.

'He's going to burn us out!' cried Katherine.

'And then shoot at us in the square, where we'll be visible,' rasped Jack. 'Bratfire's right, it's time to leave. Wait by the front door while I try to block his way through and hold him back a little. Get all the clothes you have on your backs and I'll be with you at once.'

Jack ran towards the far stairs, mounted them two at a time and, reaching the floor above, was in time to see the human passing an open door, scattering liquid from a container as he went. The smell of it was nearly overpowering.

Jack raised his stave and hurled it after the human, willing it to attack him and come back to him when it was done.

The others had retreated to the now-open doors and those that had spare garb put it on.

'*Tie* caps on,' ordered Barklice.

When Stort was ready he helped Blut, taking his opportunity to renew his enquiry, which he did in a very urgent voice. 'My Lord, this may be a matter of some importance. What was that date Arthur mentioned to you, the one at which things might still be reversible? Do you remember it precisely?'

'I do,' said Blut, and told him. 'But it means nothing to me, though perhaps it does to you, Stort?'

Stort shook his head, puzzled.

'He said nothing more about it than that? Just a date?'

'Does it *matter*, Stort?' said Katherine testily.

'I think it may. As would the occasion or name, if **you** can perhaps remember . . .'

They repeated it to her and a distant memory stirred within her.

'I can remember the name,' she said, 'but really, Stort, not now . . .'

'What was it?' he said, almost angrily.

She gave it, but that too meant nothing to either Stort or Blut, nothing at all.

'What does it *mean*?' cried Stort, frustrated.

'I wasn't even born then,' said Katherine, 'but to Arthur . . .'

'Please. Try to explain,' said Stort.

But time had run out.

Jack shouted at them to get ready to make a run for it together, came running over to them, closed the inner door and then they were outside once more, hurrying down the steps into a wind so strong that as they passed the bonfire its remnants were picked up bodily and scattered southward.

'Follow Bratfire!' Jack shouted which, with each step they took, got progressively harder to do. The wind was a mighty force, the cold now painfully intense, the racing snow and ice beginning to thicken.

Only one of them stumbled and that was Ingrid.

Bohr reached down to help her up, but Jack was there, bigger and stronger, picking her up, pushing Bohr on. 'Come on!' he urged her, 'You can make it, come on!'

'Yes,' she said, as ahead of them Bohr stumbled in his turn, the ground treacherous, 'I'm all right, so help *him* . . .'

Jack stopped Bohr falling, ran on with him at his side, urging them all to flee, not seeing Ingrid slip a second time, not seeing that now she was limping, not letting Bohr turn back.

'She's all right . . . run . . .'

Moments later the wind lulled and they were able to stop and look back. Behind them they could still see the Library. Inside, there was a brief glimmer of orange light and the next moment they saw it go up in a massive, explosive conflagration.

'Ingrid!' shouted Bohr as she ran on towards them.

For a short time the fire roared even louder than the wind and seemed to clear the air of snow a little, revealing the human in silhouette on the Library steps, framed by the now-orange rectangle of its great doors.

'Ingrid . . .'

The human moved down the steps slowly, as it seemed, with all the assurance and certainty of death itself, the wind taking the flames and heat away from him. When he reached the level ground he paused and slowly raised his weapon.

A moment's stillness and Ingrid plunged forward and down to the ground as if she had been hit by a violent blow.

Only once did she manage to raise her head to look towards them, and a hand as well, and cry out a single name.

'Erich . . .'

Then she was face down on the ground, mouth whispering to ice. '*Oh, Erich,*' she murmured and was gone.

The snow thickened and swirled between them and began settling on her still form as the human moved on towards them.

Bohr stood utterly still, uncomprehending, wind and snow driving onto his face, into his shocked eyes, unable to move. But Jack, not hesitating a moment, grabbed him bodily and heaved him round and onwards.

Ten yards on Jack looked back and saw that the blizzard was growing stronger, the snow thicker, and visibility reducing fast. The light from the flames diffused like a halo all around the human before he was lost to sight, and then Ingrid too.

Bohr was rigid in Jack's arms, mouth open to the bitter wind, eyes staring, his Ingrid lost behind him.

'Noooo!' he shouted almost silently.

Jack held him powerfully, stopping him turning, stopping him looking.

'There's nothing more we can do now,' said Jack gently, 'and she would want you to save your own life.'

He pushed the numbed and unresisting Bohr on.

'Look, there!' cried Festoon ahead of them. He had recognized the ruins of his former residence, of which only the steps remained, apart from the broken wood and piled-up doors salvaged earlier by the stavermen for the fire.

Bohr slumped, kneeling, to the ground, Jack keeping a close eye on him and, looking back, realizing that the driving snow was giving them a few moments' cover to do something to escape that human. But what?

Ahead, as it seemed, there was no direction to go except to veer left past the wood and hope the wind might help them along. But they had to step carefully lest one or other of them fell down, slipping on the ice or blown straight over.

Then Bedwyn Stort stopped as if he had hit a brick wall. They all stopped as well, for not to do so meant inevitably losing sight of each other.

'Come on, Stort.'

'I am a fool, Jack!'

'No time for that now,' said Jack. 'Come *on!*'

'A very great fool am I!' he cried. 'Shelter me!'

With that and no explanation he fell to his knees by the great pile of wood. He ran his hands over it, throwing skirting boards, shelves, an empty drawer aside.

'What are you looking for?' cried Festoon.

'What I should have looked for before. They burnt the painted panel with the images of Winter but I did not see them burn the door of Winter from the Chamber of Seasons. If it is here . . .'

He peered closer still, struggled to heave one door aside, which Terce helped him do and then another before he cried, 'There, my friends! There may be salvation. Free it and we might yet escape!'

All they saw was the corner of a thick and battered door frame, the hinges of the door itself intact.

Katherine saw Stort's intent at once. 'Get it free! Heave it upright!'

With willing hands they got more loose wood and another door away and freed the bigger one beneath and there it lay, a massive mahogany door, frame and all, on the top part of which was inscribed in Gothic script a single word: *Winter*.

Jack looked back, the blizzard snow all orange with the flames beyond. A bullet fizzed out of the murk and nicked Festoon's leg.

'By the Mirror!' he cried powerfully, 'the High Ealdor of Brum does not yield to that! Come on one and all, heave this door upright as Stort commands!'

Jack shouted, 'I'm going back to stall the human. Bohr, help them!'

Like an automaton glad of something to do, Bohr did so.

The door of Winter . . . the last remnant of the Chamber of Seasons, ā Faroün's greatest architectural triumph. A door never before opened. A door that was old with time, its handle corroded, its hinges surely useless now, its wood either rotten or stuck to the frame around it, which even in the midst of such destruction had remained closed until its time had come.

All the other doors of the seasons had led those who opened them to the end of their quest, now it was Winter's turn. Together, they pushed it upright, frame and all, battling with its weight on the one hand and the driving wind on the other.

The wind blew ice against it, the lettering began to be lost under it.

'*Jack!*' Katherine realized that Jack was standing between them and where the human would surely soon come, silhouetted against the flames and snow.

'Katherine, help us!'

She turned back to help with the door, terrible fear in her breast.

Jack strained to see the human, knowing as he did so that he was already getting too cold and tired to use his crossbow effectively. He flexed his right hand where his stave should be and found it wasn't there. He reached his hand up for it, but it did not come flying through the wind.

The play of ice and flames before him took form and *was* the human, advancing steadily, treading carefully, nearer now, near enough for Jack to see he had a weapon and was going down to one knee to more easily raise the rifle and steady the aim he was beginning to take.

Jack took three more steps forward to reduce the human's lines of sight to his friends and stood firm. He raised his crossbow, trying to steady it against the terrible wind, trying to get the sight on the human only yards ahead, trying to still his mind and breathe deeply, hoping, wishing his stave to be there too, to help him when he needed it.

But his fingers were cold, his mind wandering and slow, the shivering beginning, his strength dying, his will weakening as the cold ate into him with each flake and shard of ice that battered his hands and eyes.

The human, stolid and grey before him, now came at last into Jack's bow sight, clear and good. Jack moved his frozen fingers, trying to find a way to hold it all together against the wind and fire true.

'Oh Mirror help me, *help me . . .*' he whispered through swollen lips, and fired.

42
PEACE

Reece's head ached badly out there in the cold, from where the dwarf's stick-thing came whirling and caught him hard on the temple. Ached and throbbed like his head was bursting. His eyes wouldn't focus, he was seeing everything with shadows, seeing double. In fact, just opening his eyes was painful.

'Bastards,' he had screamed as the place went up behind him and he had stumbled down the steps, the heat at his back, the snow clearing for a moment, knowing he must not lose sight of them.

Bastards was his mantra. It was his fix upon the entire universe and now on them, the enemy, little freaks, who should not have had a chance in hell against his force yet were still alive and fighting.

They had stopped and he could see them, the wind trying to knock him down.

What the hell are they doing now?

He knelt down, staring, trying to disentangle them from their shadows and from each other, the cold hitting his temple where the stick had, like a knife thrust.

His eyes were beginning to focus at last and his vision cleared enough for him to see that one of them was coming back. The freak had come *back* and now he was nearer, was blocking the others from view, was raising a weapon, the wind fighting him.

Reece's training kicked in.

He still could not see as clearly as he needed to to get a perfect shot but he could see enough to know what he must do. He knelt, he steadied, he raised his weapon. But it wasn't easy because now the wind was like a hundred hands grabbing at the barrel, pulling it back and forth, the sight wandering, the one in front of him a black thing, his bow steadying. Reece breathed deeply and stilled, put aside the pain in his head, stared at the two images he could see, took aim plumb centre between them both and, as another cold knife thrust into his skull, he fired.

He did not see the target slump back, because simultaneously a crossbow bolt caught him in his hip, and he slumped himself. Winded or wounded? He was so damned cold he could not tell.

But not damn well out of it. Not yet. Bastard.

Jack fell back, not immediately aware he had been shot. Only that something had buffeted him hard in the side, very hard.

His stave?

He felt for it with his right hand and there it was, apologetic, huffing and puffing like a mortal. But in the snow, already whipped by wind, was his blood.

He struggled to rise with the help of the stave, but he only made it to his knees. He could find neither strength nor balance to get a purchase on the slippery ground and push himself upright.

He peered round towards the human and saw that he was down and was also finding it hard to get back up.

'Come on, Jack,' cried Katherine, reaching him, helping him up and supporting him towards the great door that now stood black and wavering in the wind with Winter scribed above it. Terce and the others had used planks to prop it up against the wind, leaving space enough to open the door, if it *would* open.

'Stupid,' said Jack, annoyed with himself for being hit, '*stupid*. Open the damn thing, Stort, and let's try to get out of here.'

They gathered around him again to keep the wind and icy snow off as he put a hand on the corroded handle and turned.

'It won't.'

Festoon, limping, tried, then Terce with two hands, then Katherine. Finally Barklice and even Bohr, broken by the loss of Ingrid though he was.

It was stuck fast.

'You try,' shouted Barklice at Bratfire.

He reached two hands to it, the adults pressing from behind, and the handle turned like it had been just fixed and oiled ten minutes before.

'You turned the wrong way,' said Bratfire shaking his head.

'Maybe,' said Stort, 'and maybe not.'

'Now push it open,' said Jack, the buffet to his side now turning to deep pain.

Stort pushed open the door of Winter but all he saw on the far side was the same white-out they were already in.

'Useless,' said Katherine.

'We'll see . . .' growled Jack. He pushed Bratfire through, shouting, 'Hold your pa's hand and don't let go . . . nobody let go of the hand they take else you'll end up somewhere else.'

If it works, he thought.

Barklice followed, and then Terce.

Bohr, still in a state of shock, followed numbly and without protest, Blut after him.

'Jack, you next . . .'

'No, me last . . .'

Katherine brooked no argument and pushed him through and could not but follow because he had her hand.

'Stort . . .' cried Festoon, 'this is my city, I go last – you go now.'

Blut reached his hand to Stort, and Festoon, wanting to be last, pushed Stort ahead of him.

'My Lord,' cried Stort, reaching back through the door, '*my Lord!*'

Reece had been right, he was down but by no means out.

He left the bolt right where it was. Painful, but the safest thing to do. Pull it out and blood flows. Leave it in and there might be a way to staunch it if he could only get out of the wind and cold.

He rolled onto his front, pulled his weapon close to keep it from freezing, and peered forward to see where they were. He could not, he literally could not, believe his eyes.

They were insane, or their world was.

They had somehow heaved a great door up despite the wind, and having opened the effing thing they were piling through it, the freak-heads. As he watched, a big one looked like he was thrusting a tall thin one through. Reece's vision had cleared.

His head too.

Oh yes, oh *yees*.

It was painful but not difficult getting his weapon ready, it being much easier lying down with the bipod out and settled into the icy snow, the sight steady.

No messing, he could get both now and then follow to take the rest. Except that the sight line on the second was now blocked by the first one. What the hell, it would have been easy enough to get both but one is better than none.

Reece raised his weapon, got the sight plumb perfect on the one he could see and fired. He would have had to be dead himself to miss and he didn't: the hydden slewed straight across the gaping door and was down.

A pause, a moment to steady his aim on the one already half through the door and into the blizzard beyond.

'Think you can slip away from me do you?'

The view was not perfect but he got the sight clear on his retreating shoulder, and stilled himself to fire.

Stort had felt Festoon's grip on his arm slacken and then seen the look of surprise on his face as he fell sideways, his eyes glazing.

He felt a yank as Katherine's right hand tugged at his and he fell back and found himself watching Festoon slowly hit the ground on the far side of the door as time . . . time . . . time slowed to nearly nothing, time between the world of here and there, ice worlds both, a world of difference as Stort looked up and back at the human on the ground, a silhouetted head against huge flames.

He thought of a date and a name he did not know and said to himself quite gently, 'Yes, of course, that will be it . . .'

He saw the muzzle of the weapon fire and the bullet coming towards him, shining and turning, reflecting ice and fire and blood and all things as it came, continuing to turn in the blizzard of slow time between here and there, back there, oh yes, he understood what he must try to do but it would be hard, so hard but but but . . .

He turned to follow Katherine and felt the bullet smash through his left shoulder and an agony of pain and loss as he tumbled forward towards the place, the date, the moment Blut and Katherine had told him about.

'Not yet,' he whispered, for there were things still to do, 'not yet!'

Reece stared and saw one down and the other ... disappear into the snow beyond the door. The wind was like a hundred thousand shards of ice, made orange by the flames behind.

He swore with the pain, got up and walked slowly towards the open door, weapon at the ready to finish them off. They wouldn't get far.

'No need to hurry,' he murmured when he got to the door where one small form hunched down in death. He shot that one again anyway, for the dark pleasure of it. Another moment of release from the eternal pain he felt.

Now for the second one . . .

Reece looked at the door, puzzled.

From afar it looked normal size; close-to it was half size. A trick of scale and perspective. It was a freak door just like them, and, bending down, stepping over the body, he peered through and saw nothing but the blizzard wind, darker here because the flame-light was blocked by the door frame itself.

Weird, curious, nobody, no one beyond at all. They had disappeared, which wasn't possible.

He was about to rise and go round when he decided, his mind numbing a little, his head hurting again, to heave his shoulder through to see if his eyes were playing tricks. He did so, squeezed some more and fell forward, half through onto his hands and knees. Vulnerable now, not good.

He scrambled hastily forward, dragging his rifle with him, until he was able to stand up once more. But when he finally did he stared, puzzled, because the wind had suddenly weakened at ground level and his feet were not on the debris of a building but on snow-encrusted grass; and things weren't right.

Grass?

More bewildering still his weapon had grown heavier. He looked down at it and nearly smashed his forehead into its muzzle. It had grown longer too.

He stepped back, fear mounting, and looked at it. The rifle had become giant-size. He looked about wild-eyed, then up to where the wind raged loud among bending, whipping, leafless treetops far above his head.

Where am I . . . ?

He examined his rifle more closely for confirmation it was really his and saw his initials on it, no question. It was just that they were now twice as big as before.

He stared at his hands and feet and felt an existential horror as he realized what he was.

'*You bastards*,' screamed Reece as he dropped the rifle and felt the blood oozing from where the crossbow bolt had hit him.

'*You've made me one of you!*' he cried.

The bolt in his side shifted, blood began to flow but he no longer cared. He lay bleeding and dying with no interest in recovery, no wish to survive, no wish for anything. Release from himself was what he wanted, a final, blessed release.

The trees were a circle above him, the sky beyond as grey as the ice that now entered into him and he saw a woman staring down at him. Large or small he had no idea. He didn't care.

'Where am I?'

'Woolstone.'

'No, *where* am I?'

'You're in the Hyddenworld.'

'They . . . they . . . made . . . they . . . fr . . . fr . . . I . . .'

But the old words, the old hate words, the old poison dried up in his mouth under her scrutiny.

He had only to look at her to know she had suffered more than he ever could.

She was old, so old, a form withered by time, with hands whose swollen, bent knuckles were raw blue and red with the cold; hideous. Oh, she had suffered more. Her eyes were the loneliest he had ever looked into and they put in him something he had forgotten and left behind long, long before, something simple. Something he wanted to say, because until he did he could never be at peace and for that, time had all but run out.

'I . . . I . . .' he tried to say as with great difficulty she bent down to hear him better.

'You . . . ?' she whispered. 'What did you do?'

'I killed my brother,' Reece said, weeping like the boy of sixteen he had once been, 'and I *miss* him . . .'

'I know,' she said, reaching her hand to his cheek, her hurt, bent, tortured hand. 'I know, my dear.' And he knew she did.

'I want to forget.'

'You will forget everything,' she said softly, letting him reach his hand to her, that he was not alone any more as the cold, cold wind carried the sound of the Chimes over him and he travelled on with it to the *musica*, a mortal on his final journey, one of the very last, as the Mirror-of-All finally broke asunder and the End of Days began.

43
TO THE TOP

'Where are Festoon and Stort?'

It was Katherine's voice, desperate against the wind. She had been the last to hold Stort's hand when they left the door behind but couldn't see him now.

Oh, but Mirror she was cold!

Where are the last two?

Her mind was working so slowly she could no longer get the words out very loudly, or find the energy to call to those in front, or begin to think about going back to seek them out in the glacial wastes behind.

She could hardly push one foot in front of the other along the rutted, icy ground they were on. So far as she could see the rest of the party at all through the snow they were frowning, heads down, tramping ever more desperately on, grey figures hunched against the wind, each step difficult.

Night had turned to day, but what time of day was impossible to tell.

Terce kicked at the snow, banged on the rucked ice, saw soil.

Bratfire, over to one side, went on his hands and knees, stabbed at the ground and found grass. He peered from low down up the slight slope. He, at least, seemed half alive.

'We're on a path.'

'Where are Stort and Festoon?' screamed Katherine again, her voice thinned to nothing by the wind.

They all finally stopped, and slowly turned, their expressions ones of such cold, fatigue and listlessness that they looked as if they were close to giving up all hope for themselves and one another. They just stood there, buffeted by the harsh wind, looking back the way they had come, waiting for their friends.

When Stort finally came they saw he was alone. He looked as he had on distant Pendower Beach: battered, nearly engulfed, on the very edge of what a mortal can any longer bear. His cap gone, his left arm loose and blowing about, his slow tread more wander than walk. Yet when he too paused, staring up the slight slope towards them, he was for a moment Stort again. His fingers flickered in recognition, his dull eyes momentarily brightened; it seemed he was trying to speak.

They went back to him and saw at once the mess that was his shoulder where he had been shot – the torn jacket, the blood, the protruding bone. His face was grey, his freckles nearly black, his eyes hollow with pain. Yet there was no despair.

'Lie down,' said Katherine, but he laughed a broken, cracked kind of laugh, shook his head and looked about. To lie down was to die.

He raised his good hand and, finding Jack, grasped his jacket, pulled himself nearer and rasped, 'You must try to get me there. Festoon was not able to come . . . but there is a way. Get me there.'

Where and for what he did not, or could not, say.

But Festoon . . . *left behind*.

Grief was out there in the cold, and a terrible numbness.

Jack's face was blue-white and his right hand held his side; between its fingers there was blood, congealed and fresh.

'Bar . . . Bark . . . Barklice?'

Barklice came and the three stood together like menhirs in the snow, cleaving to each other as they had through time. They stood windswept and bleak, words slow.

'Tell us . . . where are we?' Jack asked, the pain of trying to shout against the wind making him wince. 'Stort needs to know.'

Barklice pulled free of them again and looked about, as far as that was possible. Alone of all of them but Bratfire, he still seemed to have his natural strength. Wiry, spare, used to all conditions, honed down to all he needed to be, no more nor less. A survivor.

As he tried to make sense of what he could see, so too did they all as far as their individual strengths allowed, which wasn't much. Bohr, shattered by the loss of Ingrid, was withering before their eyes.

Blut looked weak and leaned on Terce's arm, though the chorister was half dead as well, his head dropped forward and eyes peering, his mouth open and lips swollen, as fragments of a tuneless song struggled out of his throat.

They seemed to be in an icy wilderness, the only feature being the fences on either side of the path they trekked. The ground sloped up against the wind, not steep but steadily, which was the way their collective wyrd took them.

'This place I know not,' said Barklice finally, pulling Bratfire closer to protect him from the cold and checking that his jacket was as tight and buttoned as it could be, 'but the direction we are going in feels right. Perhaps somewhere ahead we'll find a place to rest, where we can tend to Stort and Jack.'

'Continue against the wind?' said Terce. 'Surely . . .'

'Against the wind,' said Jack resolutely, 'if Barklice wants it.'

'Yes . . . yes . . .' said Barklice, himself blown sideways for a moment, Bratfire keeping him from falling. 'I'll lead the way.'

'Can you go on, Stort?' asked Katherine.

Stort nodded and whispered, 'I can, I must, we have a gem to find . . . it is . . . this is . . . the time . . .'

He struggled to get out his chronometer and failed and Blut did so instead.

'It is the last day of January . . .'

This information seemed to revive Stort a little.

'I thought it was too late,' he said.

'Afternoon,' mumbled Blut, his chronometer slipping from his frozen fingers onto the icy snow, 'middle of . . .'

He made no attempt to pick it up so Bratfire did it for him.

'Keep it,' said Blut, waving his hand, 'you'll have more use for it than I.'

'If it is only the afternoon of January 31st,' repeated Stort, with something like his old spirit, though his voice was no more than a rasp, 'then we have time to get wherever we are going, lots of time . . .'

He cracked an ironic laugh. His fingers were blanched white, his knuckles an ill-coloured maroon.

'Terce . . .' called Katherine.

She took Blut's arm on one side, and Jack's on the other, helping them both to move on.

Terce supported Stort, one singing, the other humming.

'Worst choir in the world,' muttered Jack, stumbling at Katherine's side.

Bratfire dropped back to help Bohr, Barklice staying in front. Any one of them might have fallen over in such conditions and never got up again but together they soldiered on, heads down to the wind, going ever more slowly, minds numbing and playing tricks, eyes seeing nothing but the hard path beneath, the iced barbed wire of the fences and shadowed hallucinations far ahead . . .

Then . . . dogs racing around, mastered by Reivers, in and out of their vision and the sound of her ancient screaming, telling them to be respectful, cursing where they went. She was there, was the Shield Maiden, waiting maybe, watching perhaps, urging more like, angry it had taken them so long to get to this day and this place that she was almost dead herself . . .

'Woolstone Down,' said Katherine to Jack suddenly, the path, the parallel fences, the dip slope of the escarpment up towards which they were going, 'that's where we are. Remember?'

He half looked up, he made a noise, no more.

He was dying, she could feel him dying, could feel his strong body frail now against her, his voice little more than weak rasps.

'We're on the far side from the Horse,' she said, her lips warm and urgent to his ear, doing her best against her own dreadful fatigue. 'We walked down this way more than once. We're on the gallops of Woolstone Down. Jack, we're nearly home.'

'I can't . . .' he whispered, 'I can't protect them any more, Katherine, I can't . . .'

'You can,' she said, 'you always have . . . you got us through. I think we'll make it there. Keep on going, my love, we're nearly home.'

Then, striving to make the others hear, she called out those same words again: 'Keep on going, we're nearly home.'

'Look . . .' said Bohr, eyes screwed up against the wind, cheeks now chapped and raw and bleeding at his mouth and eyes, 'look!'

In his brief and terrible time in the Hyddenworld he had never felt such fear.

The Reivers charged in on their fearsome dogs, seemingly impervious to cold, raced in and out of the blizzard wind, laughing, their foul dogs slavering, their mistress so old now they seemed to have lost their fear of her.

She was alone, without support. Even the White Horse had deserted her in old age, it seemed.

So they ran and they charged, teeth bared, her own dog Morten no longer hers but loose, leading the others, ahead of the hydden, then to the sides, mocking their slow progress up the hill by showing how easy it was whichever way they did it.

'Stop that!' Judith cried, asserting her old strength. 'You know what I can do to you! Stop it! And my once beautiful dog, *come here!*'

Morten came, a scabby cur now with only a distant hint of what he too had been, a reflection of his mistress. With his tail between his legs, he went to heel.

The cruel eyes of the Reivers and their dogs widened in surprise and fear, for they had thought Judith was so old and weak now she had forgotten how to command.

They chased each other away to a crest on the near horizon and huddled whining there in what bitter little bit of shelter they could find, the intense cold having finally got even to them. They too, they knew, were near death.

The hydden moved on, one after another . . . knowing now they could not make it, not back home, not to warmth again, not to life, not that place Katherine mentioned.

'Too far,' Terce finally said and Bohr agreed.

'Too far and too late,' said Blut.

Their steps slowing as they reached the crest, and the wind, as cold until then as it had ever been, and stronger too, grew colder yet.

For what it was worth, which was nothing at all, Katherine had been right. They had trekked up the gallops and having reached the Ridgeway, which stretched away impossibly to right and left, they faced the ramparts of Uffington Fort straight ahead. The edge of the escarpment was on the far side, where the White Horse was.

The cold wind cut through their clothes and bodies, it made their ears ache and felt as if it was tearing off their skin.

Barklice came to Stort.

'What day is it?' asked Stort, his mind wandering.

'The last, my dear friend. Is the gem near?'

'What time is it?'

Good Barklice smiled and took Stort's arm from Terce.

'Stort, there's still time. The season does not turn until midnight and then there's the hours betwixt and between but . . . my . . . you *do* cut it fine and scare us all!'

He took Stort's hand in his own to warm it, but it was stiff now, white now.

'Stort, my dear old friend,' said Barklice, his voice breaking.

Stort slowed and whispered, 'Barklice, there may be something I must ask of you . . .'

'Anything . . .'

'Something . . .'

But Stort was unable to concentrate and say just then what it was. All he could do was what he often did when he fretted and stressed and got lost in his mind. His fingers reached to his neck and touched the chime that still hung there, which Judith had given him when she was a child.

'What can I do for you?' asked Barklice.

'I . . . maybe . . . I . . . am . . . not . . . yet . . . sure.'

They did not talk very much as they struggled on. Except for mumbles now and then as they shuffled on past the ramparts into a wind that was icier yet, to the high place on the edge from where, in spring, after the snows have gone and sunshine returned, all Englalond stretches forth below in welcome.

Not so now. Grey winter was all they saw, the worst ever known and likely the very last.

Nearly home?

'I don't think so,' Katherine might have said when she was younger, but not any more; she too looked old, they all looked old and coming to their end with nowhere left to go.

The ramparts of the Iron Age fort faded behind them, lost in swirling wind.

'We might have sheltered in among them, Stort,' said Barklice, but he spoke to deaf ears now. The only hope was getting off the hill, down to Woolstone, to the sheltering henge.

But life was slipping away faster than any chronometer could show. The only life in the vast landscape, apart from their own group moving towards the edge of the hill, was that of the Reivers and their dogs, chastened by what they saw, knowing that they too would die if the End of Days was reached and no gem found to give to their decrepit mistress.

She, Judith, unable to help, unable to look, fearing that, after all, after all the long journeying, her beloved wouldn't find what she herself could not, waited.

Stort saw her but was so weak now he could not even raise a hand or smile or feel. Then he wasn't looking any more, he was stopping, his eyes were closing.

'Barkl . . . Barklice . . . what time is it?'

'There's time.'

'Kath . . . Ka . . .'

'I'm here, Stort, I'm holding you . . .'

'I saw Judith . . .' he whispered, 'I need to feel her touch just once in my life . . .'

Which she, hearing his words on the wind, feeling them through the ground, seeing each precious memory in the shards of ice that shot between them both, knew she must not, could not, respond to him while there was still hope. A mortal and immortal cannot be.

Her dog pressed his harrowed body against her leg. The Reivers shook their heads and a lone tree shivered in the wind.

44

THE LAST PORTAL

It was Bohr who saw the tree, that same solitary tree under which
Jack and Katherine had sometimes sat in better days. In spring its
blossoms all creamy white; in summer its leaves dancing with light;
in autumn its tiny berries red as the deepest sunset.

Now, in winter, the hawthorn was a black old thing, with gnarled
branches and twigs and twisted roots exposed and open to the skies.

One way was the White Horse carved in chalk, the lone tree was the
other.

'It might give us shelter, it might be home,' mumbled Erich Bohr.

They began turning towards it as one, even Jack, but Stort shook his
head. Leaning his hurt, weak body into those who held him, he turned
towards the escarpment edge below which the White Horse galloped
eternally across the sward where, when humans and hydden were at
peace, they and their leader had cut and scoured it.

'There is a way,' said Stort, 'but . . . but . . . I'm not sure yet. Take
me so I can see the Horse.'

They gave all of their final strength to get him there, until, reaching
the edge, where they knew they could see it, all Englalond a waste of
ice beneath them, they saw that the Horse was not visible.

The icy snow had covered it and nothing was to be seen.

Stort shuddered then and something in him seemed to go, as it
did in all of them. He pulled back out of the cruel wind and then
some more until, unable to support him any more, they laid him
down.

Nothing more to do, nothing more to see.

'Have I failed?' he asked.

It is said that, reaching the point of death, many creatures choose to be alone, as befits a mortal's return to the Mirror's light.

So now up there on White Horse Hill.

Stort lay on the ground as each of the others, seeking their own way back to a Mirror cracked beyond repair, set off alone.

Even Katherine, separate from Jack.

Bohr, alone.

Niklas Blut, great Emperor that he was, dying now, alone upon the ground murmuring the names of those he had loved: his spouse, his kinder and Lord Sinistral, progenitor of so much.

'My Lord . . .' he whispered finally, but said no more. Sinistral for good and ill, but finally mainly good, was gone, and now even memory of him as of all else was fading fast.

Blut reached for his spectacles but even that was too much at the end, so they shone where he lay, white reflected orbs of sky, bright as his mind and nature had always been.

While Terce, trying still to find the song that once he sang, his voice failing him, slumped to his knees, unable to go on.

'Barklice,' whispered Stort, 'are you there?'

Barklice came, Bratfire hanging back, staring at the fallen ones.

'Where is Judith . . . ? I saw her and now . . . I . . . for one last time.'

Judith, who was now no more than a husky, ragged thing, barely recognizable, came then and knelt by them both. She wanted to reach to him at last, knowing she could and he was dying and age had torn all fear out of her.

'No!' said Stort. 'No!'

She pulled back her twisted hand, eyes bleak.

'There is still a way,' said Stort, 'I glimpsed it, I felt it, though now I have no strength at all to find it.'

His torn, broken shoulder shivered in the wind, blood black now, none flowing any more.

'If we . . . if I . . .'

'If what, my friend?' asked Barklice.

'If we could have reached the tree henge again I could have . . .'

'What?'

'Journeyed on. I could have, couldn't I?'

Barklice nodded because he supposed he could. But journey to where he had no idea.

'I could have stopped the End of Days if I'd been able to reach one last henge!'

Judith nodded, because her beloved might well have changed the world. But now? He was dying too soon.

Yet even then, so close to death, Stort smiled his gentle smile of wonder and surprise, challenge and questioning.

'Trouble is,' he whispered in his old way, 'once there and all that done, how would I ever find my way back home to you?'

Few words could have touched her more.

'Worse still, if I go to the Mirror, I will forget.'

She nodded for she knew it was so. She searched for comfort in something as final as his loss of memory of her and she said, 'My dear love, to remember all that is lost in a life such as yours would be an agony too great for a mortal to bear.'

Stort stared at her and finally shook his head.

'I don't want to forget everything,' he whispered fiercely. 'I am my memory, I am my friends, I am my love of you. Without them I am not. With them, pain and all, I can be everything.'

He lay quietly for a time, thinking. Then, though so close to death, Stort roused in himself a little of the spirit of old.

'In fact,' he said, 'I refuse to forget! Therefore, my love and my dear friend, leave me in peace while I try to find a way . . . I am sure I can . . . leave me, Barklice. I would like to believe that you and Bratfire are both still on the green road in case I have need of you. Judith . . . you too must go so I can find the way by myself. But how to come back? How do I find you again if I have forgotten who you were though you were all my life?'

The wind died a little and the snow fell more thickly, drifting across where he lay and the others too. When Barklice looked back it seemed to him that all he saw was Stort and Judith. Even their friends, like the Horse, were lost now beneath a pall of white.

He saw Stort reaching a hand to his beloved, as she to him, until, not quite touching, each forever alone, she wept out her loss. Finally she too departed into the waste of that unimaginable winter, leaving Stort alone. Then, the snow thickening, Barklice could see them no more.

Stort lay alone, hearing a tuneless sound.

'Terce,' he whispered, 'if you can't sing in tune don't sing at all. I'm dying and I would very much prefer . . . I mean to say I had always thought . . .'

He struggled and heaved in the thrall of death, trying to sit up, to prop himself for a brief moment on his good arm to see the world he loved once more and the people he had loved as well.

He tried . . . and time is relative.

A moment can be eternal.

In that moment Stort looked at where Terce was, on the ground now, trying to sing.

He looked around to where Katherine lay amidst the snow, then on to Jack, utterly still, as if asleep.

Then on round to Bohr and Blut . . . and then Terce once more. Stort was circled by his friends as if they were sheltering him.

He had thought that if they could have reached the protection of the henge of Woolstone, maybe then he could have journeyed on.

His mind clarified and, having seen before what it was he had to do, he now saw how he might do it.

'There is a way!' he tried to shout.

It was there all around him, rising before him as it seemed.

'Terce!' he commanded, 'sing true!'

Which Terce did, as if very slowly waking, rising as a living being once again.

'Katherine,' cried Stort, 'we need your help! Listen!'

Then Katherine, so proud, rose tall before him, she heard the *musica* and rose.

Jack too, solid as rock, his stave glinting and shining brighter than the crystals in the snow.

On around to Bohr, cast down by sorrow, risen now with hope at the *musica* he heard.

'Sing, Terce, sing!' and at last Terce did, the voice that he had lost and never quite fully recovered, bursting forth now like a clear mountain stream.

He sent out a wondrous song that spiralled up into the skies of the then and now, of all time and the Universe. A song beyond all songs, which held for a moment its monophony before building into a harmony with all around them that expressed the boundlessness and joy of all creation.

At which Blut, bold Blut, spectacles and all, rose to the challenge he was given and gave his all.

Stort stared at the circle that they made, amazed and fearful, for few though they were, they were enough, forming about him as powerful a living henge as ever was.

'Terce, do not stop, my friend, *musica* alone can mend this broken world!' Stort cried, moaning, groaning, complaining as he too heaved himself upright, taller than them all, smiling as exquisite sound healed his hurt shoulder.

'What foolishness not to see it before! Of course . . . there is a way and there may yet be time, if only . . .'

If only I can dance the henge and find a way to journey back to that time and place where Arthur said, and Blut and Katherine agreed, things might be reversed and a new course set.

'But if I get there how to get back! I can take nothing to remind me of this world and if I succeed in this last task *this* world, this End of Days, will never be for I will have . . .'

He nearly stumbled then and fell back to the ground, but he knew he must not. The time to go was now, the place he must reach was *then*.

'Mirror, cracked you may be but try to help me this last time,' cried Stort, 'and show me that reflection I must become to be in the time and place where things could still be changed. *Help me!*'

With enormous difficulty he put chilled fingers to his neck to shed his last connection with all he knew. He found the golden thread from which hung the Chime Judith had given him when she was young, and broke it free. Then, reluctantly and yet with hope as well, he dropped it in the snow in the centre of the circle remembering he could take nothing with him, not even the Chime and its memory.

'And yet, my dear friend Barklice, I have always been able to rely on you to guide me home!'

Which said, Stort turned finally to those things he had to do if he was to complete the task in hand: *Now, where was I, what was I trying to do? Dance! That was it. I was trying to dance.*

Then Stort *did* dance, he danced the *musica* Terce sang, he danced the henge they made of themselves, he danced right out through them into the swirling wind, forgetting all and who and what he was, Stort went, leaving it behind, even she he loved most in all the world, as he set off to stop the End of Days.

While behind him the snow fell, drifting over the circle where he had been, little by little covering the Chime which was the last connection, the final memory, of the life he once had in the Hyddenworld.

45

THE END OF DAYS

Barklice, holding Bratfire close to him, looked back a final time at where Stort had risen before what seemed a swirl of snow took him and he was no more.

The Shield Maiden was long gone, the ramparts a dark wall to their right, their friends were a subtle circle on the flat ground a little above where the Horse lay hidden beneath the snow.

Barklice too was weakening and he knew it, but if they could just continue far enough to find shelter then Bratfire might survive.

But then, as he struggled against the wind on the high ridge of White Horse Hill, he stopped, a thought occurring.

'I'm an idiot, Bratfire, your pa is growing old like the rest of them. We do not need to fight our way along the Ridgeway, we can go down to Woolstone, where we . . . might . . .'

He fell silent, a look of astonishment on his face. He sat down, shook his head and closed his eyes, muttering in his fatigue, 'I think . . . why *yes* . . . I *am* an idiot!'

'Pa, what is it? What's wrong?'

Barklice felt himself shaken awake.

Barklice looked up at his son.

'You'm been sitting down too long and mustn't sleep. Come on, Pa!'

'What day is it?'

'The last day of Samhain.'

'What time?'

'Getting dark.'

'Help me up, and don't let me sit down again, even for an instant. I've been a fool. He said there must be a way . . . and there *is* a way . . .'

'A way to what?'

'To help Mister Stort, of course! To help him find his way home when his work of saving us is done. The least he deserves is to give him the means to find her again!'

Bratfire considered this and finally said, 'Well, Pa, I bain't sure I know what yer on about but if you'm can't do whate'er it be, no one can.'

They turned and began retracing their steps, their progress slow, the light fading and the wind making one last effort to blow them off the hill.

'Come on, Pa, nearly there.'

Their friends lay on open ground, covered in snow, their bodies forming a wide circle around . . . around nothing at all. Barklice went closer, ordering Bratfire to stay back, and checked them all for signs of life. He found none and nor did he find the body of Bedwyn Stort, nor any footprints or other indication that he had found the strength to rise and leave.

He stood shocked and puzzled and whispering. Barklice thought he had found a way to help Stort at the last but if he wasn't there . . . if he had gone . . . he could not do what he had thought he might.

'You went on, Mister Stort,' cried Barklice in despair, 'but how are you to find your way home if I'm not there? I might have . . . if only . . . if . . . only . . .'

He stared at the centre of the circle, where he guessed Stort might have been, with an alternating look of hope and finally despair as, going closer, he saw nothing but a drift of virgin snow.

He peered closer still, shook his head and finally knelt down, took off his pack and took his lantern and tinder box from it.

'Come and light it for me, lad. My fingers are too numb.'

Bratfire did as he was told.

'Now . . . hold it just so on that snow, a single open shutter will do.'

'There be nothing there, Pa, nothing I can see.'

'Hold it closer, lad. Now . . . closer still.'

They saw it together, just beneath the shining, white crystals of the snow, a glitter of gold thread, a myriad of dark colours.

'What be that, Pa?'

'That's a message. That's a cleverness. That's Mister Stort paying me the compliment that I'd understand what he meant and what I might do. That's a kind of miracle. Now . . .'

He scooped away the snow and took up the Chime.

'You be smiling, Pa,' said Bratfire, 'with all this death about.'

'I am, lad, because if there's one thing Stort knew to do, it was to make me smile. There's a scrap of hope and life here after all. He's found his onward journey but is liable to get lost. So now we're going to help him find the route back home to where he needs to be because at *that* he was never very good.'

'So it be important, Pa?'

'It's his way back,' came the reply.

'Yes but what be it *really?*'

Barklice patted his son's shoulder knowing that some things cannot be easily explained.

'It's a memory,' he said softly, 'which Mister Stort might need.'

This seemed to satisfy Bratfire who turned to a more practical question.

'What now?' he asked.

'Extinguish that light and help me up.'

Bratfire stood up, hauled Barklice upright and they stood in silence, saying their farewells. Then, composed once more, they headed towards where the escarpment was at its steepest.

'Pa, look!'

It was Jack's stave, lying in the snow.

Nervously, for he knew its powers to hurt those who were not Stavemeister, he picked it up.

'Just temporarily,' he said, 'until I can give it back!'

They went on to the edge, where the wind roared up at them and nearly threw them backwards.

'We wait until it weakens and when it does you hold on to my belt so I don't fall down!'

'Yes, Pa!'

The wind lightened and the sky cleared as the last light fled the day.

'Now, hold on!'

Which Bratfire did, with all his might, as Barklice raised his arm and threw the Chime up and out into the cold wind and lowering sky, as hard as he could, hard enough to reach the first winking star.

'That was a throw and a half, Pa!'

'It needed to be,' said Barklice.

'Where and when will it land?'

'Where and when my friend needs it to,' the verderer replied.

'And now?'

'We wait and we don't talk.'

'For what,' whispered Bratfire.

'For something I saw once with Jack and Katherine and Stort, across the Malvern Hills. It was called the Scythe of Time and it . . .'

'You told me, Pa. You've told me lots of things. It was big and loud.'

'Big as the Universe,' said Barklice.

As they waited, time elided into itself and before they knew it the moon shone on a world of which there was nothing now but pure white snow, turning pale blue and glistening with stars beneath them, as if whichever way they looked was only Universe.

Yet their feet were solid on the ground and they lived still.

'Be we the last?' said Bratfire.

'I think we are. Now, be ready . . . it will happen very fast.'

Bratfire stared at the sky and gasped.

'Like that!'

'Like that,' replied Barklice, taking his hand.

It started as the thinnest sliver of steely light, arcing from the furthest point in the night sky above to the lowest point of Mother Earth below. It grew bright, it turned, it began to curve and stretch until it looked sharper than the sharpest knife, swinging unstoppably across the Universe and hissing as it came, straight towards them.

'What now?'

'Stand behind me and hold on to my belt like before. Jack's stave will protect us!'

He held it before them, stood firm to the ground and waited.

The Scythe's roaring hiss was overtaking them, its steel edge sharp as the coldest light.

'Hold fast!' cried Barklice. 'Hold on!'

Wind, light, bitter cold, their hair streaming, their feet off the ground as the Scythe cut each of them together into a hundred thousand fleeting shards; and then there came the darkness of forgetting and nothing more.

The Scythe of Time passed on, cutting the world as it went, leaving the Earth and all the hydden in it, and the humans too, as if they had never been.

Just the light, bright as snow, and the dark, blacker than night, blacker than the deepest cave, blacker even than the gem of Winter and nothing and nobody but *musica* in between.

PART II
STORT'S FINAL JOURNEY

46

THE VAGRANT

One sunny morning in Texas, USA, 1963, a young man in ill-fitting clothes and wearing a pair of home-made boots found himself walking along a railtrack in a city whose name he did not know. Nor did he know the day, the date or even what country he was in.

He was suffering severe amnesia and in a state of extreme anxiety.

He knew there was something he had to do but could not remember what it was. When someone shouted at him to get off the track he clambered over a fence and found himself in a car park. But once there he was told by a different official to move on.

In a state of growing bewilderment he arrived at a grassy knoll in the shadow of some trees and bushes. He stood with his back to a picket fence, behind which was the car park he had just left.

About ten yards in front of him, a few feet lower down, was a highway. On either side of it he saw a lot of people standing and cheering. Some were waving flags, others taking photographs, a few had cine cameras.

A second or two after he arrived but before he could take in much else an impressive motorcade began passing directly in front of him.

He had no time to look at it in detail because at that same moment he both felt and heard a shot fired from beyond the fence behind him. He actually felt the bullet whizz by his ear. It was loud and very frightening and hearing it – more accurately feeling it – most people would have dived for cover.

But he knew he could not do that. Instead, and against every normal instinct and rule of common sense, he deliberately moved to his left and back a bit and so into the line of fire of a second shot. It caught him on the left shoulder like a sledgehammer and he fell sideways to the right. The bullet was a dum-dum, which meant it exploded on impact, and his blood and bone and fragments of the bullet itself showered to the left.

But such was the state of panic in the crowd along the road in front of him, because important people in the vehicles going by had been injured, no one noticed him fall or his first attempts to get up. This was difficult because his left arm was useless. Eventually, by crawling to the fence behind him and using his right hand and arm, he got himself upright and staggered off, using the fence for support.

He was found twelve minutes later, having collapsed again from shock and blood loss on a road nearby. There were a great many police in the area, and one of them called an ambulance. His injury was not life-threatening but it required surgery and it was several days before he regained some sense of equilibrium and his mind cleared of the drugs he had been given.

He did not know it but during that time he was interviewed several times by the police and the CIA and was moved from a civilian to a military hospital. There, conscious again, he was interviewed several times more. From his clothes and shoes he was judged to be a vagrant and from his mild, soft accent, and occasionally odd use of a word, he was put down as an illegal foreign immigrant.

But he gave no name and no papers were found on him. In fact he had no possessions at all beyond his clothes and home-made boots. After extensive psychological assessment, during which he continued to be held securely and saw no one apart from police and the military, it was concluded that his amnesia was real, possibly the result of long-term alcoholism, of which his extreme thinness was taken as a symptom, aggravated by the shock of being shot. He was deemed to be a threat only to himself. He had no known or traceable friends or relatives, no back history, and he was unable to recall his past or, it would seem, function very well in normal society.

The records described him as tall and thin with fine red hair. He was very freckled and had fine clear eyes. His disposition, once the initial trauma was over, was described as gentle, friendly and helpful. His IQ was exceptionally high and he had a strong practical streak. He was obviously attached to his home-made boots and was allowed to keep them.

But he was diagnosed as being prone to anxiety and mild depression with associated delusions. He seemed to think he had something important to do that might, as he put it, 'change the human world' but he did not know what it was. He also claimed he had lost something, and during his occasional bouts of depression he sometimes wept.

At these times, however, it was hard to comfort him because he claimed 'it was not allowed' or 'he might die if touched' and also that it might prevent him from doing the important things he had to do.

All this added up to being sufficient grounds for the patient with no name to be committed to state care, on the basis that, if and when he was rehabilitated and deemed ready to live normally, he would be released.

Four months after being shot in Dallas he was moved to the Terrell State Hospital, formerly the North Texas Lunatic Asylum, and it was there, among the patients, that he got his name: Mister Boots.

47

DÉJÀ VU

Forty years after Mister Boots appeared suddenly in Dallas, Texas, and then disappeared into a mental care facility, one of the world's foremost authorities on the Cosmos, Arthur Foale, retired from his position as Professor of Astral Archaeology at Cambridge University, England.

There was no reason why he should have known anything about someone called Boots or ever suspect that he had a direct connection with the anonymous vagrant.

But what the two most definitely had in common was they each had a powerful – almost painful – sense of having experienced a life other than the one they knew. Strangely, it was this sense that enabled Foale not to mind very much that, in all probability, after he left Cambridge, much of his life's work would soon be forgotten. No doubt, for a time, he would be invited back for anniversary college dinners but he had seen that happen to others and how forlorn they were and he did not intend that it should happen to him. He resolved not to go back.

But he hoped at least that some of the many colleagues and past students who gave him affectionate eulogies during his last days would take up his courteous suggestion that if they were in the area they might want to visit him and his wife, herself a retired professor, at their home in Woolstone, Berkshire. A few did, for a time. But soon, apart from Christmas cards and the occasional call, that connection with his academic past dried up as well.

But for Arthur retirement did not mean an end, rather a new beginning. His Renaissance mind was one of the most active of his generation and he knew that the Latin word 'Emeritus' did not strictly speaking mean a title for merit, as many seemed to think.

'No, my dear,' he told his wife on the first day of his retirement, 'it means "to serve out or complete one's service", as someone once told me.'

'I did,' said Margaret, who knew her Latin better than most, 'and I am now going to make a pot of tea and we can sit wherever you wish in the garden and you can tell me how, precisely, you are going to "complete your service". I wish to be the first to know. I had rather hoped we might go on holiday somewhere warm for a change.'

They sat where Arthur most liked to sit, which was at the bottom of their lawn near two great coniferous trees adjacent to his errant tomato plants and also to what they called the Chimes, shards of glass suspended by golden threads in amongst the shrubbery there, which made delightful music in the slightest breeze.

'They've always been there,' she had told him years before, 'but please don't ask me where they come from or where they go because I don't know.'

It was to that familiar music that they had their first tea in retirement and there that Arthur declared, 'You know perfectly well, my dear, what work it is I have to complete!'

And she did.

But he reminded her anyway.

'Well then,' she said two hours later, the sun going in and it getting chilly, 'that's the next few years sorted out!'

Then, leaning closer and taking his hands, because she knew the aspect of his work on which he now intended to concentrate touched something deep within him, causing a frustration and distress which none of his colleagues ever guessed at, she added, 'My love, I hope and pray you find the proof you need before . . . before . . .'

Before one or other of them passed on, was what she meant.

'I believe I will,' he said.

The research he resumed then concerned the experience that many people of all ages, cultures and periods had which was commonly called 'déjà vu'. It was often described as something someone imagines they have 'seen before', but Arthur's view was that it was better understood as something actually *experienced* before. Where his ideas differed from most interpretations was that he was convinced that at least some of those who had – or suffered, as he thought of it – a déjà vu experience had actually 'been there' in alternative lives. This had inspired some of his work as an astral archaeologist: he looked at evidence in the cosmological data that there have been many different versions of the same universe.

His interest in the subject was informed by his own personal experience, which was, as it happened, directly connected with Margaret.

They had met as students at Cambridge through a common interest in eighteenth-century dance. The moment he saw his future wife he believed he already knew her. When he finally visited her at her home in Berkshire the déjà vu feeling intensified. He felt he knew the house, the garden, the Chimes and Uffington Hill; these were all places he felt sure he had seen and known before.

The timing of that first visit in the mid-1960s and ones in the three years before their marriage coincided with various worldwide movements for change in which they were separately and actively involved. Arthur's special interest was in climatic change induced by human activity; Margaret's had to do with the dangers of factory farming of food. Both believed that the global economy was based on false premises which, as neo-Marxist economists were already forecasting, were not sustainable.

They had common views too on religions of all kinds, which they thought had become authoritarian control mechanisms in some societies or philosophically and actively so feeble in others as to have become irrelevant. Both veered towards religion's prehistoric roots, favouring animism, paganism and a love of nature peppered – by Margaret mainly – with Buddhism.

The only fundamental difference between them resulted in a painful decision: whether or not it was philosophically justified in an over-populated world to have children. Margaret wanted them, Arthur did not. In the end he gave her the choice and she decided against, because she felt she could only do so with his fullest, deepest support. It was a decision they regretted but by the time they changed their minds it was too late. By then their fertility had lessened and Margaret never conceived.

Meanwhile, the world had changed radically and, long before Arthur's retirement, their home in Woolstone became their haven from it.

The debates and arguments of the 1960s were won through a combination of extraordinary leadership in the West by many people high and low, much civic strife and a good deal of bloodshed. In Britain particularly, but in other formerly 'developed' countries too, a form of moral rearmament took place. The factory farming argument was mainly won, resulting in a rapid decline of the meat industry in the West by the late 1980s and the rise of vegetarianism. The climate change debate was won in the 1990s, resulting in a rapid decline in oil and solid fuel consumption at home and in industry. The sale of cars decreased and their useful lives were greatly extended. Successive governments banned the expansion of television, marginalized smoking and drinking and fiercely resisted global importation in favour of local production.

The result of these extraordinary changes was that, by the time Arthur retired, Britain and many parts of Western Europe still had the feel of the early 1950s about them. The population had declined but was happier by most measures. Obesity was nearly non-existent; more people walked and cycled than drove cars, and home entertainment in the sense of music making, reading, family gatherings and dancing – the Foales' first love – was the norm.

In contrast, in the same period China, Japan, Brazil and much of Pacific Asia had embraced the excesses, as the West had come to see it, of capitalism.

The only problem, which the Foales and many of their friends often discussed with growing concern, was that these great changes left countries like Britain vulnerable to Eastern imperialism. A generation that could still just remember Hitler and National Socialism shuddered at the prospect of economic invasion from the East.

'What we need but lack now,' Arthur would say, 'is a belief system which unites us behind leaders we can follow! But where that comes from and where the leaders are I have no idea!'

No wonder the ageing couple was content to remain in graceful retirement in Woolstone and cut back their travel to nothing more than bracing hikes up Uffington Hill, along the Ridgeway Path and back again. Before their final descent they would stop to drink water and share some food on top of the hill, and talk, as they had talked all their adult lives.

'I would die a happy man,' Arthur often said as they sat shoulder to shoulder watching the setting sun, 'if I could only get out of my head that I have been here before. I would also be happier to find the answer to the question that has eluded us both so long.'

'Ah, yes, *that!*' sighed Margaret, still as baffled as she had always been.

For Uffington Hill was also called White Horse Hill, which had given its name to the great vale that spread before them to north and east and west, giving them the impression that they surveyed a nearly magical world all their own. But it made no sense. The name was meant to derive from the fact that there had once been a figure of a beautiful horse cut into the turf on the escarpment. Now there was no horse there at all and according to their considerable researches there never had been. If it had once been there, all trace of it was now gone.

'If only,' Arthur would say, the last rays of the sun on his cheerful ruddy cheeks, and making his beard as white as snow, 'I knew what it had looked like. How much easier to imagine it!'

'And to follow it, my love, for a horse does not stand still for long. It goes somewhere, I suppose. Do you imagine that our horse, if we ever found it, would walk or canter?'

'I think it would probably gallop like hell,' said Arthur, 'anxious to get to a better place than this old world of ours! But come on, down the hill once more, I have work to do!'

It was a conversation they continued to have many times in many different ways until, one day, three years into Arthur's retirement, a girl of fourteen came into their lives who changed everything.

It happened when the work on the phenomenon of déjà vu had produced an interesting result. Arthur had been able to show that experiences of déjà vu were connected with what he called discontinuities of time. In other words, people who thought they had experienced things before often reported a gain or loss of actual time as a result of the experience.

From this he looked more carefully at apparent time shifts in the geological record from the prehistoric Pleistocene to the Holocene and on into the historical record. Time shifts, if that's what they were, seemed to be associated with major discontinuities in history, when the speed of events, or the direction they took, suddenly changed dramatically and without apparent reason.

'Of course,' he said over dinner one evening when he was full of these ideas, 'conventional historians earn their money finding reasons why quite extraordinary changes *had* to happen when, actually, they easily might not have. The decline of the Roman Empire; the Renaissance; and in our own time the Holocaust or even, dare I say it, the radical changes in Western society in our own lifetime we have experienced. Were these things really inevitable? Or are they the result of discontinuities and time shifts which, had they gone a different way, might have produced very different societies than the one we are now in?

'From that we might argue . . .'

'Arthur, please, you are boring our guests.'

'Ah . . . yes . . . I'm sorry, I get carried away . . . now what exactly . . . I mean to say, what is it that . . . ?'

The guests in question were not quite welcome ones.

The next-door neighbours, who had connections with the Scout and Guiding movement, had a small troop of Guides camping in their garden. Two of them had been invited over by Margaret along with the neighbours. Both were fourteen and in the presence of Arthur, and despite Margaret's gentle enquires, they had remained more or less tongue-tied. This explained Arthur's volubility, for he found the silence and lack of conversation very awkward and, not knowing how to talk to teenage girls, he had filled it with his own voice.

'So . . .' he said, as Margaret turned to one and he to the other, 'have you been here before . . . um . . . er . . . I'm sorry, I've forgotten your name?'

'Kate.'

'Have you been here before?'

They stared at each other, her eyes wide.

'No, I . . .'

'You haven't, then? Well it is . . .'

'I mean I . . .'

'You have! Ah . . .'

'Do you know,' she suddenly asked, somehow cutting through every-thing, 'why it is called White Horse Hill?'

It would be hard to say what it was about the tone of her voice, or the way she looked, or, from the others' perspective, what it was about Arthur and Kate together that stilled the room and silenced everyone.

'I . . . am . . . not . . . sure . . .'

'Kate's got a thing about white horses,' said her friend.

The silence deepened, yet not awkwardly. It was as if there was a comfortableness about it, and Arthur, his heart beating faster, for the first time in years had a feeling of déjà vu.

'Do you?' he said.

The friend said, 'She carries one around with her everywhere.'

'Oh!' said Arthur. 'I mean . . . do you mean . . . have you got it with you now?'

'I could get it,' said Kate and before they could stop her she was up and out of the room, out of the front door, running through the dark from one house to another, into her tent, grabbing her horse, and running back again, breathless, her hair dishevelled, the cloth horse in her hand.

She laid it on their great big dining table among the empty sweet dishes, the used glasses and the faded napkins. It was old and worn and it had a long, lean body like a single brushstroke, galloping legs, a head and pricked ears and a single eye. It was, beyond question, as prehistoric as a megalith but infinitely more beautiful.

'Where did you get it?' asked Arthur.

'A boy gave it to her,' said her friend grinning.

Kate grinned back.

There was an air of profound ease and comfort in the room.

For the first time in her life Margaret Foale felt like a mother, which was inexplicable.

As for Arthur, all stiffness had gone.

'What was his name?' he asked.

'Jack,' she replied.

The horse galloped between them, full of life.

'I think,' said Arthur, 'that I would very much like to talk to your Jack.'

Your Jack.

For the first time Kate flushed, but she didn't mind.

'So would I,' she said.

48
JACK

He came with the slow and steady inevitability of a change in weather after a period of unnatural quiet, so that, when he finally arrived at Woolstone they were all expecting him one way or another. It was his manner of arrival that was the surprise.

Kate had moved in, which felt as natural to the Foales as breathing. She had been fostered after her parents were killed in a car accident when she was six, the same day that she said she met the boy called Jack and acquired the toy horse.

'He gave it to me in my father's surgery in Thirsk, North Yorkshire, without me asking, but I knew why. It was protection and it worked. I asked his name. He said it was Jack. He asked for mine. I said "Katherine". I knew I'd meet him again one day and I still believe that.'

The fostering had been happy enough but Katherine, as she decided they should call her, was always restless.

'I felt I was not where I should be. They said it was because I missed my parents but they were a blur and Jack wasn't. That night of the crash when our car burst into flames I was holding the horse and it leapt from my hand and told me to follow it outside. I crawled after it through the broken window because it galloped away so fast I thought I'd lose it. I thought it would take me to Jack but it didn't. Yet I believed I'd find him one day.'

Katherine was a bright girl with a social conscience. Guiding, volunteering, raising money were what she chose to do.

'Got me out of the house, away from them. They were just . . . dull. I was never their child and I feel mean for saying that. I didn't belong.

The White Horse was where I belonged so I collected white horses. It was only a matter of time before someone mentioned White Horse Hill and Uffington. I chose where to come for the camping. The first thing we did was climb the hill. When I stood up there I felt I was home.

'When I came to this house for the first time I knew I had been here before. The hill was home, this was my shelter. And Jack . . . well, he was coming. Whe— *If* he does . . .'

'You mean "When he does", I think,' said Margaret.

'Yes.'

'When he comes,' said Arthur, 'I shall ask him a great many questions.'

Katherine smiled her lovely smile. It lit up a face which, in repose, expressed the depth of the loss she had suffered when so young. Confident and warm outside, unsure and a little prickly within.

'When he comes,' she said, 'I shall give him back the horse. He only loaned it to me to do a job, which it did.'

Sometimes Katherine played her music too loud.

Sometimes she got angry and shouted.

Sometimes she banged doors.

Sometimes she went back to see her foster parents because, as the months went by, she understood that they would like it, dull though they might be to her.

Sometimes she sat by herself in the garden, listening to the Chimes and not minding when Arthur joined her; and Margaret watched them and let them be, three people who by chance, as it seemed, knew how to be at peace together.

And once she said, 'I'm very tired and a bit frightened of what was, what might be. I think time's running out.'

When Jack came it was autumn after a dry summer and the grass on the hill was husky grey-yellow, the evenings balmy.

Margaret was finding it hard to climb straight up the hill any more so when she came they took the easier zig-zag way. Up to the top, along the Ridgeway to Wayland's Smithy, standing there, listening to the rush of the breeze in the great circle of trees, and then back for the traditional stop, which was under the hawthorn tree in the lee of the ramparts, the edge of the escarpment about fifteen yards away.

It was along the edge he came, striding purposefully with a big stick, which made Arthur notice him.

'Alpenstock,' he muttered. 'I have one. Edelweiss. We enjoyed ourselves.'

'That was a long time ago,' murmured Margaret, 'and the "we" didn't include me.'

'Was that before your time, my love?' said Arthur ingenuously, patting her thigh.

But by then Katherine was not listening, she was staring with fascinated alarm at the young male walker with a stick. She was waiting for him to turn one way or another so she could see his profile. As it was he stood staring out into what, from where they sat, looked like infinite space.

For him too, the Vale of the White Horse, for miles and miles, seemed a magical land.

He stood like a rock, a feeling made more real by the skylark high, high over his head, right up there, singing and fluttering so hard that eventually he looked up.

Jack stared, put a hand to his eyes to shield them against the afternoon glare and then, still though he had been, he became yet more still. His hand dropped down, he looked back along the edge as if he had just registered he had lost something, like a glove or a map. He looked puzzled, he shook his head, and then, glimpsing the tree from the corner of his eye, he turned and looked at them.

By then they were as astonished as Katherine – and as him as well, it seemed. Fearful too, as if the world had just changed.

Then, without seeming to think it odd in any way, he came closer and stared at them for a moment and then came nearer still.

Finally, he was about fifteen feet away and paying no attention at all to Arthur or Margaret, he said, 'Hello, Katherine.'

'Hello, Jack.'

'I've got something for you,' she said and she stood up and gave him the white horse which she had carried for so long in her backpack for just this moment and which already, while she was staring at him, she had taken from her pack.

He took it as easily as she gave it.

He looked at it, ran his hands over it as she had a million times and he said, 'I've missed it.'

Katherine felt she was there and wasn't there.

She felt her heart like it was a hammer inside.

She could hardly breathe.

Jack just the same.

'I would like you both to meet an old friend,' she managed to say finally, rather stiffly but with a lot of charm. 'Arthur, Margaret, this is Jack.'

He shook their hands firmly.

'You will come to supper,' commanded Margaret, which made him laugh.

'Yes, ma'am,' he said, as if he were a US Marine.

'And I . . .' began Arthur.

'He,' said Katherine, 'has a lot of questions.'

When they got to the house, sorted out that Jack would camp in the garden, got food onto the table and told each other about themselves, Jack finally raised the question most on his mind.

'What do you know about Mister Boots?' he asked.

49

TESTIMONY

Arthur had never heard of Mister Boots and nor had Katherine.
Maybe if they still had television then, or Arthur had continued to travel abroad, they might have come across him. But they had not, and that first night and in the weeks following as his stay with them extended until finally it became more permanent, Jack enlightened them by telling them what he had been able to find out about Mister Boots. From this, and the occasional mention of Mister Boots in the news, they came to believe and understand why it must be that he might be on his way to Woolstone. But they weren't expecting his arrival any time soon. Mister Boots was a law unto himself in the nicest possible way.

The trouble with Jack was that he was no storyteller. He was a doer rather than a talker. So his account of Mister Boots came out in fits and starts, and now and then, adding facts and ideas through time until eventually they decided it was easiest for Arthur to treat him like one of the subjects of his research into déjà vu and interview him.

Which was right in a way, because where Boots was concerned an almost ungovernable and painful sense of déjà vu was what Jack was all about.

Arthur had suffered the same intense kind of déjà vu when he came to Woolstone, and so had Katherine. It was as if people who shared something but which they had forgotten were congregating at Woolstone one by one for something important that still had to happen.

'Maybe we're all waiting for Mister Boots,' said Jack one day.

'Who's waiting?' wondered Arthur.

'Maybe the whole world,' said Katherine.

'. . . and maybe it's time to get all that Jack knows down,' said Arthur, 'and see what there is to learn from it.'

So they recorded Jack, transcribed it, and Katherine put it into order. It's as well she did, for it was a record of something that might otherwise have been lost and forgotten, like so much else about Mister Boots.

I was raised on the North York Moors in England, where I was found one day outside a children's home, *Jack began*. It wasn't what people would call a *real* home: no parents, no place to call my own. Just that toy horse I gave to Katherine.

I had nothing left of my past after that, so I hoped one day I'd see her again. Then I'd know my gift was one worth making and my loss worth suffering. From then on I was looking for somebody or some place or something I could attach to again.

It was a craving, a yearning. It wasn't a bad kind of feeling but I don't think it was very good! It left me restless and dissatisfied.

I would look at passers-by to see if they were the one. They never were. Later I would search illustrated books and magazines and old encyclopaedias to see if I could find the place. But I never did, maybe because I made the mistake of looking too far afield, thinking, like people do, that the grass is greener over there. It isn't. I didn't know the place I was looking for was nearer than I thought.

Maybe if we had had television or later what they call the internet in some countries, I might have found my place sooner. But the consensus moved against those things in England and Western Europe and later in America, when it was realized that together they were a form of highly destructive mass addiction to passive lifestyles and pornography. True they were used under strict conditions for education and official communication but I myself never got to see and use them until I was nearly adult. I didn't miss much but I did miss finding that place.

As for finding something to attach to, that was easier. I collected stones and rocks; I collected labels off bottles and then the bottles themselves. There were bright-orange and green fishing floats; old coins; Enid Blyton books and then one day, one very special day, old

Ordnance Survey maps, which are numbered from 1 to 204 in the edition I had, so they were very collectible.

I found them in jumble sales and junk shops. I couldn't afford to buy them new.

They were no substitute for my horse, which I still missed, but they opened my mind to places in England, Scotland and Wales. Friends of mine read books; I read maps. They had stories, I had journeys. It wasn't long before I went off to find the places on the maps near to me. That taught me to read them even better and make bolder journeys. I don't mean real ones, because I only had a bike. I mean ones in my imagination.

One day I bought some fish and chips in Scarborough, to where I had biked from our home with some friends. I was twelve.

I'm told that before what our teachers called the Greening of Britain had begun in the early 1970s some shops had special paper in which they wrapped their fish and chips. Like wrapping paper, but creamy white. They gave up old newspaper, saying that it looked better.

Well that was soon put a stop to. Why have special paper when you can re-use newspaper? Stupid.

So anyway, there I was, sitting on the beach, and as I dug into my chips a headline caught my eye. It read: 'Urban Legend "Boots" Turns up Briefly in Germany'. I had no idea what 'Boots' meant but Germany had always interested me. I didn't know why but, whenever I saw that country's name, or heard its language spoken, my inner ear pricked up.

Anyway, I saw the headline, ate the rest of the chips, smoothed out the now-greasy, vinegary newsprint and looked at the story. One second later I looked so astonished, or maybe so totally shocked, that one of my friends actually asked me if anything was wrong. I said it wasn't – and it wasn't *wrong*. Something was very right, so right that I felt funny all over and in a daze.

It was the image that went with the story that did it.

Of course it was only black and white because after the Greening few newspapers had colour print any more. It showed a man on a road and he had a big untidy backpack. The story was all about him. They called him 'Boots' because he wouldn't give his proper name. I didn't know then what an urban legend was, but he was one of those. He had quite a following, not that he wanted it, the story said. That was because when he turned up things happened. Good things mostly.

None of that interested me then, though later it was those things that happened – or sometimes did not happen in fact – which became my obsession. It was the picture of the man himself that grabbed my attention.

He looked old, maybe seventy.

He was tall and he had long, untidy hair which the newspaper said was still red in parts but mainly grey. He was gangly, sort of skewed over and in the picture he was setting off on the road again but looking back because the photographer had asked him to. In fact the story said he didn't like his picture being taken, which was why there were so few ever taken throughout his long and extraordinary life, but on this occasion he said he didn't mind.

But that's not the point.

The moment I looked into that man's eyes as he looked at me through the media of camera and newsprint, I knew I had met him before. By 'before' I mean *before* my first memory. I knew it as surely as I knew my name was Jack.

I also knew without being able to explain it that there were a whole lot of other things around him that I had known. Like people, like places, like things; and I knew I would meet him again one day.

I also knew it was important that I didn't try to meet him because I felt sure that the journey he was on meant *he was coming home to me*. To me!

You can say, 'How can you have known all that just from seeing a photograph?'

I will reply because we forget far, far more than we know and sometimes something triggers a flood of memory. That's what happened that day for me.

I was intrigued by how he got his nickname. Apparently it was because his boots were home-made out of car tyres bound up with twine. He absolutely refused to wear proper boots. He said that using leather for boots was a crime on animals killed for the purpose. All life, he said, is sacred. He admitted that using synthetic material for shoes was a waste of resources but since he had not yet found a way to change the fact that humankind, as he put it, uses rubber and its equivalents for tyres and then discards them he thought he'd set an example by recycling the worn treads.

From the moment I first read about Boots and recognized I knew him, I began collecting the many stories and anecdotes – and myths as well – that had been told about him over the years and which explained his near-legendary status among some people by the time I heard about him. I collected these stories with the same persistence as I collected Ordnance Survey maps.

As I did so and my collection of cuttings and suchlike about him grew, I created a filing system for them. I began by doing it by newspaper and magazine where they appeared. Then I did it country by country, because I built up a list of pen-pals, other collectors of other things. I found other stuff for them, they found Boots material for me.

Finally I realized that I had enough in my collection to refile everything in chronological order going right back to when he was much younger. I wanted to see if there was a pattern in terms of where he started, where he travelled to and where he thought he was going next. As I said before, I had known already what his final destination was; I had from the first moment I saw his picture – he was on his way to me. But I wanted to know what his life had been before that and, if possible, why he was as he was.

My pursuit of Boots was obsessional but it had one rule above all else – and interestingly I found, as time went by and I heard of other people who shared my interest, that they abided by this rule too, as if Boots, without trying, had made it up himself and announced it worldwide. You didn't try to contact Boots, you let him get on with it. The thing that emerged from all my research into Boots was that he had such natural dignity that people automatically treated him with respect. Without it, given the dangerous places he went, he would probably have been dead long ago.

The only people who interfered with him were officials of various kinds trying to move him along or the media wanting interviews and pictures. He handled them with such gracious indifference that he was rarely troubled for long. He made a good story when there was nothing else about and, though he seemed eccentric in much of what he did, most people who came to know about him realized that maybe he was the sanest man alive.

But his followers like me did nothing.

We waited.

Eventually I had a fairly complete picture of the chronology of Boots's life for something more than five decades, from 1968 on. In that year he was, judging by the evidence, about twenty-eight or -nine. Try as I might, I could not find anything before that, nothing. It was as if his previous life had disappeared entirely, or he had.

I was sure that if I looked hard enough I would eventually find something earlier, maybe even before he got the name by which his band of devoted followers, like me, knew him. But I already knew a very great deal about Boots, from the reports made, the stories told and from reading between the lines.

There's one important thing to repeat here. It came to me in that moment I first connected with his image and looked into his eyes: I knew that he was searching for something and that's why he was a restless wanderer. I knew Boots would carry on wandering until he found it or he died. I knew that his greatest fear was *not* finding whatever it was he was looking for before he died. I knew that because in one of the reported interviews with him he said words that rang so true to me that they felt like there was a truth there for all of us: 'I lost something a long time ago but I cannot remember what it was, however far I travel, however hard I try. I know I will only find it when I stop looking. But when you long for something so much, when you've lost something so deep, how do you stop, how do you ever stop?'

I knew the truth of what he said because that's how I felt. I had lost something too, which was my past. Talking of which, I never stopped collecting Ordnance Survey maps and reading them like books. The day I came across Map 174 and found White Horse Hill and Uffington and Woolstone I knew I had to go there. Two days later I did. I wasn't surprised to meet Katherine and get my horse back. That day I met Margaret and you, Arthur, and heard the Chimes for the first time. That day I found a home.

The Foales had regretted not having children but in retirement they had gained two.

Margaret had been ill on and off for two or three years. She was getting tired and feeling weary. She had struggled on because she hated to think that Arthur would be left alone if she went first. Maybe that was why she had wanted children.

But when Jack moved in, big and protective as he was, she weakened, as if she could afford to now that she knew her Arthur would not be alone and would always have someone to help.

She didn't want to go, but she no longer needed to stay. So a few months after Jack had lit up their lives, doing things around the place the others couldn't, carrying Margaret up and down the stairs because he was good like that and one memorable day getting a wheelchair and pushing her all the way up White Horse Hill so she could see the view a final time . . . a little while after that she passed away.

Arthur didn't say much and nor did they. The Chimes said more. He would wander about and in good weather go down and sit with his tomatoes.

Jack would mow the lawn or climb ladders and lie looking at the trees. Katherine would take them off for hikes and they would listen to Arthur theorizing about time, discontinuity and his sense of imminence.

Eventually, most days, one of other of them would make tea, find the biscuits, like Margaret always did, and they would end up together chatting, reading, musing, being family to each other.

But always, always, there was the sense between them that they had been there before and they could not rest content until they knew how and why.

50

MISTER BOOTS

Mister Boots lived at Terrell State Hospital for nearly five years after his first appearance in Texas, until the spring of 1968. Up to that date he had no desire to leave and nor was he ever any trouble. Rather the opposite.

In fact Boots became something of a legend quite soon and though the hospital was tough, especially on the potentially weak young men, he had an extraordinary capacity for making supportive friends. He was a natural teacher and willing and able to help others solve problems and make things. He spoke with what seemed a refined accent to most residents and used language that was quaint, as if he came from another age.

Any impression that his amnesia and initial assessment gave, that he was in some way mentally frail, was soon dispelled. He had a facility to learn languages, which he did very quickly from other patients at the hospital whose first language was not English. By the time he left he spoke French, German, Spanish and Italian nearly fluently and had some knowledge of Mandarin and Russian.

He also taught some of his fellow patients a language which they used at those moments when they wished to talk among themselves and not be understood by other patients or hospital staff and officials. No one could identify it at that time but years later, long after he had left the hospital, it was still in use at Terrell and a linguist from Berkeley University identified it as a combination of Gaelic, Welsh and a variant of Pictish, but in a form that made it a fully functioning language on its own account.

He was by nature a problem solver and seemed to understand better than the janitors how Terrell's complex and arcane electrical system worked. He also took over the running of the hospital's irrigation system for its extensive and famous gardens and in his fourth year built an outdoor sculpture, not unlike a simple prehistoric stone henge, which he claimed was his means of escape, should he ever need one.

By 'escape' it was assumed he meant his habit of sitting in the middle of his sculpture and humming, a common strategy adopted by some patients to block the real world out.

In May 1968 Boots was tracked down by the journalist Robert Eckram, then working for the *Los Angeles Times*, who was researching a story concerning an attempt that April to assassinate the President, John F. Kennedy, who was by then serving his second term. Eckram was working on the theory that there might have been a link with an earlier attempt which had involved, it was said, a cover-up by the police and CIA. This first attempt had taken place in Dallas, Texas, on November 22nd 1963 on the same day, in the same place and at exactly the same time that Boots was shot.

Eckram was able to demonstrate that four bullets were fired that day, from two different locations, only one of which passed through Kennedy's body and from which he recovered. Police and hospital records as well as photographic evidence enabled the journalist to show that Boots was on the grassy knoll from which two of the shots were fired. He had compelling evidence to support his theory that had the second shot, which hit Mister Boots, hit the President it was highly unlikely that he could have survived.

As is well known, it was this near-death experience that radically transformed the President's life. The legislation he forced through during his two terms of office, for environmental change, civil liberties and the weeding out of vested interests in US politics, followed by his later environmental work with the United Nations, pushed the world in new directions. It kick-started the movement towards austerity and environmental common sense which was responsible for the Greening of many countries in Western Europe and North America but especially England, where the movement first took off.

The first story ever to appear anywhere in the world about Mister Boots was the one by Eckram in the *Los Angeles Times* a month after his visit to Terrell. Its headline was, 'The Man Who Saved the President's Life and Changed the World'.

The unwanted celebrity this brought for Mister Boots and his friends at Terrell upset him. He asked to be discharged and was told that, though it was a certainty, he needed a final assessment.

He did not wait for it but left the hospital without formal permission sometime during the night of October 31st and November 1st 1968 during a patient firework display celebrating Hallowe'en. He was last seen in the centre of his stone circle at Terrell and, according to one of his friends, he appeared to be perfectly happy. In fact, they said, he was doing something they had never seen him do before. He was dancing.

Mister Boots did not surface again for seven years.

When he did it was as a dishwasher in one of the restaurant outlets of the New York-based Rap's Beef restaurant group. In that capacity he met and became friends with Lance Rap, son of Eike, the founder, a scion of the meat industry and one of its celebrity supporters. Mister Boots turned the son into a vegetarian.

When Eike died, Lance took over and in a few months pushed through one of the most extraordinary transformations of any major restaurant and food groups in the USA. Rap was notoriously narcissistic, vain and snobbish but he was also a culinary genius. He turned the group into a vegetarian delight.

He frequently credited Mister Boots with his anti-meat philosophy and also with the partnership that turned Rap's international. When the non-English-speaking wife of the hotelier Juan Carlos Festone turned up for a meal and was unable to make sense of the menu, Boots was summoned from the kitchen to translate into Portuguese. He so charmed her that the following day she brought Festone to meet him – and to taste the food. The resulting Rap-Festone Group, it was said, 'turned the world off meat'.

Boots moved to Paris with Rap and stayed there on and off for ten years, by when the Rap chain had spread worldwide and had become the most profitable anti-meat lobby in the world. Rap always credited Boots with its success but when in 1984, after an episode of depression, Boots disappeared and a body was found in the River Seine it was identified as his.

Rap's memorial speech was one of the few statements about Mister Boots on the record by someone who knew him personally. He said, 'He was a friend like no other, without pretension, unwilling to accept any reward for the inspiration he gave. We offered him anything he wanted but we could not give him peace of mind. He always said that he had important work to do and could never accept the idea that perhaps he had done it already. Did he not save a President's life? Did he not inspire a revolution in eating? Did he not do countless small things for people, mainly unrecorded, which changed their lives and perhaps the world as well?

'My friend's inexplicable sadness lay in the fact that he felt he had lost something and he could not find it, because he could not remember what it was. This might be a joke to some, but to him it was a continuing agony. If I could have helped our friend fulfil that quest I would willingly have given up all I have and travelled across the world to do so.'

Mister Boots's memorial service in Paris was attended by over five hundred people from all over the world.

Along with their public sentiments Festone and Rap added a strange private instruction to the managers and staff of all their outlets worldwide, from the humblest eatery to the finest five-star hotel. It was born of Rap's personal belief that his old friend was not and could not be dead and the identification was a mistake. They told their staff if ever a man answering Mister Boots's unique description turned up and asked for help he was to be given it at once, in a manner and with a style that befitted any normal customer.

This instruction had an unexpected outcome for, of course, every down-and-out alive began turning up at Rap restaurants and hotels, usually at the back door. All were cared for, within reason, and many other restaurant groups followed Rap's lead. In this way Mister Boots changed the world for vagrants like himself.

Three years later, Lance Rap had a late-night call.

It was from the manager of one of their two hotels in Bhutan. A tall, thin man with freckles and red hair who spoke English when he wasn't conversing in Nepalese had turned up at the door. He had asked for refreshment and 'That is the problem, Mister Rap, I am sorry to trouble you but . . .'

'What is the problem? Give him whatever he asked for.'

'You have said we must give him that but I do not understand "brew". What is that please?'

Rap, to his credit, laughed.

'It is . . . it is . . . is he there?'

He was and they spoke, Boots treating the conversation as if he had left yesterday. They spoke for a long time and Boots answered some questions but not others. He said he had not yet found what he was looking for but he had not given up hope. Also the mountain air had done him good and he had decided he preferred cold climates and was planning to come 'home' – a word he had never used before with Rap. But where that was he would not say.

Later Rap spoke to his manager again.

'It will be better if you let Mister Boots make his own brew. Admit him to the kitchen, give him what he needs and he will make it for himself.'

'But, sir, he is an honoured guest.'

'Exactly,' said Rap, 'he is. Very honoured. So you let him do as he needs to do. Which may include the washing-up. That's how he is. And . . . one more thing.'

'Sir?'

'When he leaves, please ask him the same question I did. He might give you the answer he would not give me. Ask him where he's heading for. Fax me if he tells you.'

'Yes, sir.'

A fax came two months later. It read, 'Sir, our honoured guest is walking to Oslo to talk with Mr K. Larsen.'

It was a message that went round the world. Larsen was the secretive billionaire arms dealer whose group, it was said, supplied both sides of many conflicts with weapon systems of all kinds. Mister Boots decided to go and see him, choosing a roundabout route through some of the most dangerous war zones in the world, including Afghanistan, Iraq and the Middle East, several African states and three South American countries notorious for the power of their drug lords.

Mister Boots perambulated through them all over a period of six years with a startling lack of concern for his personal safety and saying very little except that he would like to talk with Mr Larsen. What started as a little-known act of insane eccentricity ended up with the triumphal march of Mister Boots and nearly ten thousand followers, many wearing home-made boots and not much more, into the Moss suburb of Oslo, where Larsen had his heavily guarded home.

A folk festival for peace took place on its doorstep and three days later the security gates opened to admit Boots. He and the billionaire had a vegetarian meal for two prepared and flown in by the Rap-Festone Group, an extravagance about which Boots mildly complained. But the astonishing outcome was the Larsen Group's decision to diversify its activities towards building the infrastructures of peace, not sowing the seeds of war.

The press-shy Larsen had nothing but praise for his nemesis and said, as others had before, that Mister Boots had seemed very fit after his long walk but 'sad', adding that, as he himself now knew, 'There are some things money cannot buy and a cure for depression is one of them. This gentleman appears to be able to help everyone but himself.'

To his relief the media lost interest in Mister Boots after this, apart from an occasional report of the kind that Jack had first seen in a German newspaper.

The years passed and no more was heard of him until a year before Jack had arrived at Woolstone. An elderly vagrant was found wandering in a confused state in Digbeth, Birmingham whom somebody recognized as Mister Boots. A local reporter followed the story up and found him sleeping rough on Waseley Hill and saying, as often before, that he had lost something but he didn't know what.

'He would accept no help, nor was he able to say what he had lost,' the reporter said. 'He seemed quite unaware of the impact he had had on others and was grateful for the support the city of Birmingham had briefly given him but he felt it was time to move on. Asked why, he replied that there was much to see and do. "Mother Earth," he said, "is full of infinite possibilities."'

Jack, Katherine and Arthur looked at the image that went with the report. Mister Boots was old now, more stooped than he was in earlier pictures of him Jack had found.

Two years after Jack arrived at Woolstone he and Katherine became lovers. Young though they were, it seemed the right and natural thing to do and Arthur was a pragmatist. Sleeping arrangements were altered in the house to give them privacy, but that was all.

Then, one afternoon, Mister Boots arrived.

Arthur saw him first, the other two having gone out and away across the Downs. In fact Arthur heard him humming, as he sat enjoying his tea by the Chimes. It was a tuneless, odd sort of hum, slightly other-worldly, and Arthur couldn't work out what it was or where it came from. He got up a little nervously, searched about a bit, and eventually found a tall, white-haired man standing in amongst the trees between the two conifers, a shady place, a kind of sanctuary.

Arthur knew him the moment he saw him.

Mister Boots said, 'Very fine, very fine! I wonder if I might have a glass of water?'

'Better still,' cried Arthur, 'come and sit down and have a cup of tea!'

'I am not sure,' said Mister Boots. 'I shall stand here and see what transpires.'

'Well I . . . I mean we wouldn't want . . .'

'Oh, I shan't go. At least until I have had the water, if I may. Not tea, if you please.'

Arthur hurried off and hurried back, anxious lest Mister Boots had left. But he was still there, drank the water, stood awhile staring at the trees and said finally, 'I think perhaps I would indeed like to sit.'

Arthur took him to the garden chairs by the Chimes.

'Sit in any one of them,' he said.

Mister Boots took a chair and after some hesitation placed it between the tomatoes and the Chimes and sat down.

He didn't talk at all but sat peacefully with a very slight smile on his face. He was indeed thin, he was certainly freckled, and his hair, though mainly white, had a reddish tinge here and there.

Arthur did not know what to say but it didn't matter.

The sadness that everybody who met him had spoken of was there. But so was a kind of simple joy in the present moment which induced calm in Arthur, who soon stopped thinking about when Jack and Katherine were coming back. In their own time, no doubt.

Mister Boots just sat.

'It is a very long time,' he said suddenly, 'since I did nothing. If I may I will sit a little longer.'

'Please . . . of course . . . I would like . . .'

Jack and Katherine joined them twenty minutes later, laughing as they did so, calling out to Arthur and when he did not reply coming to find him.

He looked at them mutely as if to say, 'I have nothing to say. There is nothing to say. He is here.'

Mister Boots looked at them and slowly stood up.

'I have forgotten my name,' he said very simply, 'but people call me Mister Boots, though, as you see, I have a reasonably healthy pair of boots on my feet.'

He didn't offer his hand, nor they theirs.

He just stood and stared at them.

'I am rather tired,' he said, 'for I have walked a long way to get here. I . . . wonder . . . what are your names?'

'Jack.'

'Katherine.'

'I realize,' he said, swaying on his feet, 'that I am more tired than I thought. I did not think it would take so long to get here. I had things to do, you see, and I have been looking for something which I once lost.'

He paused for a little, frowning slightly, and added, 'I cannot remember how long ago I lost it but I do not think I can find it now.'

It was Katherine who knew what to say and do and it was not what she would normally have said at all. But then she had never in her life been in the presence of someone who had such a sense of innocence and goodness who had so clearly reached the absolute limit of all he could do physically, mentally and spiritually. Which he had done with grace, nobility and infinite courage.

'Would you like to *sleep*?' she asked him.

'Sleep,' he murmured as if it was not a word he had heard spoken, or considered the meaning of, or believed quite possible, for a very long time, 'sleep?'

'You're with friends, Mister Boots,' she said, 'and you're safe. You can sleep now, you can sleep.'

'Sleep,' he said, 'is something I would very much like to do.'

51

THE CHIME

Sometime then, in the weeks after Mister Boots came to live his last days at Woolstone House, Katherine fell pregnant. They knew when and where it happened: up there on the hill, amongst the long grass, one August evening. Though the White Horse had gone from the place to which it gave its name, it roamed still that lovely night as the stars came out above them and their child was made.

While Katherine bloomed some days and felt sick on others through the months ahead, Boots slowly recovered from his journeying, able eventually to walk up the hill, he and Arthur together.

He worried often about the important things he felt he still had to do, never able to remember what they were. When he got distressed Katherine, able to get closer to him than any of them, so much so that he would sometimes let her take his arm, would say, 'Mister Boots, you have done more than enough in your long life. Some say you saved the world.'

'Do they? Did I?'

'Many of us think so.'

Then, too, he suffered sadness for what he felt he had forgotten and what he thought he had lost. Just once in a while he seemed to catch a glimpse of that other world he had convinced himself he once knew better than the present one.

'I think, Arthur,' he once said suddenly as they headed out of the garden down the private path that led to the bottom of the hill, 'that there used to be a pilgrim road here which went all the way to Brum.'

'A pilgrim road?'

'I think so.'

'Brum? Where's that?'

'I don't exactly know,' he replied. 'but I think it may be an old name for Birmingham.'

It was when Katherine was very near her time, towards the end of April, that he remembered something else. Spring was in the air again, the old garden filled with early flowers and Katherine restless, walking up and down, sitting, standing, hands to her aching back.

She sat down and found Mister Boots staring at her bump.

'He's moving,' she said.

'It's a she,' replied Mister Boots without hesitation.

'Would you like to feel . . . him, her or it?'

He nodded, unable to speak.

Katherine took his hand and placed it on the tight, round bulge that was her child. She held his hand there and waited until the baby moved. A foot, a hand, who knew? Across her belly it went, from one side to another, life moving across its Universe.

'There! Did you feel it?'

'I did,' he said. And then without any explanation he said: 'Her name is Judith. It always was.'

She stared at him dumbfounded and held on to his hand. She knew he was right, but how and why?

'Was that the name of the person who you once . . .'

The baby moved again and he took his hand away.

'Her name is Judith,' he said again, 'but more . . . I dare not say . . . but that *is* her name.'

Then, though he did not weep, she had never felt so close to the vastness of his loss, whatever it had been; nor loved him so much.

'Do you like the name Judith?' she asked Jack later. 'And do *you*?' she added, looking at Arthur.

Perhaps they replied, perhaps they didn't. They didn't seem to have to. It seemed that one way and another Judith was always going to be her name.

She was born a fortnight later at home during the night of the season's turn, at the start of May Day morning.

Jack, standing at the window of their bedroom, looking out across the lawn, mother and baby sleeping, Arthur and Mister Boots, having been allowed to have a look, saw the fox come from out among the trees at first light, bold as brass, staring.

'I've seen you before,' said Jack softly.

He didn't know why, nor did he question it, but later, as the sun rose, he took the placenta across to the trees, went among them and put it on the ground right in their centre.

'Why?' asked Katherine later.

'It felt like the right thing to do. Like calling Judith "Judith".'

Katherine had been right when she said others thought that Mister Boots had done enough and could rest now. In the following years of Judith's growing, happy years for all of them, Arthur and Boots ageing, arguing, laughing, and Jack and Katherine maturing, the world beyond began to recognize what he had achieved.

Letters came and gifts, most of which he gave away.

The media sought him out and he would sometimes give them a little time.

People came, a few who had met him in the past, many who never had but felt grateful or inspired by what he had done. He saw his visitors if he could, waving aside the frequent protestations of Katherine and Jack, listening graciously to what people said to him. Nodding his head, saying he was sorry he was not quite well enough to accept their invitations to visit them in their homes.

'Thank you,' he would say, 'but I think I have journeyed enough and I must conserve my energy.'

'For what, Mister Boots?' they asked.

'We all have one last journey to make and ... well ... I have something I must do and something I must find.'

'You did everything, Mister Boots! What more could you do?'

'Something,' he would murmur, 'but I don't know what.'

Little Judith loved him as she loved them all. As happy, as joyful and as beautiful as a child could ever be. Each year taller, each year exploring more.

With Arthur she was all over the place, attacking his bulk with all she had and he laughing as he struggled more and more to pick her up.

'Not because I'm getting older, which I am, but because you're a pudding!'

'I'm not!'

With Mister Boots she was quite different. It was as if she understood he needed care.

Arthur she pulled along, Boots she guided carefully.

'Be careful! It's steep! Don't fall down!'

She developed normally, year by year, until there came a time when she was five or so, when it was Judith who got them up the hill.

Once in a while up there, sitting all together, they would see a passing walker hovering, too shy or nervous to say hello.

'Er excuse me but . . . well . . . *is* he . . . ?'

'Ask him yourself,' Jack would say.

'Are you Mister Boots?'

'I am,' he would reply, his smile warm, his gaze a little opaque. He was and he wasn't, that was the truth. He was Mister Boots so long as he couldn't remember his name.

In those days, in the West, in Britain especially, there were no celebrities to speak of. People got on and did what they had to without expectation or favour. They did what was right to do.

But he was a celebrity and people came to see him, and finding that sometimes they were not allowed to because he was too tired or simply poorly, they got into the habit of climbing the hill and looking down towards Woolstone House, where he was living out his 'retirement', quietly, without saying much. Then they stared across England and from there to the world.

But some visitors he saw, some even stayed.

Lance Rap, one of the most famous chefs in the world, flew in, his helicopter landing on the lawn and nearly blowing them all over.

'Mon ancien ami!' he cried in his ridiculous Franglais, 'I 'ave come to cook for you! So, where is la cuisine! Mon Dieu! Disgusting! Please, 'elp, Katherine – is that your name? Et toi . . .'

'Me?' said Judith.

'Oui, you. Carry zis outside!'

Which Judith did, at the double.

'To my friend!' said Rap more normally, splendid in his whites and tall chef's hat, 'I propose a toast!'

Mister Boots sipped the wine, a rare thing.

He ate the food.

He laughed.

'Mister Boots laughed!' said Judith surprised.

'I can cry too,' he replied.

'Can't!' rejoined Judith, mildly outraged.

'No,' said Mister Boots softly and with an infinite sadness that eluded her. 'No.'

Honours continued to come and honorary degrees and boots, plenty of pairs of boots.

But of all the gifts he received in those last years the one he liked best came along with the person who gave it, family and all. His name was Dorji and he arrived unannounced at Woolstone House.

'Please to tell Mister Boots that Dorji is come from Thimphu, Bhutan, with a gift.'

'Dorji is *here!?*' cried Mister Boots with delight. 'Well then, I must . . .'

'He's here but so are his family and there are quite a lot of them. In four cars. I will get them.'

But Boots shook his head.

'I will welcome them at the door, they have come a long way and that is the Bhutanese way.'

Mister Boots went to greet them and, as it was the end of summer and warm, Dorji made his gift outside, using the utensils he had brought with him.

How busy his family and servants were, how colourful. How aromatic the gift he made.

When he was ready Dorji put what he had made on a tray with a golden goblet, his children scattering petals, sweets and herbs all about.

'First, please, for Mister Boots to give his testimonial of quality and perfection. Then we make more. Long time ago this kind gentleman teach Dorji how to make brew. Dorji said he will one day come to Mister Boots's home and make brew for him. Here I am, here it is. Enjoy. My chillen will sing and dance!'

As they sang and danced, with Judith joining in, Mister Boots supped the brew and pronounced it as good as any he had ever tasted.

'That is good testimonial! It is already on the bottle! Look!'

To their astonishment Dorji produced a bottle of Dorji's Brew for each of them, on which was a picture of Mister Boots, smiling.

'Now Dorji is rich and famous in Bhutan and northern India but he knows always for Mister Boots that money is not important. What do with it, important. Dorji gives it away with Mister Boots's name on every wish and dream it makes! Like brew?'

'The best,' said Mister Boots, 'the very best.'

That summer was warm, the autumn beautiful and the harvests across England munificent, better than for years past.

Down by the Chimes, where the tomatoes were small and ripe and their special scent good in the middle of the day, they sat as a family, remembering. But they lingered now on the rich memories of years just past, of being together.

Arthur had less energy, Boots was quieter.

Katherine and Jack were worried by the world, for the East was rising, threatening, and the West seemed to not have the spirit to fight back. For parents with a young child the times were darkening.

'Leadership, that's the thing,' Arthur said. 'Cometh the hour, cometh the man, eh, Boots?'

'Perhaps,' he said.

'You could make some boots and set off and change the world again,' said Arthur.

Boots only shook his old head. The day was good, the sun warm, abundance and darkness were in the air together. The Chimes were quiet and getting quieter.

'Yum, yum,' said Judith popping a tiny tomato in her mouth, 'yum!'

She gave one to Katherine and then to Jack.

'Arthur . . .'

He shook his head.

'Dentures,' he growled. 'Tricky.'

'Mister Boots?'

She held it out to him and he stared at it, frowning, as if puzzled by the tiny, shiny red tomato in her hand. Remembering.

'Yummy,' she said and he smiled and opened his mouth and she popped it in.

Then he bit and the tomato exploded in his mouth and as it did so, so did memory explode in his mind, a whole universe of it.

And across the Universe it flew, the shard and its golden thread that Mister Barklice had thrown towards the stars in the distant hope, fearful indeed, that it might one day guide Stort back to where he needed to go. Flying across the face of the Mirror-of-All, reflecting, turning, a star itself, on and on through time, thin as light, sharp as the Scythe, beginning its sound, seeking its place and its eternal moment of time until it knew where it must go to be just where and when it had to be.

The Shield Maiden saw it and reached for it as it rushed on by, and called his name in joy, whom she had lost and still waited for though her task was now surely done.

Isn't it? she whispered to herself.

The Modor didn't think such things, trying to salvage something from the darkness of her long winter by murmuring names of hydden who in better days had made her smile: Leetha, Borkum Riff and Sinistral. Stort?

Always doing things, you are, she grumbled, *even to the last . . .*

As Mister Boots, tasting the fruit of the Earth, feeling the explosion of the tomato in his mouth, astonished by the suffusion of taste within him and the memories it triggered, saw as they all did, as the Chimes fell silent, another one come out of the sky, like a star descending until it landed there, above his head among the verdant branches, near where he sat, catching the light of the sun, reflecting the Fires of the Universe.

Mister Boots stood up and reached his hand to the Chime that had once been his and had come back home, touched it and let it touch him. The silence ended, the Chimes sounded loud and louder as he arched his back in pain, his mouth opening wide to express the agony he cried out to the Universe itself.

'Mister Boots . . . *Mister Boots?*'

He reached to them as they to him, his grief so overwhelming that it felt as though his body was being racked and torn apart, broken, stretched, in pain beyond pain as he wept and shouted, 'I know who I am, I remember what I have lost, I am my memory again. I am Bedwyn Stort.'

In rediscovering this he discovered all he had known and all he had lost and his grief was an entire universe. He cried then inconsolably and they held him and held him until, his grief abating, he dared cry again, 'I am my memory, I am Bedwyn Stort.'

Never, ever, had any of them been witness to loneliness like his then.

Yet finally one there found for him a consolation.

As again and again he spoke his name, Judith, reaching her hand to his, and shaking her head because she could not understand, whispered unhappily, 'No, you're Mister Boots.'

'That too,' he whispered in return, his eyes gentling, 'that too, my dear.'

52
MEMORIES

But Stort *was* Stort and he was remembering.

He was Stort, and he was old.

He was Stort and all his friends, every last one, had gone and he had nothing now and was in a world where even Jack and Katherine did not know who he really was because they did not know who they had been.

Before he left the Hyddenworld, Judith had warned that forgetting was best because remembering would be pain inconsolable.

'I am my memory,' he had said, and it had been true and now it was breaking him.

Bedwyn Stort saw no one that autumn when he fell into a troubled silence.

How could Jack know that he wasn't the Jack Stort knew?

Or Katherine?

How could he talk with Arthur and not share the Hyddenworld?

He responded only to Judith, who, calling him Mister Boots still, asked him once in a while who Mister Stort was.

'Is he a friend?'

'He was.'

'Is he dead?'

'I think he is.'

'Where does he live?'

'A long way off.'

Samhain, as he now thought of it again, came and it was the start of his winter. Stort doubted he could make it through to another spring. He was now as old as Judith had been when he saw her for the last time, but he was human and hydden no more and she . . . she was gone from his world, lost to him forever and he had failed in the quest and so failed her too.

Sometimes he would mutter his thoughts to her, sitting alone as he thought, the Chimes no consolation now.

'Are you talking to him?' asked Judith.

'I'm talking to her.'

'His wife?'

'The Shield Maiden.'

'Tell me about her.'

'Tell me.'

'Please, Mister Boots . . .'

'Leave him be, Judith, he's sleeping.'

Judith shook her head and said, 'No, he's sad, aren't you, Mister Boots?'

I'm drifting now, my love, drifting back to the cold that took me before, just drifting . . .

That winter was wet, not cold.

Floods in December, floods at the Solstice, which they made into a kind of Christmas, and a miserable one too, floods in January.

No chance of Arthur and Mister Boots going up the hill again. It was treacherous even for Jack and Katherine, yet when they made it the view was astonishing. The Vale was flooded and, the day those two went, which was in mid-January, the temperature dropped and the flooded fields were grey-white with ice, reflecting the grey sky.

'Excuse me . . .'

A voice from the ramparts of the Iron Age fort.

Jack looked up: a man, a woman, wrapped up tight.

'Are you here for the same reason we are?'

Jack climbed up to them.

'And that is?' he asked.

'Mister Boots. We heard he was dying. We came to pay our respects. You knew he lived here, didn't you?'

'Yes,' said Jack.

'It's that house down there.'

'Is it?'

'A great man, did great things.'

'Who told you he was dying?'

'Just knew. Pity, he might have had an answer.'

'To what?'

'These dangerous times.'

'You mean the threat of countries in the East . . .'

'That's exactly what I mean. Times are hard enough economically as they squeeze and squeeze us but it won't be long before the military threats become real.'

Jack did not doubt it. They had it easy and simple in England and lived in a bubble, protected by isolation and independence, but times were changing. Before Judith came, Katherine and he had been able to ignore such things, staying out of the mainstream. But a child brought new responsibilities, new fears.

The passer-by had a point and Jack stared at him wondering what to say.

'The thing is,' said the stranger, 'Mister Boots would have known what to do like he did before but now . . . well . . . if he's passing others will have to take up where he left off.'

'They will,' Jack found himself agreeing, 'and they must.'

'That's right, they must.'

Those four words from a stranger were Jack's wake-up call, reaching into that giant-born part of him which he had buried deep inside.

Maybe when . . . if . . . Jack was astonished to find himself thinking, *I might myself take a lead.*

Jack glimpsed the future, though he had no idea how he was going to get there.

They all stared at each other and maybe thoughts crystallized in their minds as they now did forcefully in Jack's.

Me, a leader? he asked himself. No sooner was the question formulated than he knew its answer. He had always known it and that somehow or other Mister Boots, now Bedwyn Stort, was a part of it. A stage on the journey. A starting point.

'Thank you,' said Jack.

'For what?'

'Showing me . . . um . . . the house.'

The cold deepened. As it got into the third week of January the numbers on the hill increased, trekking up there daily until some began to camp and in the final days of the month, more and more people came. So many that the light of the lanterns and fires lit up the hill at night.

He was dying and they wanted to show their respects.

He was dying and they wanted to light his way to the stars.

Mister Boots was passing on and the world would have been a far worse place had he not walked its way.

Jack and Katherine knew that it was so, the grief he had cried out had hollowed him, leached him, scoured him out.

Leaving nothing much at all where he lay in bed, staring out of the open window at the hill from which even the horse had gone. Even that had gone! He stirred and frowned and listened.

Outside, the grey day gave way to sunshine and he heard Jack call, 'Katherine?'

'Mum's working.'

He heard Arthur laugh.

He heard the rooks in the great coniferous trees.

'Are you awake?' whispered Katherine, leaning close, her hand on his frail shoulder, startling him, 'I have some soup.'

He heard her voice and, surprising himself, he grinned.

He had heard the world again, heard it anew.

'Katherine?'

She sat back, surprised.

'When I came I had a backpack.'

His voice was good.

'Er . . . yes . . .'

'In one of the pockets . . . I think the bottom one. Bring it here if you can find it.'

He might as well have said 'at once!' for the tone he used.

Wondering, she went and got the pack.

By the time she got back he was propped up and waiting impatiently.

'Ah ... yes. Mister Boots's pack,' he pronounced, dismissively. 'No good! I wanted Stort's. Fool that I am. Getting my worlds mixed up.'

'What did you want, from your pack?' she asked, quietly suppressing her irritation. Up and down was a long way.

He had a touch of colour in his cheeks, a brightness to his eye, an impatience to his look.

'Soup is all very well but what I need is a brew, rather stronger than the one Dorji brought. As a matter of fact, I invented one once, a sort of pick-me-up. Mister Barklice used to drink it rather too liberally but it did the trick.'

'Who was Mister Barklice?'

'A good friend. But ... help me up ... I'll have to make a brew myself.'

'Mister Boots ...' she said warningly, for it did not seem wise for him to get up.

'Bedwyn Stort is my name, Katherine. Boots was a good companion along the way but now I have no need of him any more.'

He laughed a raspy, coughy laugh.

'Help me up ...'

'Later,' she said firmly.

'Later is usually too late in my experience,' he said more firmly still, getting himself out of bed.

Later that evening Stort sat scowling in the kitchen. He was in disgrace and felt that nobody liked him much.

He had found it difficult to find the ingredients needed for a brew, in fact nigh impossible. The coffee and tea they offered was quite disgusting, though Mirror knew he had been imbibing it for the past few years. Now he knew it was poison.

They had herbs of a sort, but dried-up, desiccated things in bags and little boxes, shadows of herbs as it seemed to him. Still, peppermint was useful and thank goodness that Katherine had agrimony and lovage, garnered from the garden.

'But, Mister B ...'

'Stort, if you please.'

'Stort then. For the last few years you have drunk tea perfectly happily.'

'For the last several years I have been asleep. I cannot begin to imagine who I was. Now I am awake and it is not a very nice world I have woken into. I am a hydden, not human. I cannot seem to make you understand.'

'Mister Stort is a hydden,' repeated Judith. 'Mister Boots has gone away.'

'Where has he gone?' asked Katherine tightly, her kitchen a mess, the concoction he had made a disgusting thing in a pan, smelling of . . . *brew*.

'He has gone to the human world,' said Stort, keeping hold as best he could of the new remembrance of himself as he once was.

Jack came in, cold, wet and blustered up by wind, his hair all over the place.

'Kitchen's a mess,' he said cheerfully.

He smelt the brew.

'What's *that*? Yuk!'

'Yuk!' repeated Judith. 'Mum's cross.'

'My dear fellow!' cried Arthur, entering, 'you're up and about and . . . and er . . . making . . . *something*.'

'Brew.' Judith nearly spat out the word.

The pyjamas that Stort wore were very ancient, bought for Arthur decades before from a shop called Marks and Spencer. They were pink-striped and had a cord to hold them together and, for some reason, a slit down the front that revealed all.

'Mister B . . .' began Katherine.

'Stort,' he said, unaware.

'Mister . . .'

'*Stort*,' said Judith . . .

Katherine lost her temper as Jack laughed and indicated the problem with a meaningful glance, which Arthur caught and understood at once.

'Bloody things!' he said, 'never could stand 'em.'

'Then why, for goodness sake, keep them?' snapped Katherine.

A moment's silence as Stort, struggling, managed to tie his thumb to the cord until, peering more closely, he stood up to get a better view, skewed sideways, began to fall, and the handle hit his pan which shot his brew onto the floor.

Katherine and Jack caught him at the same time. At which Judith began to laugh, really laugh, and one by one, they all did too.

'What Margaret used to say,' said Arthur affectionately a little later, 'is that at moments like this there is nothing better than a cup of tea.'

'Or,' said Jack, delving into a cupboard and producing a bottle, 'for those who don't like tea, a good brew as Mister Stort calls it.'

'Ah,' said Stort forgetting himself, 'a hydden after my own heart!'

That evening, with the wind howling around the old house as if to keep them safely in, they gathered by the fire in the drawing room. They had warm stews and pottages and all kinds of things they had all made together, Stort included. They ate and stared at the fire and they talked as they had never done before since his coming.

They talked about the feelings of déjà vu they had and Stort listened, nodded and understood. They did remember the world he thought he had lost; it was just that they glimpsed it through a filter of their different human world, the world to which he now knew he had journeyed on a quest.

'That was my wyrd, you see,' he said.

'Explain,' said Katherine.

'Well to do that I need to explain about the Arthur that I knew before I met this one and how he did something very extraordinary for a human, very extraordinary indeed. But then he was always going to, I suppose. I would have to explain about green roads and all kinds of things I have nearly forgotten. Like Waseley Hill and Brum . . .'

'Which you mentioned once before, I believe,' said Arthur.

'Did I? Perhaps I did, struggling as I was then to find my world again.'

'What was Brum?' asked Jack.

'Why, Jack, how strange that you should ask that! You were the city's Stavemeister and of course you took over from Master Brief . . . you remember . . . ah no, of course you do not.'

'Tell us,' said Katherine gently, 'tell us *all* of it. And, too . . .'

'I'll tell you about her as well,' he said.

'Who?' asked Judith.

'The Shield Maiden,' replied Stort, ruffling her hair.

They stoked the fire and made him comfortable on the big sofa, which they moved nearer to them all. They let him sleep when talking made him tired and they brought him food and Dorji's Brew. They came and went and listened; they prompted where they had to, they asked for explanation where things made no sense and gradually they began to see who it really was had come into their midst, what he was and how much he had loved the world and all his friends. How great, therefore, his grief.

The gale outside blew on for several days, rain and sleet pelting around the house as the last days of January slipped by and Bedwyn Stort, fading now, remembering his life, told them at last about the Hyddenworld.

'But then,' he said as the last day of the month dawned and the storm outside died away to leave clear air and dripping trees, 'I never did fulfil the quest and find that final gem. Yet, as Mister Barklice once said to me, "My word, Mister Stort, you do cut it fine!" There it is, there it was, and now, well . . .'

They let him sleep, his tale well told.

Sun shone into the conservatory, the sky was blue, the drips and puddles drying up. Winter finishing early for once.

Jack built up the great fire and kept the curtains half closed, shafts of winter sunlight angling across the carpet and touching for a little Stort's thin, white hair and his gentle, closed eyes.

At dusk there was a knock on the front door.

A man and woman were there, some others at the gate.

'We were wondering . . . we have been waiting . . . on the hill . . .'

'We've noticed,' said Jack. 'We've seen the lights.'

'We're wondering. Is he . . . ?'

'He's fading,' conceded Jack.

'We wanted to say that we couldn't light candles these three nights past. Such rain and wind! But we wanted him to know, perhaps for him to see that we are there still.'

'Are there many of you?' asked Katherine.

The man smiled.

'Hundreds,' he said. 'You should come and see. More come every day, every hour. All sorts. It's peaceful up there, even in the wind. Now it's died down and, tonight being the end of the month and for the pagans among us the start of spring, we just wanted you to know. There's not a person up there will not light a candle for him tonight.'

'Thank you,' said Jack.

'Um ... I'm sorry, we were asked to ask. People wanted to know. Did he ever find what he said he lost? Did he finally do what he had to do?'

Jack looked at Katherine and she at him.

'What time is it?' said Jack.

The man looked at his watch.

'Gone five.'

'The answer to your question is that he found many things but not what he lost and we're not sure that he thinks he did what he had to do but ... but ...' and Jack smiled, 'we can tell you this. If it's only just gone five I think he might say there's still enough time.'

As they left Jack impulsively called after them, a smile in his voice, 'Tell your friends, tell them all ... he does tend to cut things fine!'

53

By Candlelight

Dying Stort might be, dead he was not.

Weak, very, but the spirit was still there and for what he had to do that was nearly everything.

'There are people, Mister Stort, and lights as well, up on the hill. They are there for you.'

'What time is it?'

'Eight . . . Nine . . . gone nine.'

Stort was downstairs on the sofa. The fire was alight, the lights were off, the curtains open, the bright stars showing, but the hill was out of sight from that room.

'Would you like to go outside and look?' said Katherine. 'It's cold but as you can see the rain's all gone. We could carry you.'

'I can walk,' he said crossly, adding with more courtesy, 'with help.'

He was lightly dressed, the embarrassing pyjamas long since discarded in favour of trousers. They helped him off with his dressing gown and bundled him into a fleece and jacket. He sat down again and Katherine put thick socks on his feet and offered him the trainers he wore around the house.

'Something more robust I think. Where are my boots?'

'You have lots of pairs these days . . .'

'My own,' he said, patting her shoulder, 'they have served me well. They shall serve me to the last.'

'There's no "last" about it quite yet!' said Katherine.

'There is, my dear.'

They got his boots. Old things, worn and often repaired, the bits of black tyre tied up with green twine and occasionally red.

'Aah . . .' he said pleasurably as he put them on, 'that's better! Now please, Katherine, help me up.'

Arthur was dressed warmly and holding Judith's hand.

'Why are we going out?'

'Mister Stort is going outside and we're all going with him. He thinks he can manage it.'

'Can I take this?'

It was Jack's horse. Lately she liked to have it close by. 'I can put it in my backpack.'

'We're not going for long . . .' said Katherine.

'*Please* . . .'

They togged her up from top to toe so she was all ponies and pinks.

Then, when they were ready, they assembled like an expedition going up to the mountains.

Jack said, 'We'll turn off the lights, all the better to see folk's lights up on the hill.'

They emerged from the house, the air cold and the ground moist but not frozen.

Katherine held Stort's arm, Jack hovered nearby to help.

'Look!'

The great conifers were silhouetted against a glowing sky, the base of the hill was dark, or seemed so, and the top aglow. The sky above shone darkly with the moon and stars, a hundred million million of them.

Only slowly, as their eyes adjusted to the dark, did they see that the lights on the edge of the hill were not the only ones there. There were others lower down, candles in jars perhaps, some moving along the road beyond the garden and others on the shallow slopes on the far side. Yet more were wending their way up the steep escarpment side to join those on top, pinpoints of moving light that made the hill come alive.

'There are so many of them,' gasped Jack.

'Hundreds and hundreds,' said Katherine.

Stort stood staring, the lights so many, and the night so clear, that his face and eyes shone with them all. He was pondering, nearly humming, thinking hard, scratching his head, tempted almost to stand on one leg had he been able. He was almost the Stort of old.

'It is a pity,' he said, 'that all trace of the horse once carved into the hill has gone, for surely it meant a great deal to the world I knew. I was thinking that on such a night as this, with all that light along the hill's edge and elsewhere too, I fancy you would see its wondrous shape. Judith! Let me have that horse of Jack's!'

She gave it to him and he held it up, as if against the dark canvas of the hill.

'See how well it fits, Jack. If you hold it so . . . yes . . . and you stand so, Katherine . . . there! Ah, I cannot pick you up, Judith, but your father can and if I hold the horse . . . so! . . . I'm sure that you can vaguely see . . .'

'It's galloping!'

'It is.'

'Did you ever see the real horse, the one the Shield Maiden rode?'

'I did. It was as big as the sky itself, bigger actually. The only thing that was bigger was the Scythe of Time which we . . . which I saw with . . . my friends . . . on the Malvern Hills. Now that was big! It was also terrifying.'

'But you could beat it, Mister Stort!'

'The only being that ever "beat it", as you put it, was my dog, who I told you about when we talked about the Hyddenworld.'

'The one called Georg without an "e"?'

'That one.'

'What happened was he faced the Scythe to protect us and was cut into a million shards, like chimes. Perhaps they were chimes. Certainly they were memories and reflections.'

'Where did he go?'

'Who knows, Judith.'

'Do you miss him too?'

Stort stood in silence, staring at the far-off candles on the hill.

'Yes,' he said, 'I do. But that's what happens when you get old. You miss what you lost and sometimes you miss what you never realized you had.'

They moved slowly across the lawn, past the Chimes, in among the trees, which in another time, another world, had been the henge.

'Are you all right?' asked Katherine.

Stort was breathless, his steps uncertain, his eyes wandering, sadness returning.

'I am . . . unsure which way to go, you see. I am not sure I can remember the way any more.'

They were at the boundary fence beyond the trees. Ahead was the pasture, which dipped to the little stream and copse, and the path that led on across the road and finally up to the hill.

'I think perhaps this is as far as we need go,' said Katherine. 'Mister Stort can rest here, but be careful of the barbed wire. Judith, hold my hand.'

He did need to rest, taking shallow breaths, leaning against a rickety post, sizing up the pasture ahead, the hill above and the wandering lights between.

'Listen!' whispered Arthur. 'Can you hear it?'

It was like a singing, a fluting and a piping and a music that held an allure like nothing they had heard before.

'Bilgesnipe music,' said Stort in wonder at the sudden memory. 'We are not the only ones here tonight. It wouldn't surprise me if there are many hydden hereabout, for they – we – celebrate the season's turn, especially this night when spring returns again.'

'As we are doing,' said Jack, 'thanks to you.'

'Ah, yes . . . but I mean *celebrate*! Not watching passively but singing and dancing and – I'm sorry, Katherine – supping good brew.'

She squeezed his thin hand.

The music came and went with the light breeze and to their left, wending their way upon the green pilgrim road, came more lights.

'Hydden,' whispered Stort, 'come for this night of nights.'

A deep momentary hush, the trees behind, music, lights, stillness together, a moment for always.

'If I knew where to go and what to do I would go and do it,' said Stort suddenly. 'I had a glimmer of it before but it's fled my mind. I do believe I am almost too afraid now to try to find my way, but perhaps, Katherine, if we just . . .'

'No, really,' she laughed, 'this is far enough. It gets dark below the hill . . .'

'Well,' grumbled Stort, 'I never was much good at finding a route without Barklice and I am very tired. Yet . . . what time is it?'

'Nearly ten, I should think,' said Jack. 'Long, long past your bedtime, Judith.'

She, looking to stay on no doubt, hoping to drag the excitement out, searched among the stars for inspiration and, pointing, finally said, 'Is it as big as . . . as . . . as that?'

'What?'

'The Scythe thing.'

'What are you looking at?'

'*That!*'

Stort bent a little, one hand for balance on the fence post, the other on Judith's shoulder as she pointed again.

It was a thin arcing line of light, the colour of steel, and as they stared they saw, as Judith had, that it reached from the furthest star to the far eastern horizon of the Earth.

'It's moving, changing, getting bigger,' said Jack, adding with slight alarm, 'and it's getting nearer.'

They closed ranks and instinctively stepped back, the fence posts and the barbed wire stolid and silvery before them in the night. A measure of protection.

'It's getting even nearer,' said Katherine nervously.

'It's hissing,' cried Arthur, pulling Judith back further still, for the sound was loud now and the speed of its approach terrifying.

'What is it?' she asked.

Stort smiled thinly.

'It is the Scythe of Time,' he said, 'and I think it might be wise if we . . . we . . . retreated a little more . . .'

He had almost to shout to be heard as the hissing and snicking and ripping of the air grew ever louder and the arc of the Scythe, its edge hair-thin, came at them from above, from the side and round, and round again so that had they run, whichever way, it would have got them, cut them, sliced them. So they stood stock still and terrified.

Then it was sweeping right through them, the blade razor-sharp, flattening out as it came, as vast as the Earth, shining as it cut snicker-snack with sound that began far off over there and hissed right into their ears and on to the end of the world, all in a moment of time.

And the only sound left as their blinking eyes tried to see in the dazzling dark after that swishing light were the five thuds of the wooden posts of the fence before them, cut through at their bases, like through butter, the barbed wire still attached, wringling and wrangling as they all fell to the ground.

Vision returned and with it the sight of two people standing before them as blinded and bemused as they were.

One was a man, the other a boy.

They each carried a stave and the adult had a spare one roped to his back. The other, the smaller of the two, wiry and fit-looking, said, 'Pa! Can't see very well and feel weird. Where'm we be?'

His father was Mister Barklice himself, come at last to the human world and now looking about and trying to get his bearings.

'Bratfire, I'm right here. Let your eyes adjust!'

He stared about himself a little more, stepping this way and that as if in hope of finding where he was until, standing stock still once more, he cried out in consternation, 'Oh no! We're alive, which is good, but we're not our normal selves, which is bad, *very* bad.'

He turned around again more slowly, looking about, but not yet seeing his old friend standing in the shadows, nor the others with him.

Bratfire, his red hair highlighted by the candles and stars, went close to him, tugged at his sleeve and said, '*What* be bad?'

'I have a very horrible feeling,' replied Barklice, 'that we are not quite as we were. Be prepared for a shock. I think we are if not quite human, then no longer of hydden size. If Mister Stort were here . . .'

'I *am* here, Barklice.'

'Bratfire, the lantern please,' cried Barklice with hope and joy in his voice. 'Hand it to me!'

Barklice opened the shutter and a beam of yellow light was cast upon the curious scene. The tangle of barbed wire and wood at their feet, the lit-up hill behind, the henge trees in front at whose base stood figures he knew and loved: Stort, Jack, Katherine and Arthur and . . . Mirror above! Judith when young.

'Pa, what's *that*!?'

Two big eyes, quite frightening in their way, stared at them from the pasture to one side, a shiny nose in front.

'Georg,' said Barklice.

'What be he?'

'Mister Stort's dog.'

'You'm never spoke of 'im to me afore, Pa.'

Bratfire sounded aggrieved. Georg advanced into the light, sniffed about, and padded quietly to Stort's side.

'The Scythe took him and now it's delivered him back,' said Barklice, 'like it's delivered us. He comes and he goes, does Georg. Now . . .'

He approached Stort and held up the lantern such that each could see the other.

'Mister Stort,' he said finally, 'I've said it before and you know it well and it does make my heart pound, but you do have a tendency to leave things *very* late. Eh, Bratfire?'

'He do seem to, Pa.'

'Master Jack, Mistress Katherine and you too, Arthur, if I may – Professor to you, lad – I won't beat about the bush. Where we're going isn't far but it'll take a bit of hyddening. Seeing as you're humans now and therefore slow and clumsy, begging your pardon, we better get started right away if we're going to get Mister Stort up there in time to find the gem he needs to give to the Shield Maiden.'

'Where are we going, Barklice?' asked Stort.

'Up the hill by the shortest route, so prepare to be puffed.'

'Is she here before us?'

'Haven't seen her but I heard she was too old to ride a horse, especially that one. Last time I saw her she was on foot. Dragging along as if age had finally caught up with her. But then Mister Stort . . .'

He came closer and examined Stort's face and looked into his eyes.

'You're older now, white haired!'

'You've not aged at all,' responded Stort, 'which in a way does not surprise me since . . .'

Barklice raised a hand.

'This is not the time for scientific explanations, Stort, and anyway I have some more important things to say which I wish I'd said before. You're my oldest friend, that's what you are and when we spoke of love, which we often did, I'm not sure we said what we were to each other. Maybe we didn't need to, Mister Stort.'

'I don't think we did.'

'Well,' Barklice went on, 'maybe and maybe not but while there's still time there was something I wanted to say. You were always the best of friends to me, by the Mirror you were.'

'You too, Barklice. The best.'

Lives well lived smile with wrinkles and love. So then, Barklice and Stort.

'The time's come for our last journey together and I intend to guide you well and make it a good one,' said Barklice warmly. 'We have a little way to go, Stort, if I'm to get you to the right place at the right time in one piece. Are you ready for the climb?'

'Jack . . . ?' whispered Katherine uncertainly.

'Arthur . . . ?' growled Jack.

'Up the hill?' cried Arthur, addressing his remarks to Barklice in the dark. 'To do what?'

It seemed a long way to all of them.

'I have no idea and never did have, where Mister Stort is concerned. He makes it up as he goes along so far as I can see and all I do is see he's all right. So here we are, there it is, now let's get going. Where's Master Jack?'

Jack found himself saying, 'I'm over here.'

'You take up the rear as you always liked to. As for Stort . . .'

He looked at Katherine and said, 'It's best if I now take his hand. I know him better than I know myself and he knows he'll not stumble with me. He's work to do, he always has, an important thing to do, that's sure. The thing is to get him there. He does the rest.'

There was no further debate and in the wyrd of that night there couldn't be.

54

DISCOVERY

They followed Barklice and Stort down the pasture in the dark, over the stream, in among the trees and up the road, Barklice watching over Stort's hesitant progress every step of the way.

When they reached the road there were folk with candles all about, pilgrims for Stort every one.

Seeing who it was, and not knowing his hydden name, they said, 'We'll light your way, Mister Boots, we'll light every step of the way. Will it be zig-zag or straight, easy or hard?'

'The quickest,' said Barklice, 'for we've little time. Bratfire, hold that lantern so we can see this steep sward. Judith, there's a candle in a jar offered by that man. Take it. Jack, you stay close behind with the others.'

'I am doing just that, Mister Barklice, and all is well.'

'Always was, mostly, when you were about.'

They climbed steadily, Barklice helping his friend, Katherine with her hands just behind, the hill steepening, the word going before them that, far from being dead, Mister Boots as was had arrived on the hill.

More lights, more folk scampering back and forth, and the Bilgesnipe music sensuous along the contours and the terracettes, beating to the rhythm of the old lynchets, the laughter and lights and ribbons of that friendly folk streaming in the dark.

'How far, Mister Stort, how far do we need to go?' asked Barklice who, having got him there, was not sure where to stop.

'This is not an exact science,' puffed Stort, 'but a little way more if you please.'

Up and up they went, slow and steady, folk not believing what they saw. In awe of the stars and moon above and Mister Boots coming up from below with all his friends and family, for that's what they seemed to be.

While Stort looked about, knowing he still had something important to do, hoping the lights would help him remember.

'Ah!' he cried, 'I do believe . . . goodness me, how could I forget? Eh, Jack? You should know and you too, Katherine! Arthur, surely you can remember?'

'What, Mister Stort?' said Judith.

'I'll show you,' he replied.

'*What?*' she demanded.

'You'll see. Now . . . What's the time? Is it midnight yet?'

'Minutes to go . . .'

'Then there's time, for if we get started before the midnight hour, the Mirror will rest content that we're on the way, so to speak. If we're a mite late doing the last few things there'll be no harm done. It is betwixt and between is this time of the season but, you see, that's what makes our worlds come close.'

He stopped climbing.

'Here, we'll start here . . . but who will begin?'

Any one of five thousand people on the hill would have been willing to but Stort knew who it must be. In another life, another place, which wasn't far from where they were just then, in fact it was right there, she had known the White Horse better than anyone. She had been its Rider and this night her work was done and the time of the Peace-Weaver was returning.

'Judith,' said Stort, 'you stand here and hold your candle high because others need to see. Yes, so!'

'See what?'

'You'll soon find out . . .'

'Now, who else will lend a helping hand? You, sir, good, stand next to Judith, don't slip for the sward curves round and is steep in places. Yes, you too, madam . . . Come here . . . yes . . . and you too, all of you, make a sinewy line . . .'

'What's he doing?' whispered Katherine.

'Search me,' said Bratfire, 'but whate'er it be 'tis important work.'

'What exactly are we doing, Stort?' asked Barklice.

'We're lighting the horse across the hill,' he replied. 'Its long, long body, its galloping legs . . . yes, there, three of you must move along *please* and up a step, yes up . . . well *obviously* . . . You're an ear, not its head, that's . . . that's . . . well then, if you must . . .'

He turned to Arthur.

'There are times,' he said, 'when I despair! Folk don't do what they ought to do. Folk are wilful and errant. Still, needs must and we're getting there!

'Yes . . . all of you there . . . That is indeed its head and its pricking ears and its eye, of course . . . Very good. What are we doing, Mister Barklice? We're lighting the horse on this special night because the Shield Maiden's work is done but she's old and cannot see and needs our help if she is to find her way home.'

He was alive again, doing the thing he had forgotten he must do, drawing a horse to lighten the darkness for his beloved.

'I'm not sure I understand,' said Jack.

'I'm not sure we need to,' replied Katherine, 'except in our hearts.'

'Nearly done,' cried Bedwyn Stort, dancing about as if he was indeed young again, directing the last candles to where they should be. 'What's the time?'

'Gone past the midnight hour,' said Barklice. 'Have you nearly finished?'

'We've certainly begun!' cried Stort happily. 'This is – yes that's right, you three are the last of the longest leg and please, no, you're backs, not ears . . . good, excellent . . . and this is the end of the beginning, my dear Barklice, the rest is up to them.'

He pointed up to the edge of the hill, where hundreds waited, wanting to help.

'Where's Jack?'

He came.

'Got your stave? No? This is the one you should be carrying, I think.'

Barklice withdrew the stave stuck through the back of his belt and gave it to Jack. One moment it seemed no more than an ordinary stave but the next, alive once more in Jack's hand, its energy flowing into him, it caught the light of the stars in its depths.

Jack trembled for a moment and then, as it seemed to them all, stood taller and more proud; stronger and more purposeful.

Barklice smiled.

'You're ready to be a leader again, Jack, and to show them the way. Folk need to know what it is they have to do.'

'I'm not sure I know myself yet, but it'll come, it'll come.'

The stave glimmered brighter still and as it did Stort stumbled, his brief youth fleeing, fearful age showing in his eyes.

'Are you all right?' asked Jack.

'He's scared, Master Jack,' murmured Barklice, 'always was worried by love, for that's his final journey and I can't help him with that. We can show the way, me on the green road, like I've trained young Bratfire to do, and you with folk to keep 'em safe and show them things I never could. But now Stort's afeared of the journey he'll have to make alone, now his job is almost done on Earth . . . but I'll stay with him as long as I can.'

Of all the candles there only one wavered then.

'What will I see?' asked Judith. 'My arm's tired. I can't see a horse, just candles and candles all along the hill. No ears, no head, it's all jumbled up.'

'It just feels that way,' said Stort, 'help me to her, Barklice. I'll show her.'

Then . . . 'Look,' he said, putting his hands on Judith's shoulders and she coming close, 'look and hold your candle high for you'll see it soon, reflected in the night sky . . .'

What he saw came down slowly across the far horizon and had a thin, bright edge to it. For a moment his heart jolted, as it reminded him of the Scythe, but almost at once he knew it was not. It was something larger, something greater, and it covered the whole Universe.

But it came closer, stretching, curving, ever bigger, forcing them to look up and up and higher still, craning their necks to right and left. It was dark like an eclipse of life itself.

Slowly it seemed to come, though in fact its speed was the speed of light but it being so vast and the distances too, so beyond the scale of mortal mind, it seemed to move barely at all until, the darkness complete and then held awhile, they saw a softer light, flickering and gentle, reaching across the Universe as if a horse was there that was made of candlelight, with elongated legs, the long thin stretch of a body, ears that pricked, a mouth all open and a single eye.

'But that's the horse which Stort has made,' whispered Katherine. 'That's this horse here.'

It turned above them, as big as the sky itself, and they turned with it, unable to see it all, it was so vast. An immortal horse made of mortal candlelight, moving slowly as they stared.

'That isn't a horse,' said Stort, 'it's a reflection of what we've made. That's the Mirror itself passing overhead.'

It really was above them, moving at the pace of the Universe itself, the Mirror-of-All was overhead and the wondrous sound it made was the *musica*, vast, beyond their minds to think it, but that as it passed they saw the horse they had made galloping across the sky, one way, all ways, exquisite in its form.

Jack's horse.

Katherine's for a time.

Judith's now.

Everyone's.

Then, the Mirror, tilting as if some great hand was touching it, reflected the light over the hill, the horse galloping fast to light the dark of Englalond, over the sea where Borkum Riff lives, catching Leetha in her dance, there where all the others are and it lights the slow path of she whom Stort most loved, who waited for him so long.

There she too goes, the light from the Mirror soft at her stumbling feet, for the path is steep where the Modor lives and her door is ajar and she is not yet home.

The White Horse, who never speaks, following close to see she's safe, says, 'Modor, your work as Shield Maiden is nearly done. One last task and you can love him until the end of time.'

Oh, she is old now and she can barely put one foot in front of the other to get to her own front door.

'He said he wouldn't take long when he left,' whispered the Modor, going inside, 'but he's been gone a whole lifetime. If he ever comes back, White Horse, will he remember what I was before I became what I am now?'

What the Modor had been, in that universe in which Bedwyn Stort had had his life, was Judith the Shield Maiden. What Stort was in the Mirror's light, which is greater than all things, was the Wita, the Modor's consort. But shifts of time and place, shimmers among the Mirror's universes, can make a Bedwyn Stort forget, and even a Modor uncertain.

So the Modor now. She peered back outside, as best she could, and stared at the mist among the trees where the White Horse had been.

Jack knew what he had to do and got them working at once, cutting the sward so the chalk began to show, following the lines of the horse whose image Stort had lighted across the hill with candles, the horse that galloped across the slow Mirror's face as it passed over their heads, confirming faith and establishing memory.

They hewed, they cut, they lifted up, those hundreds of humans and hydden alike, right through the early hours and ahead of the sun rising on the first spring day while they still had time.

Following the lights, cutting the lines deep and true, creating the horse in its beauty with the sweat and sinew of all they were, in heart, body and spirit.

Until old Barklice said, 'Stort, it's nearly done.'

'It is indeed,' said Stort kneeling by the new-carved eye of the Horse, 'yet not quite so. There is still a mote in its eye and it's best we remove it so that it sees all the better what it *must* see now and ever more.'

Yet it was no mote they found, no scrap of a thing, no mite of grit within the chalk, black as night though it was.

Stort knelt down by the eye of the Horse, reached forward and dug out what he saw, grunting with the effort of doing so. For, small though it was, the moment he took it up he knew, as did Barklice as well, what it truly was and that in any other hand it might have weighed as heavy as winter itself. Then, when he put it in his palm it began to wake from its years of sleep.

He trembled as it did so, for he held the gem of Winter in his hand at last, vivified by light, its rays of dark majesty shining in his eyes.

He shuddered too, seeming about to fall until Barklice took his arm and steadied him.

'It is too much for me to hold, Barklice, too much . . .'

But Barklice shook his head.

'You bore the other gems, Mister Stort, and you've borne the winter of two lives. You're strong enough to take the gem now to she who has waited these long years . . .'

'Am I?' said Stort rather fearfully.

'You are. Now put it out of sight lest it begins to darken our spirits . . .'

Stort put the gem in an inside pocket, as he had the others he had found. The darkness and the cold it brought eased away.

'That's better,' said Barklice, helping Stort to his feet once more. 'Not a minute too soon!'

'Just so,' agreed Stort.

They stood together with their friends by the eye of the Horse as the sky lightened with the rays of the rising sun. They saw that the Mirror was gone, the Horse was free to gallop on through time as the spring, not yet quite there but holding its breath, was now ready to come.

Just so.

It is said Stort insisted that he climbed to the top without help and alone which, reluctantly, Barklice allowed him to do.

It is said that winter, reluctant to leave, sent a scattering of snow right across the hill, as if to try to obliterate the fresh-cut horse in chalk, to hide it in crystalline white.

But spring breathed out and the sun cast its warm rays across the hill. All there saw what happened then: the snow evaporated into a million tiny threads and curls of mist which, turning and thickening, reached to the White Horse already above them, or maybe became the Horse before their eyes. The rising mists became its mane, caught by the soft breeze like dappling leaves; became its great flank and legs and hooves; became its wondrous head and gentle eyes as, knowing that Bedwyn Stort's journey was finally done, it knelt upon the hill to which it gave its name and awaited his coming.

Tall he was but not tall enough when he reached up to that great Horse.

'Mister Barklice! I need a hand. Help me if you will!'

Which, with an affectionate shake of his head and a smile, Barklice climbed up the hill to do, content to provide that last service for Mister

Bedwyn Stort, scrivener of Brum, seer of things great and small, lover of life, beloved of Judith the Shield Maiden, Wise One now.

Very old, the Modor, old as time.

Her consort, the Wita as some called him, had gone off saying he had things to do, but that was a long time ago. A lifetime even. Two lifetimes perhaps.

Even the wise get lonely. They too wither and die.

Mortal or immortal, all life needs touch and a word of love and a smile.

Lonely was the Modor, her head bent to her chest, her hands hooked, her hair thin and lank and her doubts very great. What was there left to love any more, she wondered, in one as old as she?

He had seen her age as Shield Maiden, but she had only ever seen him young.

Her beloved, how he had made her smile.

But not to be able to touch him, or feel his touch, that had been her agony, the price she paid to help him save the Universe and mortalkind.

Old the Modor today, grumpy too.

Shuffling about and muttering.

'Doing things? If he comes back . . . I'll . . .'

But she had no idea what she'd do. So, muttering, she went outside and stood staring.

'Where's that damn horse?'

I've not finished with you yet! One last thing to do. If he comes. Which he probably won't.

She moved back inside and closed the broken old door and stared about.

Food? She wanted none now. Hadn't eaten in years.

Drink? She shook her head.

Sleep? Can't.

Sit? Weep.

Sit then, remembering, yearning, longing for his firm touch.

'*Doing things!* What he's been doing all these years has nearly been the death of me!'

55

THE JOURNEY ON

The White Horse would have gone faster, but this Rider is old. And tottery. Nearly fell off over the Channel. Hung on for dear life on the great silver way of the stars. Cried out in fear at the final descent, and fell off exhausted.

He was fearful, too.

What to say? What to do? Everyone suffers nerves before the face of love, especially him.

The White Horse clip-clopped in the snow.

'Snow still here?' cried Stort. 'Can't stand the stuff! Slows my brain.'

The White Horse stamped not once but twice and then a third time for good measure and the snow riffled off the trees of their mountain home and the new sun, risen already across the world, rose there where he and his beloved had lived their many lives.

But each time was new and this time Bedwyn Stort was especially nervous.

He arrived with a gift, but it didn't seem much.

He came in hope, but that seemed forlorn.

He was old now, stiff, and he needed the spring sun to liven him up, but she'd not love him if he was so old he couldn't get on the Horse without help, let alone ride it. As for getting off that . . . was . . . no . . . joke!

He stood finally outside their old shack of a humble, glad to have the ground firmly back under his boots again. Here he was and here he would stay if only she'd agree to have him back!

The day's new warmth cheered his face. He looked at their old home and then beyond it in every direction and he saw the new world rising.

'Better get it over,' said Stort aloud. 'Better do it.'

He straightened himself as best he could. He adjusted his jerkin and trews. He scowled at his boots but thought better of retying his laces. Too far to get down, too hard to get up.

He saw some remnant snow on a branch and had an idea. Scooping it up, he rubbed it into his hair in the hope of making it sleeker than it had been for a while.

Then, knowing he had delayed enough, his heart beating most painfully, words deserting him, with only his gift to cling on to, he went to the Modor's door and wondered if he should knock by way of warning or just open the door with a cough to announce his arrival and walk straight in.

'What would she prefer?' he murmured as a good lover should.

He walked straight in.

Dark was their home, winter still lingering, shadows still thick, cold staying put.

He could hardly see her but when he did she was sitting, head to her chest, old and lonely, half blind now, she who had been Judith and was Modor once more was barely able to hear him or didn't dare to.

Stort stared at her and his heart filled with love.

She was his beloved and she was most beautiful.

He went near slowly, not wanting to frighten her, and knelt down and took her hands. Warm were his own but cold were hers, and fretful too.

'I have something for you,' he said, digging in his pocket and taking out the gem, its dark light shining, its fearful light most terrible.

She saw it in his hands but dared not look up into his eyes for fear he was not there at all, but just an imagining, a hope.

Stort reached to her neck and found the golden chain that held the pendant Beornamund had made. He freed it gently, and saw the gems of Spring and Summer and Autumn shimmering, waiting, wanting, yearning to be made whole again.

'This is my gift to you,' he declared, and he put the gem of Winter into the setting made so long before by Beornamund.

'There!' said Stort.

The gems united and the Fires of the Universe were at one again as the Modor took his hand and looked into his eyes once more.

'You are,' said Stort, his heart back to normal, his knees knobbly on the rough floor, his life returning, 'most beautiful to me and I have missed you every day I have been gone. *Every* day.'

She looked at Stort and at how the gems, coming to life now, cast the colour of the seasons in his bright eyes and across his lovely face. Spring, Summer, Autumn and Winter, all were there for her to see in him.

'You are my beloved,' she said, 'and your name is Bedwyn Stort and always was. Mister Boots, indeed!'

Winter left her, autumn too, and summer fled back across her face and turned to the spring.

'Boots served his purpose for a time,' he said. 'He and I had things to do!'

He got up, which was easier now than he thought it might be, and they opened the shutters, opened the door and went outside.

'Where's that Horse!?' she said. 'I am the Modor, you are the Wita and by the rights of all the stars and the sun and the moon it should do our bidding.'

The White Horse came and knelt.

Judith, young as spring itself, took off the heavy pendant which had worn her down so long.

She took some strands of the horse's mane and entwined them with the golden chain. Stort helped her, and their fingers, getting more nimble by the moment, working together, tied the cunning knot.

'There!' she said.

'There indeed, my love!'

'Now go,' she commanded the Horse, 'and find she who'll wear it best of all. The time of the Peace-Weaver has come again. Tell her that if she needs advice she can come to us.'

'The White Horse doesn't speak,' said Stort.

'The White Horse has its ways,' said Judith as it left, adding, as she took Stort's hand, 'as we have ours.'

Jack saw it, they all did, galloping across the sky. The colours of spring up there in the clouds, new seasons on the way.

He hummed a song he had heard and murmured its words: '. . . *and the snow falls, and the wind calls and the year turns round again.*'

'Where's it going?' asked Bratfire.

'The White Horse, if that's what we saw?' Jack replied. 'To the East, if it's got any sense. As Mister Stort told us, they have more need of the Peace-Weaver than us!'

They were on the hill again, only a few folk lingering now, the scouring of the horse long over and only a final packing up of tents to be done.

Jack had decided it was time to travel on, take the lead, show others the way of the White Horse that they had been shown. Their packs were full and ready; they were well shod.

'Barklice, shake my hand,' said Jack, 'for you're going a different way from us.'

'A different way, Jack? I'm going to a different world! But my lad's young, he'll stay in the human world awhile and help see you on your path. But I'll not be alone, Arthur's coming with me.'

'I am, my dear Jack,' declared Arthur. 'Retirement does not suit me. Much as I will miss you all, Mister Barklice here says that he is going to show me a better dance than I ever danced before and that, if I learn it well enough, it will take me into the Hyddenworld. Do you know . . . I am inclined to believe him!'

Barklice and Bratfire hugged their long goodbye.

'He'll guide you well, Jack.'

'I know he will and where we're going he'll need to. Now . . . you leave first, Mister Barklice, Arthur . . .'

They saw them go slowly down the hill, Arthur preferring the zig-zag way as the first sunshine of spring had not been warm enough to dry the ground underfoot. When they reached the bottom they stopped to wave. Then Jack and Katherine watched as they went in among the trees of the henge, as once it had been and might be again. After that they saw them no more.

They turned back to the hill, Jack and his stave, Katherine, Judith, and the errant dog called Georg, eager to be gone.

'So . . . which way, Bratfire?'

Bratfire knew that the Ridgeway was the oldest green road known to hydden and human, in use for three thousand years. He looked right and then he looked left and after a while he said, 'I be having a think!'

He walked a little way from them and sniffed at the air, as his father always did. He kicked the ground and closed his eyes and felt the way the breeze blew and listened to what the season said.

'We'm not goin' right and we bain't goin' left,' he finally pronounced, 'not in and out o' them old ruts. We'm going a new way now!'

'Well then,' said Jack, 'lead on!'

Which Bratfire did, steady and true, not looking back until, quite soon, they left the Ridgeway far behind.

56

EPILOGUE

One April morning many years later, Judith lay in Stort's freckly arms listening to the sounds of a new spring.

The first and most exquisite of the seasons came late to the high forests of the Harz Mountains in Germany, where they had their home. It was the drip-drip-drip of melting snow from the roof onto the slate flags outside their door that woke her and the music of the thaw-streams all about that made her smile.

His breathing too, his warmth, his life, as restless as the new season's sound. It was the feel and sound of him that put the happiness in the crinkle of her eyes and at the corners of her mouth.

She stirred at the chatter of siskin and crossbill at the edge of their garden, and sat up to listen to the coo of the stock dove, the drum of the black woodpecker and the far-off mating calls of the raptors gyring on the balmy winds across the steep slopes and grey rock faces above the tree-line.

But it was a more urgent and insistent sound that suddenly had her rousing Stort from his slumbers.

'Wake up, my love! Wake now!'

He stirred, frowning, her tangled limbs half his, her warmth his too, her voice his joy, her lips whispering at his ears, his pleasure.

'Wake up!'

The Modor and the Wita were neither old nor young, for wisdom knows no bounds of age. They just *were* and she was eager to get up and he reluctant.

'What?' he said finally.

'Listen! That Horse is back and he wants us up and about and off.'

She was right.

The hoofs of the White Horse rang from one side of spring right through to the other, clattering about the forest with a few snorts thrown in, wanting to be heard.

'Off to where? And for what?' demanded Stort.

Her answer was elusive.

'That's the sound of something unfinished, something unrequited. Which is something we two know all about.'

Stort woke, sat up, pulled the plaid about them both, cocked an ear to one side to listen to the Horse until, after a pause for thought, he said, 'But nothing was left unfinished, all was requited. We are one and we are wise and there's nothing more to say or do about all that happened in the Hyddenworld *I'm* thinking of . . . and *anyway* . . .'

Stort smiled, his red hair tousled, his nightshirt crumpled.

'I can't go off just like that – I have things to do.'

Judith shook her head and said, 'My dear, I think the Horse is telling us that you left something undone. Or maybe you took a wrong turn. Perhaps you think you went one way when in fact you went another without realizing it. He's restless and needs us to be away on his broad back to see to something you forgot.'

'I forgot nothing.'

'Let's go and find out if that's true, my love.'

Stort took his time and, in truth, Judith took hers. The Horse clipped and clopped and snorted until, finally impatient, it leaned its vast weight against their old wooden cabin so that it swayed this way and that until they emerged breathless, laughing, spring in their steps, pleasure in their eyes and faces.

'Do I have to?' said Stort, his complaint not very real.

I do, he told himself, answering his own question.

But in any case, as Judith and the Horse might well have guessed, he was now curious to know what it was he had forgotten and that was always an impulse Stort could not resist.

'What's unfinished and what's unrequited?' he cried out against the cold, clear wind that blew through their hair and riffled their garb as the Horse carried them off.

'Where are we going?' he called into Judith's ear, holding her tight, his long legs keeping her safe.

'Englalond,' she replied, 'because that's where you left something undone.'

'England, I think,' he replied finally, when the Horse set them down, for whatever they were when they left, they were in the human world when they arrived and there were humans about.

Some even stared, seeing the Horse, or rather glimpsing its sheen and its shadow, not sure what they saw at all. Staring as well at the two who remained standing there after it had gone across the fields, smiling as brightly at something or other as if they were the sun itself.

'Where are we, Stort, and why are we here?' asked Judith, who was glad they had come but also had no idea why. It felt like a break. Like a holiday from being the Modor and the Wita. Like a chance to be, well, normal for a little while.

Which, indeed, they looked, except for the easy sense of love and joy that radiated from them both, which was too rarely seen in the troubled human world.

Stort and Judith had seen to that between them and now, for a little while, they were a couple out for the day who held hands now and then, which made them seem a touch younger than perhaps they were.

'We are . . .' began Stort looking about, his voice going quiet with thought, 'we are . . . somewhere . . . I have been . . . before!'

The White Horse, having made itself scarce, had come back, or at least stopped nearby, across a field or two. Hard to say with the Horse, it had a habit of seeming to be near and far, to be the wraith on the mountain top or the reflection of white sky in the puddle at folks' feet.

Just then there were no mountains, nor any puddles. They were on one side of a natural amphitheatre formed by wide ramparts with a nice, bright stream rilling nearby.

'We're at Durrington,' said Stort finally, turning to point, 'and just over there . . .'

Over there was Woodhenge, which when he last visited it in another life, had posts made of concrete to mark where once the prehistoric posts had been.

'Over one hundred of them,' he announced, 'except that then they were concrete and now they are wood, which is what they would have been three thousand years ago and should have been when Katherine and Jack and I came here and were witness to two humans trying to perform the complex dance through the portal of the henge. It was, as I remember, going dangerously awry and we had to help them.'

'And did you help them?'

'We did.'

'Are you quite sure of that?'

'I am . . . I think.'

'You think!'

'Well, *I thought* . . .'

'Stort!'

'I daresay they . . .'

'*Stort!*'

'My dear?'

'Look . . . over there . . .'

A man stood hesitating on one side of the henge, staring at the wooden posts. He went in among them, feeling his way from one to the next as if trying to find a route he was not sure of. He was middle-aged, of medium height and he wore a baseball cap of the quality sort which members of US corporations wear when they are working hard at being on vacation.

'Excuse me, sir . . .'

He turned from the henge, came out from among the posts and approached Stort.

Stort stared down at him affably. Judith watched from a little way off. They both looked friendly and approachable.

'Sir, I was wondering if you know about this henge?'

'I know something,' said Stort.

'You look as if you do.'

'Do I?'

'He does,' said Judith coming closer. 'May we help you?'

'I doubt that, unfortunately. You're British?'

Stort nodded ambiguously.

'I'm American,' said the stranger, 'but with German parentage.'

'Yes,' said Stort, as if he knew, which he did. He had met many people in his different lives but Erich Bohr he remembered very well. This, to within a few feet more or less, was where they had first met.

'This is my third visit here in three years,' announced Bohr.

'Any special reason?' wondered Stort, who very much feared there was.

Things undone, wrong turns made . . .

'It's déjà vu. I feel sure I have been here before. And to other places. Each year I come back, trying to remember.'

'Something unfinished?' wondered Stort, who knew that what Erich Bohr couldn't remember was much darker than something simply unfinished.

'Feels like it.'

'Where else do you visit, in search of your memory?'

'White Horse Hill. Heard of it?'

'I have. And Brum?'

Erich Bohr looked puzzled.

'Birmingham.'

Bohr looked astonished.

'How did you know that?'

'Do you remember me?' asked Stort.

Bohr stepped back, nearly fell over a post, stared at Stort and, passing his hand over his eyes and forehead as if to brush away cobwebs, said, 'I can't say I do, exactly. But . . .'

'We met here,' said Stort, 'and I think we made a mistake. We took a wrong turn when we were sure we were taking the right one.'

Bohr looked bewildered but also, in some way, determined. He was searching for the connection and wasn't going to give up.

'So . . .' he said, 'you do know about this henge?'

Stort took a deep breath and said, 'The key thing is that we are two and a half miles from Stonehenge. This is the henge for the living, that is the one for the dead. I think, Doctor Bohr . . .'

'How did you . . . ?'

'. . . I think that you are looking in the wrong place. I think . . .'

Off and away the White Horse stamped.

Bohr looked from Stort to Judith, his alarm turning to bewilderment as the earth trembled and the air shimmered and time shifted.

There had been people about when the conversation had started moments before and the day then had been bright. Now there was no one and the sky was darkening and the air was taking on a chill.

Judith smiled and nodded.

Erich Bohr's puzzlement eased. He had never seen quite such kindly, reassuring eyes as these two had. He felt his natural caution weakening, resistance slipping, an opening-up occurring, and for him that was unusual. He felt spacey, light and almost ready to do something he had not done in years. From where the idea of it came he had no idea. He felt like dancing.

'I think that it is not a memory you have lost,' continued Stort, 'so much as a person. Sometimes there is only one person in the whole Universe with whom we are, as it were, at one with everything. Is that what you're trying to remember?'

Bohr could only stare at him, suddenly moved, for with the letting go had come emotion.

'You come back repeatedly because it's here that you believe yourself nearest to what you lost.'

Now Bohr most definitely could not speak.

'Yes,' said Stort, 'I do know about this henge and many others too. As for this particular one it is in a sense *your* henge in a rather important way. Now listen . . . if you are to find what you lost you'll have to reverse what you did before – or rather what I and two of my friends, Jack and Katherine, inadvertently helped you do. We danced you out of this place . . .'

Bohr's eyes widened in surprise, his bewilderment returning, laced once more with alarm.

Stort smiled and raised a hand, as reassuring now as Judith.

'What I am saying will seem strange but without a great many explanations and demonstrations, for which we have not the time, I doubt that it would ever make much sense. Just know now that it's up to us to dance you back into this henge so that, with luck, you'll come back to where you first began with she whom you lost.'

'In Birmingham,' said Bohr impulsively, to his own surprise. 'That's where I lost her.'

'That was the place,' said Stort, as much to Judith as Bohr. 'In a blizzard. There were plenty of those that winter, were there not?'

'There were, Stort.'

'That's right,' said Bohr, 'it was a blizzard.'

'You remember?'

'Not quite, the image of one just came out. It's like I saw it as a glancing thing, a reflection in a mirror.'

'Ah! Perfect! It's exactly like that, Erich, because that's exactly what it is. But if I were to dance you back here logic dictates that you'd have to start somewhere else. Fortunately not Brum or Birmingham. No, all you have to do is walk with us for a while, along the banks of the Avon here, then by way of the ancient cursus that leads to the mordant shadows of Stonehenge.'

Bohr shook his head.

'Can't. Not today. Went there earlier.'

Stort smiled, Judith laughed and the White Horse snorted irritably.

'Your instincts are in the right place, then.'

Still Bohr shook his head.

'When I say "can't", I mean it. Stonehenge is closed.'

'Not to us it's not.' said Stort. 'Otherwise you might as well say that the Sahara desert is closed to the sun, or the sea to the wind, or the . . .'

'*Stort . . .*' murmured Judith, stopping him.

'Yes, well, let's go, then.'

The walk to Stonehenge from Durrington took them nearly an hour and during that time they passed through all the seasons of the year so that by the time they got there, winter was on them, cold and hard.

'Erich, hold my hand tight,' said Judith, 'the blizzard gets worse before it gets better. Hold *tight.*'

Stort was good at some things, Judith at others. At blizzards, and flying into the face of them, she was very good indeed.

'Stort, hang on to my other hand or you'll get lost . . . *Stort!*'

She had to shout and hold hands with them both as tight as could be, so they didn't fly off from each other or the wrong way, as they flew through space and time between the megaliths of Stonehenge, like the wind.

Amongst the dark stones they went, enshadowed with death, enshrouded in bleak resonance, which took in the dead from the whole world and Universe and held them as fractured memories, broken grief, still and silent and stuck forever when unrequited and unfinished.

Amongst the frozen shards Stort saw Ingrid running, her hair bright with reflections of the fire of the Library behind, the silhouette of Reece raising his weapon to take aim, the image horribly sharp though the blizzard raced across it. On either side, as it seemed, then in front and behind as well, black megaliths rose up, forest-like and impenetrable.

All was suddenly as still as ice and felt like death corporeal.

He turned Bohr to look and said, 'This is where we made a *faux pas*, as some might say. This here, this now. No hurry, time is with us, the dance dictates its own graceful measures. Judith, take his hand, show him the steps, dance him back, help him to help Ingrid dance safely out of the megaliths and back . . . back . . . *back* . . .'

The dark day lightened, the air shimmered, the ground shook and the White Horse stamped again but backwards, as if taking its hoofs off the Earth.

Bohr stood with Judith, holding her hand for a moment before, realizing he was doing so and it being strange to do it with a virtual stranger, he let it go.

Stort stood frowning and a little puffed.

'That was the theory,' said Stort, 'but where's the lady?'

'My love,' chided Judith, 'you should trust yourself more.'

He looked about, half expecting to see Jack and Katherine, their dance having been so like the time before. But now was different: same place, same couple and different version of the same world.

Bohr said, 'I thought that someone was coming, a female . . .'

'You'll know her when you see her and when you do, for Mirror's sake, this time take your opportunity!' said Judith.

Then: 'Stort!'

'Judith!'

Older they were now, ready for a nap back in their own bed.

The Horse knelt, they mounted and Stort said, 'Wait a little, just a moment, just to see. I'm curious.'

They watched from across the river, from the spot where, many lives before, Stort had camped with his good friends and they first spied Erich Bohr and Ingrid Hansen begin their fatal dance. A different time, for now he stood alone, bewildered by the day and the thought he had been there before and that he was waiting for someone whose name he did not even know; whose life had not yet crossed his in this particular world but which resonated still from another.

'Déjà vu,' he muttered as they watched him almost giving up, but not quite. 'She'll probably not come.'

A rented car came down the little hill from Durrington, bright and shiny like the spring. It tootled along hesitatingly, its driver no more than a shape behind a windscreen that reflected the white sky.

Bohr watched in trepidation as it pulled into the car park, stood idling a moment; then, the engine stopped, a tall young woman got out. She stood staring, her eyes everywhere, trying to make sense of what she felt, where she was and why it didn't seem strange at all that the man who stood there, as if he had been waiting there forever trusting that one day she would finally come, raised a hand in shy greeting and began to walk towards her.

Nor did it feel strange that she, her heart beating, found herself walking towards him.

He reached out a hand and she took it.

'I'm Erich Bohr,' he said.

'Ingrid,' she replied.

But Stort and Judith only half saw that moment and none of what followed because the White Horse was up and away and over the hills, knowing, as it usually did, that they had things to do.

ACKNOWLEDGEMENTS

A four-book series like Hyddenworld is always a significant project for a publisher and my first thanks go to Pan Macmillan for supporting it – and me – in so many ways from concept to publication. In particular the three editors involved: Peter Lavery, Julie Crisp and Bella Pagan. Without their combined efforts and patience over six years or so this story would not exist. To their names I want to add that of Will Atkins, who has been what the trade calls my structural editor for *Winter* and *Harvest*, meaning the person who reads the final draft and points out the many errors of its ways and enables their correction. He has been a pleasure to work with.

I have been lucky, indeed blessed, to have a different sort of 'structural editor' in Jackie Brockway, whose friendship and unwavering editorial eye have been with me constantly for the last three books of the series. Without her, Hyddenworld would not have emerged in its present form. Nor would it have been anything like the fun to write. Her unseen but not quite silent presence in and around the creative process would surely be a joy for any author but has been far more than that for me.

The work of two academics in particular inform Hyddenworld. Professor David Harvey of the City University of New York was one of my tutors at Bristol University when I was an undergraduate studying Geography with Economics. His lectures were then, and remain still, models of clarity and vision; and his huge and powerful body of work critiquing urban systems and capitalism underlies the human aspect of the Hyddenworld. He has made sense for me of the economic chaos of a troubled world, created by the governments we ourselves have given power to. I am grateful, too, to Professor Mike Parker-Pearson of the UCL's Institute of Archaeology. His warm and exciting elucidations of the rich prehistoric landscape near which I live, through talks and books describing the findings of the Stonehenge Riverside Project, inform the hydden view of henges as between-world portals. My interpretation of his work and that of the many other archaeologists involved is, of course, my own.